SINISTER STREET

By COMPTON MACKENZIE

Volume I

My dear Mr. Stone,

Since you have on several occasions deprecated the length of my books, I feel that your name upon the dedicatory page of this my longest book deserves explanation, if not apology.

When I first conceived the idea of 'Sinister Street,' I must admit I did not realize that in order to present my theme fully in accord with my own prejudice, I should require so much space. But by the time I had written one hundred pages I knew that, unless I was prepared against my judgment to curtail the original scheme, I must publish my book in a form slightly different from the usual.

The exigencies of commercial production forbid a six shilling novel of eight or nine hundred pages, and as I saw no prospect of confining myself even to that length, I decided to publish in two volumes, each to contain two divisions of my tale.

You will say that this is an aggravation of the whole matter and the most impenitent sort of an apology. Yet are a thousand pages too long for the history of twenty-five years of a man's life, that is to say if one holds as I hold that childhood makes the instrument, youth tunes the strings, and early manhood plays the melody?

The tradition of the English novel has always favoured length and leisure; nor do I find that my study of French and Russian literature leads me to strain after brevity. I do not send forth this volume as the first of a trilogy. It is actually the first half of a complete book. At the same time, feeling as I do that in these days of competitive reading, the sudden vision of over a thousand pages would be inevitably depressing, I give you the opportunity of rest at the five-hundredth page, which reaches a climax at least as conclusive as any climax can be that is not death. I do not pretend that I shall not be greatly disappointed if next January or February you feel disinclined to read 'Dreaming Spires' and 'Romantic Education,' which will complete the second volume. Yet I will be so considerate as to find someone else to bear the brunt of dedication, and after all there will be no compulsion either upon you or upon the public to resume.

Yours ever affectionately,

Compton Mackenzie.

Let me add in postscript that 'Sinister Street' is a symbolic title which bears no reference to an heraldic euphemism.

Phillack, August 3, 1913.

VOLUME ONE

CONTAINING

THE PRISON

. HOUSE

CLASSIC

I. EDUCATION

"The imagination of a boy is healthy, and the mature imagination of a man is healthy; but there is a space of life between, in which the soul is in a ferment, the character undecided, the way of life uncertain, the ambition thick-sighted."

JOHN KEATS.

BOOK ONE
THE PRISON HOUSE

"What youth, Goddess—
what guest
    Of Gods or mortals?"
        Matthew Arnold.

"Slow on your dials the
shadows creep,
    So many hours for food and

sleep.
*So many hours till study tire.
So many hours for heart's
desire."*
Robert Bridges.

Chapter I: *The New World*

FROM a world of daisies as big as moons and of mountainous green hillocks Michael Fane came by some unrealized method of transport to the thin red house, that as yet for his mind could not claim an individual existence amid the uniformity of a long line of fellows. His arrival coincided with a confusion of furniture, with the tramp of men backwards and forwards from a cavernous vehicle very dry and dusty. He found himself continually being lifted out of the way of washstands and skeleton chests of drawers. He was invited to sit down and keep quiet, and almost in the same breath to walk about and avoid hindrance. Finally, Nurse led him up many resonant stairs to the night-nursery which at present consisted of two square cots that with japanned iron bars stood gauntly in a wilderness of oilcloth surrounded by four walls patterned with a prolific vegetation. Michael was dumped down upon a grey pillow and invited to see how well his sister Stella was behaving. Nurse's observation was true enough: Stella was rosily asleep in an undulation of blankets, and Michael, threatened by many whispers and bony finger-shakes, was not at all inclined to wake her up. Nurse retired in an aura of importance, and Michael set out to establish an intimacy with the various iron bars of his cage. For a grown-up person these would certainly have seemed much more alike than even the houses of Carlington Road, West Kensington: for Michael each bar possessed a personality. Minute scratches unnoticed by the heedless adult world lent variety of expression: slight irregularitiesinfused certain groups with an air of deliberate consultation. From the four corners royal bars, crowned with brass, dominated their subjects. Passions, intrigues, rumours, ambitions, revenges were perceived by Michael to be seething below the rigid exterior of these iron bars: even military operations were sometimes discernible. This cot was guarded by a romantic population, with one or two of whose units Michael could willingly have dispensed: one bar in particular, set very much askew, seemed sly and malignant. Michael disliked being looked at by anybody or anything, and this bar had a persistent inquisitiveness which already worried him. 'Why does he look at me?' Michael would presently ask, and 'Nobody wants to look at such an ugly little boy,' Nurse would presently reply. So one more intolerable question would overshadow his peace of mind.

Meanwhile, far below, the tramp of men continued, until suddenly an immense roar filled the room. Some of the bars shivered and clinked, and Michael's heart nearly stopped. The roar died away only to be succeeded by another roar from the opposite direction. Stella woke up crying. Michael was too deeply frightened so to soothe himself, as he sat clutching the pointed ears of the grey pillow. Stella, feeling that the fretful tears of a sudden awakening were insufficient, set up a bellow of dismay. Michael was motionless, only aware of a gigantic heart that shook him horribly. At last the footsteps of Nurse could be heard, and over them, the quick 'tut-tut-tuts' that voiced her irritation.

"You naughty boy, to wake up your little sister."

"What was that noise?" asked Michael.

"Your own noise," said Nurse sharply.

"It wasn't. It was lions."

"And if it *was* lions, what next?" said Nurse. "Lions will always come, when little boys are naughty. Lions don't like naughty boys."

"Michael doesn't like lions."

He took refuge in the impersonal speech of earlier days, and with a grave obstinacy of demeanour resisted the unreasonableness of his nurse.

"What was that noise, Nanny? Do tell me."

"Why a train, of course. There's a molly-coddle. Tut-tut!"

"A train like we rode in from down in the country?"

"Yes, a train like we rode in from down in the country!" Nurse mimicked him in an outrageous falsetto.

"Not lions at all?"

"Not if you're a good boy."

"Nor bears—nor tigers—nor wolverines?"

The last was a dreadful importation of fancy from some zoological gift-book.

"Now that's enough," Nurse decided.

"Nor laughing hyenas?"

"Am I to speak to you again? As if there wasn't enough to do without children why-why-whying morning, noon and night."

Michael recognized finality of argument. The mention of morning, noon and night with their dreary suggestion of the infinite and unattainable plunged him into silence. Nurse, gratified by her victory and relieved to find that Stella was crooning happy mysteries to a rag doll, announced that she was prepared in return for the very best behaviour to push the two cots against the window. This done, she left the children to their first survey of London airs, to silent wonder amid the cheeping of countless sparrows.

Stella sat blinking at the light and the sailing clouds. She soon began to chant her saga. Primitive and immemorial sounds flowed from that dewy mouth; melodies and harmonies, akin to the day itself, voiced the progress of the clouds; and while she told her incommunicable delight there was actually no one to say 'Stella, will you stop that 'umming?' Michael could not compete with his sister in her interpretation of the clouds' courses. He had, indeed, tried once or twice; but Stella either stopped abruptly, leaving him to lag for a while with a lame tune of his own, or else she would burst into tears. Michael preferred an inspiration more immediately visual to Stella's incomprehensibly boundless observations. Michael would enjoy holding in his hand a bunch of blue cornflowers; Stella would tear them to pieces, not irritably, but absently in a seclusion of spacious visions. On this occasion Michael paid no attention to Stella's salutation of light; he was merely thankful she showed no sign of wishing to be amused by 'peep-bo,' or by the pulling of curious faces. Both these diversions were dangerous to Michael's peace of mind, because at some period of the entertainment he was bound, with disastrous results, to cross the line between Stella's joy and Stella's fear. Michael turned to look out of the window, finding the details of the view enthralling. He marked first of all the long row of poplar trees already fresh and vivid with young May's golden green. Those trees, waving with their youthfulness in the wind, extended as far as could be observed on either side. Three in every garden were planted close to the farthest wall. How beautiful they looked, and how the sparrows hopped from branch to branch. Michael let his eyes rove along the pleasant green line whose slightness and evenness caressed the vision, as velvet might have caressed a hand running lightly over the surface. Suddenly, with a sharp emotion of shame, Michael perceived that the middle tree opposite his own window was different from the rest. It was not the same shape; it carried little blobs such as hang from tablecloths and curtains; it scarcely showed a complete leaf. Here was a subject for speculation indeed; and the more Michael looked at the other trees, the more he grew ashamed for the loiterer. This problem would worry him interminably: he would return to it often and often. But the exquisite pleasure he had taken in the trim and equable row was gone; for as soon as the eye caressed it, there was this intolerably naked tree to affront all regularity.

After the trees, Michael examined the trellis that extended along the top of a stuccoed wall without interruption on either side. This trellis was a curiosity, for if he looked at it very hard, the lozenges of space came out from their frame and moved about in a blur—an odd business presumably inexplicable for evermore like everything else. Beyond the trellis was the railway; and while Michael was looking a signal shot down, a distant roar drew near, and a real train rumbled past which, beheld from Michael's window, looked like a toy train loaded with dolls, one of whom wore a red tam-o'-shanter. Michael longed to be sitting once again in that moving wonderland and to be looking out of the window, himself wearing just such another red tam-o'-shanter. Beyond the railway was surely a very extraordinary place indeed, with mountains of coal everywhere and black figures roaming about; and beyond this, far far away, was a very low line of houses with a church steeple against an enormous sky.

"Dinner-time! Tut-tut," said Nurse, suddenly bustling into the room to interrupt Stella's saga and Michael's growing dread of being left alone in that wilderness beyond the railway lines.

"Could I be left there?" he asked.

"Left where?"

"There." He pointed to the coal-yard.

"Don't point!" said Nurse.

"What is that place?"

"The place where coal comes from."

"Could I be left there?" he persisted.

"Not unless one of the coalmen came over the wall and carried you off and left you there, which he will do unless you're a good boy."

Michael caught his breath.

"Can coalmen climb?" he asked, choking at the thought.

"Climb like kittens," said Nurse.

A new bogey had been created, black and hairy with yellow cat's eyes and horrid prehensile arms.

Michael and Stella were now lifted out of the cots and dumped on to the cold oilcloth and marched into the adjacent bathroom, where their faces and hands were sponged with a new sponge that was not only rough in itself, but also had something that scratched buried in one of the pores. During this operation, Nurse blew violent breaths through her tightly closed lips. When it was over, Stella was lifted up into Nurse's arms; Michael was commanded to walk downstairs in front and not to let go of the banisters; then down they went, down and down and down—past three doors opening into furniture-heaped rooms, past a door with upper panels of coloured glass in a design of red and amber sparrows upon a crude blue vegetation—a beautiful door, Michael thought, as he went by. Down and down and down into the hall which was strewn with bits of straw and shavings and had another glass-panelled door very gaudy. Here the floor was patterned with terra-cotta, yellow, black and slate-blue tiles. Two more doors were passed, and a third door was reached, opening apparently on a box into which light was let through windows of such glass as is seen round the bottom of bird-cages. This final staircase was even in the fullest daylight very dim and eerie, and was permeated always with a smell of burnt grease and damp cloths. Half-way down Michael shrunk back against Nurse's petticoats, for in front of him yawned a terrible cavern exuding chill.

"What's that?" he gasped.

"Bless the boy, he'll have me over!" cried Nurse.

"Oh, Nanny, what is it—that hole? Michael doesn't like that hole."

"There's a milksop. Tut-tut! Frightened by a coal-cellar! Get on with you, do."

Michael, holding tightly to the banisters, achieved the ground and was hustled into the twilight of the morning-room. Stella was fitted into her high chair; the circular tray was brought over from behind and thumped into its place with a click: Michael was lifted up and thumped down into another high chair and pushed close up to the table so that his knees were chafed by the sharp edge and his thighs pinched by a loose strand of cane. Nurse, blowing as usual through closed lips, cut up his meat, and dinner was carried through in an atmosphere of greens and fat and warm, milk-and-water and threats of Gregory-powder, if every bit were not eaten.

Presently the tramping of furniture-men was renewed and the morning-room, was made darker still by the arrival of a second van which pulled up at right angles to the first. In the course of dinner, Cook entered. She was a fat masculine creature who always kept her arms folded beneath a coarse and spotted apron; and after Cook came Annie the housemaid, tall and thin and anæmic. These two watched the children eating, while they gossiped with Nurse.

"Isn't Mrs. Fane coming at all, then?" enquired Cook.

"For a few minutes—for a few minutes," said Nurse quickly, and Michael would not have been so very suspicious had he not observed the nodding of her head long after there was any need to nod it.

"Is mother going to stay with us?" he asked.

"Stay? Stay? Of course she'll stay. Stay for ever," asserted Nurse in her bustling voice.

"Funny not to be here when the furniture came," said Cook.

"Yes, wasn't it?" echoed Annie. "It *was* funny. That's what I thought. How funny, I thought."

"Not that I suppose things will be what you might call properly arranged just yet?" Cook speculated.

"Everything arranged. Everything arranged," Nurse snapped. "Nothing to arrange. Nothing to arrange."

And as if to stifle for ever any ability in Michael to ask questions, she proceeded to cram his mouth with a dessert-spoonful of rice pudding from her own plate, jarring his teeth with the spoon when she withdrew it.

Then Michael's lovely mother in vivid rose silk came into the room, and Cook squeezed herself backwards through the door very humbly and so quietly that Annie found herself alone before she realized the fact; so that in order to cover her confusion and assist her retreat she was compelled to snatch away Michael's plate of rice pudding before he had finished the last few clotted grains. Michael was grateful to Annie for this, and he regarded her from that moment as an ally. Thenceforth he would often seek her out in what she called 'her' pantry, there to nibble biscuits, while Annie dried cups and swung them from brass hooks.

"How cosy you all look," said mother. "Darling Stella, are you enjoying your rice pudding? And, darling Michael," she added, "I hope you're being very good."

"Oh, yes," said Nurse, "Good! Yes. He's very good. Oh, yes. Tut-tut! Tut-tut!"

After this exhalation of approval Nurse blew several breaths, leaned over him, pulled down his blue and white sailor-top, and elevated his chin with the back of her hand.

"There's no need to bother about the drawing-room or the dining-room or my bedroom or, in fact, any of the rooms except the night-nursery and the day-nursery. You're quite straight in here. I shall be back by the end of June."

Nurse shook her head very violently at this, and Michael felt tears of apprehension welling up into his eyes. Mrs. Fane paused a moment doubtfully; then she waved beautiful slim gloves and glided from the room. Michael listened to delicate footsteps on the stairs, and the tinkle of small ornaments. A bleak silence followed the banging of the front door.

"She's gone away. I know she's gone away," he moaned.

"Who's She?" demanded Nurse. "She's the cat's mother."

"Mother! Mother!" he wailed. "She always goes away from Michael."

"And no wonder," said Nurse. "Dear, dear! Yes—tut-tut!—but goodness gracious, she won't be gone long. She'll be back in June."

"What's June?" Michael asked.

"If you ask any more silly questions you'll go to bed, young man; but if you're a good boy, I'll tell you a story."

"A real story? A nice long story?" asked Michael.

"I'll tell you a story about Jack o' my Nory And now my story's begun. I'll tell you another about Jack and his brother And now my story's done."

Nurse twiddled her thumbs with a complacent look, as she smacked her palate upon the final line.

"That isn't a story," said Michael sullenly. "When will mother be back?"

"In June. That's enough," said Nurse.

Michael went to sleep that night, trying to materialize this mysterious June. It came to mean a distant warmth of orange light towards which he waited very slowly. He lay awake thinking of June in the luminousness of a night-light shielded from his direct vision by a basin. His hands were muffled in fingerless gloves to prevent thumb-sucking. Suddenly upon the quiet came a blaze of light. Had he reached June? His sleepy eyelids uncurled to the scented vision of his beautiful mother. But it was only gaslight playing and fluttering over the figure of anæmic Annie taking hairpin after hairpin from her hair. Yet there was a certain interest in watching Annie undress. Her actions were less familiar than those of Nurse. Her lips were softer to kiss. Then the vision of June, rising and falling with Annie's breath, recurred from distances unattainable, faded again into the blackness of the night, and after a while came back dazzling and golden. It was morning, and in a chirping of sparrows and depth of quiet sunlight Michael began to wonder why he was sleeping beside Annie in a big bed. It was an experience that stood for a long time in his memory as the first adventure of his life.

The adventure of Annie was a solitary occasion. By the following night the regular night-nursery was ready for occupation, and the pea-green vegetation of the walls was hidden by various furniture. Nurse's bed flanked by the two cots occupied much of its space. Round the fire was a nursery fender on which hung perpetually various cloths and clothes and blankets and sheers which, as it was summer at the time, might all have been dried much more easily out of doors. Pictures were hung upon the wall—pictures that with the progress of time became delightfully intimate experiences. They were mostly framed chromolithographs saved from the Christmas numbers of illustrated papers. There was Cherry Ripe—a delicious and demure girl in a white dress with a pink sash, for whom Michael began to feel a romantic affection. There was the picture of a little girl eating a slice of bread-and-butter on a doorstep, watched by a fox terrier and underneath inscribed 'Give me a piece, please.' Michael did not know whether to feel more sorry for the little girl or the dog; some sort of compassion, he thought, was demanded. It was a problem picture insoluble over many years of speculation. The night-nursery seemed always full of Nurse's clothes. Her petticoats were usually chequered or uniform red, preternaturally bright in contrast with the blackness of the exterior apparel. The latter of heavy serge or similar material was often sown with jet bugles which scratched Michael's face when he played 'Hide-Oh' among the folds of such obvious concealment. Apart from these petticoats and skirts, the most individual possession of Nurse's wardrobe was a moon-shaped bustle of faded crimson which Michael loved to swing from the bedpost whence out of use it was suspended. There was also in a top drawer, generally unattainable, a collection of caps threaded with many different velvet ribbons and often coquettish with lace flowers. Michael was glad when Nurse put on her best cap, a proceeding which took place just before tea. Her morning cap was so skimpy as scarcely to hide the unpleasant smoothness of her thin hair. In the amber summer afternoons or blue spring twilights, Nurse looked comparatively beautiful under the ample lace, with a softer apron and a face whose wrinkles were smoothed out by the consciousness of leisure and the pleasant brown teapot. Mostly, Michael was inclined to compare her with a monkey, so squab was her nose, so long her upper lip, and such a multitude of deep furrows twisted up her countenance. That Nurse was ever young, Michael could not bring himself to believe, and daguerreotypes framed in tin-foil which she produced as evidence of youth from a square box inlaid with mother-o'-pearl, never convinced him as a chromolithograph might have convinced him. At the same time the stories of her childhood, which Nurse was sometimes persuaded to tell, were very enthralling; moreover, by the fact of her obvious antiquity, they had the dimness and mystery of old fairy-tales.

On the whole Michael was happy in his pea-green nursery. He was well guarded by the iron soldiers of his cot. He liked the warmth and the smallness of the room; he liked to be able to climb from his cot on to Nurse's bed, from Nurse's bed into Stella's cot, and with this expanse of safe territory he felt sorry for the chilly and desolate and dangerous floor. Michael also liked the day-nursery. To begin with, it possessed a curious and romantic shape due to its nearness to the roof. The ceiling sloped on either side of the window almost to the floor. It was not a room that was square and obvious, for round the corner from the door was a fairly large alcove which was not destined to lose its romance for many years. The staircase that led up to the day-nursery was light and cheerful owing to the skylight in the roof. Yet this skylight Michael could have wished away. It was a vulnerable spot which made the day-nursery just a little uneasy at dusk—this and the cistern cupboard with its dark boomings and hammerings and clankings and utter inexplicableness. However, the day-nursery was a bright room, with a cosy atmosphere of its own. The pleasantest meal of the day was taken there, and in a black cupboard lived the golden syrup and the heraldic mugs and the dumpy teapot and the accessories of tea. What a much pleasanter cupboard this was than the smaller one in the night-nursery which revealed, when opened, slim and ugly ipecacuanha, loathsome Gregory-powder with wooden cap and squat cork, wicked envelopes of grey powders and slippery bottles of castor-oil. There, too, was the liver-coloured liquorice-powder, the vile rhubarb and the deceitful senna. In fact, apart from a bag of jaded acid-drops, there were only two pleasant inmates of this cupboard—the silvery and lucent syrup of squills and a round box of honey and borax. There were no pills because Nurse objected to pills. She was always telling Michael as he listened, sick at heart, to the stirring-up of the Gregory-powder with a muffled spoon, so different from the light-hearted tinkle and quick fizz of magnesia, to be thankful he was not on the verge of taking a pill. That she represented as something worthy of a struggle. Michael imagined the taking of a pill to be equivalent to swallowing a large painted ball full of a combination of all the nastiest medicines in the world. Even the omnipotent, omniscient Nanny could not take a pill.

There were other jolly cupboards in the day-nursery—one in particular pasted over with 'scraps' and varnished—a work of art that was always being added to for a treat. There was a patchwork hearthrug very comfortable to lie upon beside the cat and her two black kittens. There was Nanny's work-table in the window, gay with coloured silks and wools. There was a piano locked up until Michael's first lesson, but nevertheless wonderful on account of the smooth curve of the lid that allowed one moment's delicious balance and then an equally delicious slide on to the floor.

Certainly the day-nursery was the best room in the tall thin house, just as the morning-room was the worst. The morning-room was odious. In it were eaten breakfast and dinner, both nasty meals. Near it was the coal-cellar and the area-door with its grinning errand boys. The windows afforded foothold to strange cats that stared abominably with yellow eyes. Tramps and sweeps walked past the area-railings or looked in evilly. Horrid gipsies smirked through the window, and pedlars often tapped. The morning-room was utterly abominable, fit only for the boiled mutton and caper sauce and suet puddings that loaded its table.

The kitchen, although it was next to the morning-room, was a far pleasanter resort. So far as any ground-floor now could be considered safe, the kitchen was safe. It looked out upon its own fortified basement whose perforated iron staircase had a spiked door at the top, which could be securely shut. The kitchen contained a large number of objects of natural interest, among which was a shallow cupboard that included upon an attainable shelf jars of currants,sultanas, and rice much more edible in the raw state than cooked. There was the electric-bell case, recording with mysterious discs a far-off summons. There was the drawer in the kitchen table that contained, besides knives and forks, a rolling-pin, a tin-opener, a corkscrew, skewers and, most exciting of all, a club-shaped cage for whipping eggs. There was also a deep drawer in the dresser which held many revelations of the private history of Annie and Cook. Michael could easily have spent days in the kitchen without exhausting its treasures, and as for Cook, gross though she was and heavily though she smelt of onions and beer, her tales were infinitely superior to anything ever known in the way of narration.

Towards the end of June, Mrs. Fane came back. Her arrival was heralded by the purchase of several pots of marguerites and calceolarias—the latter to Michael a very objectionable flower because, detecting in it some resemblance to his dearly loved snapdragons, he pressed open the mouth of a flower and, finding inside a small insect, had to drop the whole pot in a shudder. This brought the punishment of not being allowed to watch from the steps for his mother's cab rounding the corner into Carlington Road, and made calceolarias for ever hateful. However, Mrs. Fane arrived in the richness of a midsummer twilight, and Michael forgot all about calceolarias in his happiness. All day long for many golden days he pattered up and down the house and in and out of all the rooms at his mother's heels. He held coils of picture-wire and hooks and hammers and nails and balls of wool and reels of silk and strands of art-muslin and spiders of cotton-wool and Japanese fans and plumes of pampas grass and all the petty utilities and beauties of house arrangement. By the end of July every room was finally arranged, and Michael and Stella with their mother, accompanied by Nurse and Annie, went down to the seaside to spend two wonderful months. Michael was often allowed to sit up an extra half-hour and even when he went to bed his mother would come to hear him say his prayers. She would sit by him, her lovely face flushed by the rose-red August sunsets that floated in through the open window on a sound of sea-waves. As it grew darker and, over the noise of happy people walking about in the cool evening, a distant band played music, his mother would lean over and kiss him good night. He would be loath to let her go, and just as she was closing the door quietly he would call her back and whisper 'One more kiss,' and because that good-night kiss was the most enchanting moment in his day, he would whisper as he held her to him very close, 'Only one more, but much, much, much the longest kiss in all the world.'

They were indeed two very wonderful months. In the morning Michael would sit beside his mother at breakfast, and for a great treat he would be given the segment she so cleverly cut off from the tip of her egg. And for another treat, he would be allowed to turn the finished egg upside down and present it to her as a second untouched, for which she would be very grateful and by whose sudden collapse before the tapping of the spoon, she would be just as tremendously surprised. After the egg would always come two delicious triangles of toast, each balancing a single strawberry from the pot of strawberry jam. After breakfast, Michael would walk round the heap of clinkers in the middle of the parched seaside garden while his mother read her letters, and very soon they would set out together to the beach, where in time they would meet Nurse and Stella with the perambulator and the camp-stools and the bag of greengages or William-pears. Sand castles were made and boats were sailed or rather were floated upside down in pools, and just as the morning was getting too good to last, they would have to go home to dinner, joining on to the procession of people returning up the cliffs. Michael would be armed with a spade, a boat with very wet sails, and sometimes with a pail full of sea-water and diminutive fish that died one by one in the course of the afternoon heat. After dinner Mrs. Fane would lie down for a while, and Michael would lie down for a great treat beside her and keep breathless and still, watching the shadows of light made by the bellying of the blind in the breeze. Bluebottles would drone, and once to his bodeful apprehension a large spider migrated to another corner of the ceiling. But he managed to restrain himself from waking his mother.

One afternoon Michael was astonished to see on the round table by the bed the large photograph in a silver frame of a man in knee-breeches with a sword—a prince evidently by his splendid dress and handsome face. He speculated during his mother's sleep upon this portrait, and the moment Annie had left the cup of tea which she brought in to wake his mother Michael asked who the man was.

"A friend of mine," said Mrs. Fane.
"A prince?"
"No, not a prince."
"He looks like a prince," said Michael sceptically.
"Does he, darling?"
"I think he does look like a prince. Is he good?"
"Very good."
"What's wrote on it?" Michael asked. "Oh, mother, when will I read writing?"
"When you're older."
"I wish I was older now. I want to read writing. What's wrote on it?"
"Always," his mother told him.
"Always?"
"Yes."
"Always what? Always good?"
"No, just plain 'always,'" said Mrs. Fane.
"What a funny writing. Who wrote it?"
"The man in the picture."
"Why?"
"To please mother."
"Shall I write 'always' when I can write?" he asked.
"Of course, darling."

"But what is that man for?"

"He's an old friend of mother's."

"I like him," said Michael confidently.

"Do you, darling?" said his mother, and then suddenly she kissed him.

That evening when Michael's prayers were concluded and he was lying very still in his bed, he waited for his mother's tale.

"Once upon a time," she began, "there was a very large and enormous forest——"

"No, don't tell about a forest," Michael interrupted. "Tell about that man in the picture."

Mrs. Fane was staring out of the window, and after a moment's hesitation she turned round.

"Because there *are* fairy-tales without a prince," said Michael apologetically.

"Well, once upon a time," said his mother, "there lived in an old old country house three sisters whose mother had died when they were quite small."

"Why did she die?"

"She was ill."

Michael sighed sympathetically.

"These three sisters," his mother went on, "lived with their father, an old clergyman."

"Was he kind to them?"

"According to his own ideas he was very kind. But the youngest sister always wanted to have her own way and one day when she was feeling very cross because her father had told her she was to go and stay with an aunt, who should come riding along a lane but——"

"That man," interrupted Michael, greatly excited.

"A rider on horseback. And he said good morning, and she said good morning, though she had no business to."

"Why hadn't she?"

"Because it isn't right for girls to speak to riders on horseback without being introduced. But the rider was very handsome and brave and after that they met very often, and then one day he said, 'Won't you ride away with me?' and she rode away with him and never saw her father or her sisters or the old house any more."

Mrs. Fane had turned her face to the sunset again.

"Is that all?" Michael asked.

"That's all."

"Was they happy ever afterwards?"

"Very happy—too happy."

"Are they happy now?"

"Very happy—too happy."

"Did they live in a castle?"

"Sometimes, and sometimes they lived in a beautiful ship and went sailing away to the most beautiful cities in the world."

"Can't Michael go with you?" he asked.

"Darling boy, it's a fairy-tale."

"Is it?" he said doubtfully.

The two wonderful months were over. One long day of packing up was the end of them, and when they got back to London there was more packing up, after a few days of which Mrs. Fane took Michael in her arms and kissed him good-bye and told him to be very good. Michael tried not to cry; but the tears were forced out by a huge lump in his throat when he saw a cab at the door, pointing the other way from London. He could not bear the heaped-up luggage and Nurse's promises of sitting up late that evening for a great treat. He did not want to sit up late, and when his mother whispered there was a surprize for him in the drawing-room, he did not care at all for a surprize. But nothing could make the minutes stay still. He was allowed to watch the cab going down the road, but he had no heart to wave his handkerchief in farewell, and when presently he went back with Nurse into the thin red house and was triumphantly led into the drawing-room, he was not raised to any particular happiness by the lancer's uniform, displayed on a large square of cardboard. He suffered himself to be dressed up and to have the scarlet breast-plate strapped around him and the plumed helmet to be pushed over his nose and the sabre-tache to be entangled with his legs; but there was no spirit of hope and adventure flaming in his breast—only an empty feeling and a desire to look out of the night-nursery window at the trains going by with happy people inside.

Chapter II: *Bittersweet*

HIS mother's absence made very sad for Michael the tall thin house in Carlington Road. He felt enclosed in the restraint from which his mother had flown like a bird. Time stretched before him in unimaginable reckonings. It was now the beginning of autumn, and the leaves of the lime trees, falling to lie stained and unlovely in sodden basements, moved Michael with a sense of the long winter before him, with the unending black nights and the dark wet dawns. From the window of the night-nursery he recognized for the first time the beauty of the unsymmetrical plane tree that now, when the poplars were mere swishing bundles of twigs, still defied the October winds with wide green leaves. Soon, however, by a damp frost the plane tree was conquered, and its blobs jigged to November gusts. Fogs began, and the morning-room was always gaslit, even for dinner at one o'clock. Stella was peevish, and games became impossible. The two black kittens were an entertainment and took part with Michael in numberless dramas of revenge and punishment, of remorse and exaggerated cherishing. These histrionic pastimes became infused with a terrible reality, when one day the favourite kitten jumped from Michael's arms over the banisters and fell on to the tiled floor of the hall, hurting herself internally so that she had to be poisoned. He stood by her grave in the blackened mould of the garden, and wished poignantly that he had never spoken harshly to her, had never banished her to a waste-paper basket prison for the length of a long foggy afternoon.

Christmas arrived with more uniforms, with a fishmonger's shop and a mechanical mackerel which when wound up would click in finny progress from one end of the bath to the other and back. It was wound up every Sunday afternoon for a treat, and was afterwards replaced in a high corner-cupboard that always attracted Michael's extreme curiosity and was the object of many vows to solve its secret, when he grew bigger. All these presents came from his mother together with half a dozen books. He received no other presents except from the household. Nurse gave him a china house, romantic when illuminated by a night-light; Annie shyly placed before him a crystal globe that when shaken gave a wonderful reproduction of a snow-storm falling upon a weather-worn tin figure with a green face, blue legs and an unpainted coat. Mrs. Frith the cook gave him a box of tops, none of which he or she or anyone else could spin. In addition to these presents Santa Claus allowed him on a still December night an orange, an apple, a monkey on a stick, five nuts (three of them bad) and a selection of angular sweets. As Michael with foresight had hung up two of Nurse's stockings as well as his own socks, he felt slightly resentful towards Santa Claus for the meagre response.

Christmas passed away in a week of extravagant rain, and a visit was paid to the pantomime of Valentine and Orson at the Surrey Theatre that reduced Michael to a state of collapse owing to the fight between the two protagonists, in which Orson's fingers were lacerated by the glittering sword of Valentine. Nurse vainly assured him the blood was so much red paint. He howled the louder and dreamed ghastly dreams for a month afterwards.

About this time Michael read many books in a strange assortment. Nurse had a collection of about a dozen in her trunk from which Michael was allowed to read three to himself. These were The Lamplighter, The Arabian Nights in a small paper-bound volume of diminutive print, and a Tale of the Black Rising in Jamaica which included an earthquake. In The Arabian Nights he read over and over again the stories of Aladdin, The Forty Thieves and Sinbad, owing to their familiarity through earlier narratives. On Sunday afternoons Nurse always read aloud from Baring-Gould's Lives of the Saints and Mrs. Gatti's Parables from Nature, and told the story of Father Machonochie's death in Argyll and of his faithful Skye terriers, whose portraits she piously possessed in Oxford frames. Michael's own books included at this period several zoological works, the Swiss Family Robinson, Holiday House, Struwwelpeter, Daddy Darwin's Dovecote, Jackanapes, The Battles of the British Army and an abbreviated version of Robinson Crusoe.

The winter and cold wet spring dragged by. Day by day life varied very little. In the morning after breakfast, if it was fairly fine, a visit would be paid to Kensington Gardens, a dull business; for the Round Pond was not visited, and indeed the Gardens were only penetrated as far as the Palace, with occasional promenades along the flower-walk for a treat. Treats were important factors in Michael's life. Apparently anything even mildly pleasant came under the category of treats. It was a treat to walk on the grass in the Gardens; it was a treat to help to push Stella's perambulator; it was a treat to have the sponge floating beside him in the bath, to hum, to laugh, to read, to stay up one minute after half-past six, to accompany Nurse on her marketing, and most of all to roll the slabs of unbaked dough down in the kitchen. The great principle of a treat was its rarity. As anything that had to be asked for became a treat automatically and as the mere fact of asking was made a reason for refusing to grant a treat, the sacred infrequency of the treat was secured. The result of this was that the visit to Kensington Gardens instead of being the jolly business it seemed to be for other children, became a tantalizing glimpse of an unattainable paradise. Michael would stand enraptured by the March winds, every impulse bidding him run and run eternally through the blowy spring weather; yet if he so much as climbed the lowest rung of the scaly part-railings, if he dallied one moment to watch a kite launched on the air, Nanny would haul him back to the perambulator's side. As for talking to other children, not even could the magic treat effect that. If Nurse was to be believed, conversation with strange children was the lowest depth to which human nature could sink. The enforced solitariness of his life bred in Michael a habit of contemplation. Much of his morning walk was passed in a dream, in which he seemed to be standing still while the world of houses and trees and railings and people swam by him unheeded. This method of existence led to several unpleasant shocks, as when he walked into a lamp-post and bruised his nose. Nanny used to jeer at him, calling him Little Johnny Head-in-air; but Michael was so much used to her derogatory opinions that he cared very little and made no attempt to cure himself of the habit, but even encouraged himself to put himself into these nihilistic trances.

It was probably owing to this habit that one morning Michael, looking round in Kensington Gardens, could discern no familiar figure. He was by himself in the middle of a broad gravel walk. Nurse and the perambulator had vanished. For a moment a sickening horror seized him. He would never see Carlington Road again; he would never see Stella or his mother; he would never go to the seaside; he was lost. Then he recalled to himself the knowledge of his name and address: he reassured himself by repeating both aloud, Charles Michael Saxby Fane, 64 Carlington Road, Kensington. A name and address he had often been warned was a talisman to enlist the service of policemen. His heart beat more gently again; his breathing became normal. He looked around him at the world seen for the first time with freedom's eyes. With waves of scent the beds of hyacinths impressed themselves upon his memory. He was free under a great gusty sky, free to climb railings, to pick up shells from the gravel walk, to lie on his back in the grass and brood upon the huge elm-trees that caught the clouds in their net. Michael wandered along to a drinking-fountain to which, access had often been forbidden. He drank four cups of water from the captive metal mug: he eyed curiously the many children who, as free as himself, ran up and down the steps of the fountain. He wished for barley-sugar that he might offer it to them and earn their approbation and company. He was particularly attracted to one group consisting of three funny little girls with splashed pinafores and holes in their stockings, and of two little boys with holes in their knickerbockers and half-peeled sticks. The group moved away from the fountain and Michael followed at a distance. The group turned somersaults over the highest railings and Michael watched it hungrily. The group strolled on, the girls nonchalant and enlaced, the boys still peeling their sticks with perseverance. Michael squeezed through the railings, and followed in the group's wake. The two boys finished peeling their sticks and pushed over in a heap the three little girls. There was laughter and shouting, and a confusion of pinafores and black stockings and hair and caps. Michael stood close to them, wide-eyed with admiration. Suddenly the group realized his propinquity and flocked together critically to eye him, Michael became self-conscious and turned away; he heard giggling and spluttering. He blushed with shame and began to run. In a moment he fell over a turret of grass and the group jeered openly. He picked himself up and fled towards the gate of the

Gardens, anxious only to escape ridicule. He ran on with beating heart, with quickening breath and sobs that rose in his throat one after another like bubbles, breaking because he ran so fast. He was in Kensington High Street, among the thickening crowds of people. He seemed to hear pursuing shouts and mocking laughter. At last he saw a policeman whose tunic he clutched desperately.

"What's all this about?" demanded the constable.

"Please, my name is Charles Michael Saxby Fane and I live at 64 Carlington Road and I want to go home."

Michael burst into tears and the policeman bent over and led him by a convulsed hand to the police station. There he was seated in a wooden chair, while various policemen in various states of undress came and talked kindly to him, and in the end, riding on the shoulder of his original rescuer, he arrived at the tall thin house from whose windows Nurse was peering, anxious and monkey-like.

There seemed to be endless talk about his adventure. All day the affair was discussed, all day he was questioned and worried and scolded and threatened. Treats faded from possible granting for months to come. Restrictions and repressions assumed gigantic proportions, and it was not until Nanny went upstairs to put Stella to bed and left Michael in the kitchen with Mrs. Frith and Annie that his adventure came to seem a less terrible breach of natural law. Away from Nurse, the cook and the housemaid allowed a splendid laxity to gild their point of view.

"Well, what a fuss about nothing," said Mrs. Frith comfortably. "I declare. And what was *she* doing? That's what some people would like to know. You can't lose a child the same as you might lay down a thimble. I call it very careless."

"Yes. What a shame!" Annie agreed. "Supposing he'd of been run over."

"He might of been run over a dozen times," said Mrs Frith. "It's all very fine to put all the blame on the poor child, but what was *she* doing?"

Then Mrs. Frith closed her right eye, tightened her mouth and very slowly nodded her head until the most of her pleated chin was buried in the bib of her apron.

"That's what I thought," said Annie mysteriously.

"What did you think, Annie?" Michael asked fretfully.

"She thought you hadn't no business to be so daring," said Mrs, Frith. "But there! Well! And I was daring myself. Very daring *I* was. Out and about. Hollering after boys. The slappings I've had. But I enjoyed myself. And if I sat down a bit tender, that's better than a sore heart, I used to think."

"I expect you enjoyed yourself," said Annie. "I was one of the quiet ones, I was. Any little trip, and I was sick."

"Couldn't bear the motion, I suppose?" Cook enquired.

"Oh, it wasn't the travelling as did it. It was the excitement. I was dreadfully sick in the crypt of St. Paul's Cathedral."

"What a grand place it is, though," said Mrs. Frith, nodding. "Oh, beautiful. So solemn. I've sat there with my late husband, eating nuts as peaceful as if we was in a real church. Beautiful. And that whispering gallery! The things you hear. Oh—well. I like a bit of fun, I do. I remember——"

Then Nurse came downstairs, and Michael was taken up to bed away from what he knew would be an enthralling conversation between Annie and Cook. It was hateful to be compelled to march up all those stairs farther and farther away from the cheerful voices in the basement.

August arrived without bringing Michael's mother, and he did not care for the days by the sea without her. Stella, to be sure, was beginning to show signs of one day being an intelligent companion, but Nurse under the influence of heat grew more repressive than ever, and the whole seaside ached with his mother's absence. Michael was not allowed to speak to strange children and was still dependent on rare treats to illuminate his dulness. The landlady's husband, Mr. Wagland, played the harmonium and made jokes with Nurse, while Mrs. Wagland sang hymns and whispered with Nurse. A gleam of variety came into Michael's life when Mr. Wagland told him he could catch birds by putting salt on their tails, and for many afternoons, always with a little foolscap of salt, Michael walked about the sunburnt-grass patch in front of the house, waiting for sparrows to perch and vainly flinging pinches of salt in the direction of their tails.

Church was more exciting by the seaside than at home, where every Sunday morning during the long sermon Michael subsided slowly from a wooden bench in the gallery on to a disembowelled hassock, or languished through the Litany with a taste of varnish in his mouth caused by an attempt to support his endurance by licking the back of the pew in front. Nurse told him of wonderful churches with music and incense and candles and scarlet and lace, but, for some reason of inexplicable contrariness, she took Michael to an old Calvinistic church with a fire-breathing vicar, a sniffling vicar's wife and a curate who sometimes clasped Michael's head with a damp hand that always felt as if it were still there when it had long been removed, like a cold linseed poultice. Now at the seaside, Michael went to a beautiful church and was so much excited by the various events that he pressed forward, peering on tiptoe. Luckily the two ladies in front of him were so devout and bobbed up and down so often that he was able to see most of what was happening. How he longed to be the little boy in scarlet who carried a sort of silver sauce-boat and helped to spoon what looked like brown sugar into the censer. Once during a procession, Michael stepped out into the aisle and tried to see what actually was carried in the boat. But the boat-boy put out his tongue very quickly, as he walked piously by, and glared at Michael very haughtily, being about the same size.

After submitting without pleasure to a farewell kiss from Mrs. Wagland, and after enduring much shame on account of Stella's behaviour in the crowded railway carriage, Michael came back to Carlington Road. During the space between arrival and bed-time he was gently happy in welcoming his toys and books, in marvelling at the quick growth of the black kitten and in a brief conversation with Mrs. Frith and Annie; but on the next morning which was wet with a wetness that offered no prospect of ever being dry, he was depressed by the thought of the long time before Christmas, by the foreboding of yellow days of fog and the fact that to-morrow was Sunday. He had been told to sit in the dining-room in order to be out of the way during the unpacking and, because he had been slow in choosing which book should accompany him, he had been called Mr. Particular and compelled to take the one book of all others that he now felt was most impossible even to open. So Michael sat in the bay-window and stared at the rainy street. How it rained, not ferociously as in a summer storm, when the surface of the road was blurred with raindrops and the water poured along the gutters, carrying twigs and paper and orange-peel towards the drain, and when there almost seemed a chance of a second flood, an event Michael did not fear, having made up his mind to float on an omnibus to the top of the Albert Hall which had once impressed him with its perfect security. Now it was raining with the dreary mediocrity of winter, dripping from the balcony above on to the sill below, trickling down the window-panes, lying in heavy puddles about the road, a long monotonous grey soak. He sighed as he looked out of the window at the piece of waste ground opposite, that was bordered in front by a tumble-down fence and surrounded on the three other sides by the backs of grey houses. A poor old woman was picking groundsel with a melancholy persistence, and the torn umbrella which wavered above her bent form made her look like a scarecrow. Presently round the corner a boy appeared walking very jauntily. He had neither coat nor waistcoat nor shoes nor stockings, his shirt was open in front, and a large piece of it stuck out behind through his breeches; but he did not seem to mind either the rain or his tattered clothes. He whistled as he walked along, with one hand stuck in his braces and with the other banging the wooden fence. He went by with tousled hair and dirty face, a glorious figure of freedom in the rain, Michael envied him passionately, this untrammelled fence-banging whistling spirit; and for a long time this boy walked before Michael's aspirations, leading them to his own merry tune. Michael would often think of this boy and wonder what he was doing and saying. He made up his mind in the beeswaxed dining-room that it was better to be a raggle-taggle wanderer than anything else. He watched the boy disappear round the farther corner, and wished that he could disappear in such company round corner after corner of the world beyond the grey house-backs.

The climax of this wet morning's despair was reached when a chimney-sweep came into sight, whooping and halloaing nearer and nearer. Of the many itinerant terrors that haunted polite roads, Michael dreaded sweeps most of all. So he hastily climbed down from the chair in the window and sat under the dining-room table until the sound had passed, shivering with apprehension lest it should stop by Number Sixty-four. It went by, however, without pausing, and Michael breathed more freely, but just as he was cautiously emerging from the table, there was an extra loud postman's knock which drove him back in a panic, so that when Nurse came fussing in to fetch him to wash his hands for dinner, he had to invent a plausible excuse for such a refuge. As he could not find one, he was told that for a punishment he could not be allowed to hear the message his mother had written at the end of what was evidently a very important letter, to judge by the many tut-tuts the reading of it provoked Nurse to click.

However, under the influence of tea Nanny softened, and the message was read just as the rain stopped and the sun glittered through the day-nursery window right across the room in a wide golden bar.

Como.

Darling Michael,

You are to go to kindergarten which you will enjoy. You will only go for the mornings and you will have to learn all sorts of jolly things—music and painting and writing. Then you'll be able to write to Mother. I'm sure you'll be good and work hard, so that when Mother comes home at Christmas, you'll be able to show her what a clever boy she has. You would like to be in this beautiful place. As I write I can see such lovely hills and fields and lakes and mountains. I hope darling Stella is learning to say all sorts of interesting things. I can't find any nice present to send you from here, so I've told Nanny that you and she can go and buy two canaries, one for you and one for Stella—a boy canary and a girl canary. Won't that be fun? Love and kisses from

Mother.

Michael sat in a dream when the letter was finished. It had raised so many subjects for discussion and was so wonderful that he could scarcely speak.

"Will mother really come home at Christmas?" he asked.

"You heard what I said."

"Christmas!" he sighed happily.

"Aren't you glad to go to school?" Nurse wanted to know.

"Yes, but I'd like Christmas to come," he said.

"Was there ever in this world anyone so hard to please?" Nurse apostrophized.

"When will we go to get these canaries, Nanny?"

"Plenty of time. Plenty of time."

"Soon, will we?"

"One more question and there'll be no canaries at all," said Nurse.

However, the sun shone so brightly, and the prospect of a visit to Hammersmith Broadway on a Saturday afternoon appealed so strongly to Nurse that she put on her bonnet and trotted off with Michael up Carlington Road, and stopped a red omnibus, and fussed her way into it, and held the tickets in her mouth while she put away her purse, and told Michael not to fidget with his legs and not to look round behind him at what was passing on that side of the road, until at last they arrived. The canary-shop was found, and two canaries and a bird-cage were bought, together with packets of seed and a bird's bath and a pennyworth of groundsel and plantains. Nurse told Michael to wait in the shop while the birds were being prepared for travelling, and while she herself went to the chemist to buy a remedy for the neuralgia which she prophesied was imminent. Michael talked to the canary-man and asked a lot of questions which the canary-man seemed very glad to answer; and finally Nurse, looking much better, came back from the chemist with a large bottle wrapped up in a newspaper. In the omnibus, going home, Michael never took his eyes from the cage, anxious to see how the birds bore the jolting. Sometimes they said 'sweet,' and then Michael would say 'sweet,' and a pleasant old lady opposite would say 'sweet,' and soon all the people inside the omnibus were saying 'sweet,' except Nurse, who was chewing her veil and making the most extraordinary faces.

It was very exciting to stand on tiptoe in the kitchen while Mrs. Frith cut the string and displayed the canaries in all the splendour of their cage.

"Beautiful things," said Mrs. Frith. "I'm that fond of birds."

"Don't they hop!" said Annie. "Not a bit frightened they don't seem, do they?"
"What are their names?" Mrs. Frith enquired.
Michael thought for a long time.
"What *are* their names, Mrs. Frith?" he asked at last.
"That's your business," said Cook.
"Why is it?" Michael wanted to know.
"Because they're your birds, stupid."
"One's Stella's."
"Well, Stella isn't old enough to choose for herself. Come along, what are you going to call them?"
"You call them," said Michael persuasively.
"Well, if they was mine I should call them——" Cook paused.
"What would you?" said Michael, more persuasively than ever.
"I'm blessed if I know. There, Annie, what does anyone call a canary?"
"Don't ask me, I'm sure. No," simpered Annie.
"I shouldn't call them nothing, I shouldn't," Mrs. Frith finally decided. "It isn't like dogs."
"What's the matter?" said Nurse, bustling into the kitchen. "Has one got out? Has one got out?"
"I was telling Master Michael here," said Cook, "as how I shouldn't call neither of them nothing. Not if I was he."
"Call what? Call what?" Nurse asked quickly.
"His new dicky-birds."
"Must have names. Yes. Yes. Must have names. Dick and Tom. Dick and Tom."
"But one's a girl," Michael objected.
"Can't be changed now. Must be Dick and Tom," Nurse settled, blowing rapidly as usual.

The decision worried Michael considerably, but as they both turned out to be hens and laid twenty-three eggs between them next spring, it ceased to bother him any more.

The Miss Marrows' School and Kindergarten, kept by Miss Marrow and Miss Caroline Marrow assisted by Miss Hewitt and Miss Hunt, struck Michael as a very solemn establishment indeed. Although its outward appearance was merely that of an ordinary house somewhat larger than others on account of its situation at the corner of Fairfax Terrace, it contained inside a variety of scholastic furniture that was bound to impress the novice.

At twenty minutes past nine on the first day of the autumn term, Nurse and Michael stood before a brass plate inscribed

> The Misses Marrow
> School and Kindergarten

while a bell still jangled with the news of their arrival. They were immediately shown into a very small and very stuffy room on the right of the front door—a gloomy little room, because blinds of coloured beads shut out the unscholastic world. This room was uncomfortably crowded with little girls taking off goloshes and unlacing long brown boots, with little boys squabbling over their indoor shoes, with little girls chatting and giggling and pushing and bumping, with little boys shouting and quarrelling and kicking and pulling. A huddled and heated knot of nurses and nursemaids tried to help their charges, while every minute more little boys and more little girls and more bigger girls pushed their way in and made the confusion worse. In the middle of the uproar Miss Marrow herself entered and the noise was instantly lulled.

"The new boys will wait in here and the new girls will *quietly* follow Helen Hungerford down the passage to Miss Caroline's room. Nurses need not wait any longer."

Then a bell vibrated shrilly. There was a general scamper as the nurses and the nursemaids and the old boys and the old girls hurried from the room, leaving Michael and two other boys, both about two years older than himself, to survey each other with suspicion. The other boys finding Michael beneath the dignity of their notice spoke to each other, or rather the larger of the two, a long-bodied boy with a big head and vacant mouth, said to the other, a fidgety boy with a pink face, a frog-like smile and very tight knickerbockers:

"I say, what's your name?"

The pink-faced boy gulped "Edward Ernest Arnott."

"What is it then?" asked the long-bodied boy.

"Arnott is my surname. Edward and Ernest," he gulped again, "are my Christian names."

"Mine's Vernon Brown. I say, what's your father?"

"A solicitor," said Edward. "What's yours?"

"A cricket—I mean a critic," said Vernon.

"What's that?"

This seemed to upset the long-bodied boy, who replied:

"Coo! Don't you know what a cricket is? I mean critic. You must be a kid."

Michael thought this was the most extraordinary conversation he had ever heard. Not even Mrs. Frith and Annie could be so incomprehensible.

"I don't believe you know yourself," said the pink-faced boy, deepening to crimson.

"Don't I? I bet I do."

"I bet you don't."

"I know better than you anyway."

"So do I than you."

Michael would have found a conversation between two fox-terriers more intelligible. It ended abruptly, however, with the entrance of Miss Marrow, who waved them all to follow her to the severity of her own room. Edward Arnott and Vernon Brown were despatched upstairs to take their places in the class above the Kindergarten for which Michael was destined and whither he followed Miss Marrow, wondering at the size and ugliness of her. Miss Marrow's base was a black bell, on which was set a black cushion, above which was Miss Marrow's round beetroot-coloured face. Miss Caroline was like a green curtain through the folds of which seemed to have burst a red face like her sister's but thinner. Miss Caroline was pleasanter than Miss Marrow and never shouted, perhaps because she was never without a cold in the head.

Michael was handed over to the care of Miss Hewitt, the Kindergarten mistress, who was very kind and very jolly. Michael enjoyed the Kindergarten. There he learned to write pothooks and hangers and very soon to write proper letters. He learned to sew alternate red and blue lines of wool upon a piece of cardboard. He learned to weave bookmarkers with shining slips of chocolate and yellow paper, and to pleat chequered mats of the same material: these, when term was over, appeared at the prize-giving, beautifully enhanced with paper frills cut by the clever Miss Hewitt. He learned to paint texts and to keep his pencil-box tidy and to play the treble of a very unmelodious duet with Miss Hunt, in whose bony fingers his own fingers would from time to time get entangled. He tried the treble without the bass accompaniment at home on Stella, but she cried and seemed as Annie, who was in charge, said 'to regular shudder.' Altogether Kindergarten was a pleasure to Michael, and he found the days went by more quickly, though still far too slowly.

About a week before Christmas his mother came back, and Michael was happy. All the rooms that were only used when she was at home changed from bare beeswaxed deserts to places of perfect comfort, so rosy were the lamp-shades, so sweet was the smell of flowers and so soft and lovely were his mother's scattered belongings. Christmas Day brought presents—a box of stone bricks, a rocking-horse, a doll's house for Stella, boxes of soldiers, a wooden battleship, and books—Hans Andersen and Grimm and the Old French Fairy-tales. As for the stockings that year, it was amazing how much managed to get into one stocking and how deliciously heavy it felt, as it was unhooked from the end of the cot and plumped down upon the bed in the gaslight of Christmas morning. There was only one sadness that hung over the festivities—the thought that his mother would be going away in two days. Boxing Day arrived and there were ominous open trunks and the scattered contents of drawers. To-morrow she was going. It was dreadful to think of. Michael was allowed the bitter joy of helping his mother to pack, and as he stood seriously holding various articles preparatory to their entombment, he talked of the summer and heard promises that mother would spend a long long time with Michael.

"Mother," he said suddenly, "what is my father?"

"What makes you ask that?"

"The boys at Miss Marrow's all ask me that. Have I got a father? Must boys have fathers? Oh, mother, do tell me," pleaded Michael.

Mrs. Fane seemed worried by this question.

"Your father was a gentleman," she said at last.

"What is a gentleman?"

"A good man, always thoughtful and considerate to others."

"Was that man in the photograph my father?"

"What photograph?" Mrs. Fane parried.

"By your bed at the seaside?"

"I don't remember," she said, "Anyway, your father's dead."

"Is he? Poor man!" said sympathetic Michael.

"And now run to Nanny and ask her if she remembers where mother put her large muff."

"Nanny," said Michael, when he had received Nurse's information, "why did my father die?"

"Die? Die? What questions. Tut-tut! Whatever next?" And Nurse blew very violently to show how deeply she disapproved of Michael's inquisitiveness.

That evening, just when Michael was going to bed, there came a knock at the door, and a tall fair man was shown into the drawing-room.

"How d'ye do, Mrs. Fane? I've come to ask you if you'll go to the theatre to-night. Saxby is coming on later."

"Oh, thank you very much, Mr. Prescott, but I really think I must stay in. You see," she said smilingly, "it's Michael's last night of me for a long time."

Michael stood gazing at Mr. Prescott, hating him with all his might and sighing relief at his mother's refusal to go out.

"Oh, Michael won't mind; will you, Michael?"

Nurse came in saying 'Bed-time! Tut-tut-tut! Bed-time!' and Michael's heart sank.

"There you are," said Mr. Prescott. "Here's Nurse to say it's bed-time. Now do come, Mrs. Fane."

"Oh, I really think I ought to stay."

"Now what nonsense. Saxby will be furiously disappointed. You must. Come along, Michael, be a brave chap and tell your mother she's got to go out; and here's something to square our account."

He pressed a little gold coin into Michael's unwilling hand.

"Would you mind very much, if I went?" his mother asked.

"No," said Michael tonelessly. The room was swimming round him in sickening waves of disappointment.

"Of course he won't," decided Mr. Prescott boisterously.

While he was being undressed, Nurse asked what he was holding. Michael showed the half-sovereign.

"Spoiling children," muttered Nanny. "That's for your money-box."

Michael did not care what it was for. He was listening for his mother's step. She came in, while he lay round-eyed in his cot, and leaned over to kiss him. He held her to him passionately; then he buried his face in the bedclothes and, while she rustled away from him, sobbed soundlessly for a long while.

In the morning he watched her go away until the warm summer-time and felt abandoned as he walked through the wintry rooms, where lately he and his mother had sat by the fire. As for the ten-shilling piece, he thought no more about it. Soon afterwards he fell ill with whooping-cough, he and Stella together, and the days dragged unendurably in the stuffy nursery away from school.

Chapter III: *Fears and Fantasies*

DURING whooping-cough Michael was sometimes allowed to sit in a room called the library, which was next to his mother's bedroom on the first floor and was therefore a dearly loved resort. Here he discovered the large volume of Don Quixote illustrated by Doré that influenced his whole life. He would pore over this work for hours, forgetting everything under a spell of chivalry. He read the tale seriously and thought it the saddest tale ever known. He wept over the knight's adventures, and big teardrops would spatter the page. He had not yet encountered much more than mild teazing at the Kindergarten, that with the unreasonableness of Nurse and his mother's absence made up the sum of the incomprehensible crosses which he had to bear. But even these were enough to make him sympathize with Don Quixote. He perceived that here was a man intent upon something— he could not understand exactly what—thwarted always by other people, thwarted and jeered at and even physically maltreated. Yet he was a man whose room was full of dragons and fairies, whose counterpane was the adventurous field of little knights-at-arms, whose curtains were ruffled by dwarfs, whose cupboards held enchanters. Michael loved the tall thin knight and envied Sancho Panza.

When whooping-cough was over, and Michael went back to Kindergarten, Nurse decided that he should sleep by himself in the room next to the night-nursery. She never explained to Michael her reasons for this step, and he supposed it to be because lately he had always woken up when she came to bed. This was not his fault, because Nurse always bumped into his cot as she came, into the room, shaking it so violently that no one could have stayed asleep. She used to look at him in a funny way with angry staring eyes, and when he sometimes spoke she would blow cheese-scented breath at him and turn away and bump into the washstand.

Everything in this new room was by Michael anticipated with dread. He would go to bed at half-past six: he would settle down in the wide white bed that stretched a long way on either side of him: the gas would be turned down: the door would be left ajar: Nurse's footsteps would gradually die away and he would be left alone.

The night was divided into two portions of equal horror. First of all he had to concentrate on closing his mouth when asleep, because Annie had told him a tale about a woman who slept with her mouth open, the result of which bad habit was that one night a mouse ran down it and choked her. Then he had to explore cautiously with his feet the ice-cold end of the bed, in case he should touch a nest of mice—another likely occurrence vouched for by Annie. Then outside, various sounds would frighten him. A dog would howl in the distance: cats would spit and wail, making Michael wonder whether they were coming through his window to claw his face. Presently, far up the street, newsboys would cry hoarsely the details of a murder or suicide. As they passed beneath his bedroom window their voices would swell to a paralyzing roar, and as the voices died away round the corner, Michael would be left shaking with fear. Once he was so frightened by a succession of these murder-shouts that he got out of bed and crept forth on to the landing, whence he peered down between the banisters into the quiet red light burning in the hall far below. While he was leaning over, a door banged suddenly on the top floor, and Michael fled barefooted down the stairs, until he reached the cold tiles of the front hall. Should he dare to descend still lower and disturb Nurse at her supper in the kitchen? Or were they all lying there, Cook and Annie and Nurse, with their throats cut? The door leading to the basement stairs was open, and he stole down over the oilcloth, past the yawning cellar, past the laundry-basket in the passage, past the cupboard under the stairs, to listen by the kitchen door. There was a murmur of voices, familiar yet unfamiliar: the kitchen door was ajar and he peered round stealthily. There was Nurse with a very red face in a heap on a chair, shaking her forefinger at Mrs. Frith, who with an equally red face was talking very indistinctly to Nurse; while between them, bolt upright and very pale, sat Annie nervously shaving from the cheese very thin segments which she ate from the knife's edge. They seemed to Michael, as he watched them, like people in a nightmare, so unreal and horrible were they: they frightened him more than ever, sitting there nodding at each other in the kitchen where the blackbeetles ran slyly in and out beneath the fender. Suddenly Annie saw Michael and waved him back; he turned at her gesture and withdrew from sight. While he stood shivering in the dark passage, Annie came out and, picking him up, carried him out of hearing.

"Whatever made you come downstairs?" she panted on the first-floor landing.

"I was frightened."

"You frightened *me*."

"Who are they murdering?"

"You've been having a bad dream," said Annie.

She led him upstairs again to his room and tucked him up, and at his earnest request turned the gas a trifle higher.

"Why did Nanny and Mrs. Frith look like that?" he asked.

"They're tired," said Annie.

"Why?"

"They have to work so hard to look after you."

Then she left him alone, and he fell asleep before they all came up to bed.

Generally speaking, the first part of the night, however bad the outside noises, was not so fearful as the second part. Mostly the second portion of the night was preceded by a bad dream in which Michael's nerves were so much shaken that he had no courage or common-sense left to grapple with the long hours in the ghastly stillness of his room. There was one dream in particular which he dreaded, and indeed it was the only one that repeated itself at regular intervals without any essential change. He would find himself alone in a long street in the middle of the night. Usually it would be shining with wet, but sometimes it would be dry and airless. This street stretched as far as one could see. It had on either side lamp-posts which burned with a steady staring illumination, long rows of lamp-posts that converged in the farthest distance. The houses all seemed empty, yet everyone was in some way a malignant personality. Down this street Michael would have to walk on and on. He would meet nobody, and the only living thing was a bony hound that pattered behind him at whatever pace he went, whether he ran or whether he loitered. He would in his dream be filled with a desire to enter one of these houses, and often he would mount the steps and knock a summons on the door—a knock that echoed all over the gloom within. While he knocked, the bony hound would howl in the shadows of the basement. Every house at which he knocked Michael would be more and more anxious to pass, more and more fearful to disturb. Yet however much he struggled against it, he would ultimately be compelled to knock his loud challenge. The street would now stretch for miles of lighted lamps before and behind him, and the knowledge would gradually be borne in upon Michael that sooner or later in one of these grey houses the door would open. He would hurry along, but however fast he travelled some house would draw him inexorably to its threshold, and he would wait in agony lest slowly the great door should swing back to a dim hall. The climax of the dream would now be reached. One house would simultaneously repel and draw him more than any of those left behind. He would struggle to go by, but he would find himself on the steps with legs that refused to carry him away. He would knock: very slowly the door would swing back and, convulsed and choking and warding off horror, Michael would wake in a frenzy of fear to his own real house of ghastly stillness, where no longer did even a belated luggage-train or jingling hansom assure him of life's continuity.

He did not always wake up suddenly: sometimes he would be aware that he was slowly waking and would struggle to keep asleep, lying for a long time without moving a muscle, in order to cheat himself into the belief that he was not awake. But gradually the strain would be too much and he would have to become conscious of the room. First of all he would turn on to his left side and view apprehensively the door ajar. This would seem to tremble, as he looked, to some invisible hand trying it. Then along the wall the wardrobe would creak, and every knot of its varnished surface would take on a fantastic countenance. He would wonder what was inside, and try to gain comfort and the sense of commonplace daytime existence by counting the cats swinging on a roundabout in one of Louis Wain's Christmas pictures. In the corner beyond the wardrobe was a large clothes-basket that crackled and snapped and must surely hold somebody inside, hidden as the Forty Thieves were hidden in the oil-jars. The fire-place, opposite the foot of the bed, seemed a centre for the noise of mice. How he hoped they would be content to play upon the hearth and not venture to leap over the fender and scuttle about the room. Then the door would begin to frighten him again, and Michael would turn very quietly on to his back, staring at the luminous ceiling where the gas-jet made a huge moon whose edges wavered perpetually. But the gas-jet itself became terrifying, when looked at too long, with its queer blue base and slim solemn shape, so melancholy, so desolate, so changeless. The ceiling would very soon become unendurable because various black marks would seem with intensest contemplation more and more like spiders and beetles. Michael would have to give up lying on his back and turn upon his right side. He would count each slat of the Venetian blinds and long passionately and sadly for the grey streaks to appear at the sides in proclamation of the approach of day. Without these grey streaks the windows were unbearable, so menacing were they with the unknown infinite night behind them. The curtains, too, would quiver, and even Michael's clothes, heaped upon a chair, would assume a worm-like vitality. The washstand made him feel oppressed, so silent and white were the jug and basin and soap-dish, so cold and chill were they. There was nothing to be done but to bury his head beneath the clothes and, trembling, try to believe in the reality of guardian angels. He would shut his eyes very tightly until the wheels of coloured lights thus evoked would circle and revolve, changing their colours in some mysterious way. These dissolving spots were a great consolation and passed the time for a little while, until the dread of fire began to come. He would fling back the clothes in a paroxysm and, heedless of any other danger, sit up with staring eyes and listening ears and keen nostrils, dreading and imagining and doubting. Surely he could hear a crackle; he could smell smoke. The house was on fire; yet not for anything could he have got out of bed to reassure himself. What might not be underneath, a burglar, a dead body, a murderer, a skeleton, a mad dog?

Underneath the clothes he would plunge, and then he would be sure that someone was coming into the room to smother him. He held his breath, waiting; with an effort he flung back the clothes again. There was nothing but the ghastly stillness and the solemn gaslight and the viewless blinds and the expectant door ajar. The bedposts would now take on a sort of humanity. They would look at him and wink and shiver. The wall-paper, normally a pattern of rosebuds and roses, began to move, to swim with unnatural life. The cistern upstairs began to clank; the bath began to drip. It must be blood—Nanny had been murdered. The blood was dripping slowly. Michael choked with horror. Somebody was tapping at the window-pane, yes, somebody was tapping. It was horrible this endless tapping. Cats must be coming in. The wardrobe creaked and rapped and groaned. Some of his clothes slid off the chair on to the floor with a soft plump; Michael tried to shriek his dismay; but his tongue was dry. Underneath him a knife was being pushed through the bed. A death-watch was ticking in the fastness of the wall at his head. A rat was gnawing his way into the room. Black-beetles were coming up the stairs.

Then along the edge of the Venetian blinds appeared a blue streak. It widened. It became more luminous. It turned from blue to grey. It turned from grey to dimmest silver. Hark! 'Cheep, cheep, cheep, cheep!' The sparrows were beginning. Their chorus rose. Their noise was cool as water to Michael's fever. An early cart rattled cheerfully down the road. It was morning.

Chapter IV: *Unending Childhood*

AFTER whooping-cough came chicken-pox, and it was settled that Michael should leave the Kindergarten where these illnesses were caught. A French governess was to teach him every morning and to walk with him every afternoon. Mrs. Fane wrote to Nurse to tell her of this decision and to announce that a Madame Flauve would on Monday next arrive at 64 Carlington Road to superintend the education of Michael. This news reached Nurse on the preceding Friday and threw her into an agitation. The whole house was turned upside down: curtains were changed; floors were beeswaxed; furniture was polished; pictures were dusted. All Saturday and Friday a great cleaning took place, and on Sunday every cushion was smoothed and patted; chairs were adjusted; mats were shaken; flowers were distributed, until in the evening Nurse and Cook and Annie, followed by Michael, marched over the house and examined their handiwork.

"Well, I hope we shall see something worth looking at," said Mrs. Frith. "I never worked so hard in all my natural."

"Oh, yes. Must get the place nice. Not going to have strange people come here and grumble," said Nurse.

"What is this Madame Flauve? Is she a lady?" Cook asked.

"Oh, yes. Yes. A lady. French. Very particular," Nurse replied.

Michael wondered what his governess would be like. He never remembered to have seen Nanny so reverently excited before.

"I've heard a lot about these French women," said Mrs. Frith. "A lot about them, I have. They live very gay, don't they?"

"Doesn't matter how they live. No. No. Must have everything at its best," Nurse insisted.

By the time the scouring of the house was done, Michael was prepared for the advent of a creature so lovely that he made up his mind the mere sight of her would fill him with joy. He had not settled exactly which princess she would most nearly resemble. As he turned over the pages of his fairy-books, he would fancy with every illustration that here was to be seen the image of his beautiful French governess. As he lay awake in his bed on a quiet Sunday evening, so pleasant was the imagination of her radiancy that fears and horrors were driven away by the power of her beauty's spell. The night acquired something of the peace and sanctity of Christmas Eve, when the air was hallowed by Santa Claus on his jovial pilgrimage. He had never felt so little oppressed by the night, so confident in the might of good.

On Monday morning Michael jigged through his dressing, jigged downstairs to breakfast, jigged through the meal itself and jigged upstairs to the dining-room to watch for the splendid arrival. He tambourinated upon the window-pane a gay little tune, jigging the while from foot to foot in an ecstasy of anticipation.

Nurse had decided that the morning-room was not a fit place for such a paragon to perform her duties. Nor did she feel that the day-nursery was worthy of her. So, even while Michael jigged at his vigil, Nurse was arming the dining-room table for an encounter with greatness. Inkpots were dusted and displayed; blotting-pads, including one poker—worked with a view of Antwerp Cathedral, were unfolded. Pens and pencils and pieces of india-rubber and pen-wipers and boxes of nibs and drawing-pins were lavishly scattered about the green tablecloth. Various blue exercise-books gleamed in the April sunlight and, to set the seal upon the whole business, a calendar of Great Thoughts was roughly divested of ninety-eight great thoughts at once, in order that for this rare female a correct announcement should celebrate the ninth of April, her famous date. At five minutes to ten Nurse and Michael were both in a state of excitement; Cook was saying that she had never regretted the inadequacy of the kitchen arrangements of Sixty-four until this moment; and Annie was bracing herself for the real effort, the opening of the door to Madame Flauve. The only calm person was Stella who, clasping a rubber doll with tight curly rubber hair and a stomachic squeak, chanted to herself the saga of Madame Flauve's arrival.

At two minutes past ten Michael said somebody was coming up the steps, and a ring confirmed his assertion. The door was opened. Madame Flauve was heard rubbing her boots on the SALVE of the mat, was heard putting away her umbrella in the peacock-blue china umbrella-stand, was heard enquiring for Mrs. Fane and was announced inaudibly by Annie.

Michael's heart sank when he beheld a fat young French-woman with a bilious complexion and little pig's eyes and a dowdy black mantle and a common black hat. As for Nurse, she sniffed quite audibly and muttered an insincere hope that Madame Flauve would find everything to her liking. The governess answered in the thick voice of one who is always swallowing jujubes that without a doubt she would find everything, and presently Nurse left the room with many a backward glance of contempt towards Madame Flauve.

When the lessons began (or rather before they began) a time-table was drawn up by Madame Flauve:

```
            ⎡           1       Frenc
        Mo  ⎢  0—11     h                    2
nday        ⎢  11—12    Geography        .30—4    alk
            ⎣  12—1     History
```

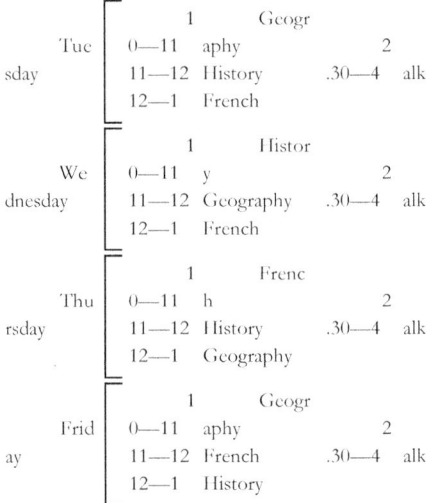

		1	Geography	2	
Tuesday	0—11				
	11—12	History		.30—4	alk
	12—1	French			
Wednesday	0—11	1	History	2	
	11—12	Geography		.30—4	alk
	12—1	French			
Thursday	0—11	1	French	2	
	11—12	History		.30—4	alk
	12—1	Geography			
Friday	0—11	1	Geography	2	
	11—12	French		.30—4	alk
	12—1	History			

Michael, when he saw the programme of his work, felt much depressed. It seemed to lack variety and he was not very much cheered up to hear that at meals only French would be spoken. Those meals were dreadful. At first Nurse and Stella were present, but when Nanny found that Madame wanted to teach Stella the French for knife and fork, she declined to have dinner downstairs any longer, and Michael and Madame Flauve were left to dine tête-à-tête on dull food and a languishing conversation.

"Madam indeed," Nurse would sniff, when the governess had left after tea, "I never heard of such a thing in all my life. Madam! A fine Madam!"

"What an imperence," agreed Mrs. Frith. "Fancy, a ordinary volgar thing like that to go calling herself Madam, whatever shall we come to?"

"It does seem a cheek, don't it?" said Annie.

"I never!" Cook gasped. "I never! Madam! Well, I could almost laugh at the sauce of it. And all that cleaning as you might say for a person as isn't a scrap better than you and me."

"Oh, I've written to Mrs. Fane," said Nurse. "I said there must be some mistake been made. Oh, yes, a mistake—must be a mistake."

Michael did not much enjoy the walks with his governess. He was always taken to a second-hand furniture-shop in the Hammersmith Road, not a pleasant old furniture-shop with Toby mugs and stuffed birds and coins; but a barrack full of red washing-stands and white-handled chests of drawers. Madame Flauve informed him that she was engaged in furnishing at that moment, and would immediately show him a locket with the portrait of her husband inset. Michael could not gain any clear idea of what M. Flauve was like, since all that remained was a nebulous profile smothered by a very black moustache. Madame Flauve told him that M. Flauve was 'tout-à-fait charmant, mais charmant, mon petit. Il était si aimable, si gentil et d'un cœur très très bon.' Michael grew very tired of being jostled outside the furniture-shop every afternoon, while his governess grubbed around the ugly furniture and argued with the man about the prices. The only article she ever bought was a commode, which so violently embarrassed Michael that he blushed the whole way home. But Madame Flauve often made him blush and would comment upon subjects not generally mentioned except by Mrs. Frith, and even by her only in a spirit of hearty coarseness that did not make Michael feel ashamed like this Frenchwoman's suggestion of the nasty. He was on one occasion very much disgusted by her remarks on the inside of an egg that was slightly set. Yet while he was disgusted, his curiosity was stimulated by the information imparted, and he made further enquiries from Nurse that evening. Nanny was horrified, and said plainly that she considered this governess no better than a low beast and that she should write accordingly to Mrs. Fane.

After a month or two Michael was sent back to school in the morning, though the afternoon walks still continued for a time. When Michael returned to the Misses Marrow, he was promoted to the class above the Kindergarten and was set to learn the elements of Latin in a desultory and unpractical way, that is to say he was made to learn—

	Nom	m	a
inative,	ensa,	table	
	Voca	m	C
tive,	ensa,	table	
	Accu	m	a
sative,	ensam,	table	

and the rest of the unintelligible rigmarole. He had no clear notion what Latin was, and so far as he could make out nobody else at the Miss Marrows' school had any clearer notion. Indeed, the only distinct addition to his knowledge of life was gained from Vernon Brown who with great ingenuity had hollowed out a cork and by the insertion of several pins in the front had made of it a miniature cage in which he kept a fly. All the other boys were much impressed by Vernon Brown's achievement, and very soon they all came to school with flies captive in excavated corks. Michael longed to be like these bigger boys and pined for a cage. One day Edward Arnott gave him one, and all the rest of that day Michael watched the fly trying to escape. When he showed it to Madame Flauve, she professed herself shocked by the cruelty of it and begged him to release the fly, asserting that she would find him a substitute which would deceive all the other boys. Michael agreed to release his captive and the long-imprisoned fly walked painfully out of his cell. Then Madame Flauve chipped off a little piece of coal and tied it round with one of her own hairs and showed Michael how by cunningly twisting this hair, the coal would gain the appearance of mobility. Michael was doubtful at first, but Madame's exaggerated encouragement led him to suppose that it was safe to practise the deception on his companions. So on the next day he proceeded to exhibit his 'fly.' But everybody knew it was coal and jeered at Michael and made him very unhappy and anxious never again to attempt to differentiate himself or his actions from the rest of mankind.

Michael's mother came home towards the end of July, and Madame Flauve vanished to her husband and house and furniture. Michael did not regret her. Mrs. Fane asked him many questions and particularly she wanted to know if he was perfectly happy. Michael said 'yes,' and his mother seemed satisfied. She was now very much taken up with Stella, who was a lovely little girl with grey eyes and light brown glinting hair. Michael did not exactly feel jealous of his sister, but he had an emotion of disappointment that no longer could he be alone with his mother in a fragrant intimacy from which the perpetually sleeping Stella was excluded. Now Stella no longer slept all the time, but, on the contrary, was very much awake and very eager to be entertained. Michael also felt a twinge of regret that Stella should be able out of her own self to entertain grown-up people. He wished that he could compose these wonderful, endless songs of hers. He could not but admit that they were wonderful, and exactly like real poetry. To be sure their subjects were ordinary enough. There was no magic in them. Stella would simply sing of getting up in the morning and of the morning bath and the towel and the bread and milk for breakfast. She would sing, too, of the ride in the perambulator and of the ladies who paid her compliments as she passed. It was a little galling to Michael that he, so long his mother's only companion, should have to share her love with such an insidious rival. Curious men with long hair came to the house, apparently just to see Stella; for they took no notice at all of Michael. These long-haired visitors would sit round in the drawing-room, while Stella played at the piano pieces that were not half so hummable as those which Michael had already learned to play in violent allegretto. Stella would sit upright in her starchiest frock and widest sash and play without any music a long and boring noise that made Michael feel very fidgety. He would endure it for a while and then he would have to go out of the room. The first time he had done this he had expected somehow that people would run after him to bring him back. But nobody moved. Everyone was intent upon Stella and her noise. They were all grunting and clearing their throats and making unintelligible exclamations. Michael was glad that they had begun to build houses in the waste ground opposite. It was better to watch men climbing up ladders and walking over planks and messing with lumps of mortar than to sit there among those guttural men in an atmosphere of Stella worship. He felt sometimes that he would like to pinch Stella's legs— they looked so sleek and well-behaved, as she sat there playing the piano. Michael was never invited to play on the drawing-room piano. He was only allowed to play up in the day-nursery, with merely the ambition of one day being able to reach the pedals to stir him on.

"Ach, Mrs. Vane," he heard these long-haired men declare. "Your daughter is wonderful. Ach! Ach! Ach! She is a genius. She will be the great pianist of the new generation. Ach! Ach! Ach!"

Michael began to feel that his love for his mother or her love for him did not matter. He began to feel that only what he himself thought and wanted did matter; and when she went away again he was sorry, but not so sorry as he used to be. One of these long-haired men now began to come every day to give Stella lessons on the drawing-room piano. He would give a very loud knock and hang up a wide-brimmed black hat in the hall and clear his throat and button up his coat very tightly and march into the drawing-room to wait for Stella to be brought down. Stella would come down the stairs with her grey eyes shining and her hair all fuzzy and her hands smelling of pink soap, while Nurse would blow very importantly and tell Michael not to peep round corners. Stella's music lessons were much grander than Michael's in the stuffy back-room of Miss Marrow's. Besides, Michael's music lessons were now particularly unpleasant, because Miss Hunt, his mistress, had grown two warts on her first finger during the summer holidays, which made him feel sick during their eternal duets.

The withdrawal of Madame Flauve from the superintendence of Michael's afternoon walks was apparently a great blow to Nurse. She had acquired a habit either of retiring to the night-nursery or of popping out of the back-door on secret errands. Stella in the charge of Annie was perfectly happy upstairs, and Nurse resented very strongly Michael's enquiries as to where she was going. Michael had no ulterior reasons for his questions. He was sincerely interested by these afternoon walks of Nurse, and speculated often upon her destination. She would always return very cheerful and would often bring him home small presents—a dark blue bird on a pin at boat-race time (for Nurse was staunchly Oxford), a penny packet of stamps most of which were duplicates inside, penny illustrated books of Cock Robin or Tom Thumb; and once she brought him home a Night Companion. This Night Companion was a club-headed stick, very powerful and warranted to secure the owner from a murderous attack. It was one of a row in the window of a neighbouring umbrella-shop, a long row of Night Companions that cost one shilling each. Michael liked his stick and took it to bed with him and was comforted, when he woke up, by the sight of its knotted head upon the bolster. He grew very intimate with the stick and endowed it with character and temperament and humanity. He would often stare at the still unpurchased Night Companions in the shop, trying to discover if any other of them were so beneficent and so pleasant a companion as his own. In time he took a fancy to another, and begged Nurse to be allowed to buy this for Stella. Nurse was gratified by his appreciation of her present and gave him leave to break into the ten-shilling piece to endow Stella with a Companion. Michael himself carried it home, wrapped in a flimsy brown paper and tied up as he thought unnecessarily with a flimsy string. Stella was told to take it to bed with her and did so, but by some accident grazed her forehead on the Night Companion's knotty head and cried so much that it was taken away from her. This was all the better for Michael who thenceforth had two Night Companions—one on either side of him to guard him from the door and the window.

Still, notwithstanding these presents, Nurse grew more and more irritable to find Michael watching her exits from and entrances into 64 Carlington Road. Once, she was so much annoyed to see Michael's face pressed against the pane of the morning-room window that she slid all the way down the area-steps and sent Michael to bed as a punishment for peeping. At last she decided that Michael must go for walks by himself and lest he should be lost or get into mischief, every walk must be in the same direction, along the same road to the same place and back. He was to walk up Carlington Road into the Hammersmith Road and along the Kensington Road as far as the Earl's Court Road. Here he was to stop and turn round and walk back to Carlington Road on his traces.

Michael detested this walk. He would stump up the area-steps, watched by Nurse, and he would walk steadily, looking neither to the right nor to the left according to orders, as far as 44 Carlington Road. Here in the morning-room window was a small aquarium, sadly mobile with half a dozen pale goldfish, that Michael would be compelled to watch for a few seconds before he turned round and acknowledged the fact that Nurse was flicking him on with her hand. Michael would proceed past the other houses until he came to 22 Carlington Road, where a break occurred, caused by a house entirely different from any of the others, at the side of which was a huge double door. This was sometimes open, and inside could be seen men hammering with chisels at enormous statues including representations of Queen Victoria and of a benignant lion. Next to this house was a post office, not an ordinary post office where stamps could be bought, but a harum-scarum place, full of postmen running up and down and emptying bags and hammering on letters and talking very loudly and very quickly. By this office Carlington Road made an abrupt rectangular turn past a tumble-down tarred fence, through whose interstices could be seen a shadowy garden full of very long pale grass and of trees with jet-black trunks. Beyond the trees was a tumble-down house with big bare windows glinting amongst the ivy. After this Carlington Road went on again with smaller houses of a deeper red brick than those in the part where Michael lived. They had no basements, and one could see into their dining-rooms, so close were they to the road. When 2 Carlington Road was reached a tall advertisement hoarding began, and for a hundred yards the walk became absolutely interesting. Then Carlington Mansions rose majestic, and Michael, who had been told that they were flats and had heard people wondering at this strange new method of existence, loitered for a moment in order to watch a man in a uniform, sitting on a wooden chair and reading a pink newspaper. He also read the names of people who were either out or in, and settled, when he was older, to live in a flat in the security of many other families and a man in a green uniform. The roar of the Hammersmith Road burst upon him, and dreams were over for a while, as he hurried along past eight shops, at none of which he would dare to look since he read in a book of a boy who had been taken off to the police station on a charge of theft, though he was actually as innocent as Michael himself and was merely interested by the contents of a shop window. The next turning to Carlington Road was a queer terrace, very quiet except that it overlooked the railway, very quiet and melancholy and somehow unused. Nothing ever turned down here except an occasional dog or cat; no servants stood gossiping by area-gates, and at the end of it loomed the tumble-down house whose garden Michael had already seen near the post office. He used to think as he left Padua Terrace behind him that one day for a great adventure he would like to walk along under its elm-trees to discover if anyone did live in those dark houses; but he never managed to be brave enough to do so. Michael now crossed the railway bridge and looked at the advertisements: then followed a dull line of iron railings with rusty pineapples on top of each of them. These were bounded at each end by gates that were marked 'Private. No Thoroughfare,' and after the second gate came the first crossing. Michael had been told to be very careful of crossings, and he used to poise himself on the kerb for a moment to see if any carts were near. If none were even in sight, he used to run across as quickly as he could. There were three other crossings before Earl's Court Road was reached, and one of them was so wide that he was very glad indeed when it was put behind him. All the way, terrace after terrace of grim houses, set back from the high road behind shrubberies, had to be passed, and all the way Michael used to hum to himself for company and diversion and encouragement. The only interesting event was a pavement-artist, and he was very often not there. It was an exasperating and monotonous walk, and he hated it for the gloom it shed upon all his afternoons.

Sometimes Michael would arrive home before Nanny, and then he would have to endure a long cross-examination upon his route. The walk was not sufficiently interesting to invent tales about, and he resented Nurse's incredulous attitude and wrinkled obstinate face. Indeed, Michael began to resent Nurse altogether, and so far as he was able he avoided her. His scheme of things was logical: he had already a philosophy, and his conception of the wonder inherent in everything was evidently not unique, because the pictures in Don Quixote proved conclusively that what Michael thought, other people besides himself thought. He might be old-fashioned, as Nurse assured him he was; but if to be old-fashioned was to live in the world of Don Quixote, he certainly preferred it to the world in which Nanny lived. That seemed to him a circumscribed and close existence for which he had no sympathy. It was a world of poking about in medicine-cupboards, of blind unreasonableness, of stupidity and malice and blank ugliness. He would sit watching Nanny nibbling with her front teeth the capers of the caper sauce, and he would hate her. She interfered with him, with his day-dreams and toys and meals; and the only time when he wanted her presence was in the middle of the night, when she was either drinking her glass of ale in the kitchen or snoring heavily in the next room. Michael's only ambition was to live in his own world. This he would have shared with his mother, but her visits were now so rare that it was unwise to rely on her presence for happiness. He was learning to do without her: Nurse he had never yet learnt to endure. She charged ferociously into his fancies, shattering them with her fussy interference, just as she would snatch away his clay pipe, when the most perfect bubble was trembling on the edge of the bowl.

"Time for tea," she would mutter. "Time for bed," she would chatter. Always it was time for something unpleasant.

Mrs. Frith, on the other hand, was a person whose attractions grew with longer friendship, as Nurse's decreased even from the small quantity she originally possessed. As Michael month by month grew older, Mrs. Frith expanded towards him. She found him an attentive, even a breathless listener to her rollicking tales. Her life Michael plainly perceived to have been crammed with exciting adventures. In earliest youth she had been forced by cunning to outwit a brutal father with the frightening habit of coming home in the evening and taking off his belt to her and her brothers and her sisters. The house in which she lived had been full of hiding-places, and Mrs. Frith, picturing herself to Michael of less ample girth, described wonderfully how her father had actually routed for her with a broom-handle while her mother sat weeping into an apron. Then it appeared that it was the custom of small boys in the street of her youth to sell liquorice-water in exchange for pins.

"But was it nice?" asked Michael, remembering liquorice-powder.

"Lovely stuff," Mrs. Frith affirmed. "They used to go calling up and down, 'Fine liquorice-water! Fine liquorice-water! Bring out your pins and have a bottle of liquorice-water.'"

"And did you?" asked Michael.

"Did we? Of course we did—every pin in the place. There wasn't a pin in the whole street after those boys had gone by."

"What else did you do when you were little, Mrs, Frith?"

"What else? Why everything."

"Yes, but tell me what," Michael begged, clasping his knees and looking earnestly at Cook.

"Why once I went to a Sunday-school treat and got thrown off of a donkey and showed more than I meant and the boys all hollered after me going to Sunday-school and I used to stand behind a corner and dodge them. The saucy demons!"

These tales were endless, and Michael thought how jolly it would be to set out early one summer morning with Mrs. Frith and look for adventures like Don Quixote. This became a favourite day-dream, and he used to fancy Mrs. Frith tossed in a blanket like Sancho Panza. What company she would be, and it would be possible with two donkeys. He had seen women as fat as her riding on donkeys by the seaside.

One day Mrs. Frith told him she was thinking of getting married again, and on a Sunday afternoon Michael was introduced to her future husband, a certain Mr. Hopkins, who had a shining red head and an enormous coloured handkerchief into which he trumpeted continuously. Mr. Hopkins also had a daughter three or four years older than Michael—a wizened little girl called Flossie who spoke in a sort of hiss and wore very conspicuous underclothing of red flannelette. Michael and Flossie played together shyly under the admiring patronage of Mrs. Frith and Mr. Hopkins, and were just beginning to be friendly when Nurse came in and said:

"Can't be allowed. No, no. Never heard of such a thing. Tut-tut."

After this Nurse and Mrs. Frith did not seem to get on very well, and Mrs. Frith used to talk about 'people as gave theirselves airs which they had no business to of done.' She was kinder than ever to Michael and gave him as many sultanas as he wanted and told him all about the house into which she and Mr. Hopkins and Flossie would presently depart from Carlington Road.

"Are you going away?" Michael asked, aghast.

"Going to be married," said Mrs. Frith.

"But I don't want you to go."

"There, bless your heart, I've a good mind to stay. I believe you'll miss your poor old Mrs. Frith, eh, ducky?"

Everybody nice went away, Michael thought. It was extraordinary how only nasty food and nasty people were wholesome.

Mrs. Frith's departure was even more exciting than her stories. One afternoon Michael found her in the kitchen, dancing about with her skirts kilted above her knees. He was a little embarrassed at first, but very soon he had to laugh because she was evidently not behaving like this in order to show off, but because she enjoyed dancing about the kitchen.

"Why are you dancing, Mrs. Frith?" he asked.

"Happy as a lark, lovey," she answered in an odd voice. "Happy as a lark, for we won't go home till morning, we won't go home till morning," and singing, she twirled round and round until she sank into a wicker arm-chair. At this moment Annie came running downstairs with Nurse, and both of them glared at Mrs. Frith with shocked expressions.

"What ever are you doing, Cook?" said Nurse.

"That's all right, lovey. That's All Sir Garnet, and don't you make no mistake. Don't you—make no mistake."

Here Mrs. Frith gave a very loud hiccup and waved her arms and did not even say 'beg pardon' for the offensive noise.

"Michael," said Nurse, "go upstairs at once. Mrs. Frith, get up. You ignorant and vulgar woman. Get up."

"And you ought to be ashamed of yourself," said Cook to Nurse. "You old performing monkey, that's what you are."

"Annie," said Nurse, "fetch a policeman in, and go and get this woman's box."

"Woman!" said Mrs. Frith. "Woman yourself. Who's a woman? I'm not a woman. No, I'm not. And if I am a woman, you're not the one to say so. Ah, I know how many bottles have gone out of this house and come in—not by me."

"Hold your impudent tongue," said Nurse.

"I shall not hold my tongue, so now," retorted Mrs. Frith.

Michael had squeezed himself behind the kitchen door fascinated by this duel. It was like Alice in Wonderland, and every minute he expected to see Cook throwing plates at Nanny, who was certainly making faces exactly like the Duchess. The area door slammed, and Michael wondered what was going to happen. Presently there came the sound of a deep tread in the passage and a policeman entered.

"What's all this?" he said in a deep voice.

"Constable," said Nurse, "will you please remove this dreadful woman?"

"What's she been doing?" asked the policeman.

"She's drunk."

Mrs. Frith apparently overwhelmed by the enormity of the accusation tottered to her feet and seized a saucepan.

"None of that now," said the policeman roughly, as he caught her by the waist.

"Oh, I'm not afraid of a bluebottle," said Mrs. Frith haughtily. "Not of a bluebottle, I'm not."

"Are you going to charge her?" the policeman asked.

"No, no. Nothing but turn her out. The girl's packing her box. Give her the box and let her go."

"Not without my wages," said Mrs. Frith. "I'm not going to leave my wages behind. Certainly I'm not."

Nurse fumbled in her purse, and at last produced some money.

"That's the easiest way," said the policeman. "Pay her the month and let her go. Come on, my lady."

He seized Mrs. Frith and began to walk her to the door as if she were a heavy sack. Michael began to cry. He did not want Mrs. Frith to be hurt and he felt frightened. In the passage she suddenly broke loose and, turning round, pushed Nurse into the laundry-basket and was so pleased with her successful effort that she almost ran out of the house and could presently be heard singing very cheerfully 'White wings, they never grow weary,' to the policeman. In the end her trunk was pushed down the front-door steps, and after more singing and arguing a four-wheeler arrived and Mrs. Frith vanished for ever from Carlington Road.

The effect of this scene on Nurse was to make her more repressive and secretive. She was also very severe on vulgarity; and all sorts of old words were wrapped up in new words, as when bread and dripping became bread and honey, because dripping was vulgar. The house grew much gloomier with Mrs. Frith's departure. The new cook whose name Michael never found out, because she remained the impersonal official, was very brusque and used to say: "Now then, young man, out of my kitchen or I'll tell Nurse. And don't hang about in the passage or in two-twos you'll be sorry you ever came downstairs."

It was autumn again, and the weather was dreary and wet. Michael suffered a severe shock one morning. It was too foggy to go to school and he was sitting alone in the window of the morning-room, staring at the impenetrable and fearful yellowness of the air. Suddenly he heard the cry, 'Remember, remember the Fifth of November, and gunpowder, treason and plot,' and, almost before he had time to realize it was the dreaded Guy Fawkes, a band of loud-voiced boys with blackened faces came surging down the area steps and held close to the window a nodding Guy. Michael shrieked with fear and ran from the room, only to be told by Nurse that she'd never heard such old-fashioned nonsense in all her life.

During that November the fogs were very bad and, as an epidemic term had compelled the Misses Marrow to close their school, Michael brooded at home in the gaslit rooms that shone dully in the street of footsteps. The long morning would drag its length out, and dinner would find no appetite in Michael. Stella seemed not to care to play and would mope with round eyes saddened by this eternal gloom. Dusk was merely marked by the drawing down of the blinds at the clock's hour without regard to the transit from day to night. Michael used to wonder if it were possible that this fog would last for ever, if for ever he would live in Carlington Road in this yellow twilight, if his mother had forgotten there ever was such a person as Michael Fane. But, at any rate, he would have to grow up. He could not always be the same size. That was a consolation. It was jolly to dream of being grown-up, to plan one's behaviour and think of freedom. The emancipation of being grown-up seemed to Michael to be a magnificent prospect. To begin with it was no longer possible to be naughty. He realized, indeed, that crimes were a temptation to some grown-ups, that people of a certain class committed murders and burglaries, but as he felt no inclination to do either, he looked forward to a life of unbroken virtue.

So far as he could ascertain, grown-up people were exempt from even the necessity to distinguish between good and evil. If Michael examined the Commandments one by one, this became obvious. *Thou shalt have none other gods than me.* Why should one want to have? One was enough. The Children of Israel must be different from Michael. He could not understand such peculiar people. *Make not to thyself any graven image.* The only difficulty about this commandment was its length for learning. Otherwise it did not seem to bear on present-day life. *Thou shalt not take the name of the Lord thy God in vain.* This was another vague injunction. Who wanted to? *Remember thou keep holy the Sabbath Day.* It was obviously a simple matter for grown-up people, who no longer enjoyed playing with toys, to keep this commandment. At present it was difficult to learn and difficult to keep. *Honour thy father and thy mother.* He loved his mother. He would always love her, even if she forgot him. He might not love her so much as formerly, but he would always love her. *Thou shalt do no murder.* Michael had no intention of doing murder. Since the Hangman in Punch and Judy he was cured of any inclination towards murder. *Thou shalt not commit adultery.* Why should he ever want to marry another man's wife? At present he could not imagine himself married to anybody. He supposed that as one result of growing up he would get married. But, forewarned, he would take care not to choose somebody else's wife. *Thou shalt not steal.* With perfect freedom to eat when and where and what one liked, why should one steal? *Thou shalt not bear false witness.* It would not be necessary to lie when grown up, because one could not then be punished. *Thou shalt not covet thy neighbour's ox.* He would covet nothing, for when he was grown up he would be able to obtain whatever he wanted.

This desire to be grown up sustained him through much, even through the long foggy nights which made his bedroom more fearfully still than before. The room would hardly seem any longer to exist in the murk which crept through it. The crocus-shaped jet of the gas burned in the vaporous midnight with an unholy flame somehow, thought Michael, as candles must look, when at the approach of ghosts they burn blue. How favourable to crime was fog, how cleverly the thief might steal over the coal-yard at the back of the house and with powerful tools compel the back-door to open. And the murderers, how they must rejoice in the impenetrable air as with long knives they stole out from distant streets in search of victims. Michael's nerves were so wrought upon by the unchanging gloom of these wintry days that even to be sent by Nurse to fetch her thimble or work-bag before tea was a racking experience.

"Now then, Michael, run downstairs like a good boy and fetch my needle and cotton which I left in the morning-room," Nurse would command. And in the gathering dusk Michael would practically slide downstairs until he reached the basement. Then, clutching the object of his errand, he would brace himself for the slower ascent. Suppose that when he reached the hall there were two skeletons sitting on the hall chest? Suppose that on the landing above a number of rats rushed out from the housemaid's closet to bite his legs and climb over him and gnaw his face? Suppose that from the landing outside his own room a masked burglar were stealing into his room to hide himself under the bed? Suppose that when he arrived back at the day-nursery, Stella and Nurse were lying with their heads chopped off, as he had once seen a family represented by a pink newspaper in the window of a little shop near Hammersmith Broadway? Michael used to reach his goal, white and shaking, and slam the door against the unseen follower who had dogged his footsteps from the coal-cellar. The cries of a London twilight used to oppress him. From the darkening streets and from the twinkling houses inexplicable sounds floated about the air. They had the sadness of church-bells, and like church-bells they could not be located exactly. Michael thought that London was the most melancholy city in the world. Even at Christmas-time, behind all the gaiety and gold of a main road lay the trackless streets that were lit, it seemed, merely by pin-points of gas, so far apart were the lamp-posts, such a small sad circle of pavement did they illuminate. The rest was shadows and glooms and whispers. Even in the jollity of the pantomime and comfortable smell of well-dressed people the thought of the journey home through the rainy evening brooded upon the gayest scene. The going home was sad indeed, as in the farthest corner of the jolting omnibus they jogged through the darkness. The painted board of places and fares used to depress Michael. He could not bear to think of the possibilities opened up by the unknown names beyond Piccadilly Circus. Once in a list of fares he read the word Whitechapel and shivered at the thought that an omnibus could from Whitechapel pass the corner of Carlington Road. This very omnibus had actually come from the place where murders were done. Murderers might at this moment be travelling in his company. Michael looked askance at the six nodding travellers who sat opposite, at the fumes of their breath, at their hands clasped round the handles of their umbrellas. There, for all he knew, sat Jack the Ripper. It happened that night that one of the travellers, an old gentleman with gold-rimmed eye-glasses, alighted at the corner and actually turned down Carlington Road. Michael was horrified and tugged at Nanny's arm to make her go faster.

"Whyever on earth are you dancing along like a bear for? Do you want to go somewhere, you fidgety boy?" said Nurse, pulling Michael to her side with a jerk.

"Oh, Nanny, there's a man following us, who got out of our bus."

"Well, why shouldn't he get out? Tut-tut. Other people besides you want to get out of buses. I shan't ever take you to the pantomime again, if you aren't careful."

"Well, I will be careful," said Michael, who, perceiving the lamp in their front hall, recovered from his fright and became anxious to propitiate Nanny.

"So I should think," muttered Nurse. "Tut-tut-tut-tut-tut." Michael thought she would never stop clicking her tongue.

About this time with the fogs and the rain and the loneliness and constant fear that surrounded him, Michael began to feel ill. He worried over his thin arms, comparing them with the sleek Stella's. His golden hair lost its lustre and became drab and dark and skimpy. His cheeks lost their rose-red, and black lines ringed his large and sombre blue eyes. He cared for little else but reading, and even reading tired him very much, so that once he actually fell asleep over the big Don Quixote. About two hundred pages were bent underneath the weight of his body, and the book was taken away from him as a punishment for his carelessness. It was placed out of his reach on top of the bookcase and Michael used to stand below and wish for it. No entreaties were well enough expressed to move Nurse; and Don Quixote remained high out of reach in the dust and shadows of the ceiling. Nurse grew more and more irrational in her behaviour and complained more and more of the neuralgia to which she declared she was a positive martyr. Annie went away into the country because she was ill and a withered housemaid took her place, while the tall thin house in Carlington Road became more grim every day.

Then a lucky event gave Michael a new interest. Miss Caroline Marrow began to teach him the elements of Botany, and recommended all the boys to procure window-boxes for themselves. Michael told Nurse about this; and, though she muttered and clicked and blew a great deal, one day a bandy-legged man actually came and fitted Michael's window-sills with two green window-boxes. He spent the whole of his spare time in prodding the sweet new mould, in levelling it and patting it, and filling in unhappy little crevices which had been overlooked. Then on a fine spring morning he paid a visit to the old woman who sold penny packets of seeds, and bought nasturtiums, mignonette, Virginia stocks and candytuft, twelve pansy roots and twelve daisy roots. Michael's flowers grew and flourished and he loved his window-boxes. He liked to turn towards his window at night now. Somehow those flowers were a protection. He liked to lie in bed during the sparrow-thronged mornings of spring and fancy how the birds must enjoy hopping about in his window-boxes. He was always careful to scatter plenty of crumbs, so that they should not be tempted to peck up his seeds or pull to pieces the pansy buds. He was disappointed that neither the daisies nor the pansies smelt sweet, and when the mignonette bloomed, he almost sniffed it away, so lovely was the perfume of it during the blue days of June. He had a set of gardening tools, so small and suitable to the size of his garden that rake and hoe and spade and fork were all originally fastened to one small square of cardboard.

But, best of all, when the pansies were still a-blowing and the Virginia stocks were fragrant, and when from his mother's window below he could see his nasturtium flowers, golden and red and even tortoiseshell against the light, his mother came home suddenly for a surprise, and the house woke up.

"But you're not looking well, darling," she said.

"Oh, yes, quite well. Quite well," muttered Nurse, "Quite well. Mustn't be a mollycoddle. No. No."

"I really must see about a nice governess for you," said Mrs. Fane. Nurse sniffed ominously.

Chapter V: *The First Fairy Princess*

MISS CARTHEW'S arrival widened very considerably Michael's view of life. Nurse's crabbed face and stunted figure had hitherto appropriately enough dominated such realities of existence as escaped from the glooms and shadows of his solitary childhood. Michael had for so long been familiar with ugliness that he was dangerously near to an eternal imprisonment in a maze of black fancies. He had come to take pleasure in the grotesque and the macabre, and even on the sunniest morning his imagination would turn to twilight and foggy eves, to basements and empty houses and loneliness and dust. Michael would read furtively the forbidden newspapers that Nurse occasionally left lying about. In these he would search for murders and crimes, and from their association with thrills of horror, the newspapers themselves had gradually acquired a definitely sinister personality. If at dusk

Michael found a newspaper by Nurse's arm-chair, he would approach it with beating heart, and before he went over to read it where close to the window the light of day lingered, he would brood upon his own daring, as if some Bluebeard's revenge might follow.

When Michael's mother was at home, he was able to resume the cheerfulness of the last occasion on which her company had temporarily relieved his solitude; but always behind the firelit confidences, the scented good mornings and good nights, the gay shopping walks and all the joys which belonged to him and her, stood threatening and inevitable the normal existence with Nurse in which these rosy hours must be remembered as only hours, fugitive and insecure and rare. Now came Miss Carthew's brisk and lively presence to make many alterations in the life of 64 Carlington Road, Kensington.

Michael's introduction to his governess took place in the presence of his mother and, as he stood watching the two women in conversation, he was aware of a tight-throated feeling of pleasure. They were both so tall and slim and beautiful: they were both so straight and clean that they gave him the glad sensation of blinds pulled up to admit the sun.

"I think we're going to be rather good friends," said Miss Carthew.

Michael could only stare his agreement, but he managed to run before Miss Carthew in order to open the door politely, when she was going out. In bed that night he whispered to his mother how much he liked Miss Carthew and how glad he was that he could leave the Miss Marrows' for the company of Miss Carthew all day long.

"And all night?" he asked wistfully.

"No, not at present, darling," she answered. "Nanny will still look after you at night."

"Will she?" Michael questioned somewhat doubtfully.

After Mrs. Fane went away, there was a short interval before the new-comer assumed her duties. During this time Michael hummed incessantly and asked Nurse a thousand questions about Miss Carthew.

"Goodness gracious, what a fuss about a governess," commented Nanny. "Tut-tut. It might be the Queen of England. She'll be here quite soon enough for everyone, I dare say."

It fell out that Miss Carthew was to arrive on Valentine Day, and Michael with a delicious breathlessness thought how wonderful it would be to present her with a Valentine. He did not dare tell Nurse of his intention; but he hoped that by sending Valentines to every inmate of the house he might be allowed to include Miss Carthew. Nurse was agreeable to the notion of receiving a token, and in her company Michael set out to a neighbouring stationer's shop to make his purchases. A Valentine for Cook was bought, and one of precisely the same design for Gladys the withered housemaid, and a rather better one for Stella, and a better one still for Nurse.

"Come along now," said Nanny.

"Oh, but can't I get one for Miss Carthew? Do let me."

"Tut-tut-tut. What nonsense. I do declare. Whatever do you want to give her a Valentine for?" Nurse demanded, as she tried to hustle Michael from the shop.

"Oh, do let me, Nanny."

"Well, come along, and don't be all day choosing. Here, this will do," said Nurse, as she picked one from the penny tray.

But Michael had other ideas. He had noticed an exquisite Valentine of apple-green satin painted with the rosiest of Cupids, the most crimson of pierced hearts, a Valentine that was almost a sachet so thick was it, so daintily fringed with fretted silver-paper.

"That one," he declared, pointing.

"Now what have I told you about pointing?"

"That large one's a shilling," said the stationer.

"Come along, come along," grumbled Nurse. "Wasting good money."

"But I want to have that one," said Michael.

For the first time in his life he did not feel at all afraid of Nurse, so absolutely determined was he to present Miss Carthew with the Valentine of his own free choice.

"I will have that one," he added. "It's my money."

"You will, will you, you naughty boy? You won't, then. So now! You dare defy me. I never heard of such a thing. No, nothing more this morning, thank you," Nurse added, turning to the stationer. "'The little boy has got all he wants. Say 'thank you' to the gentleman and 'good morning,'" Nurse commanded Michael.

"I won't," he declared. "I won't." Scowling so that his nose nearly vanished into his forehead, and beating back the tears that were surging to his eyes, Michael followed Nurse from the shop. As he walked home, he dug his nails wrathfully into the envelope of Valentines, and then suddenly he saw a drain in the gutter. He hastily stooped and pushed the packet between the bars of the grating, and let it fall beyond the chance of recovery. When they reached their house, Nurse told him to give her the cards, so that they might not be soiled before presentation.

"I've dropped them," said Michael sullenly.

"Dropped them? Dropped them? What do you mean—dropped them?"

"I threw them away," said Michael.

"On purpose?"

"Yes. I can do what I like with my own things."

"You ungrateful wicked boy," said Nurse, horrified by such a claim.

"I don't care if I am," Michael answered. "I wanted to give Miss Carthew a Valentine. Mother would have let me."

"Your mother isn't here. And when she isn't here, I'm your mother," said Nurse, looking more old and wrinkled and monkey-like than ever.

"How dare you say you're my mother?" gasped the outraged son. "You're not. You're not. Why, you're not a lady, so you couldn't ever be my mother."

Hereupon Nurse disconcerted Michael by bursting into tears, and he presently found himself almost petting her and declaring that he was very sorry for having been so unkind. He found a certain luxury in this penitence just as he used to enjoy a reconciliation with the black kittens. Perhaps it was this scene with Nurse that prompted him soon afterwards to the creation of another with his sister. The second scene was brought about by Stella's objection to the humming with which Michael was somewhat insistently celebrating the advent of Miss Carthew.

"Don't hum, Michael. Don't hum. Please don't hum," Stella begged very solemnly. "Please don't hum, because it makes my head hurt."

"I *will* hum, and every time you ask me not to hum, I'll hum more louder," said Michael.

Stella at once went to the piano in the day-nursery and began to play her most unmelodious tune. Michael ran to the cupboard and produced a drum which he banged defiantly. He banged it so violently that presently the drum, already worn very thin, burst. Michael was furious and immediately proceeded to twang an over-varnished zither. So furiously did he twang the zither that finally he caught one of his nails in a sharp string of the treble, and in great pain hurled the instrument across the room. Meanwhile, Stella continued to play, and when Michael commanded her to stop, answered annoyingly that she had been told to practise.

"Don't say pwactise, you silly. Say practise," Michael contemptuously exclaimed.

"Shan't," Stella answered with that cold and fat stolidity of demeanour and voice which disgusted Michael like the fat of cold mutton.

"I'm older than you," Michael asserted.

Stella made no observation, but continued to play, and Michael, now acutely irritated, rushed to the piano and slammed down the lid. Stella must have withdrawn her fingers in time, for there was no sign of any pinch or bruise upon them. However, she began to cry, while Michael addressed to her the oration which for a long time he had wished to utter.

"You are silly. You are a cry-baby. Fancy crying about nothing. I wouldn't. Everybody doesn't want to hear your stupid piano-playing. Boys at school think pianos are stupid. You always grumble about my humming. You are a cry-baby.

What are little boys made of?
Sugar and spice and all that's nice,
That's what little boys are made of.
What are little girls made of?

Slugs and snails and puppy-dogs' tails, Ugh! that's what little girls are made of."

"They're not," Stella screamed. "They're not!" Michael's perversion of the original rhyme made her inarticulate with grief and rage. "They're not, you naughty boy!"

Michael, contented with his victory, left Stella to herself and her tears. As he hummed his way downstairs, he thought sensuously of the imminent reconciliation, and in about ten minutes, having found some barley-sugar buried against an empty day, Michael came back to Stella with peace-offerings and words of comfort.

Miss Carthew arrived on the next morning and the nervous excitement of waiting was lulled. Miss Carthew came through the rain of Valentine Day, and Michael hugged himself with the thought of her taking off her mackintosh and handing it to Gladys to be dried. With the removal of her wet outdoor clothes, Miss Carthew seemed to come nearer to Michael and, as they faced each other over the schoolroom table (for the day-nursery in one moment had become the schoolroom), Michael felt that he could bear not being grown up just for the pleasure of sitting opposite to his new governess.

It was not so much by these lessons that Michael's outlook was widened as by the conversations he enjoyed with Miss Carthew during their afternoon walks. She told him, so far as she could, everything that he desired to know. She never accused him of being old-fashioned or inquisitive, and indeed as good as made him feel that the more questions he asked the better she would like it. Miss Carthew had all the mental and imaginative charm of the late Mrs. Frith in combination with an outward attractiveness that made her more dearly beloved. Indeed Miss Carthew had numberless pleasant qualities. If she promised anything, the promise was always kept to the letter. If Michael did not know his lesson or omitted the performance of an ordained task, Miss Carthew was willing to hear the explanation of his failure and was never unreasonable in her judgment. One morning very soon after her arrival, Michael was unable to repeat satisfactorily the verse of the psalm Venite Adoremus set for him to learn.

"Why don't you know it, Michael?" Miss Carthew asked.

"I had to go to bed."

"But surely you had plenty of time before you went to bed?" Miss Carthew persisted.

"Nanny wanted to go out, and I went to bed early," Michael explained.

For a moment or two Miss Carthew considered the problem silently. Then she rang the bell and told withered Gladys that she wished to speak to Nurse. Presently Nurse came in, very aggressive and puckered.

"Did Michael have to go to bed very early last night?" Miss Carthew enquired.

"Oh, yes. Yes," Nurse blew out. "Early last night. Wednesday night. Yes. I had to go out. Yes."

"What time did he go to bed?" Miss Carthew went on.

"What time?" repeated Nurse. "Why the proper time, of course."

"Don't be insolent," said Miss Carthew very tranquilly.

Nurse blustered and wrinkled her nose and frowned and came very close to Miss Carthew and peered up into her face, blowing harder than ever.

"The arrangements can't be altered for governesses," said Nurse. "No. Tut-tut. Never heard of such a thing."

"The arrangements *will* be altered. In future Michael will go to bed at half-past seven. It's not good for him to go to bed earlier. Do you understand?"

"Do I understand? No, I don't understand," Nurse snapped.

"Very well," said Miss Carthew. "You need not wait, Nurse."

Nurse blinked and peered and fumed, but Miss Carthew paid so little attention that Michael felt himself blushing for her humiliation. However, he did not go to bed that night till half-past seven and at the end of the week could rattle off the Venite in two breaths. It was extraordinary how Nurse shrank into nothing at Miss Carthew's approach, like a witch in the presence of a good fairy.

The nights were still a trial to Michael, but gradually they became less terrible, as Miss Carthew's conversation gave him something better to meditate upon than the possibilities of disaster and crime. On the afternoon walks would be told stories of Miss Carthew's youth in the West Country, of cliffs and sea-birds and wrecks, of yachting cruises and swimming, of golden sands and magical coves and green islands. Miss Carthew's own father had been a captain in the Royal Navy and she had had one brother, a midshipman, who was drowned in trying to save the life of his friend. By all accounts the Carthews must have lived in as wonderful a house as was ever known. From the windows it was possible to look down into the very sea itself, and from the front door, all wreathed in roses, ran a winding path edged with white stones down to the foot of the cliff. Day and night great ships used to sail from the harbour, some outward bound with the crew singing in the cool airs of a summer morning, some homeward bound, battered by storms. Miss Carthew, when a little girl, had been the intimate friend of many coastguards, had been allowed to peep through their long telescopes, had actually seen a cannon fired at close quarters. Before her own eyes the lifeboat had plunged forth to rescue ships and with her own hands she had caught fish on quiet sunny mornings and on windless nights under the moon. Her most valuable possession, however, must have been that father who could sit for hours and never tell the same tale twice, but hold all who heard him entranced with a narrative of hostile Indians, of Chinese junks, of cannibals and wrecks and mutinies and bombardments. It was sad to hear that Captain Carthew was now dead: Michael would have been glad to make his acquaintance. It was sad to hear that the Carthews no longer lived in the West within the sound of waves and winds; but it was consoling to learn that they still lived in the depth of the country and that some time, perhaps during this very next summer, Michael should certainly pay Mrs. Carthew a visit. He would meet other Miss Carthews, one of whom was only fourteen and could obviously without ceremony be hailed immediately as Nancy. Of Joan and May, who were older, Michael spoke in terms of the familiar Christian name with embarrassment, and he was much perplexed in his own mind how he should address them, when actually they met.

"I wish you were going to take us away for our holidays to the seaside," Michael said.

"Perhaps I will another time," Miss Carthew replied. "But this year you and Stella are going with Nurse, because Stella isn't going to begin lessons with me till you go to school."

"Am I really going to school?"

"Yes, to St. James' Preparatory School," Miss Carthew assured him.

In consideration of Michael's swiftly approaching adventure, he was allowed to take in the Boy's Own Paper monthly, and as an even greater concession to age he was allowed to make friends with several boys in Carlington Road, some of whom were already scholars of St. James' Preparatory School and one of whom actually had a brother at St. James' School itself, that gigantic red building whose gates Michael himself would enter of right one day, however difficult at present this was to believe.

What with the prospect of going to school in the autumn and Miss Carthew's tales of freedom and naval life, Michael began to disapprove more than ever of Nurse's manners and appearance. He did not at all relish the notion of passing away the summer holidays in her society. To be sure, for the end of the time he had been invited by Mrs. Carthew's own thin writing to spend a week with her in Hampshire; but that was at least a month away, and meanwhile there was this month to be endured with Nurse at Mr. and Mrs. Wagland's lodgings, where the harmonium was played and conversation was carried on by whispers and the mysterious nods of three heads. However, the beginning of August arrived, and Miss Carthew said good-bye for a month. Wooden spades, still gritty with last year's sand, were produced from the farthest corners of cupboards: mouldy shrimping nets and dirtied buckets and canvas shoes lay about on the bed, and at last, huddled in paraphernalia, Nurse and Stella and Michael jogged along to the railway station, a miserable hour for Michael, who all the time was dreading many unfortunate events, as for the cabman to get down from his box and quarrel about the fare, or for the train to be full, or for Stella to be sick during the journey, or for him and her to lose Nurse, or for all of them to get into the wrong train, or for a railway accident to happen, or for any of the uncomfortable contingencies to which seaside travellers were liable.

During these holidays Michael grew more and more deeply ashamed of Nurse, and more and more acutely sensitive to her manners and appearance. He was afraid that people on the front would mistake him and Stella for her children. He grew hot with shame when he fancied that people looked at him. He used to loiter behind on their walks and pretend that he did not belong to Nurse, and hope sincerely that nobody would think of connecting him with such an ugly old woman. He had heard much talk of 'ladies and gentlemen' at the Kindergarten, and since then Miss Carthew had indirectly confirmed his supposition that it was a terrible thing not to be a gentleman and the son of a gentleman. He grew very critical of his own dress and wished that he were not compelled to wear a sailor-top that was slightly shabby. Once Mr. and Mrs. Wagland accompanied them to church on a Sunday morning, and Michael was horrified. People would inevitably think that he was the son of Mr. Wagland. What a terrible thing that would be. He loitered farther behind than ever, and would liked to have killed Mr. Wagland when he offered him the half of his hymn-book. This incident seemed to compromise him finally, to drag him down from the society of Miss Carthew to a degraded status of unutterable commonness. Mr. Wagland would persist in digging him with his elbow and urging him to sing up. Worse even, he once said quite audibly 'Spit it out, sonny.' Michael reeled with shame.

September arrived at last, and then Michael realized suddenly that he would have to make the journey to Hampshire alone. This seemed to him the most astonishing adventure of his life. He surveyed his existence from the earliest dawn of consciousness to the last blush caused by Nurse's abominable habits, and could see no parallel of daring. He was about to enter upon a direct relationship with the world of men. He would have to enquire of porters and guards; he would have to be polite without being prodded to ladies sitting opposite. No doubt they would ask questions of him and he would have to answer distinctly. And beyond this immediate encounter with reality was School. He had not grasped how near he was to the first morning. A feeling of hopelessness, of inability to grapple with the facts of life seized him. Growing old was a very desperate business after all. How remote he was getting from Nurse, how far away from the dingy solitude which had so long oppressed his spirit. Already she seemed unimportant and already he could almost laugh at the absurdity of being mistaken for a relation of hers. The world was opening her arms and calling to him.

On the day before he was to set out for Hampshire, he and Nurse and Stella and Mr. Wagland and Mrs. Wagland drove in a wagonette to picnic somewhere in the country behind the sea. It had been a dry August and the rolling chalk downs over which they walked were uniformly brown. The knapweed was stunted and the scabious blooms drooped towards the dusty pasture. Only the flamy ladies' slippers seemed appropriate to the miles of heat that flickered against the landscape. Michael ran off alone, sliding as he went where the drouth had singed the close-cropped grass. The rabbits ran to right and left of him, throwing distorted shadows on the long slopes, and once a field-mouse skipped anxiously across his path. On the rounded summit of the highest hill within reach he sat down near a clump of tremulous harebells. The sky was on every side of him, the largest sky ever imagined. Far away in front was the shining sea, above whose nebulous horizon ships hung motionless. Up here was the sound of summer airs, the faint lisp of wind in parched herbage, the twitter of desolate birds, and in some unseen vale below the bleating of a flock of sheep. Bumble-bees droned from flower to flower of the harebells and a church clock struck the hour of four. The world was opening her arms and calling to Michael. He felt up there in the silver weather as the ugly duckling must have felt when he saw himself to be a radiant swan. Michael almost believed, in this bewitching meditation, that he was in a story by Hans Christian Andersen. Always in those tales the people flew above the world whether in snow-time or in spring-time. It was really like flying to sit up here. For the first time Michael flung wide his arms to grasp the unattainable; and, as he presently charged down the hill-side in answer to distant holloas from the picnic party, he saw before him a flock of sheep manœuvring before his advance. Michael shouted and kept a swift course, remembering Don Quixote and laughing when he saw the flock break into units and gallop up the opposite slope.

"Tut-tut," clicked Nurse. "What a mess you do get yourself into, I'm sure. Can't you sit down and enjoy yourself quietly?"

"Did you see me make those silly old sheep run away, Nanny?" Michael asked.

"Yes, I did. And I should be ashamed to frighten poor animals so. You'll get the policeman on your tracks."

"I shouldn't care," said Michael boastfully. "He wouldn't be able to catch me."

"Wouldn't he?" said Nurse very knowingly, as she laid out the tea-cups on a red rug.

"Oh, Michael," Stella begged, "don't make a policeman come after you."

Michael was intoxicated by the thought of his future. He could not recognize the ability of any policeman to check his desires, and because it was impossible to voice in any other way the impulses and ambitions and hopes that were surging in his soul, he went on boasting.

"Ha, I'd like to see an old policeman run after me. I'd trip him up and roll him all down the hill, I would. I'd put his head in a rabbit hole. I would. I can run faster than a policeman, I can."

Michael was swaggering round and round the spread-out cups and saucers and plates.

"If you put your foot on those jam sandwiches, you'll go straight back to the carriage and wait there till we've finished tea. Do you hear?"

Michael considered for a moment the possibility that Nanny might execute this threat. He decided that she might and temporarily sobered down. But the air was in his veins and all tea-time he could not chatter fast enough to keep pace with the new power which was inspiring him with inexpressible energy. He talked of what he was going to do in Hampshire; he talked of what he was going to do on the journey; he talked of what he was going to do at school and when he was grown up. He arranged Stella's future and bragged and boasted and fidgeted and shouted, so that Nurse looked at him in amazement.

"Whatever's the matter with you?" she asked.

Just then a tortoiseshell butterfly came soaring past and Michael, swinging round on both his legs to watch the flight, swept half the tea-cups with him. For a moment he was abashed; but after a long sermon of reproof from Nurse he was much nearer to laughter than tears.

A gloomy reaction succeeded, as the party drove home through the grey evening that was falling sadly over the country-side. A chilly wind rustled in the hedgerows and blew the white dust in clouds behind the wagonette. Michael became his silent self again and was now filled with apprehensions. All that had seemed so easy to attain was now complicated by the unknown. He would have been glad of Miss Carthew's company. The green-shaded lamp and creaking harmonium of the seaside lodgings were a dismal end to all that loveliness of wind and silver so soon finished. Nevertheless it had made him very sleepy and he was secretly glad to get to bed.

The next day was a dream from which he woke to find himself clinging affectionately to Miss Carthew's arm and talking shyly to Nancy Carthew and a sidling spaniel alternately, as they walked from the still country station and packed themselves into a pony-chaise that was waiting outside behind a dun pony.

Chapter VI: *The Enchanted Palace*

THE dun pony ambled through the lanes to the village of Basingstead Minor where Mrs. Carthew and her four daughters lived in a house called Cobble Place. It stood close to the road and was two stories high, very trim and covered with cotoneaster. On either side of the door were two windows and above it in a level row five more windows: the roof was thatched. On the left of the house were double doors which led into the stable-yard, a large stable-yard overlooked by a number of irregular gables in the side of the house and continually fluttered by white fantail pigeons. Into the stable-yard the dun pony turned, where, clustered in the side entrance of Cobble Place under a clematis-wreathed porch, stood Mrs. Carthew and Miss May Carthew and Miss Joan Carthew, all smiling very pleasantly at Michael and all evidently very glad to see him safely arrived. Michael climbed out of the chaise and politely shook hands with Mrs. Carthew and said he was very well and had had a comfortable journey and would like some tea very much, although if Nancy thought it was best he was quite ready to see her donkey before doing anything else. However, Nancy was told that she must wait, and soon Michael was sitting at a large round table in a shady dining-room, eating hot buttered tea-cake and chocolate cake and macaroons, with bread-and-butter as an afterthought of duty. He enjoyed drinking his tea out of a thin teacup and he liked the silver and the satin tea-cosy and the yellow Persian cat purring on the hearthrug and the bullfinch flitting from perch to perch of his bright cage. He noticed with pleasure that the pictures on the wall were full of interest and detail, and was particularly impressed by two very long steel engravings of the Death of Nelson and the Meeting of Wellington and Blücher on the field of Waterloo. The only flaw in his pleasure was the difficulty of addressing Miss May Carthew and Miss Joan Carthew, and he wished that his own real Miss Carthew would suggest a solution. As for the bedroom to which he was taken after tea, Michael thought there never could have been such a jolly room before. It was just the right size, as snug as possible with its gay wall-paper and crackling chintzes and ribboned bed. The counterpane was patchwork and therefore held the promise of perpetual entertainment. The dressing-table was neatly set with china toilet articles whose individual importance Michael could not discover. One in particular like the antler of a stag stuck upright in a china tray he was very anxious to understand, and when he was told it was intended for rings to hang upon, he wished he had a dozen rings to adorn so neat a device.

After he had with Miss Carthew's help unpacked and put his clothes away, Michael joined Nancy in the stable-yard. He stroked the donkey and the dun-coloured pony and watched the fantail pigeons in snowy circles against the pale blue sky. He watched the gardener stirring up some strange stuff for the pig that grunted impatiently. He watched the pleasant Carthew cook shelling peas in the slanting sunlight by the kitchen door. The air was very peaceful, full of soft sounds of lowing cows, of ducks and hens and sheep. The air was spangled with glittering insects: over a red wall hung down the branch of a plum tree, loaded with creamy ovals of fruit, already rose-flushed with summer. Nancy said they must soon go into the garden.

"Is there a garden more than this?" Michael asked. His bedroom window had looked out on to the stable-yard.

"Through here," said Nancy. She led the way to a door set in the wall, which when open showed a green glowing oblong of light that made Michael catch his breath in wonder.

Then together he and Nancy sauntered through what was surely the loveliest garden in the world. Michael could scarcely bear to speak, so completely did it fulfil every faintest hope. All along the red walls were apples and pears and plums and peaches; all along the paths were masses of flowers, phloxes and early Michaelmas daisies and Japanese anemones and sunflowers and red-hot pokers and dahlias. The air was so golden and balmy that it seemed as though the sunlight must have been locked up in this garden for years. At the bottom of the vivid path was a stream with real fish swimming backwards and forwards, and beyond the stream, safely guarded and therefore perfectly beautiful, were cows stalking through a field beyond which was a dark wood beyond which was a high hill with a grey tower on the top of it. Some princess must have made this garden. He and Nancy turned and walked by the stream on which was actually moored a punt, a joy for to-morrow, since, explained Nancy, Maud had said they were not to go on the river this afternoon. How wonderful it was, Michael thought, to hear his dearest Miss Carthew called Maud. Never was spoken so sweet a name as Maud. He would say it to himself in bed that night, and in the morning he would wake with Maud calling to him from sleep. Then he and Nancy turned from the tempting stream and walked up a pleached alley of withies woven and interarched. Over them September roses bloomed with fawn and ivory and copper and salmon-pink buds and blossoms. At the end of the pleached alley was a mulberry tree with a seat round its trunk and a thick lawn that ran right up to the house itself. On the lawn Nancy and Michael played quoits and bowls and chased Ambrose the spaniel, until the sun sent still more slanting shadows across the garden and it was possible to feel that night was just behind the hill beyond the stream. The sun went down. The air grew chilly and Miss Carthew appeared from the door, beckoning to Michael. She sat with him in the dusky dining-room while he ate his bread and milk, and told him of her brother the midshipman, while he looked pensively at the picture of the Death of Nelson. Then Michael went to the drawing-room where all the sisters and Mrs. Carthew herself were sitting. He kissed everybody good night in turn, and Mrs. Carthew put on a pair of spectacles in order to follow his exit from the room with a kindly smile. Miss Carthew sat with him while he undressed, and when he was in bed, she told him another story and kissed him good night and blew out the candle, and before the sound of pleasant voices coming upstairs from the supper-table had ceased, Michael was fast asleep.

In the morning while he was lying watching the shadows on the ceiling, Nancy's freckled face appeared round the door.

"Hurry up and dress," she cried. "Fishing!"

Michael had never dressed so quickly before. In fact when he was ready, he had to wait for Nancy who had called him before she had dressed herself. Nancy and Michael lived a lifetime of delight in that golden hour of waiting for breakfast.

However, at Cobble Place every minute was a lifetime of delight to Michael. He forgot all about everything except being happy. His embarrassment with regard to the correct way of addressing May and Joan was terminated by being told to call them May and Joan. He was shown the treasures of their bedrooms, the butterfly collections, the sword of Captain Carthew, the dirk of their brother the midshipman, the birds' eggs, the fossils, the bones, the dried flowers, the photographs, the autographs, in fact everything that was most absorbing to look at. With Mrs. Carthew he took sedate walks into the village, and held the flowers while she decorated the altar in church, and sat with her while she talked to bed-ridden old women. With Nancy on one memorable day he crossed the river and disembarked on the other side and walked through the field of cows, through the meadowsweet and purple loosestrife and spearmint. Then they picked blackberries and dewberries by the edge of the wood and walked on beneath the trees without caring about trespassing or tramps or anything else. On the other side they came out at the foot of the high hill. Up they walked, up and up until they reached the grey tower at the top, and then, to Michael's amazement, Nancy produced the key of the tower and opened the door.

"Can we really go in?" asked Michael, staggered by the adventure.

"Of course. We can always get the key," said Nancy.

They walked up some winding stone steps that smelt very damp, and at the top they pushed open a trap-door and walked out on top of the tower. Michael leaned over the parapet and for the second time beheld the world. There was no sea, but there were woods and streams and spires and fields and villages and smoke from farms. There were blue distances on every side and great white clouds moving across the sky. The winds battled against the tower and sang in Michael's ears and ruffled his hair and crimsoned his cheeks. He could see the fantail pigeons of Cobble Place circling below. He could look down on the wood and the river they had just crossed. He could see the garden and his dearest Miss Carthew walking on the lawn.

"Oh, Nancy," he said, "it's glorious."

"Yes, it is rather decent," Nancy agreed.

"I suppose that's almost all of England you can see."

"Only four counties," said Nancy carelessly. "Berkshire and I forget the other three. We toboggan down this hill in winter. That's rather decent too."

"I'd like to come here every day," sighed Michael. "I'd like to have this tower for my very own. What castle is it called?"

"Grogg's Folly," said Nancy abruptly.

Michael wished the tower were not called Grogg's Folly, and very soon Nancy and he, shouting and laughing, were running at full speed down the hill towards Cobble Place, while the stalks of the plantains whipped his bare legs and larks flew up in alarm before his advance.

The time of his stay at Cobble Place was drawing to a close: the hour of his greatest adventure was near. It had been a visit of unspoiled enjoyment; and on his last night, Michael was allowed for a treat to stay up to supper, to sit at the round table rose-stained by the brooding lamp, while the rest of the room was a comfortable mystery in which the parlour-maid's cap and apron flitted whitely to and fro. Nor did Michael go to bed immediately after supper, for he actually sat grandly in the drawing-room, one of a semicircle round the autumnal fire of logs crackling and leaping with blue flames. He sat silent, listening to the pitter-pat of Mrs. Carthew's Patience and watching the halma board waiting for May to encounter Joan, while in a low voice Nancy read to him one of Fifty-two Stories of Adventure for Girls. Bed-time came at the end of the story and Michael was sad to say good night for the last time and sad to think, when he got into his ribboned bed, that to-morrow night he would be in Carlington Road among brass knobs and Venetian blinds and lamp-posts and sounds of London. Then came a great surprize that took away nearly all the regrets he felt at leaving Cobble Place, for Miss Carthew leaned over and whispered that she was coming to live at Sixty-four.

"Oh!" Michael gasped. "With us—with Stella and me?"

Miss Carthew nodded.

"I say!" Michael whispered. "And will Stella have lessons when I'm going to school?"

"Every morning," said Miss Carthew.

"I expect you'll find her rather bad at lessons," said Michael doubtfully.

He was almost afraid that Miss Carthew might leave in despair at Stella's ineptitude.

"Lots of people are stupid at first," said Miss Carthew.

Michael blushed: he remembered a certain morning when capes and promontories got inextricably mixed in his mind and when Miss Carthew seemed to grow quite tired of trying to explain the difference.

"Will you teach her the piano now?" he enquired.

"Oh dear, no. I'm not clever enough to do that."

"But you teach me."

"That's different. Stella will be a great pianist one day," said Miss Carthew earnestly.

"Will she?" asked Michael incredulously. "But I don't like her to play a bit—not a bit."

"You will one day. Great musicians think she is wonderful."

Michael gave up this problem. It was another instance of the chasm between youth and age. He supposed that one day he would like Stella's playing. One day, so he had been led to suppose, he would also like fat and cabbage and going to bed. At present such a condition of mind was incomprehensible. However, Stella and the piano mattered very little in comparison with the solid fact that Miss Carthew was going to live in Carlington Road.

On the next morning before they left, Michael and Mrs. Carthew walked round the garden together, while Mrs. Carthew talked to him of the new life on which he was shortly going to enter.

"Well, Michael," she said, "in a week, so my daughter tells me, you will be going to school."

"Yes," corroborated Michael.

"Dear me," Mrs. Carthew went on. "I'm glad I'm not going to school for the first time; you won't like it at all at first, and then you'll like it very much indeed, and then you'll either go on liking it very much or you'll hate it. If you go on liking it—I mean when you're quite old—sixteen or seventeen—you'll never do anything, but if you hate it then, you'll have a chance of doing something. I'm glad my daughter Maud is going to look after you. She's a good girl."

Michael thought how extraordinary it was to hear Miss Carthew spoken of in this manner and felt shy at the prospect of having to agree verbally with Mrs. Carthew.

"Take my advice—never ask questions. Be content to make a fool of yourself once or twice, but don't ask questions. Don't answer questions either. That's worse than asking. But after all, now I'm giving advice, and worst of anything is listening to other people's advice. So pick yourself some plums and get ready, for the chaise will soon be at the door."

Nurse was very grumpy when he and Miss Carthew arrived. She did not seem at all pleased by the idea of Miss Carthew living in the house, and muttered to herself all the time. Michael did no more lessons in the week that remained before the autumn term began; but he had to go with Miss Carthew to various outfitters and try on coats and suits and generally be equipped for school. The afternoons he spent in Carlington Road, trying to pick up information about St. James' Preparatory School from the boys already there. One of these boys was Rodber, the son of a doctor, and probably by his manner and age and appearance the most important boy in the school. At any rate Michael found it difficult to believe that there could exist a boy with more right to rule than this Rodber with his haughty eye and Eton suit and prominent ears and quick authoritative voice.

"Look here," said Rodber one evening, "can you borrow your mail-cart? I saw your sister being wheeled in one this morning. We've got three mail-carts and we want a fourth for trains."

Michael ran as fast as he could back to Sixty-four, rushed down the area steps, rang the bell half a dozen times and tapped continuously on the ground glass of the back door until Cook opened it.

"Whatever's the matter?" said Cook.

Michael did not stop to answer, but ran upstairs, until breathless he reached the schoolroom.

"Please, Miss Carthew, may we have Stella's mail-cart? Rodber wants it—for trains. Do let me. Rodber's the boy I told you about who's at school. Oh, do let us have the cart. Rodber's got three, but he wants ours. May I, Miss Carthew?"

She nodded.

Michael rushed downstairs in a helter-skelter of joy and presently, with Cook's assistance in getting it up the steps, Michael stood proudly by the mail-cart which was of the dogcart pattern, very light and swift when harnessed to a good runner. Rodber examined it critically.

"Yes, that's a fairly decent one," he decided.

Michael was greatly relieved by his approval.

"Look here," said Rodber, "I don't mind telling you, as you'll be a new kid, one or two tips about school. Look here, don't tell anybody your Christian name and don't be cocky."

"Oh, no, I won't," Michael earnestly promised.

"And don't, for goodness' sake, look like that when chaps speak to you, or you'll get your head smacked."

This was the sum of Rodber's advice, and presently Michael was stationed as signalman by the junction which was a pillar-box, while Rodber went off at express speed, bound for the next station which was a lamp-post. A signalman's life on the Carlington Road line was a lonely one, and it was also a very tiring one, when any obstruction caused the signals to be up. Michael's arm ached excruciatingly when Rodber's train got entangled with Garrod's train and Macalister's train had to be kept from running into them. Moreover, the signalman's life had none of the glories of controlling other people; a signalman on the Carlington Road line was dependent on the train for his behaviour. He was not allowed to interfere with the free running of any freight, but if the engine-driver insisted he had to let him go past, and if there was an accident, he was blamed. A signalman's life was lonely, tiring, humiliating and dangerous.

These few fine days of mid-September went quickly by and one evening Rodber said casually, almost cruelly it seemed to Michael:

"Well, see you to-morrow in the break, young Fane."

Michael wondered what on earth a 'break' was; he longed to ask Rodber, but he dared not display at the very beginning of his career what would evidently be a disgraceful ignorance, and so he said that he would see Rodber in the 'break' to-morrow. He asked Miss Carthew when he got home what a 'break' was, and she told him it was a large wagonette sometimes driven by four horses. Michael was very much puzzled, but thought school would be fun if large wagonettes were commonplace objects of school life, and dreamed that night of driving furiously with Rodber in a gigantic mail-cart along the Hammersmith Road.

At breakfast Miss Carthew asked Michael if he would like her to come with him. He thought for a moment, and wished that Rodber had invited him to accompany him that first morning.

"You know, it's for you to choose, Michael," said Miss Carthew.

"Well, I would like you to come," said Michael at last.

So at ten minutes past nine they set out. All sorts of boys were going to school along the Hammersmith Road, boys of every size carrying satchels or bags or loose bundles of books. Most of them wore the Jacobean cap, and Michael eyed them with awe; but many wore the cap of St. James' Preparatory School, and these Michael eyed with curiosity as well as awe. He spoke very little during the walk and felt all the way a sinking of the heart. When actually he reached the gate of Randell House, the less formal appellation of St. James' Preparatory School, he longed to turn back with Miss Carthew, as he thought with sentimental pangs of the pleasant schoolroom and of Stella sitting by Miss Carthew, learning to read through a sunlit morning.

"Don't come in with me," he whispered.

"Quite right," said Miss Carthew approvingly. "Much better without me."

"And don't wave, will you?" he begged. Then with an effort he joined the stream of boys walking confidently through the big gate.

In the entrance hall a ginger-haired foxy-faced man in a green uniform said sharply: "New boy?"

Michael nodded.

"Stand on one side, please. Mr. Randell will see you presently."

Michael waited. He noticed with pride that the boy next to him had brought with him either his mother or his sister or his governess. Michael felt very superior and was glad he had resisted the temptation to ask Miss Carthew to come in with him. He noticed how curiously the other boys eyed this lady and fancied that they threw contemptuous glances at the boy who had introduced her. Michael was very glad indeed that he had let Miss Carthew turn back.

Chapter VII: *Randell House*

THE preliminaries of Michael's career at St. James' Preparatory School passed in a dream-like confusion of thought and action. First of all he waited anxiously in the Headmaster's study in an atmosphere of morocco-leather and large waste-paper baskets. Like every other room in which Michael had waited, whether of dentist or doctor, the outlook from the window was gloomy and the prospect within was depressing. He was glad when Mr. Randell led him and several other boys towards the First Form, where in a dream, peopled by the swinging legs of many boys, he learnt from a scarlet book that while Cornelia loved Julia, Julia returned Cornelia's affection. When this fact was established in both English and Latin, all the boys shuffled to their desks and the record of a great affection was set down largely and painfully.

Cornelia

. Juliam amat.

Julia

. Corneliam amat.

Blotted and smudged and sprawling though it ultimately appeared, Michael felt a great satisfaction in having dealt successfully with two nominatives, two accusatives and a verb. The first part of the morning passed away quickly in the history of this simple love. At eleven o'clock a shrill electric bell throbbed through the school, and Michael, almost before he knew what was happening, was carried in a torrent of boys towards the playground. Michael had never felt supreme loneliness, even at night, until he stood in the middle of that green prairie of recreation, distinguishing nobody, a very small creature in a throng of chattering giants. Some of these giants, who usually walked about arm in arm, approached him.

"Hullo, are you a new kid?"

Michael breathed his 'yes.'

"What's your name?"

With an effort Michael remembered Rodber's warning and replied simply:

"Fane."

"What's your Christian name?"

This was a terribly direct attack, and Michael was wondering whether it would be best to run quickly out of the playground, to keep silence or to surrender the information, when the quick and authoritative voice of Rodber flashed from behind him.

"Fish and find out, young Biden."

"Who are you calling young, young Rodber?"

"You," said Rodber. "So you'd jolly well better scoot off and leave this kid alone."

"Church said I was to collar all the new kids for his army," Biden explained.

"Did he? Well, this kid's in our army, so sucks! And you can tell young Church that Pearson and me are going to jolly well lam him at four o'clock," announced Rodber very fiercely.

"Why don't you tell him yourself?" asked Biden, whose teeth seemed to project farther and farther from his mouth as his indignation grew.

"All right, Toothy Biden," jeered Rodber. "We'll tell the whole of your rotten army at four o'clock, when we give you the biggest lamming you've ever had. Come on, young Fane," he went on, and Michael, somewhat perturbed by the prospect of being involved in these encounters, followed at his heels.

"Look here," said Rodber presently, "you'd better come and show yourself to Pearson. He's the captain of our army; and for goodness' sake look a bit cheerful."

Michael forced an uncomfortable grin such as photographers conjure.

Under the shade of a gigantic tree stood Pearson the leader, languidly eating a very small and very unripe pear.

"Hullo, Pinky," he drawled.

"I say, Pearson," said Rodber in a reverent voice, "I know this kid at home. He's awfully keen to be allowed to join your army."

Pearson scarcely glanced at Michael.

"All right. Swear him in. I've got a new oath written down in a book at home, but he can take the old one."

Pearson yawned and threw away the core of the pear.

"He's awfully glad he's going to join your army, Pearson. Aren't you, young Fane?"

"Yes, awfully glad," Michael echoed.

"It's the best army," said Pearson simply.

"Oh, easily," Rodber agreed. "I say, Pearson, that kid Biden said Church was going to lam you at four o'clock."

The offended Pearson swallowed a large piece of a second unripe pear and scowled.

"Did he? Tell the army to line up behind the lav. at four o'clock."

Rodber's eyes gleamed.

"I say, Pearson, I've got an awfully ripping plan. Supposing we ambush them."

"How?" enquired the commander.

"Why, supposing we put young Fane and two or three more new kids by the tuckshop door and tell them to run towards the haunted house, we could cop them simply rippingly."

"Give the orders before afternoon school," said Pearson curtly, and just then the bell for 'second hour' sounded.

"Wait for me at half-past twelve," Rodber shouted to Michael as he ran to get into school.

Michael grew quite feverish during 'second hour' and his brain whirled with the imagination of battles, so that the landing of Julius Cæsar seemed of minor importance. Tuckshops and haunted houses and doors and ambushes and the languid pale-faced Pearson occupied his thoughts fully enough. At a quarter-past twelve Mr. Whichelo the First Form master told Michael and the other new boys to go to the book-room and get their school caps, and at half-past twelve Michael waited outside on the yellow gravel for Rodber, splendidly proud of himself in a blue cap crested with a cockleshell worked in silver wire. He was longing to look at himself in the glass at home and to show Miss Carthew and Stella and Nanny and Cook and Gladys his school cap.

However, before he could go home Rodber took him round to where the tuckshop ambush would ensue at four o'clock. He showed him a door in a wall which led apparently into the narrow shady garden of an empty house next to the school. He explained how Michael was to hang about outside this door and when the Churchites demanded his presence, he told him that he was to run as hard as he could down the garden towards the house.

"We'll do the rest," said Rodber. "And now cut off home."

As soon as Michael was inside Number 64 he rushed upstairs to his bedroom and examined himself critically in the looking-glass. Really the new cap made a great difference. He seemed older somehow and more important. He wished that his arms and legs were not so thin, and he looked forward to the time when like Rodber he would wear Etons. However, his hair was now pleasantly and inconspicuously straight: he had already seen boys woefully teazed on account of their curls, and Michael congratulated himself that generally his dress and appearance conformed with the fashion of the younger boys' dress at Randell's. It would be terrible to excite notice. In fact, Michael supposed that to excite notice was the worst sin anybody could possibly commit. He hoped he would never excite notice. He would like to remain perfectly ordinary, and very slowly by an inconspicuous and gradual growth he would thus arrive in time at the dignity and honour enjoyed by Rodber, and perhaps even to the sacred majesty that clung to Pearson. Already he was going to take an active part in the adventures of school; and he felt sorry for the boys who without Rodber's influence would mildly go straight home at four o'clock.

Indeed, Michael set out for afternoon school in a somewhat elated frame of mind, and when he turned into the schoolyard, wearing the school cap, he felt bold enough to watch a game of Conquerors that was proceeding between two solemn-faced boys. He thought that to try to crack a chestnut hanging on a piece of string with another chestnut similarly suspended was a very enthralling pastime, and he was much upset when one of the solemn-faced antagonists suddenly grabbed his new school-cap and put it in his pocket and, without paying any attention to Michael, went on with the game as if nothing had happened. Michael had no idea how to grapple with the situation and felt inclined to cry.

"I say, give me my cap," he said at last.

The solemn-faced boys went on in silence with the game.

"I say, please give me my cap," Michael asked again.

No notice was taken of his appeal and Michael, looking round in despair, saw Rodber. He ran up to him.

"I say, Rodber, that boy over there has got my cap," he said.

"Well, don't come sneaking to me, you young ass. Go and smack his head."

"Am I to really?" asked Michael.

"Of course."

Michael was not prepared to withstand Rodber's advice, so he went up to the solemn-faced boy and hit him as hard as he could. The solemn-faced boy was so much surprized by this attack that he did not for a moment retaliate, and it was only his friend's gasp 'I say, what fearful cheek,' that restored him to a sense of what had happened.

In a moment Michael found himself lying on his back and almost smothered by the solemn-faced boy's whole body and presently suffering agony from the pressure of the solemn-faced boy's knees upon his arms pinioned cross-wise. Excited voices chattered about him from an increasing circle. He heard the solemn-faced boy telling his horrified auditors that a new kid had smacked his head. He heard various punishments strongly recommended, and at last with a sense of relief he heard the quick authoritative voice of the ubiquitous Rodber.

"Let him get up, young Plummer. A fight! A fight!"

Plummer got up, as he was told, and Michael in a circle of eager faces found himself confronted by Plummer.

"Go on," shouted Rodber. "I'm backing you, young Fane."

Michael lowered his head and charged desperately forward for the honour of Rodber; but a terrible pain in his nose and another in his arm and a third in his chin brought tears and blood together in such quantity that Michael would have liked to throw himself on to the grass and weep his life out, too weak to contend with solemn-faced boys who snatched caps.

Then over his misery he heard Rodber cry, 'That's enough. It's not fair. Give him back his cap.' The crowd broke up except for a few admirers of Rodber, who was telling Michael that he had done tolerably well for a new kid. Michael felt encouraged and ventured to point out that he had not really blabbed.

"You cocky young ass," said Rodber crushingly. "I suppose you mean 'blubbed.'"

Michael was overwhelmed by this rebuke and, wishing to hide his shame in a far corner of the field, turned away. But Rodber called him back and spoke pleasantly, so that Michael forgot the snub and wandered for the rest of the dinner-hour in Rodber's wake, with aching nose, but with a heart beating in admiration and affection.

Within a fortnight Michael had become a schoolboy, sharing in the general ambitions and factions and prejudices and ideals of schoolboyhood. He was a member of Pearson's victorious army; he supported the London Road Car Company against the London General Omnibus Company, the District Railway against the Metropolitan Railway; he was always ready to lam young boarders who were cheeky, and when an older boarder called him a 'day-bug' Michael was discreetly silent, merely registering a vow to take it out of the young boarders at the first opportunity. He also learnt to speak without blushing of the gym. and the lav. and arith. and hols. and 'Bobbie' Randell and 'my people' and 'my kiddy sister.' He was often first with the claimant 'ego,' when someone shouted 'quis?' over a broken pocket-knife found. He could shout 'fain I' to be rid of an obligation and 'bags I' to secure an advantage. He was a rigid upholder of the inviolableness of Christian names as postulated by Randellite convention. He laid out threepence a week in the purchase of sweets, usually at four ounces a penny; while during the beggary that succeeded he was one of the most persistent criers of 'donnez,' when richer boys emerged from the tuckshop, sucking gelatines and satin pralines and chocolate creams and raspberry noyau. As for the masters, he was always ready to hear scandalous rumours about their un-official lives, and he was one of the first to fly round the playground with the news that 'Squeaky' Mordaunt had distinctly muttered 'damn' beneath his breath, when Featherstone Minor trod on his toe towards the close of first hour. Soon also with one of the four hundred odd boys who made up the population of this very large private school, Michael formed a great friendship. He and Buckley were inseparable for sixteen whole weeks. During that time they exchanged the most intimate confidences. Buckley told Michael that his Christian names were Claude Arnold Eustace, and Michael told Buckley that he was called Charles Michael Saxby, and also that his mother was generally away from home, that his father was dead, that his governess was called Miss Carthew, that he had a sister who played the piano and that one day when he grew up he hoped to be an explorer and search for orchids in Borneo. Sometimes on Saturday or Wednesday half-holidays Buckley came to tea with Michael and sometimes Michael went to tea with Buckley, and observed how well Buckley kept in order his young brothers and kiddy sisters. Buckley lived close to Kensington Gardens and rode to school every morning on a London Road Car, which was the reason of Michael's keen partizanship of that company. In the eleven o'clock break between first and second hours, Michael and Buckley walked arm in arm round the field, and in the dinner-hour Michael and Buckley shared a rope on the Giant Stride and talked intimately on the top of the horizontal ladder in the outdoor gymnasium. During the Christmas holidays they haunted the banks of the Round Pond and fished for minnows and sailed capsizable yachts and checked keepers. Every night Michael thought of Buckley and every night Michael hoped that Buckley thought of him. Even in scholarship they were scarcely distinguishable; for when at the end of the autumn term Michael was top of the class in Divinity and English, Buckley headed the Latin list. As for Drawing they were bracketed equal at the very bottom of the form.

Then towards the middle of the Lent term Randell House was divided against itself; for one half of the school became Oxford and the other half Cambridge, in celebration of the boat-race which would be rowed at the end of March. When one morning Michael saw Buckley coming into school with a light blue swallow pinned to the left of his sailor-knot and when Buckley perceived attached to Michael's sailor-top a medal dependent from a dark blue ribbon, they eyed each other as strangers. This difference of opinion was irremediable. Neither romance nor sentiment could ever restore to Michael and Buckley their pristine cordiality, because Michael was now a despised Oxtail and Buckley was a loathed Cabbage-stalk.

They shouted to one another from the heart of massed factions mocking rhymes. Michael would chant:

"Oxford upstairs eating all the cakes; Cambridge downstairs licking up the plates."

To which Buckley would retort:

"Cambridge, rowing on and on for ever; Oxford in a matchbox floating down the river."

Snow fell in February, and great snow-ball fights took place between the Oxtails and the Cabbage-stalks in which the fortunes of both sides varied from day to day. During one of these fights Michael hit Buckley full in the eye with a snow-ball alleged to contain a stone, and the bitterness between them grew sharper. Then Oxford won the boat-race, and Buckley cut Michael publicly. Finally, owing to some alteration in the Buckley home, Buckley became a boarder, and was able with sneering voice to call Michael a beastly 'day-bug.' Such was the friendship of Michael and Buckley, which lasted for sixteen weeks and might not indeed have so much wounded Michael, when the rupture was made final, if Buckley had proved loyal to that friendship. Unfortunately for Michael's belief in human nature Buckley one day, stung perhaps by some trifling advantage gained by day-boys at the expense of boarders, divulged Michael's Christian names. He called out distinctly, "Ha! ha! Charles Michael Saxby Fane! Oh, what a name! Kiddy Michael Sacks-of-coals Fane!"

Michael regretted his intimacy with one who was not within the circle of Carlington Road. In future he would not seek friends outside Carlington Road and the six roads of the alliance. There all secrets must be kept, and all quarrels locally adjusted, for there Christian names were known and every household had its skeleton of nurse or governess.

Meanwhile, Mrs. Fane did not come home and Miss Carthew assumed more and more complete control of Number 64, until one day in spring Nurse suddenly told Michael that she was leaving next day. Somehow, Nurse had ceased to influence Michael's life one way or the other, and he could only feel vaguely uncomfortable over her departure. Nurse cried a good deal particularly at saying good-bye to Stella, whom she called her own girl whatever anybody might say. When Michael perceived Nurse's tears he tried hard to drag up from the depths of his nature a dutiful sentimentality. For the last time he kissed that puckered monkey-like face, and in a four-wheeler Nurse vanished without making any difference in the life of Sixty-four, save by a convenient shifting about of the upstair rooms. The old night-nursery was redecorated and became for many years Michael's bedroom. Miss Carthew slept in Michael's old big lonely front room, and Stella slept in a little dressing-room opening out of it. Down in the kitchen, whence withered Gladys and the impersonal cook had also vanished, Michael gleaned a certain amount of gossip and found that the immediate cause of Nurse's departure was due to Miss Carthew's discovery of her dead drunk in a kitchen chair. It seemed that Miss Carthew, slim and strong and beautiful, had had to carry the old woman up to her bedroom, while Michael lay sleeping, had had to undress and put her to bed and on the next day to contend with her asseverations that the collapse was due to violent neuralgia. It seemed also that for years the neighbourhood had known of Nurse's habits, had even seen her on two occasions upset Stella's perambulator. Indeed, so far as Michael could gather, he and Stella had lived until Miss Carthew's arrival in a state of considerable insecurity.

However, Nurse was now a goblin of the past, and the past could be easily forgotten. In these golden evenings of the summer-term, there was too much going forward in Carlington Road to let old glooms overshadow the gaiety of present life. As Mrs. Carthew had prophesied, Michael enjoyed being at school very much, and having already won a prize for being top of his class in Divinity and English at Christmas with every prospect of being top of his class again in the summer, he was anxious to achieve the still greater distinction of winning a prize in the school sports which were to be held in July. All the boys who lived in the Carlington Confederate Roads determined to win prizes, and Rodber was very much to the fore in training them all to do him credit. It was the fashion to choose colours in which to run, and Michael after a week's debate elected to appear in violet running-drawers and primrose-bordered vest. The twin Macalisters, contemporaries of Michael, ran in cerise and eau-de-nil, while the older Macalister wore ultramarine and mauve. Garrod chose dark green and Rodber looked dangerously swift in black and yellow. Every evening there was steady practice under Rodber, either in canvas shoes from lamp-post to lamp-post or, during the actual week before the sports, in spiked running-shoes on the grass-track, with corks to grip and a temperamental stop-watch to cause many disputes. It was a great humiliation for the Confederate Roads when Rodber himself failed to last the half-mile (under 14) on the day itself. However, the Macalister twins won the sack-race (under 11) and in the same class Michael won the hundred yards Consolation Race and an octagonal napkin-ring, so Carlington Road congratulated itself. In addition to athletic practice there were several good fights with 'cads' and a disagreeable Colonel had his dining-room window starred by a catapult. Other notable events included a gas explosion at Number 78, when the front door was blown across the street and flattened a passer-by against the opposite wall. There was a burglary at Number 33 and the housemaid at Number 56 fell backwards from the dining-room window-sill and bruised her back on the lid of the dustbin in the area.

With all these excitements to sustain the joy of life Michael was very happy and, when school broke up for the summer holidays, he had never yet looked forward so eagerly to the jolly weeks by the sea. Miss Carthew and Michael and Stella went to Folkestone that year, and Michael enjoyed himself enormously. Miss Carthew, provided that she was allowed a prior inspection, offered no opposition to friendship with strange children, and Michael joined an association for asking everybody on the Leas what the time was. The association would not have been disbanded all the holidays if one of the members had not asked the time from the same old gentleman twice in one minute. The old gentleman was so acutely irritated by this that he walked about the Leas warning people against the association, until it became impossible to find out the time, when one really wanted to know. Michael moved inland for a while after this and fell into Radnor Park pond, when he returned to the sea and got stung by a jelly-fish while he was paddling, and read Treasure Island in the depths of his own particular cave among the tamarisks of the Lower Sandgate Road.

After about a fortnight of complete rest a slight cloud was cast over the future by the announcement at breakfast one morning that he was to do a couple of hours' work at French every day with a French governess: remembering Madame Flauve, he felt depressed by the prospect. But Miss Carthew found a charming and youthful French governess at a girls' school, where about half a dozen girls were remaining during the holidays, and Michael did not mind so much. He rather liked the atmosphere of the girls' school, although when he returned to Randell's he gave a very contemptuous account of female education to his masculine peers. An incident happened at this girls' school which he never told, although it made a great impression on his imagination.

One afternoon he had been invited to take tea with the six girls and Mademoiselle, and after tea the weather being wet, they all played games in the recreation-room. One of the smaller girls happened to swing higher than decorum allowed, and caused Michael to blush and to turn his head quickly and look intently at houses opposite. He knew that the girl was unaware of the scandal she had created, and therefore blushed the deeper and hoped that the matter would pass off quietly. But very soon he heard a chatter of reproof, and the poor little girl was banished from the room in disgrace, while all the other girls discussed the shameful business from every point of view, calling upon Mademoiselle and Michael to endorse their censure. Michael felt very sorry for the poor little girl and wished very much that the others would let the matter drop, but the discussion went on endlessly and as, just before he went home, he happened to see the offending girl sitting by a window with tear-stained face, Michael felt more sorry than ever and wished that he dared to say a comforting word, to explain how well he understood it was all an accident. On the way home, he walked silently, meditating upon disgrace, and for the first time he realized something of human cruelty and the lust to humiliate and submerge deeper still the fallen. At the same time he himself experienced, in retrospect of the incident, a certain curious excitement, and did not know whether, after all, he had not taken pleasure in the little girl's shame, whether, after all, he would not have liked to go back and talk the whole matter out again. However, there was that exciting chapter in Treasure Island to finish and the September Boy's Own Paper to expect. On the next day Michael, walking with Miss Carthew on the Leas, met General Mace, and girls' schools with their curious excitements and blushes were entirely forgotten. General Mace, it appeared, was an old friend of Miss Carthew's father and was staying by himself at Folkestone. General Mace had fought in the Indian Mutiny and was exactly what a general should be, very tall with a white moustache fiercely curling and a rigid back that bent inwards like a bow and a magnificent ebony walking-stick and a gruff voice. General Mace seemed to take a fancy to Michael and actually invited him to go for a walk with him next day at ten o'clock.

"Sharp, mind," said the General as he saluted stiffly. "Ten o'clock to the minute."

Michael spent the rest of the day in asking questions of Miss Carthew about General Mace, and scarcely slept that night for fear he might be late. At nine o'clock, Michael set out from the lodgings and ran all the way to the General's house on the Leas, and walked about and fidgeted and fretted himself until the clock struck the first chime of ten, when he rang the bell and was shown upstairs and was standing on the General's hearthrug before the echo of the last chime had died away.

The General cleared his throat and after saluting Michael suggested a walk. Proudly Michael walked beside this tall old soldier up and down the Leas. He was told tales of the Mutiny; he learned the various ranks of the British Army from Lance-corporal to Field-marshal; he agreed at the General's suggestion to aim at a commission in the Bengal Cavalry, preferably in a regiment which wore an uniform of canary-yellow. Every morning Michael walked about Folkestone with General Mace, and one morning they turned into a toy-shop where Michael was told to choose two boxes of soldiers. Michael at first chose a box of Highlanders doubling fiercely with fixed bayonets and a stationary Highland Regimental Band, each individual of which had a different instrument and actually a music-stand as well. These two boxes together cost seven shillings, and Michael was just leaving the shop when he saw a small penny box containing twelve very tiny soldiers. Michael was in a quandary. For seven shillings he would be able to buy eighty-four penny boxes, that is to say one thousand and eight soldiers, whereas in the two boxes of Highlanders already selected there were only twelve with bayonets, twelve with instruments and twelve music-stands. It was really very difficult to decide, and General Mace declined to make any suggestion as to which would be the wiser choice, Michael was racked by indecision and after a long debate chose the original two boxes and played with his Highlanders for several years to come.

"Quite right," said the General when they reached the sunlight from the dusty little toy-shop. "Quite right. Quality before quantity, sir. I'm glad to see you have so much common sense."

Almost before the holidays seemed to have begun, the holidays were over. There was a short and melancholy day of packing up, and a farewell visit through the rain to General Mace. He and Michael sat for a while in his room, while they talked earnestly of the Indian Army and the glories of patriotism. Michael told tales, slightly exaggerated, of the exploits of Pearson's army and General Mace described the Relief of Lucknow. Michael felt that they were in profound sympathy: they both recognized the splendour of action. The rain stopped, and in a rich autumnal sunset they walked together for the last time over the golden puddles and spangled wetness of the Leas. Michael went through the ranks of the British Army without a single mistake, and promised faithfully to make the Bengal Lancers his aim through youth.

"Punctuality, obedience and quality before quantity," said the General, standing up as tall and thin as Don Quixote against the sunset glow. "Good-bye."

"Good-bye," said Michael.

They saluted each other ceremoniously, and parted. The next day Michael was in London, and after a depressing Sunday and an exciting Monday spent in buying a Norfolk suit and Eton collars, the new term began with all the excitements of 'moving up,' of a new form-master, of new boys, of seeing who would be in the Football Eleven and of looking forward to Christmas with its presents and pantomimes.

Chapter VIII: *Siamese Stamps*

IN the Upper Fourth class, under the tutorship of Mr. Macrae, Michael began to prosecute seriously the study of Greek, whose alphabet he had learnt the preceding term. He now abandoned the scarlet book of Elementary Latin for Henry's Latin Primer, which began with 'Balbus was building a wall,' and looked difficult in its mulberry-cloth binding. This term in the Upper Fourth was very trying to Michael. Troubles accumulated. Coincident with the appearance of Greek irregular verbs came the appearance of Avery, a new boy who at once, new boy though he was, assumed command of the Upper Fourth and made Michael the target for his volatile and stinging shafts. Misfortune having once directed her attention to Michael, pursued him for some time to come. Michael was already sufficiently in awe of Avery's talent for hurting his feelings, when from the Hebrides Mrs. Fane sent down Harris tweed for Michael's Norfolk suits. He begged Miss Carthew to let him continue in the inconspicuous dark blue serge which was the fashion at Randell's; but for once she was unsympathetic, and Michael had to wear the tweed. Avery, of course, was very witty at his expense and for a long time Michael was known as 'strawberry-bags,' until the joke palled. Michael had barely lived down the Harris tweed, when Avery discovered, while they were changing into football shorts, that Michael wore combinations instead of pants and vest. Combinations were held to be the depth of effeminacy, and Avery often enquired when Michael was going to appear in petticoats and stays. Michael spoke to Miss Carthew about these combinations which at the very moment of purchase he had feared, but Miss Carthew insisted that they were much healthier than the modish pants and vest, and Michael was not allowed to change the style of his underclothing. In desperation he tied some tape round his waist, but the observant Avery noticed this ruse, and Michael was more cruelly teazed than ever. Then one Monday morning the worst blow of all fell suddenly. The boys at Randell's had on Saturday morning to take down from dictation the form-list in a home-book, which had to be brought back on Monday morning signed by a parent, so that no boy should escape the vigilance of the paternal eye. Of course, Miss Carthew always signed Michael's home-book and so far no master had asked any questions. But Mr. Macrae said quite loudly on this Monday morning:

"Who is this Maud Carthew that signs your book, Fane?"

Michael felt the pricking of the form's ears and blushed hotly.

"My mother's away," he stammered.

"Oh," said Mr. Macrae bluntly, "and who is this person then?"

Michael nearly choked with shame.

"My governess—my sister's governess, I mean," he added, desperately trying to retrieve the situation.

"Oh, yes," said Mr. Macrae. "I see."

The form tittered, while the crimson Michael stumbled back to his desk. It was a long time before Avery grew tired of Miss Carthew or before the class wearied of crying 'Maudie' in an united falsetto whenever Michael ventured to speak. Mr. Macrae, too, made cruel use of his advantage, for whenever Michael tripped over an irregular verb, Mr. Macrae would address to the ceiling in his soft unpleasant voice sarcastic remarks about governesses, while everyMonday morning he would make a point of putting on his glasses to examine Michael's home-book very carefully. The climax of Michael's discomfort was reached, when a snub-nosed boy called Jubb with a cockney accent asked him what his father was.

"He's dead," Michael answered.

"Yes, but what was he?" Jubb persisted.

"He was a gentleman," said Michael.

Avery happened to overhear this and was extremely witty over Michael's cockiness, so witty that Michael was goaded into retaliation, notwithstanding his fear of Avery's tongue.

"Well, what is your father?" he asked.

"My father's a duke, and I've got an uncle who's a millionaire, and my governess is a queen," said Avery.

Michael was silent: he could not contend with Avery. Altogether the Upper Fourth was a very unpleasant class; but next term Michael and half of the class were moved up to the Lower Fifth, and Avery left to go to a private school in Surrey, because he was ultimately destined for Charterhouse, near which school his people had, as he said, taken a large house. Curiously enough the combination of half the Upper Fourth with the half of the Lower Fifth left behind made a rather pleasant class, one that Michael enjoyed as much as any other so far, particularly as he was beginning to find that he was clever enough to avoid doing as much school-work as hitherto he had done, without in any way permanently jeopardizing his position near the top of the form. To be sure Mr. Wagstaff, the cherub-faced master of the Lower Fifth, complained of his continually shifting position from one end of the class to the other; but Michael justified himself and incidentally somewhat annoyed Mr. Wagstaff by coming out head boy in the Christmas examinations. Meanwhile, if he found Greek irregular verbs and Latin gender rhymes tiresome, Michael read unceasingly at home, preferably books that encouraged the private schoolboy's instinct to take sides. Michael was for the Trojans against the Greeks, partly on account of the Greek verbs, but principally because he once had a straw hat inscribed H.M.S. Hector. He was also for the Lancastrians against the Yorkists, and, of course, for the Jacobites against the Hanoverians. Somewhat illogically, he was for the Americans against the English, because as Miss Carthew pointed out he was English himself and the English were beaten. She used to tease Michael for nearly always choosing the beaten side. She also used to annoy him by her assertion that in taking the part of the Americans in the War of Independence, he showed that most of his other choices were only due to the books he read. She used to make him very angry by saying that he was at heart a Roundhead and a Whig, and even hinted that he would grow up a Radical. This last insinuation really annoyed him very much indeed, because at Randell House no boy could be anything but a Conservative without laying himself open to the suggestion that he was not a gentleman.

In time, after an absence of nearly two years, Mrs. Fane came home for a long time; but Michael did not feel any of those violent emotions of joy that once he used to feel when he saw her cab rounding the corner. He was shy of his mother, and she for her part seemed shy of him and told Miss Carthew that school had not improved Michael. She wondered, too, why he always seemed anxious to be playing with other boys.

"It's quite natural," Miss Carthew pointed out.

"Darling Michael. I suppose it is," Mrs. Fane agreed vaguely. "But he's so grubby and inky nowadays."

Michael maintained somewhat indignantly that all the boys at Randell's were like him, for he was proud that by being grubby and inky no boy could detect in him any inclination to differentiate himself from the mass. At Randell's, where there was one way only of thinking and behaving and speaking, it would have been grossly cocky to be brushed and clean. Michael resented his mother's attempt to dress him nicely and was almost rude when she suggested ideas for charming and becoming costumes.

"I do think boys are funny," she used to sigh.

"Well, mother," Michael would argue, "if I wore a suit like that, all the other boys would notice it."

"But I think it's nice to be noticed," Mrs. Fane would contend.

"I think it's beastly," Michael always said.

"I wish you wouldn't use that horrid word," his mother would say disapprovingly.

"All the boys do," was Michael's invariable last word.

Then, "Michael," Miss Carthew would say sharply, as she fixed him with that cold look which he so much dreaded. Michael would blush and turn away, abashed; while Stella's company would be demanded by his mother instead of his, and Stella would come into the room all lily-rosed beside her imp-like brother.

Stella was held by Michael to be affected, and he would often point out to her how little such behaviour would be tolerated at a boys' school. Stella's usual reply was to pout, a form of expression which came under the category of affectations, or she would cry, which was a degree worse and was considered to be as good as sneaking outright. Michael often said he hoped that school would improve Stella's character and behaviour; yet when she went to school, Michael thought that not only was she none the better for the experience, but he was even inclined to suggest that she was very much the worse. Tiresome little girl friends came to tea sometimes and altered Michael's arrangements; and when they came they used to giggle in corners and Stella used to show off detestably. Once Michael was so much vexed by a certain Dorothy that he kissed her spitefully, and a commotion ensued from the middle of which rose Miss Carthew, grey-eyed and august like Pallas Athene in The Heroes. It seemed to Michael that altogether too much importance was attached to this incident. He had merely kissed Dorothy in order to show his contempt for her behaviour. One would think from the lecture given by Miss Carthew that it was pleasant to kiss giggling little girls. Michael felt thoroughly injured by the imputation of gallantry, and sulked instead of giving reasons.

"I really think your mother is right," Miss Carthew said at last. "You are quite different from the old Michael."

"I didn't want to kiss her," he cried, exasperated.

"Doesn't that make it all the worse?" Miss Carthew suggested.

Michael shrugged his shoulders feeling powerless to contend with all this stupidity of opinion.

"Surely," said Miss Carthew at last, "Don Quixote or General Mace or Henry V wouldn't have kissed people against their will in order to be spiteful."

"They might," argued Michael; "if rotten little girls came to tea and made them angry."

"I will not have that word 'rotten' used in front of me," Miss Carthew said.

"Well, fat-headed then," Michael proposed as a euphemism.

"The truth is," Miss Carthew pointed out, "you were angry because you couldn't have the Macalisters to tea and you vented your anger on poor Stella and her friends. I call it mean and unchivalrous."

"Well, Stella goes to mother and asks for Dorothy to come to tea, when you told me I could have the Macalisters, and I don't see why I should always have to give way."

"Boys always give way to girls," generalized Miss Carthew.

"I don't believe they do nowadays," said Michael.

"I see it's hopeless to argue any more. I'm sorry you won't see you're in the wrong. It makes me feel disappointed."

Michael again shrugged his shoulders.

"I don't see how I can possibly ask your mother to let Nancy stay here next Christmas. I suppose you'll be trying to kiss her."

Michael really had to laugh at this.

"Why, I like Nancy awfully," he said. "And we both think kissing is fearful rot—I mean frightfully stupid. But I won't do it again, Miss Carthew. I'm sorry. I am really."

There was one great advantage in dealing with Miss Carthew. She was always ready to forgive at once, and, as Michael respected her enough to dislike annoying her, he found it perfectly easy to apologize and be friends—particularly as he had set his heart on Nancy's Christmas visit.

Carlington Road and the Confederate Roads were now under the control of Michael and his friends. Rodber had gone away to a public school: the elder Macalister and Garrod had both got bicycles which occupied all their time: Michael, the twin Macalisters and a boy called Norton were in a very strong position of authority. Norton had two young brothers and the Macalisters had one, so that there were three slaves in perpetual attendance. It became the fashion to forsake the school field for the more adventurous wasteland of the neighbourhood. At the end of Carlington Road itself still existed what was practically open country as far as it lasted. There were elm-trees and declivities and broken hedges and the excavated hollows of deserted gravel-pits. There was an attractive zigzag boundary fence which was sufficiently ruinous at certain intervals to let a boy through to wander in the allotments of railway workers. Bands of predatory 'cads' prowled about this wasteland, and many were the fierce fights at sundown between the cads and the Randellites. Caps were taken for scalps, and Miss Carthew was horrified to observe nailed to Michael's bedroom wall the filthiest cap she had ever seen.

Apart from the battles there were the luxurious camps, where cigarettes at five a penny were smoked to the last puff and were succeeded by the consumption of highly scented sweets to remove the traces of tobacco. These camps were mostly pitched in the gravelly hollows, where Michael and the Macalisters and Norton used to sit round a camp-fire on the warm evenings of summer, while silhouetted against the blue sky above stood the minor Macalister and the junior Nortons in ceaseless vigilance. The bait held out to these sentries, who sometimes mutinied, was their equipment with swords, guns, pistols, shields, bows, arrows and breastplates. So heavily and decoratively armed and sustained by the prospect of peppermint bull's-eyes, Dicky Macalister and the two Nortons were content for an hour to scan the horizon for marauding cads, while down below the older boys discussed life in all its ambiguity and complication. These symposiums in the gravel-pit tried to solve certain problems in a very speculative manner.

"There must be *some* secret about being married," said Michael one Saturday afternoon, when the sun blazed down upon the sentries and the last cigarette had been smoked.

"There *is*," Norton agreed,

"I can't make out about twins," Michael continued, looking critically at the Macalisters.

Siegfried Macalister, generally known as 'Smack' in distinction to his brother Hugh always called 'Mac,' felt bound to offer a suggestion.

"There's twenty minutes' difference between us. I heard my mater tell a visitor, and besides I'm the eldest."

Speculation was temporarily interrupted by a bout between Smack and Mac, because neither was allowed to claim priority. At the end of an indecisive round Michael struck in:

"But why are there twins? People don't like twins coming, because in Ally Sloper there's always a joke about twins."

"I know married people who haven't got any children at all," said Norton in order still more elaborately to complicate the point at issue.

"Yes, there you are," said Michael. "There's some secret about marriage."

"There's a book in my mater's room which I believe would tell us," hinted Smack.

"There's a good deal in the Bible," Norton observed. "Only it's difficult to find the places and then you can't tell for certain what they mean."

Then came a long whispering at the end of which the four boys shook their heads very wisely and said that they were sure that was it.

"Hullo!" Michael shouted, forgetting the debate. "Young Dicky's signalling."

"Indians," said Mac.

"Sioux or Apaches?" asked Smack anxiously.

"Neither. It's Arabs. Charge," shouted Norton.

All problems went to the winds in the glories of action, in the clash of stick on stick, in the rending of cad's collar and cad's belt, and in the final defeat of the Arabs with the loss of their caravan—a sugar-box on a pair of elliptical wheels.

In addition to the arduous military life led by Michael at this period, he was also in common with Smack and Mac and Norton a multiplex collector. At first the two principal collections were silkworms and silver-paper. Afterwards came postage stamps and coins and medals and autographs and birds' eggs and shells and fossils and bones and skins and butterflies and moths and portraits of famous cricketers. From the moment the first silkworm was brought home in a perforated cardboard-box to the moment when by some arrangement of vendible material the first bicycle was secured, the greater part of Michael's leisure was mysteriously occupied in swapping. This swapping would continue until the mere theory of swapping for swapping's sake as exemplified in a paper called The Exchange and Mart was enough. When this journal became the rage, the most delightful occupation of Michael and his friends was that of poring over the columns of this medium of barter in order to read of X.Y.Z. in Northumberland who was willing to exchange five Buff Orpingtons, a suit, a tennis racket and Cowper's Poems for a mechanical organ or a 5 ft. by 4 ft. greenhouse. All the romance of commerce was to be found in The Exchange and Mart together with practical hints on the moulting of canaries or red mange in collies. Cricket was in the same way made a mathematical abstraction of decimals and initials and averages and records. All sorts of periodicals were taken in—Cricket, The Cricketer, Cricketing amongst many others. From an exact perusal of these, Michael and the Macalisters knew that Streatham could beat Hampstead and were convinced of the superiority of the Incogniti C.C. over the Stoics C.C. With the collections of cricketers' portraits some of these figures acquired a conceivable personality; but, for the most part, they remained L.M.N.O.P.Q. Smith representing 36·58 an innings and R.S.T.U.V.W. Brown costing 11·07 a wicket. That they wore moustaches, lived and loved like passionate humanity did not seem to matter compared with the arithmetical progression of their averages. When Michael and Norton (who was staying with him at St. Leonards) were given shillings and told to see the Hastings' Cricket Week from the bowling of the first ball to the drawing of the final stump, Michael and Norton were very much bored indeed, and deprecated the waste of time in watching real cricket, when they might have been better occupied in collating the weekly cricketing journals.

At Christmas Michael emerged from a successful autumn term with Stories from the Odyssey by Professor Church and a chestnut that was reputed to have conquered nine hundred and sixty-six other and softer chestnuts. That nine hundred and sixty-sixer of Michael's was a famous nut, and the final struggle between it (then a five hundred and forty-oner) and the four hundred and twenty-fourer it smashed was a contest long talked of in circles where Conquerors were played. Michael much regretted that the etiquette of the Lent term, which substituted peg-tops for Conquerors, should prevent his chestnut reaching four figures. He knew that next autumn term, if all fell out as planned, he would be at St. James' School itself, where Conquerors and tops and marbles were never even mentioned, save as vanities and toys of early youth. However, he swapped the nine hundred and sixty-sixer for seven white mice and a slow-worm in spirits of wine belonging to Norton; and he had the satisfaction of hearing later on that after a year in rejuvenating oil the nine hundred and sixty-sixer became a two thousand and thirty-threer before it fell down a drain, undefeated.

After Christmas Nancy Carthew came up from Hampshire to spend a fortnight at Carlington Road, and the holidays were spent in a fever of theatres and monuments and abbeys. Michael asked Nancy what she thought of Stella and her affectation, and was surprised by Nancy saying she thought Stella was an awfully jolly kid and 'no end good' at the piano. Michael in consideration of Nancy's encomium tried to take a fresh view of Stella and was able sincerely to admit that, compared with many other little girls of the neighbourhood, Stella was fairly pretty. He decided that it would be a good thing for Norton to marry her. He told Norton that there seemed no reason why he and Stella should not come together in affection, and Norton said that, if Michael thought he should, he was perfectly willing to marry Stella, when he was grown up. Michael thereupon swapped a box of somewhat bent dragoons for a ring, and presented this ring to Norton with the injunction that he should on no account tell Stella that he was engaged to her, in case it made her cocky. He also forbade Norton to kiss her (not that he supposed Norton wanted to kiss Stella), because Miss Carthew would be annoyed and might possibly close the area door to Norton for the future.

When Nancy went back to Hampshire, Michael felt lonely. The Macalisters and the Nortons had gone away on visits, and Carlington Road was dreary without them. Michael read a great deal and by reason of being at home he gradually became less grubby, as the holidays wore on. Also his hair grew long and waved over his forehead with golden lights and shadows and curled in bunches by his ears. A new Eton suit well became him, and his mother said how charming he looked. Michael deplored good looks in boys, but he managed to endure the possession of them during the little space that remained before the Lent term began. He took to frequenting the drawing-room again as of old and, being nowadays allowed to stay up till a quarter to nine, he used to spend a rosy half-hour after dinner sitting on a footstool in the firelight by his mother's knee. She used to stroke his hair and sigh sometimes, when she looked at him.

One afternoon just before term began Mrs. Fane told him to make himself as tidy as possible, because she wanted to take him out to pay a call. Michael was excited by this notion, especially when he heard that they were to travel by hansom, a form of vehicle which he greatly admired. The hansom bowled along the Kensington Road with Michael in his Eton suit and top-hat sitting beside his mother scented sweetly with delicious perfumes and very silky to the touch. They drove past Kensington Gardens all dripping with January rains, past Hyde Park and the Albert Memorial, past the barracks of the Household Cavalry, past Hyde Park Corner and the Duke of Wellington's house. They dashed along with a jingle and a rattle over the slow old omnibus route, and Michael felt very much distinguished as he turned round to look at the melancholy people crammed inside each omnibus they passed. When they came to Devonshire House, they turned round to the left and pulled up before a grand house in a square. Michael pressed the bell, and the door opened immediately, much more quickly than he had ever known a door open.

"Is his lordship in?" asked Mrs. Fane.

"His lordship is upstairs, ma'am," said the footman.

The hall seemed full of footmen, one of whom took Michael's hat and another of whom led the way up a wide soft staircase that smelt like the inside of the South Kensington Museum. All the way up, the walls were hung with enormous pictures of men in white wigs. Presently they stood in the largest room Michael had ever entered, a still white room full of golden furniture. Michael had barely recovered his breath from astonishment at the size of the room, when he saw another room round the corner, in which a man was sitting by a great fire. When the footman had left the room very quietly, this man got up and held Mrs. Fane's hand for nearly a minute. Then he looked at Michael, curiously, Michael thought, so curiously as to make him blush.

"And this is the boy?" the gentleman asked.

Michael thought his mother spoke very funnily, as if she were just going to cry, when she answered:

"Yes, this is Michael."

"My God, Valérie," said the man, "it makes it harder than ever."

Michael took the opportunity to look at this odd man and tried to think where he had seen him before. He was sure he had seen him somewhere. But every time just as he had almost remembered, a mist came over the picture he was trying to form, so that he could not remember.

"Well, Michael," said the gentleman, "you don't know who I am."

"Ah, don't, Charles," said Mrs. Fane.

"Well, he's not so wise as all that," laughed the gentleman.

Michael thought it was a funny laugh, more sad than cheerful.

"This is Lord Saxby," said Mrs. Fane.

"I say, my name is Saxby," Michael exclaimed.

"Nonsense," said Lord Saxby, "I don't believe it."

"It is really. Charles Michael Saxby Fane."

"Well, that's a very strange thing," said Lord Saxby.

"Yes, I think it's awfully funny," Michael agreed. "Because I never heard of anyone called Saxby. My name's Charles too. Only, of course, that's quite a common name. But nobody at our school knows I'm called Saxby except a boy called Buckley who's an awful beast. We don't tell our Christian names, you know. If a chap lets out his Christian name he gets most frightfully ragged by the other chaps. Chaps think you're an awfully silly ass if you let out your Christian name."

Michael was finding it very easy to talk.

"I must hear some more about this wonderful school," Lord Saxby declared.

Then followed a delightful conversation in which due justice was done to the Macalister twins and to Norton, and to the life they shared with Michael.

"By gad, Valérie, he ought to go to Eton, you know," declared Lord Saxby, turning to Michael's mother.

"No, no. I'm sure you were right, when you said St. James'," persisted Mrs. Fane.

"Perhaps I was," Lord Saxby sighed. "Well, Valérie—not again. It's too damnably tantalizing."

"I thought just once while he was still small," said Mrs. Fane softly. "Photographs are so unsatisfactory. And you haven't yet heard Stella play."

"Valérie, I couldn't. Look at this great barrack of a house. If you only knew how I long sometimes for—what a muddle it all is!"

Then a footman came in with tea, and Michael wondered what dinner was like in this house, if mere tea were so grand and silvery.

"I think I must drive you back in the phaeton," said Lord Saxby.

"No, no, Charles. No more rules must be broken."

"Yes, I suppose you're right. But don't—not again, please. I can't bear to think of the 'ifs.'"

Then Lord Saxby turned to Michael.

"Look here, young man, what do you want most?"

"Oh, boxes of soldiers and an unused set of Siamese," said Michael.

"Siamese what? Siamese cats?"

"No, you silly," laughed Michael, "Stamps, of course!"

"Oh, stamps," said Lord Saxby. "Right—and soldiers, eh? Good."

All the way back in the hansom Michael wished he had specified Artillery to Lord Saxby; but two days afterwards dozens of boxes of all kinds of soldiers arrived, and unused sets not merely of Siamese, but of North American Tercentenaries and Borneos and Labuans and many others.

"I say," Michael gasped, "he's a ripper, isn't he? What spiffing boxes! I say, he is a decent chap, isn't he? When are we going to see Lord Saxby again, mother?"

"Some day."

"I can have Norton to tea on Wednesday, can't I?" begged Michael. "He'll think my soldiers are awfully ripping."

"Darling Michael," said his mother.

"Mother, I will try and not be inky," said Michael in a burst of affectionate renunciation.

"Dearest boy," said his mother gently.

Chapter IX: *Holidays in France*

IN Michael's last term at St. James' Preparatory School, Mrs. Fane settled that he should for the holidays go to France with Mr. Vernon and Mr. Lodge, two masters who were accustomed each year to take a few boys away with them to the coast of Brittany. Five boys were going this summer—Michael and Hands and Hargreaves and Jubb and Rutherford; and all five of them bragged about their adventure for days before school broke up. Miss Carthew drove with Michael to Victoria Station and handed him over to Mr. Lodge who was walking about in a very thick and romantic overcoat. Mr. Lodge was a clean-shaven, large-faced and popular master, and Mr. Vernon was an equally popular master, deep-voiced, heavy-moustached, hook-nosed. In fact it was impossible to say which of the two one liked the better. Mr. Lodge at once produced two packets of Mazawattee tea which he told Michael to put in his pocket and say nothing about when he landed in France, and when Hands, Hargreaves, Rutherford and Jubb arrived, they were all given packets of tea by Mr. Lodge and told to say nothing about them when they landed in France. Mr. Vernon appeared, looking very business-like and shouting directions about the luggage to porters, while Mr. Lodge gathered the boys together and steered them through the barrier on to the platform and into the train for Newhaven. The steamer by which they were going to cross was not an ordinary packet-boat, but a cargo-boat carrying vegetable ivory. For Channel voyagers they were going to be a long while at sea, calling at Havre and afterwards rounding Cherbourg and Brest, before they reached St. Corentin, the port of their destination at the mouth of the Loire. It was rough weather all the way to Havre, and Michael was too ill to notice much the crew or the boat or any of the other boys. However, the excitement of disembarking at Havre about midnight put an end to sea-sickness, for it was very thrilling at such an hour to follow Mr. Lodge and Mr. Vernon through the gloomy wharves and under their dripping archways. When after this strange walk, they came to a wide square and saw cafés lighted up and chairs and tables in the open air before the doors, Michael felt that life was opening out on a vista of hitherto unimagined possibilities. They all sat down at midnight, wrapped up in their travelling coats and not at all too much tired to sip grenadine sucrée and to crunch Petit Beurre biscuits. Michael thought grenadine sucrée was just as nice as it looked and turned to Hands, a skull-headed boy who was sitting next to him:

"I say, this is awfully decent, isn't it?"

"Rather," squeaked Hands in his high voice. "Much nicer than Pineappleade."

After they had stayed there for a time, watching isolated passers-by slouch across the wind-blown square, Mr. Lodge announced they must hurry back to the boat and get a good night's sleep. Back they went between the damp walls of the shadowy wharves, plastered with unfamiliar advertizements, until they reached their boat and went to bed. In the morning when Michael woke up, the steamer was pitching and rolling: everything in the cabin was lying in a jumble on the floor, and Rutherford and Hargreaves were sitting up in their bunks wideawake. Rutherford was the oldest boy of the party and he was soon going in for his Navy examination; but he had been so sea-sick the day before that Michael felt that he was just as accessible as the others and was no longer afraid to talk to this hero without being spoken to first. Rutherford, having been so sick, felt bound to put on a few airs of grandeur; but he was pleasant enough and very full of information about many subjects which had long puzzled Michael. He spoke with authority on life and death and birth and love and marriage, so that when Michael emerged into the wind from the jumbled cabin, he felt that to dress beside Rutherford was an event not easily to be forgotten: but later on as he paced the foam-spattered deck, and meditated on the facts of existence so confidently revealed, he began to fear that the learned Rutherford was merely a retailer of unwarranted legends. Still he had propounded enough for Michael, when he returned to Carlington Road, to theorize upon and impart to the Macalisters; and anyway, without bothering about physiological problems, it was certainly splendid to walk about the deck in the wind and rain, and no longer to hate, but even to enjoy the motion of the boat. It was exhilarating to clamber right up into the bows among coils of rope and to see how the boat charged through the spuming water. Michael nearly made up his mind to be a sailor instead of a Bengal Lancer, and looked enviously at the ship's boy in his blue blouse. But presently he heard a savage voice, and one of the sailors so much admired kicked the ship's boy down the companion into the forecastle. Michael was horrified when, late in the grey and stormy afternoon, he heard cries of pain from somewhere down below. He ran to peer into the pit whence they came, and in the half-light he could see a rope's-end clotted with blood. This sight dismayed him, and he longed to ask Mr. Lodge or Mr. Vernon to interfere and save the poor ship's boy, but a feeling of shame compelled silence and, though he was sincerely shocked by the thought of the cruel scenes acted down there in the heart of the ship, he could not keep back a certain exultation and excitement similar to that which he had felt at Folkestone in the girls' school last summer.

Soon the steamer with its cargo of vegetable ivory and tortured ship's boy and brutal crew were all forgotten in the excitement of arriving at St. Corentin, of driving miles into the country until they reached the house where they were going to spend six weeks. It was an old house set far back from the high road and reached by a long drive between pollarded acacias. All round the house were great fig trees and pear trees and plum trees. The garden was rank with unpruned gooseberry and currant bushes, untidy with scrambling gourds and grape vines. It was a garden utterly unlike any garden that Michael had ever known. There seemed to be no flowers in this overwhelming vegetation which matted everything. It was like the garden of the Sleeping Beauty's palace. The crumbling walls were webbed with briars; their foundations were buried in thickets of docks and nettles, and the fruit trees that grew against them had long ago broken loose from any restraint. It was a garden that must surely take a very long time to explore, so vast was it, so trackless, so much did every corner demand a slow advance.

When the boys had unpacked and when they had been introduced to Mrs. Wylde, the mistress of the house, and when they had presented to her the packets of Mazawattee tea and when they themselves had eaten a deliciously novel dinner at the unusual hour of six, they all set out to explore the luxuriant wilderness behind the house. Mr. Vernon and Mr. Lodge shouted to them to eat only the ripe fruit and with this solitary injunction left them to their own amusements until bed-time. Rutherford, Hargreaves and Jubb at once set out to find ripe fruit, and as the first tree they came to was loaded with greengages, Rutherford, Hargreaves and Jubb postponed all exploration for the present. Michael and Hands, who was sleeping in hisroom and with whom he had already made friends, left the others behind them. As they walked farther from the house, they spoke in low tones, so silent was this old garden.

"I'm sure it's haunted," said Michael. "I never felt so funny, not exactly frightened, you know, but sort of frightened."

"It's still quite light," squeaked the hopeful Hands.

"Yes, but the sun's behind all these trees and you can't hear anything, but only us walking," whispered Michael.

However, they went on through a jungle of artichokes and through an orchard of gnarled apple trees past a mildewed summer-house, until they reached a serpentine path between privet bushes, strongly scented in the dampness all around.

"Shall we?" murmured Hands doubtfully.

"Yes. We can bunk back if we see anything," said Michael. "I like this."

They walked on following the zigzags of the path, but stopped dead as a blackbird shrilled and flapped into the bushes affrighted.

"By Jove, that beastly bird made me awfully funky," said Michael.

"Let's go back," said Hands. "Suppose we got murdered. People do in France."

"Rot," said Michael. "Not in a private garden, you cuckoo."

With mutual encouragement the two boys wandered on, until they found farther progress barred by a high hedge, impenetrable apparently and viewless to Michael and Hands who were not very tall.

"What sucks!" said Michael. "I hate turning back. I think it's rotten to turn back. Don't you? Hullo!" he cried. "Look here, Hands. Here's a regular sort of tunnel going down hill. It's quite steep."

In a moment Hands and Michael were half sliding, half climbing down a cliff. The lower they went, the faster they travelled and soon they were sliding all the way, because they had to guard their faces against the brambles that twined above them.

"Good Lord!" gasped Michael, as he bumped down a sheer ten-feet of loose earth. "I'm getting jolly bumped. Look out, Hands, you kicked my neck, you ass."

"I can't help it," gasped Hands. "I'm absolutely slipping, and if I try to catch hold, I scratch myself."

They were sliding so fast that the only thing to do was to laugh and give way. So, with shouts and laughter and bumps and jolts and the pushing of loose stones and earth before them, Michael and Hands came with a run to the bottom of the cliff and landed at last on soft sea-sand.

"By gum," said Michael, "we're right on the beach. What a rag!"

The two boys looked back to the scene of their descent. It was a high cliff covered with shrubs and brambles, apparently unassailable. Before them was the sea, pale blue and gold, and to the right and to the left were the flat lonely sands. They ran, shouting with excitement, towards the rippling tide. The sand-hoppers buzzed about their ankles: Hands tripped over a jelly-fish and fell into several others: sea-gulls swooped above them, crying continually.

"It's like Robinson Crusoe," Michael declared.

He was mad with the exhilaration of possession. He owned these sands.

"Oh, young Hands fell down on the sands," he cried, bursting into uncontrollable laughter at the absurdity of the rhyme. Then he found razor-shells and waved his arms triumphantly. He found, too, wine-stained shells and rosy shells and great purple mussels. He and Hands took off their shoes and stockings and ran through the limpid water that sparkled with gold and tempted them to wade for ever ankle deep. They reached a broken mass of rock which would obviously be surrounded by water at high tide; they clambered up to the summit and found there grass and rabbits' holes.

"It's a real island," said Michael. "It is! I say, Hands, this is our island. We discovered it. Bags I, we keep it."

"Don't let's get caught by the tide," suggested cautious Hands.

"All right, you funk," jeered Michael.

They came back to the level sands and wandered on towards the black point of cliff bounding the immediate view.

"I say, there's a cave. I bet you there's a cave," Michael called to his companion who was examining a dead fish.

"Wait a jiffy," shouted Hands; but Michael hurried on to the cave. He wanted to be the first to enter under its jagged arch. Already he could see the silver sand shimmering upon the threshold of the inner darkness. He walked in, awed by the secrecy of this sea-cavern, almost expectant of a mermaid or octopus in the deepest cranny. Suddenly he stopped. His heart beat furiously: his head swam: his legs quivered under him. Then he turned and ran towards the light.

"Good lummy!" said Hands, when Michael came up to him. "Whatever's the matter? You're simply frightfully white."

"Come away," said Michael. "I saw something beastly."

"What was it?"

"There's a man in there and a woman. Oh, it was beastly."

Michael dragged Hands by the arm, but not before they had left the cave far behind would he speak.

"What was it really?" asked Hands, when they stood at the bottom of the cliff.

"I couldn't possibly tell anybody ever," said Michael.

"You're making it up," scoffed Hands.

"No, I'm not," said Michael. "Look here, don't say anything to the others about that cave. Promise."

Hands promised silence; and he and Michael soon discovered a pathway up the cliff. When they reached the garden, it was a deeper green than ever in the falling twilight, and they did not care to linger far from the house. It was a relief to hear voices and to see Rutherford, Hargreaves and Jubb still eating plums. Presently they played games on a lawn with Mr. Vernon and Mr. Lodge, and soon, after reading sleepily for a while in the tumble-down room which was set apart for the boys' use, Michael and Hands went to bed and, after an exciting encounter with a bat, fell asleep.

The days in Brittany went by very swiftly. In the morning at eight o'clock there were great bowls of café au lait and rolls with honey and butter waiting in the dining-room for the boys, when they came back from bathing. All the other boys except Michael had come to France to improve their French; but he worked also at the first book of Ovid's Metamorphoses and at Lucian's Charon, because he was going in for a scholarship at St. James'. However, these classical subjects were put away at eleven o'clock, when déjeuner with all sorts of new and delicious dishes was served. After this there was nothing to do until six o'clock but enjoy oneself. Sometimes the boys made expeditions into St. Corentin, where they wondered at the number of dogs to each inhabitant and bought cakes and sweets at a pastrycook's and gas-filled balloons which they sent up in the market-place. Or they would stroll down to the quays and watch the shipping and practise their French on sailors looking more like pirates than ordinary sailors.

Once, while Michael was gazing into a shop window at some dusty foreign stamps in a brass tray, a Capuchin friar spoke to him in very good English and asked if he collected stamps. Michael said that he did, and the Capuchin invited him to come back to the convent and see his collection. Michael thought this was a splendid invitation and willingly accompanied the Capuchin whom, except for a sore on his lip, he liked very much. He thought the inside of the convent was rather like the inside of an aquarium, but he enjoyed the stamps very much. The friar gave him about a dozen of his duplicates, and Michael promised to write to him, when he got home, and to send him some of his own. Then they had tea in the friar's cell, and afterwards Michael set out to walk back to St. Antoine. It was not yet six o'clock when he reached the house, but there was a terrible fuss being made about his adventure. Telegrams had been despatched, the gendarmerie had been informed, and the British Vice-consul had been interviewed. Mr. Vernon asked in his deepest voice where the deuce he had been, and when Michael told him he had been taking tea with a monk, Mr. Vernon was more angry than ever.

"Don't do things like that. Good heavens, boy, you might have been kidnapped and turned into a Catholic, before you knew where you were. Hang it all, remember I'm responsible for your safety and never again get into conversation with a wandering monk."

Michael explained about the stamps, but Mr. Vernon said that was a very pretty excuse, and would by no means hear of Michael visiting the convent again. When Michael thought over this fuss, he could not understand what it had all been about. He could not imagine anything more harmless than this Capuchin friar with the sore on his lip. However, he never did see him again, except once in the distance, when he pointed him out to Mr. Vernon, who said he looked a dirty ruffian. Michael discovered that grown-up people always saw danger where there was no danger, but when, as on the occasion when Hands and he plainly perceived a ghost in the garden, there was every cause for real alarm, they merely laughed.

The weather grew warmer as August moved on, and Michael with Mr. Vernon and Mr. Lodge used sometimes to plunge into the depths of the country, there to construe Ovid and Lucian while the other boys worked at French with the Frenchman who came in from St. Corentin to teach them. Michael enjoyed these expeditions with Mr. Vernon and Mr. Lodge. They would sit down in the lush grass of a shady green lane, close to a pool where the bull-frogs croaked. Michael would construe the tale of Deucalion and Pyrrha to Mr.

Lodge, while Mr. Vernon lay on his back and smoked a large pipe. Then a White Admiral butterfly would soar round the oak trees, and Ovid would be thrown behind them like Deucalion's stones; while Michael and Mr. Vernon and Mr. Lodge manœuvred and shouted and ran up and down, until the White Admiral was either safely bottled with the cyanide of potassium or soared away out of sight. When Ovid was finished for the day, Mr. Lodge used to light a big pipe and lie on his back, while Michael construed the Dialogue of Charon to Mr. Vernon. Then an Oak Eggar moth would fly with tumbling reckless flight beyond the pool, luring Michael and Mr. Lodge and Mr. Vernon to charge through in pursuit, not deterred by the vivid green slime of the wayside water as the ghosts were deterred by gloomy Styx. Indeed, as the hot August days went by, each one was marked by its butterflies more definitely than by anything else. Michael thought that France was a much better place for collecting them than England. Scarce Swallow-tails and Ordinary Swallow-tails haunted the cliffs majestically. Clouded Yellows were chased across the fields of clover. Purple Emperors and Camberwell Beauties and Bath Whites were all as frequent as Heath Browns at home. Once, they all went a long expedition to Bluebeard's Castle on the other side of the Loire, and, while they sat in a garden café, drinking their grenadine sucrée, hundreds of Silver-washed Fritillaries appeared over the tables. How the fat French bourgeois stared to see these mad English boys chasing butterflies in their sunny bee-haunted garden. But how lovely the Fritillaries looked, set upside down to show their powdered green and rosy wings washed by silver streaks. Perhaps the most exciting catch of all happened, close to the shutting in of a September dusk, in the avenue of pollarded acacias. Michael saw the moth first on the lowest bough of a tree. It was jet-black marked with thick creamy stripes. Neither he nor Hands had a net, and they trembled with excitement and chagrin. Michael threw a stone rather ineffectively and the moth changed its position, showing before it settled down on a higher branch underwings of glowing vermilion.

"Oh, what can it be?" Michael cried, dancing.

"It's frightfully rare," squeaked Hands.

"You watch it carefully, while I scoot for a net," commanded Michael.

He tore along up the darkening drive, careless of ghosts or travelling seamen bent on murder and robbery. He rushed into the hall and shouted, 'A terribly rare moth in the drive! Quick, my net!' and rushed back to the vigilant Hands. The others followed, and after every cunning of the hunter had been tried, the moth was at last secured and after a search through Kirby's Butterflies and Moths pronounced to be a Jersey Tiger, not so rare, after all, in fact very common abroad. But it was a glorious beast when set, richly black, barred and striped with damasked cream over a flame of orange-scarlet.

The six weeks were over. Michael had to leave in advance of the others, in order to enter for his scholarship examination at St. James'. Mr. Lodge took him to St. Malo and handed him over to the charge of Rutherford's older brother, who was already at St. James' and would see Michael safely to London. Michael could scarcely believe that this Rutherford was a boy, so tall was he, such a heavy black moustache had he and so pleasant was he to Michael. Michael thought with regret of the green and golden days in Brittany, as he waved to Mr. Lodge standing on the St. Malo jetty. He felt, as the steamer sailed across the glassy sea through a thick September haze, that he was coming back to greater adventures, that he was older and, as he paced beside Rutherford up and down the deck, that he was more important. But he thought with regret of Brittany and squeaky Hands and the warm days of butterflies. He hoped to return next year and see again the fig tree by his bedroom window and the level shore of the Loire estuary and the tangled tumble-down garden on the cliff's edge. He would always think of Mr. Lodge and Mr. Vernon, those very dearly loved schoolmasters. He would think of the ghostly Breton lanes at twilight and the glorious Sundays unspoilt by church or best clothes and of the bull-frogs in the emerald pools.

Michael disliked the examination very much indeed. He hated the way in which all the other competitors stared. He disliked the speed with which they wrote and the easy manners of some of them. However, he gained his scholarship mostly by age marks and was put in the Lower Third, the youngest boy in the class by two years, and became a Jacobean, turning every morning round the same gate, walking every morning up the same gravel path, running every morning up the same wide steps, meeting every morning the same smell of hot-water pipes and hearing every day the same shuffle of quick feet along the corridors past the same plaster cast of the Laocoön.

BOOK TWO
CLASSIC EDUCATION

"What is it then that thou hast got
 By drudging through that five-year task?
 What knowledge or what art is thine?
 Set out thy stock, thy craft declare."

Ionica.

"Sic cum his, inter quos eram, voluntatum enuntianaarum signa conmunicavi; et vitae humanae procellosam societatem altius ingressus sum, pendens ex parentum auctoritate nutuque maiorum hominum."

ST. AUGUSTINE.

Chapter I: *The Jacobean*

MICHAEL found the Lower Third at St. James' a jolly class. He was so particularly young that he was called 'Baby,' but with enough obvious affection to make the dubious nickname a compliment. To be sure, Mr. Braxted would often cackle jokes in a raucous voice about his age, and if Michael made a false quantity he would grumble and say he was paid as a schoolmaster not as a wet-nurse. However, Mr. Braxted was such a dandy and wore such very sharply creased and tight trousers and was so well set up and groomed that the class was proud of his neat appearance, and would inform the Upper Third that Foxy Braxted did, at any rate, look a gentleman, a distinction which the Upper Third could scarcely claim for their own form-master.

Michael liked the greater freedom of a public school. There were no home-books to be signed by governesses: there was no longer any taboo upon the revelation of Christian names. Idiosyncrasies were overlooked in the vaster society of St. James'. The senior boys paid no attention to the juniors, but passed them by scornfully as if they were grubs not worth the trouble of squashing. There was no longer the same zest in the little scandals and petty spitefulness of a private school. There was much greater freedom in the choice of one's friends, and Michael no longer felt bound to restrict his intimacy to the twin Macalisters and Norton. Sometimes in the 'quarter' (as the break was now called) Michael would stand on the top of the steps that led down from the great red building into the school-ground. From this point he would survey the huge green field with its archipelago of countless boys. He would think how few of their names he knew and from what distances many of them travelled each morning to school. He could wander among them by himself and not one would turn a curious head. He was at liberty even to stare at a few great ones whom athletic prowess had endowed already with legendary divinity, so that among small boys tales were told of their daring and their immortality gradually woven into the folk-lore of St. James'. Sometimes a member of the first fifteen would speak to Michael on a matter of athletic business.

"What's your name?"

"Fane," Michael would answer, hoping the while that his contemporaries might be passing and see this colloquy between a man and a god.

"Oh, yes," the hero would carelessly continue, "I've got you down already. Mind you turn up to Little Side at 1.45 sharp."

Little Side was the football division that included the smallest third of the school. Sometimes the hero would ask another question, as:

"Do you know a kid called Smith P.L.?"

And Michael with happy blushes would be able to point out Smith P.L. to the great figure.

Michael played football on Little Side with great regularity, rushing home to dinner and rushing off again to change and be in the field by a quarter to two. He could run very fast and for that reason the lords of Little Side made him play forward, a position for which the slightness of his body made him particularly unsuited. One day, however, he managed to intercept a pass, to outwit a three-quarter, to dodge the full-back and to score a try, plumb between the posts. Luckily one of the heroes had strolled down from Pelion that afternoon to criticize Little Side and Michael was promoted from the scrum to play three-quarter back on the left wing, in which position he really enjoyed football very much indeed.

It fell out that year that the St. James' fifteen was the most invincible ever known in the school's history, and every Saturday afternoon, when there was a home match, Michael in rain or wind or pale autumnal sunlight would take up his position in the crowd of spectators to cheer and shout and urge St. James' to another glorious victory. Match after match that year earned immortal fame in the school records, sending the patriotic Jacobeans of every size and age home to a happy tea in the rainy twilight. Those were indeed afternoons of thunderous excitement. How everybody used to shout—School—Schoo-oo-ol—Schoo-ol! Play up—Schoo-oo-ool! James! Ja-a-a-mes! Oh, go low. Kick! Touch! Forward! Held! Off-side! Go in yourself! Schoo-ool!

How Michael's heart beat at the thud of the Dulford forwards in their last desperate rush towards the School 'twenty-five.' Down went the School halves, and over them like a torrent swept the Dulford pack. Down went the three-quarters in a plucky attempt to sit on the ball. Ah! There was an unanimous cry of agony, as everybody pressed against the boundary rope and craned towards the touch-line until the posts creaked before the strain. Not in vain had those gallant three-quarters been smeared with mud and bruised by the boots of the surging Dulford pack; for the ball had been kicked on too far and Cutty Jackson, the School back, had fielded it miraculously. He was going to punt. 'Kick!' yelled the despairing spectators. And Jackson, right under the disappointed groans of the Dulford forwards whose muscles cracked with the effort to fetch him down, kicked the ball high, high into the silvery November air. Up with that spinning greasy oval travelled the hopes of the onlookers, and, as it fell safely into touch, from all round the field rose like a rocket a huge sigh of relief that presently broke into volleys and pæans of exultation, as half-time sounded with St. James' a goal to the good. How Michael admired the exhausted players when they sucked the sliced lemons and lay about in the mud; how he envied Cutty Jackson, when the lithe and noble fellow leaned against the goalpost and surveyed his audience. 'Sidiness' could be easily forgiven after that never-to-be-forgotten kick into touch. Why, thought Michael, should not he himself be one day ranked as the peer of Cutty Jackson? Why should not he, six or seven years hence, penetrate the serried forces of Dulford and score a winning try, even as the referee's whistle was lifted to sound 'time'? Ambition woke in Michael, while he surveyed upon that muddy field the prostrate forms of the fifteen, like statues in a museum. Then play began and personal desires were merged in the great hope of victory for the School. Hardly now could the spectators shout, so tense was the struggle, so long was each full minute of action. Michael's brain swam with excitement. He saw the Dulford team as giants bull-necked and invulnerable. He saw the School halves shrinking, the School three-quarters shiver like grass and the School forwards crumple before the Dulford charges. They were beaten: the untarnished record was broken: Michael could have sobbed for his side. Swifter than swallows, the Dulford three-quarters flew down the now all too short field of play. They were in! Look! they were dancing in triumph. A try to Dulford! Disconsolately the School team lined up behind their disgraced goal. Jauntily the Dulford half walked away with the shapely leather. The onlookers held their breath, as the ball, evilly accurate, dangerously direct, was poised in position for the kick at goal. The signal was given: the School team made their rush: the ball rose in the air: hung for a moment motionless, hit a goalpost, quivered and fell back. One goal to a try—five points to three—and St. James' was leading. Then indeed did the School play up. Then indeed did every man in the team 'go low': and for the rest of the game to neither side did any advantage incline. Grunts and muttered oaths, the thud of feet, the smack of wet leather lasted continually. In the long line-ups for the throw in from touch, each man marked his man viciously: the sweat poured down from hanging jaws: vests were torn, knees were grimed with mud and elbows were blackened. The scrimmages were the tightest and neatest ever watched, and neither scrum could screw the other a foot. At last the shrill whistle of the referee proclaimed the end of an immortal contest. There were cheers for the victors by the vanquished, by the vanquished for their conquerors. The spectators melted away into the gathering mist and rain, a flotsam of black umbrellas. In a few moments the school-ground was desolate and silent. Michael, as he looked at the grass ploughed into mud by the severe struggle, thought what superb heroes were in his School team; and just as he was going home, content, he saw a blazer left on a post. It was Jackson's, and Michael, palpitating with the honour, ran as fast as he could to the changing-room through the echoing cloister beneath the school.

"I say, Jackson, you left this on the ground," he said shyly.

Jackson looked up from a conversation with the Dulford full-back.

"Oh, thanks very much," he murmured, and went on with his talk.

Michael would not have missed that small sentence for any dignity in the world.

During his first term at St. James', Michael went on with his study of the art of dancing, begun during the previous winter without much personal satisfaction and with a good deal of self-consciousness. These dancing lessons took place in the hall at Randell's, and Michael revisited his old school with a new confidence. He found himself promoted to stay beyond the hour of pupilage in order pleasantly to pass away a second hour by dancing formally with the sisters and cousins of other boys. He had often admired last year those select Jacobeans who, buttoning white gloves, stood in a supercilious group, while their juniors clumped through the Ladies' Chain uninspired by the swish of a single petticoat. Now he was of their sacred number. It was not surprising that under the influence of the waltz and the Circassian circle and the schottische and the quadrille and the mazurka that Michael should fall in love. He was not anxious to fall in love: many times to other boys he had mocked at woman and dilated upon the folly of matrimony. He had often declared on his way to and from school that celibacy should be the ideal of every man. He used to say how little he could understand the habit of sitting in dark corners and kissing. Even Miss Carthew he grew accustomed to treat almost with rudeness, lest some lynx-eyed friend of his should detect in his relation with her a tendency towards the sentimental. However, Muriel in her salmon-coloured, accordion-pleated frock bowled Michael off his superior pedestal. He persuaded himself that this was indeed one of those unchangeable passions of which he read or rather did read now. This great new emotion was certainly Love, for Michael could honestly affirm that as soon as he saw Muriel sitting on a chair with long black legs outstretched before her, he loved her. No other girl existed, and when he moved towards her for the pleasure of the next dance, he felt his heart beating, his cheeks on fire. Muriel seemed to like him after a fashion. At any rate, she cordially supported him in a project of long-deferred revenge upon Mr. Macrae of the Upper Fourth at Randell's, and she kept 'cavé' while Michael tried the door of his empty class-room off the top gallery of the hall. It was unlocked, and Michael crept in and quickly threw the contents of Mr. Macrae's desk out of the window and wrote on the blackboard: 'Mr. Macrae is the silliest ass in England.' Then he and Muriel walked demurely back to join the tinkling mazurka down below and, though many enquiries were set on foot as to the perpetrator of the outrage, Michael was never found out.

Michael's passion for Muriel increased with every evening of her company, and he went so far as to make friends with a very unpopular boy who lived in her road, for the sake of holding this unpopular boy in close conversation by his threshold on the chance of seeing Muriel's grey muff in the twilight. Muriel was strangely cold for the heroine of such a romance, and indeed Michael only once saw her really vivacious, which was when he gave her a catapult. Yet sometimes she would make a clandestine appointment and talk to him for twenty minutes in a secluded terrace, so that he consoled himself with a belief in her untold affection. Michael read Don Quixote again on account of Dulcinea del Toboso, and he was greatly moved by the knight's apostrophes and declamations. He longed for a confidant and was half inclined to tell Stella about Muriel; but when he came to the point Stella was engrossed in a new number of Little Folks and Michael feared she was unworthy of such a trust. The zenith of his passion was attained at the Boarders' dance to which he and Muriel and even Stella were invited. Michael had been particularly told by Miss Carthew that he was to dance four times at least with Stella and never to allow her to be without a partner. He was in despair and felt, as he encountered the slippery floor with Stella hanging nervously on his arm, that round his neck had been tied a millstone of responsibility. There in a corner was Muriel exquisite in yellow silk, and in her hair a yellow bow. Boys flitted round her, like bees before a hive, and here was he powerless with this wretched sister.

"You wait here," said Michael. "I'll be back in half a jiffy."

"Oh, no," pouted Stella. "You're not to leave me alone, Michael. Miss Carthew said you were to look after me."

Michael groaned.

"Do you like ices?" he asked desperately. "You do, don't you?"

"No," said Stella. "They make my tooth ache."

Michael almost wept with chagrin. He had planned to swap with Stella for unlimited ices all her dances with him. Then he saw a friend whom he caught hold of, and with whom he whispered fiercely for a moment.

"I say, you might dance with my kiddy sister for a bit. She's awfully fond of ices, so you needn't really dance."

The friend said he preferred to remain independent at a dance.

"No, I say, do be a decent chap," begged Michael. "Just dance with her once and get another chap to dance with her after you've had your shot. Oh, do. Look here. What'll you swap for the whole of her programme?"

The friend considered the proposition in its commercial side.

"Look here," Michael began, and then, as he nervously half turned his head, he saw the crowd thickening about Muriel. He waved his arm violently in the hope that she would realize his plight and keep the rivals at arm's length. "Look here," he went on, "you know my bat with the whalebone splice?" This bat was Michael's most precious possession, and even as he bartered it for love, he smelt the fragrant linseed-oil of the steeped bandages which now preserved it for summer suns.

The friend's eyes twinkled greedily.

"I'll swap that bat," said Michael, "if you'll make sure my kiddy sister hasn't got a single empty place on her programme all the dance."

"All right," said the friend. And as he was led up to Stella, Michael whispered hurriedly, when the introduction had been decorously made:

"This chap's frightfully keen on you, Stella. He simply begged me to introduce him to you."

Then from the depths of Michael's soul a deep-seated cunning inspired him to add:

"I wouldn't at first, because he was awfully in love with another girl and I thought it hard cheese on her, because she's here to-night. But he said he'd go home if he didn't dance with you. So I had to."

Michael looked enquiringly at Stella, marked the smirk of satisfaction on her lips, then recklessly, almost sliding over the polished floor, he plunged through Muriel's suitors and proffered his programme. They danced together nearly all the evening, and alas, Muriel told him that she was going to boarding-school next term. It was a blow to Michael, and the dance programme with Muriel's name fourteen times repeated was many times looked at with sentimental pangs each night of next term before Michael went to bed a hundred miles away from Muriel at her boarding-school.

However, Muriel and her porcelain-blue eyes and the full bow of her lips and the slimness and girlishness of her were forgotten in the complexities of life at a great public school. Michael often looked back to that first term in the Lower Third as a period of Arcadian simplicity, a golden age. In his second term Michael after an inconspicuous position in the honest heart of the list was not moved up, for which he was very glad, as the man who took the Upper Third was by reputation a dull driver without any of the amenities by which Foxy Braxted seasoned scholastic life.

One morning, when the Lower Third had been pleasantly dissolved in laughter by Foxy's caustic jokes at the expense of a boy who had pronounced the Hebrides as a dissyllable, following a hazardous guess that the capital of New South Wales was New York, the door of the class-room opened abruptly and Dr. Brownjohn the Headmaster sailed in.

"Is there a boy called Fane in this class?" he demanded deeply.

The laughter had died away when the tip of Dr. Brownjohn's nose glistened round the edge of the door, and in the deadly silence Michael felt himself withering away.

"Oh, yes," said Mr. Braxted, cheerfully indicating Michael with his long forefinger.

"Tell him to pack up his books and go to Mr. Spivey in the Hall. I'll see him there," rumbled Dr. Brownjohn as, after transfixing the Lower Third with a glance of the most intense ferocity, he swung round and left the room, slamming the door behind him.

"You'd better take what you're doing to Mr. Spivey," said Mr. Braxted in his throatiest voice, "and tell him with my compliments you're an idle young rascal. You can get your books at one o'clock."

Michael gathered together pens and paper, and left his desk in the Lower Third.

"Good-bye, sir," he said as he went away, for he knew Foxy Braxted really rather liked him.

"Good-bye," cackled his late form-master.

The Lower Third followed his exit from their midst with an united grin of farewell, and Michael was presently interviewing Mr. Spivey in the Hall. He realized that he was now a member of that assorted Purgatory, the Special, doomed to work there for a term of days or weeks and after this period of intensive culture to be planted out in a higher form beyond the ordinary mechanics of promotion. Mostly in the Special class Michael worshipped the two gods εἰ and ἐάν, and his whole life was devoted to the mastery of Greek conditional sentences in their honour.

The Special form at St. James' never consisted of more than fourteen or fifteen boys, all of whom were taught individually, and none of whom knew when they would be called away. The Special was well called Purgatory. Every morning and every afternoon the inmates toiled away at their monotonous work, sitting far removed from one another in the great echoing hall, concentrated for the most part on εἰ and ἐάν. Every morning and every afternoon at a fatal moment the swinging doors of the lower end of the Hall would clash together, and the heavy tread of Dr. Brownjohn would be heard as he rolled up one of the two aisles between the long desks. Every morning and every afternoon Dr. Brownjohn would sit beside some boy to inspect his work; and every morning and every afternoon hearts would beat the faster, until Dr. Brownjohn had seized his victim, when the other boys would simultaneously work with an almost lustful concentration.

Dr. Brownjohn was to Michael the personification of majesty, dominion, ferocity and awe. He was huge of build, with a long grey beard to which adhered stale morsels of food and the acrid scent of strong cigars. His face was ploughed and fretted with indentations volcanic: scoriac torrents flowed from his eyes, his forehead was seared and cleft with frowning crevasses and wrinkled with chasms. His ordinary clothes were stained with soup and rank with tobacco smoke, but over them he wore a full and swishing gown of silk. When he spoke his voice rumbled in the titanic deeps of his body, or if he were angry, it burst forth in an appalling roar that shook the great hall. His method of approach was enough to frighten anyone, for he would swing along up the aisle and suddenly plunge into a seat beside the chosen boy, pushing him along the form with his black bulk. He would seize the boy's pen and after scratching his own head with the end of the holder would follow word by word the liturgy of εἰ and ἐάν, tapping the paper between the lines as he read each sentence, so that at the end of his examination the page was peppered with dots of ink. Dr. Brownjohn, although he had a voice like ten bulls, was himself very deaf and after bellowing in a paralyzing bass he would always finish a remark with an intoned 'um?' of tenor interrogation to exact assent or answer from his terrified pupil. When due reverence was absent from Michael's worship of εἰ and ἐάνDr. Brownjohn would frown at him and roar and bellow and rumble and thunder and peal his execration and contempt. Then suddenly his fury would be relieved by this eruption, and he would affix his initials to the bottom of the page—S. C. B. standing for Samuel Constantine Brownjohn—after which endorsement he would pat Michael's head, rumble an unintelligible joke and plunge down beside another victim.

One of Michael's greatest trials was his inability to convince Miss Carthew how unutterably terrific Dr. Brownjohn really was. She insisted that Michael exaggerated his appearance and manners, and simply would not believe the stories Michael told of parents and guardians who had trembled with fear when confronted by the Old Man. In many ways

Michael found Miss Carthew was very contentious nowadays, and very seldom did an evening pass without a hot argument between him and her. To be sure, she used to say it was Michael who had grown contradictory and self-assertive, but Michael could not see that he had radically altered since the first moment he saw Miss Carthew, now nearly four years ago.

Michael's purgatory in the Special continued for several weeks, and he grew bored by the monotony of his work that was only interrupted by the suspense of the Headmaster's invasions. Sometimes Dr. Brownjohn would make his dreadful descent early in the 'hour,' and then relieved from the necessity to work with such ardour, Michael would gaze up to the raftered roof of the hall and stare at the long lancet windows filled with the coats of arms in stained glass of famous bygone Jacobeans. He would wonder whether in those windows still unfilled a place would one day be found for his name and whether years and years hence, boys doing Greek conditional sentences would speculate upon the boyhood of Charles Michael Saxby Fane. Then Mr. Spivey would break into his dreams with some rather dismal joke, and Michael would make blushing amends to εἰ and ἐάν by writing as quickly as he could three complete conditional sentences in honour and praise of the twin gods. Mr. Spivey, the master in charge of the Special, was mild and good-humoured. No one could fail to like him, but he was not exhilarating; and Michael was greatly pleased when one morning Mr. Spivey informed him that he was to move into the Shell. Michael was glad to dodge the Upper Third, for he knew that life in the Shell under Mr. Neech would be an experience.

Chaps had often said to Michael, "Ah, wait till you get into old Neech's form."

"Is he decent?" Michael would enquire.

"Some chaps like him," the chaps in question would ambiguously reply.

When Mr. Spivey introduced Michael to the Shell, Mr. Neech was sitting in his chair with his feet on the desk and a bandana handkerchief over his face, apparently fast asleep. The inmates of the Shell were sitting, vigorously learning something that seemed to cause them great hardship; for every face was puzzled and from time to time sighs floated upon the class-room air.

Mr. Spivey coughed nervously to attract Mr. Neech's attention, and when Mr. Neech took no notice, he tapped nervously on the desk with Mr. Neech's ruler. Somewhere in the back row of desks a titter of mirth was faintly audible. Mr. Neech was presumably aroused with great suddenness by Mr. Spivey's tapping and swung his legs off the desk and, sitting bolt upright in his chair, glared at the intruders.

"Oh, the Headmaster has sent Fane from the Special," Mr. Spivey nervously explained.

Mr. Neech threw his eyes up to the ceiling and looked as if Michael's arrival were indeed the last straw.

"Twenty-six miserable boys are already having a detestable and stultifying education in this wretched class," lamented Mr. Neech. "And now comes a twenty-seventh. Very well. Very well. I'll stuff him with the abominable jargon and filthy humbug. I'll cram him with the undigested balderdash. Oh, you unhappy boy," Mr. Neech went on, directly addressing Michael. "You unfortunate imp and atom. Sit down, if you can find a desk. Sit down and fill your mind with the ditchwater I'm paid to teach you."

Mr. Spivey had by this time reached the door and with a nervous nod he abruptly vanished.

"Now then everybody," said Mr. Neech, closing his lips very tightly in a moment's pause and then breaking forth loudly. "You have had one quarter of an hour to learn the repetition you should all have learned last night. Begin, that mooncalf with a dirty collar, the boy Wilberforce, and if any stupid stoat or stockfish boggles over one word, I'll flay him. Begin! The boy Fane can sit still. The others stand up!" shouted Mr. Neech. "Now the boy Wilberforce!

Tityre tu patulæ recubans sub tegmine fagi—— Go on, you bladder of idiocy."

Michael watched the boy Wilberforce concentrate all his faculties upon not making a single mistake, and hoped that he would satisfy this alarming master. While Wilberforce spoke the lines of the Eclogue, panting between each hexameter, Mr. Neech strode up and down the room with his arms crossed behind him, wagging the tail of his gown. Sometimes he would strike his chin and, looking upwards, murmur to himself the lines with an expression of profound emotion. Wilberforce managed to get through, and another boy called Verney took up the Eclogue successfully, and so on through the class it was successfully sustained.

"You pockpuddings, you abysmal apes," Mr. Neech groaned at his class. "Why couldn't you have learned those lines at home? You idle young blackguards, you pestilent oafs, you fools of the first water, write them out. Write them out five times."

"Oh, sir," the Shell protested in unison.

"Oh, sir!" Mr. Neech mimicked. "Oh, sir! Well, I'll let you off this time, but next time, next time, my stars and garters, I'll flog any boy that makes a single mistake."

Mr. Neech was a dried-up, snuff-coloured man, with a long thin nose and stringy neck and dark piercing eyes. He always wore a frock-coat green with age and a very old top-hat and very shiny trousers. He read Spanish newspapers and second-hand-book catalogues all the way to school and was never seen to walk with either a master or a boy. His principal hatreds were Puseyism and actors; but as two legends were extant, in one of which he had been seen to get into a first-class railway carriage with a copy of the Church Times and in the other of which he had been seen smoking a big cigar in the stalls of the Alhambra Theatre, it was rather doubtful whether his two hatreds were as deeply felt as they were fervently expressed. He was reputed to have the largest library in England outside the British Museum and also to own seven dachshunds. He was a man who fell into ungovernable rages, when he would flog a boy savagely and, the flogging done, fling his cane out of the window in a fit of remorse. He would set impositions of unprecedented length, and revile himself for ruining the victim's handwriting. He would keep his class in for an hour and mutter at himself for a fool to keep himself in as well. Once, he locked a boy in at one o'clock, and the boy's mother wrote a long letter to complain that her son had been forced to go without his dinner. Legend said that Mr. Neech had been reprimanded by Dr. Brownjohn on account of this, which explained Mr. Neech's jibes at the four pages of complaint from the parents that were supposed inevitably to follow his mildest rebuke of the most malignant boy.

Michael enjoyed Mr. Neech's eccentricities after the drabness of the Special. He was lucky enough to be in Mr. Neech's good graces, because he was almost the only boy who could say in what novel of Dickens or Scott some famous character occurred. Mr. Neech had a conception of education quite apart from the mere instilling of declensions and genders and 'num' and 'nonne' and 'quin' and εἰ and ἐάν. He taught Geography and English History and English Literature, so far as the school curriculum allowed him. Divinity and English meant more to Mr. Neech than a mere hour of Greek Testament and a pedant's fiddling with the text of Lycidas. Michael had a dim appreciation of his excellence, even in the Shell: he identified him in some way with Tom Brown's Schooldays, with prints of Eton and Westminster, with Miss Carthew's tales of her brother on the Britannia. Michael recognized him as a character in those old calf-bound books he loved to read at home. Once Mr. Neech called a boy a dog-eared Rosinante, and Michael laughed aloud and when fiercely Mr. Neech challenged him, denying he had ever heard of Rosinante, Michael soon showed that he had read Don Quixote with some absorption. After that Mr. Neech put Michael in one of the favoured desks by the window and would talk to him, while he warmed his parchment-covered hands upon the hot-water pipes. Mr. Neech was probably the first person to impress Michael with the beauty of the past or rather to give him an impetus to arrange his own opinions. Mr. Neech, lamenting the old days long gone, thundering against modernity and denouncing the whole system of education that St. James' fostered, was almost the only schoolmaster with a positive personality whom Michael ever encountered. Michael had scarcely realized, until he reached the Shell, in what shadowy dates of history St. James' was already a famous school. Now in the vulgarity of its crimson brick, in the servility with which it truckled to bourgeois ideals, in the unimaginative utility it worshipped, Michael vaguely apprehended the loss of a soul. He would linger in the corridors, reading the lists of distinguished Jacobeans, and during Prayers he would with new interest speculate upon the lancet windows and their stained-glass heraldry, until vaguely in his heart grew a patriotism more profound than the mere joy of a football victory, a patriotism that submerged Hammersmith and Kensington and made him proud that he himself was veritably a Jacobean. He was still just as eager to see St. James' defeat Dulford at cricket, just as proud to read that St. James' had won more open scholarships at the Universities than some North-country grammar school; but at the same time he was consoled in the event of defeat by pride in the endurance of his school through so many years of English History.

It was about this time that Michael saw in a second-hand shop a print of the tower of St. Mary's College, Oxford. It was an old print and the people small as emmets, who thronged the base of that slim and lovely tower, were dressed in a bygone fashion that very much appealed to Michael. This print gave him the same thrill he experienced in listening to Mr. Neech's reminiscences or in reading Don Quixote or in poring over the inscriptions of famous Jacobeans. Michael had already taken it as an axiom that one day he would go to Oxford, and now he made up his mind he would go to St. Mary's College. At this moment people were hurrying past that tower, even as they hurried in this grey print and even as Michael himself would one day hurry. Meanwhile, he was enjoying the Shell and Mr. Neech's eccentricities and the prospect of winning the Junior Form Cricket Shield, a victory in which Michael would participate as scorer for the Shell.

Summer suns shone down upon the green playground of St. James' rippling with flannelled forms. The radiant air was filled with merry cries, with the sounds of bat and ball, with boyhood in action. In the great red mass of the school buildings the golden clock moved on through each day's breathless hour of cricket. The Junior Shield was won by the Shell, and the proud victors, after a desperate argument with Mr. Neech, actually persuaded him to take his place in the commemorative photograph. School broke up and the summer holidays began.

Chapter II: *The Quadruple Intrigue*

MICHAEL, although Stella was more of a tie than a companion, was shocked to hear that she would not accompany Miss Carthew and himself to Eastbourne for the summer holidays. He heard with a recurrence of the slight jealousy he had always felt of Stella that, though she was not yet eleven years old, she was going to Germany to live in a German family and study music. To Michael this step seemed a device to spoil Stella beyond the limits of toleration, and he thought with how many new affectations Stella would return to her native land. Moreover, why should Stella have all the excitement of going abroad and living abroad while her brother plodded to school in dull ordinary London? Michael felt very strongly that the balance of life was heavily weighted in favour of girls and he deplored the blindness of grown-up people unable to realize the greater attractiveness of boys. It was useless for Michael to protest, although he wasted an evening of Henty in arguing the point with Miss Carthew. Stella became primed with her own importance before she left England, and Michael tried to discourage her as much as he could by pointing out that in Germany her piano-playing would be laughed at and by warning her that her so evident inclination to show off would prejudice against her the bulk of Teutonic opinion. However, Michael's well-meant discouragement did not at all abash Stella, who under his most lugubrious prophecies trilled exasperatingly cheerful scales or ostentatiously folded unimportant articles of clothing with an exaggerated carefulness, the while she fussed with her hair and threw conceited glances over her shoulder into the mirror. Then, one day, the bonnet of a pink and yellow Fraulein bobbed from a cab-window, and, after a finale of affectation and condescension on the front-door steps for the benefit of passers-by, Stella set out for Germany and Michael turned back into the house with pessimistic fears for her future. The arrangements for Stella's transportation had caused some delay in Michael's holidays, and as a reward for having been forced to endure the sight of Stella going abroad, he was told that he might invite a friend to stay with him at Eastbourne during the remainder of the time. Such an unexpected benefaction made Michael incredulous at first.

"Anyone I like?" he said. "For the whole of the hols? Good Lord, how ripping."

Forthwith he set out to consider the personal advantages of all his friends in turn. The Macalisters as twins were ruled out; besides, of late the old intimacy was wearing thin, and Michael felt there were other chaps with more claim upon him. Norton was ruled out, because it would be the worst of bad form to invite him without the Macalisters and also because Norton was no longer on the Classical side of St. James'. Suddenly the idea of asking Merivale to stay with him occurred like an inspiration. Merivale was not at present a friend with anything like the pretensions of Norton or the Macalisters. Merivale could not be visualized in earliest Randell days, indeed he had been at a different private school, and it was only during this last summer term that he and Michael had taken to walking arm in arm during the 'quarter.' Merivale turned to the left when he came out of school and Michael turned to the right, so that they never met on their way nor walked home together afterwards. Nevertheless, in the course of the term, the friendship had grown, and once or twice Michael and Merivale had sat beneath the hawthorn trees, between them a stained bag of cherries in the long cool grass, while intermittently they clapped the boundary hits of a school match that was clicking drowsily its progress through the summer afternoon. Tentative confidences had been exchanged, and by reason of its slower advance towards intimacy the friendship of Michael and Merivale seemed built on a firmer basis than most of the sudden affinities of school life. Now, as Michael recalled the personality of Merivale with his vivid blue eyes and dull gold hair and his laugh and freckled nose and curiously attractive walk, he had a great desire for his company during the holidays. Miss Carthew was asked to write to Mrs. Merivale in order to give the matter the weight of authority; but Michael and Miss Carthew went off to Eastbourne before the answer arrived. The sea sparkled, a cool wind blew down from Beachy Head; the tamarisks on the front quivered; Eastbourne was wonderful, so wonderful that Michael could not believe in the probability of Merivale, and the more he thought about it, the more he felt sure that Mrs. Merivale would write a letter of polite refusal. However, as if they were all people in a book, everything happened according to Michael's most daringly optimistic hopes. Mrs. Merivale wrote a pleasant letter to Miss Carthew to say that her boy Alan was just now staying at Brighton with his uncle Captain Ross, that she had written to her brother who had written back to say that Alan and he would move on to Eastbourne, as it did not matter a bit to him where he spent the next week. Mrs. Merivale added that, if it were convenient, Alan might stay on with Michael when his uncle left. By the same post came a letter from Merivale himself to say that he and his uncle Kenneth were arriving next day, and that he jolly well hoped Fane was going to meet him at the railway station.

Michael, much excited, waited until the train steamed in with its blurred line of carriage windows, from one of which Merivale was actually leaning. Michael waved: Merivale waved: the train stopped: Merivale jumped out: a tall man with a very fair moustache and close-cropped fair hair alighted after Merivale and was introduced and shook hands and made several jokes and was on terms of equality before he and Merivale and Michael had got into the blue-lined fly that was to drive them to Captain Ross's hotel. During the few days of Captain Ross's stay, he and Michael and Merivale and Miss Carthew went sailing and climbed up Beachy Head and watched a cricket match in Devonshire Park and generally behaved like all the other summer visitors to Eastbourne. Michael noticed that Captain Ross was very polite to Miss Carthew and heard with interest that they both had many friends in common—soldiers and sailors and Royal Marines. Michael listened to a great deal of talk about 'when I was quartered there' and 'when he was stationed at Malta' and about Gunners and Sappers and the Service. He himself spoke of General Mace and was greatly flattered when Captain Ross said he knew him by reputation as a fine old soldier. Michael was rather disappointed that Captain Ross was not in the Bengal Lancers, but he concluded that next to being in the Bengal Lancers, it was best to be with him in the Kintail Highlanders (the Duke of Clarence's own Inverness-shire Buffs).

"Uncle Ken looks jolly ripping in a kilt," Merivale informed Miss Carthew, when on the last evening of Captain Ross's stay they were all sitting in the rubied light of the hotel table.

"Shut up, showman," said Captain Ross, banging his nephew on the head with a Viennese roll.

"Oh, I say, Uncle Kenneth, that loaf hurts most awfully," protested Merivale.

"Well, don't play Barnum," said the Captain as he twirled his little moustache. "It's not done, my lad."

When Captain Ross went away next morning, Miss Carthew at his earnest invitation accompanied the boys to see him off, and, as they walked out of the station, Merivale nudged Michael to whisper:

"I say, I believe my uncle's rather gone on Miss Carthew."

"Rot," said Michael. "Why, she'd be most frightfully annoyed. Besides, chaps' uncles don't get gone on——" Michael was going to add 'chaps' sisters' governesses,' but somehow he felt the remark was all wrong, and blushed the conclusion of the sentence.

The weather grew very hot, and Miss Carthew took to sitting in a canvas chair and reading books on the beach, so that Michael and Merivale were left free to do very much as they wanted which, as Michael pointed out, was rather decent of her.

"I say, Merivale," Michael began one day, as he and his friend, arm in arm, were examining the credentials of the front on a shimmering morning, "I say, did you notice that Miss Carthew called you Alan?"

"I know. She often does," replied Merivale.

"I say, Merivale," said Michael shyly, "supposing I call you Alan and you call me Michael—only during the hols, of course," he added hastily.

"I don't mind," Alan agreed.

"Because I suppose there couldn't be two chaps more friends than you and me," speculated Michael.

"I like you more than I do any other chap," said Alan simply.

"So I do you," said Michael. "And it's rather decent just to have one great friend who you call by his Christian name."

After this Michael and Alan became very intimate and neither held a secret from the other, as through the crowds of seaside folk they threaded their way along the promenade to whatever band of minstrels had secured their joint devotion. They greatly preferred the Pierrots to the Niggers, and very soon by a week's unbroken attendance at the three daily sessions, Michael and Alan knew the words and music of most of the repertory. Of the comic songs they liked best The Dandy Coloured Coon, although they admired almost equally a duet whose refrain was:

"We are a couple of barmy chaps, hush, not a word!
    A little bit loose in our tiles, perhaps, hush, not a word!
    We're lunatics, lunatics, everybody declares
    We're a couple of fellows gone wrong in our bellows,
    As mad as a pair of March hares."

Gradually, however, and more especially under the influence of Japanese lanterns and a moon-splashed sea, Michael and Alan avowed openly their fondness for the more serious songs sung by the Pierrettes. The words of one song in particular were by a reiteration of passionate utterance deeply printed on their memory:

"Two little girls in blue, lad,
Two little girls in blue,
They were sisters, we were brothers,
And learnt to love the two.

And one little girl in blue, lad,
Who won your father's heart,
Became your mother: I married the other,
And now we have drifted apart."

This lyric seemed to Michael and Alan the most profoundly moving accumulation of words ever known. The sad words and poignant tune wrung their hearts with the tears always imminent in life. This lyric expressed for the two boys the incommunicable aspirations of their most sacred moments. As they leaned over the rail of the promenade and gazed down upon the pretty Pierrette whose tremolo made the night air vibrant with emotion, Michael and Alan were moved by a sense of fleeting time, by thoughts of old lovers and by an intense self-pity.

"It's frightfully decent, isn't it?" murmured Michael.

"Ripping," sighed Alan. "I wish I could give her more than a penny."

"So do I," echoed Michael. "It's beastly being without much tin."

Then 'Encore' they both shouted as the Pierrette receded from the crimson lantern-light into obscurity. Again she sang that song, so that when Michael and Alan looked solemnly up at the stars, they became blurred. They could not bear The Dandy Coloured Coon on such a night, and, seeing no chance of luring Pierrette once more into the lantern-light, they pushed their way through the crowd of listeners and walked arm in arm along the murmurous promenade.

"It's beastly rotten to go to bed at a quarter past nine," Michael declared.

"We can talk up in our room," suggested Alan.

"I vote we talk about the Pierrots," said Michael, affectionately clasping his chum's arm.

"Yes, I vote we do too," Alan agreed.

The next day the Pierrots were gone. Apparently they had had a quarrel with the Corporation and moved farther along the South Coast. Michael and Alan were dismayed, and in their disgust forsook the beach for the shrubberies of Devonshire Park where in gloomy by-ways, laurel-shaded, they spoke quietly of their loss.

"I wonder if we shall ever see that girl again," said Michael. "I'd know her anywhere. If I was grown up I'd know her. I swear I would."

"She was a clinker," Alan regretted.

"I don't suppose we shall ever see a girl half as pretty," Michael thought.

"Not by a long chalk," Alan agreed. "I don't suppose there is a girl anywhere in the world a quarter as pretty. I think that girl was simply fizzing."

They paced the mossy path in silence and suddenly round a corner came upon a bench on which were seated two girls in blue dresses. Michael and Alan found the coincidence so extraordinary that they stared hard, even when the two girls put their heads down and looked sidelong and giggled and thumped each other and giggled again.

"I say, are you laughing at us?" demanded Michael.

"Well, you looked at us first," said the fairer of the two girls.

In that moment Michael fell in love.

"Come away," whispered Alan. "They'll follow us if we don't."

"Do you think they're at all decent?" asked Michael. "Because if you do, I vote we talk to them. I say, Alan, do let's anyway, for a lark."

"Supposing anyone we know saw us?" queried Alan.

"Well, we could say *some*thing," Michael urged. He was on fire to prosecute this adventure and, lest Alan should still hold back, he took from his pocket a feverish bag of Satin Pralines and boldly offered them to the girl of his choice.

"I say, would you like some tuck?"

The girls giggled and sat closer together; but Michael still proffered the sweets and at last the girl whom he admired dipped her hand into the bag. As all the Satin Pralines were stuck together, she brought out half a dozen and was so much embarrassed that she dropped the bag, after which she giggled.

"It doesn't matter a bit," said Michael. "I can get some more. These are beastly squashed. I say, what's your name?"

So began the quadruple intrigue of Dora and Winnie and Michael and Alan.

Judged merely by their dress, one would have unhesitatingly set down Dora and Winnie as sisters; but they were unrelated and dressed alike merely to accentuate, as girl friends do, the unanimity of their minds. They were both of them older by a year or more than Michael and Alan; while in experience they were a generation ahead of either. The possession of this did not prevent them from giggling foolishly and from time to time looking at each other with an expression compounded of interrogation and shyness. Michael objected to this look, inasmuch as it implied their consciousness of a mental attitude in which neither he nor Alan had any part. He was inclined to be sulky whenever he noticed an exchange of glances, and very soon insisted upon a temporary separation by which he and Dora took one path, while Alan with Winnie pursued another.

Dora was a neatly made child, and Michael thought the many-pleated blue skirt that reached down to her knees and showed as she swung along a foam of frizzy white petticoats very lovely. He liked, too, the curve of her leg and the high buttoned boots and the big blue bow in her curly golden hair. He admired immensely her large shady hat trimmed with cornflowers and the string of bangles on her wrist and her general effect of being almost grown up and at the same time still obviously a little girl. As for Dora's face, Michael found it beautiful with the long-lashed blue eyes and rose-leaf complexion and cleft chin and pouting bow mouth. Michael congratulated himself upon securing the prettier of the two. Winnie with her grey eyes and ordinary hair and dark eyebrows and waxen skin was certainly not comparable to this exquisite doll of his own.

At first Michael was too shy to make any attempt to kiss Dora. Nevertheless the kissing of her ran in his mind from the beginning, and he would lie awake planning how the feat was to be accomplished. He was afraid that if suddenly he threw his arms round her, she might take offence and refuse to see him again. Finally he asked Alan's advice.

"I say, have you ever kissed Winnie?" he called from his bed.

Through the darkness came Alan's reply:

"Rather not. I say, have you?"

"Rather not." Then Michael added defiantly, "But I jolly well wish I had."

"She wouldn't let you, would she?"

"That's what I can't find out," Michael said despondently. "I've held her hand and all that sort of rot, and I've talked about how pretty I think she is, but it's beastly difficult. I say, you know, I don't believe I should ever be able to propose to a girl—you know—a girl you could marry—a lady. I'm tremendously gone on Dora and so are you on Winnie. But I don't think they're ladies, because Dora's got a sister who's in a pantomime and wears tights, so you see I couldn't propose to her. Besides, I should feel a most frightful fool going down on my knees in the path. Still I must kiss her somehow. Look here, Alan, if you promise faithfully you'll kiss Winnie to-morrow, when the clock strikes twelve, I'll kiss Dora. Will you? Be a decent chap and kiss Winnie, even if you aren't beastly keen, because I am. So will you, Alan?"

There was a minute's deliberation by Alan in the darkness, and then he said he would.

"I say, you are a clinker, Alan. Thanks most awfully."

Michael turned over and settled himself down to sleep, praying for the good luck to dream of his little girl in blue.

On the next morning Alan and Michael eyed each other bashfully across the breakfast table, conscious as they were of the guilty vow not yet fulfilled. Miss Carthew tried in vain to make them talk. They ate in silence, oppressed with resolutions. They saw Winnie and Dora in Devonshire Park at eleven o'clock, and presently went their different ways along the mazy paths. Michael talked of subjects most remote from love. He expounded to Dora the ranks of the British Army; he gave her tips on birds'-nesting; he told her of his ambition to join the Bengal Lancers and he boasted of the exploits of the St. James' Football Fifteen. Dora giggled the minutes away, and at five minutes to twelve they were on a seat, screened against humanity's intrusion. Michael listened with quickening pulses to the thump of tennis balls in the distance. At last he heard the first stroke of twelve and looked apprehensively towards Dora. Four more strokes sounded, but Michael still delayed. He wondered if Alan would keep his promise. He had heard no scream of dismay or startled giggle from the shrubbery. Then as the final stroke of midday crashed forth, he flung his arms round Dora, pressed her to him and in his confusion kissed very roughly the tilted tip of her nose.

"Oh, you cheek!" she gasped.

Then Michael kissed her lips, coldly though they were set against his love.

"I say, kiss me," he whispered, with a strange new excitement crimsoning his cheeks and rattling his heart so loudly that he wondered if Dora noticed anything.

"Shan't!" murmured Dora.

"Do."

"Oh, I couldn't," she said, wriggling herself free. "You have got a cheek. Fancy kissing anyone."

"Dora, I'm frightfully gone on you," affirmed Michael, choking with the emotional declaration. "Are you gone on me?"

"I like you all right," Dora confessed.

"Well then, do kiss me. You might. Oh, I say, do."

He leaned over and sought those unresponsive lips that, mutely cold, met his. He spent a long time trying to persuade her to give way, but Dora protested she could not understand why people kissed at all, so silly as it was.

"But it's not," Michael protested. "Or else everybody wouldn't want to do it."

However, it was useless to argue with Dora. She was willing to put her curly golden head on his shoulder, until he nearly exploded with sentiment; she seemed not to mind how often he pressed his lips to hers; but all the time she was passive, inert, drearily unresponsive. The deeper she seemed to shrink within herself and the colder she stayed, the more Michael felt inclined to hurt her, to shake her roughly, almost to draw blood from those soft lifeless lips. Once she murmured to him that he was hurting her, and Michael was in a quandary between an overwhelming softness of pity and an exultant desire to make her cry out sharply with pain. Yet as he saw that golden head upon his shoulder, the words and tune of 'Two little girls in blue' throbbed on the air, and with an aching fondness Michael felt his eyes fill with tears. Such love as his for Dora could never be expressed with the eloquence and passion it demanded.

Michael and Alan had tacitly agreed to postpone all discussion of their passionate adventure until the blackness of night and secret intimacy of their bedroom made the discussion of it possible.

"I say, I kissed Dora this morning," announced Michael.

"So did I Winnie," said Alan.

"She wouldn't kiss me, though," said Michael.

"Wouldn't she?" Alan echoed in surprize, "Winnie kissed me."

"She didn't!" exclaimed Michael.

"She did, I swear she did. She kissed me more than I kissed her. I felt an awful fool. I nearly got up and walked away. Only I didn't like to."

"Good Lord," apostrophized Michael. He was staggered by Alan's success and marvelled that Alan, who was admittedly less clever than himself, should conquer when he had failed. He could not understand the reason; but he supposed that Dora, being so obviously the prettier, was deservedly the more difficult to win. However, Michael felt disinclined to pursue the subject, because it was plain that Alan took no credit to himself for his success, and he wished still to be the leader in their friendship. He did not want Alan to feel superior in anything.

The next day Miss Carthew was laid up in bed with a sick headache, so that Michael and Alan were free to take Dora and Winnie upon the promenade without the risk of detection. Accordingly, when they met in Devonshire Park, Michael proposed this public walk. He was the more willing to go, because since Alan's revelation of Winnie, he took a certain pleasure in denying to her the attraction of Alan's company. Winnie was not very anxious for the walk, but Dora seemed highly pleased, and Dora, being the leader of the pair, Winnie had to give way. While they strolled up and down the promenade in a row, Dora pointed out to Michael and Alan in how many respects they both failed to conform to the standards of smartness, as she conceived them. For instance, neither of them carried a stick and neither of them wore a tie of any distinction. Dora called their attention to the perfectly dressed youths of the promenade with their high collars and butterfly ties and Wanghee canes and pointed boots and vivid waistcoats.

After the walk the boys discussed Dora's criticism and owned that she was right. They marshalled their money and bought made-up bow-ties of purple and pink that were twisted round the stud with elastic and held in position by a crescent of whalebone. They bought made-up white silk knotted ties sown with crimson fleurs-de-lys and impaled with a permanent brass horseshoe. They spent a long time in the morning plastering back their hair with soap and water, while in the ribbons of their straw hats they pinned inscribed medallions. Finally they purchased Wanghee canes and when they met their two little girls in blue, the latter both averred that Michael and Alan were much improved.

Miss Carthew remained ill for two or three days; so Michael and Alan were able to display themselves and their sweethearts all the length of the promenade. They took to noticing the cut of a coat as it went by and envied the pockets of the youths they met; they envied, too, the collars that surrounded the adolescent neck, and wished the time had come for them to wear 'chokers.' Sometimes, before they undressed, they would try to pin round their necks stiff sheets of note-paper in order to gauge, however slightly, the effect of high collars on their appearance.

The weather was now steadily fine and hot, and Michael begged Miss Carthew to let him and Alan buy two blazers and cricket belts. Somewhat to his surprise, she made no objection, and presently Michael and Alan appeared upon the front in white trousers, blue and yellow blazers and cherry-coloured silk belts fastened in front by a convenient metal snake. Dora thought they looked 'all right,' and, as Miss Carthew had succumbed again to her headache, Michael and Alan were free to swagger up and down on the melting asphalt of the promenade. Miss Carthew grew no better, and one day she told the boys that Nancy was coming down to look after them. Michael did not know whether he were really glad or not, because, fond as he was of Nancy, he was deeply in love with Dora and he had a feeling that Nancy would interfere with the intrigues. In the end, as it happened, Nancy arrived by some mistake on the day before she was expected and, setting forth to look for the boys, she walked straight into them arm in arm with Dora and Winnie. Michael was very much upset, and told the girls to scoot, a command which they obeyed by rushing across the road, giggling loudly, standing on the opposite curb and continuing to giggle.

"Hullo!" said Nancy, "who are your young friends in blue cashmere?"

Michael blushed and said quickly they were friends of Alan, but Alan would not accept the responsibility.

"Well, I don't admire your taste," said Nancy contemptuously. "No, and I don't admire your get-up," she went on. "Did you pick those canes up on the beach, what?"

"We bought them," said Michael, rather affronted.

"My goodness," said Nancy. "What dreadful-looking things. I say, Michael, you're in a fair way towards looking like a thorough young bounder. Don't you come to Cobble Place with that button on your hat. Well, don't let me disturb you. Cut off to the Camera Obscura with Gertie and Evangeline. I don't expect I'm smart enough for you two."

"We don't particularly want to go with those girls," said Michael, looking down at his boots, very red and biting his under-lip. Alan was blushing too and greatly abashed.

"Well," said the relentless Nancy, "it's a pity you don't black your faces, for I never saw two people look more like nigger minstrels. Where *did* you get that tie? No wonder my sister feels bad. That belt of yours, Michael, would give a South Sea Islander a headache. Go on, hurry off like good little boys," she jeered. "Flossie and Cissie are waiting for you."

Michael could not help admitting, as he suffered this persiflage from Nancy, that Dora and Winnie did look rather common, and he wished they would not stand, almost within earshot, giggling and prodding each other. Then suddenly Michael began to hate Dora and the quadruple intrigue was broken up.

"I say, Alan," he said, looking up again, "let's bung these sticks into the sea. They're rotten sticks."

Alan at once threw his as far as it would go and betted Michael he would not beat the distance. So Michael's stick followed its companion into oblivion. Nancy was great sport, after all, as both boys admitted, and when Michael grazed his finger very slightly on a barnacled rock, he bandaged it up with his silk tie. Very soon he discovered the cut was not at all serious, but he announced the tie was spoilt and dipped it casually into a rock pool, where it floated blatantly among the anemones and rose-plumed seaweed. Alan's tie vanished less obtrusively: no one noticed when or where. As for the buttons inscribed with mottoes they became insignificant units in the millions of pebbles on the beach.

Nancy was great sport and ready to do whatever the boys suggested in the way of rock-climbing and walking, provided they would give her due notice, so that she could get into a hockey skirt and thick shoes. They had fine blowy days with Nancy up on Beachy Head above the sparkling blue water. They caught many blue butterflies, but never the famous Mazarin blue which legend in the butterfly-book said had once been taken near Eastbourne.

Michael and Alan, even in the dark privacy of their room, did not speak again of Dora and Winnie. Michael had an idea that Alan had always been ashamed of the business, and felt mean when he thought how he had openly told Nancy that they were his friends. Once or twice, when Michael was lying on his back, staring up at the sky over Beachy Head, the wind lisping round him sadly made him feel sentimental, but sentimental in a dominion where Dora and Winnie were unknown, where they would have been regarded as unpleasant intruders. Up here in the daisy's eye, the two little girls in blue seemed tawdry and took their place in the atmosphere of Michael's earlier childhood with Mrs. Frith's tales and Annie's love-letters. For Michael the whole affair now seemed like the half-remembered dreams which, however pleasant at the time, repelled him in the recollection of them. Moreover, he had experienced a sense of inequality in his passion for Dora. He gave all: she returned nothing. Looking back at her now under the sailing clouds, he thought her nose was ugly, her mouth flabby, her voice odious and her hair beastly. He blushed at the memory of the ridiculous names he had called her, at the contemplation of his enthusiastic praise of her beauty to Alan. He was glad that Alan had been involved, however unwillingly. Otherwise he was almost afraid he would have avoided Alan in future, unable to bear the injury to his pride. This sad sensation promoted by the wind in the grasses, by the movement of the clouds and the companionship of Alan and Nancy, was more thrilling than the Pierrette's tremolo in the lantern light. Michael's soul was flooded with a vast affection for Alan and for Nancy. He wished that they all could stay here in the wind for ever. It was depressing to think of the autumn rain and the dreary gaslit hours of afternoon school. And yet it was not depressing at all, for he and Alan might be able to achieve the same class. It would be difficult, for Michael knew that he himself must inevitably be moved up two forms, while Alan was only in the Upper Third now and could scarcely from being ninth in his class get beyond the Lower Fourth, even if he escaped the Shell. How Michael wished that Alan could go into the Special for a time, and how pleasant it would be suddenly to behold Alan's entrance into his class, so that, without unduly attracting attention, he could manage to secure a desk for Alan next to himself.

But when Michael and Alan (now again the austere Fane and Merivale) went back to school, Michael was in the Middle Fourth, and Alan just missed the double remove and inherited Michael's scrabbled desk in the Shell.

Chapter III: *Pastoral*

THE new term opened inauspiciously; for Miss Carthew fell ill again more seriously, and Michael's mother came back, seeming cross and worried. She settled that, as she could not stay at home for long, Michael must be a boarder for a year. Michael did not at all like this idea, and begged that Nancy might come and look after him. But Mrs. Fane told him not to make everything more difficult than it was already by grumbling and impossible suggestions. Michael was overcome by his mother's crossness and said no more. Mrs. Fane announced her intention of shutting up the house in Carlington Road and of coming back in the summer to live permanently at home, when Michael would be able to be a day-boy again. Mrs. Fane seemed injured all the time she had to spend in making arrangements for Michael to go to Mr. Wheeler's House. She wished that people would not get ill just when it was most inconvenient. She could not understand why everything happened at exactly the wrong moment, and she was altogether different from the tranquil and lovely lady whom Michael had hitherto known. However, the windows of Number 64 were covered with newspapers, the curtain-poles were stripped bare, the furniture stood heaped in the middle of rooms under billowy sheets, and Michael drove up with all his luggage to the gaunt boarding-house of Mr. Wheeler that overlooked the School ground.

Michael knew that the alteration in his status would make a great difference. Long ago he remembered how his friendship with Buckley had been finally severed by the breaking up of Buckley's home and the collapse of all Buckley's previous opinions. Michael now found himself in similar case. To be sure, there was not at St. James' the same icy river of prejudice between boarders and day-boys which divided them so irreparably at Randell's. Nevertheless, it was impossible for a boarder to preserve unspoilt a real intimacy with a day-boy. To begin with, all sorts of new rules about streets being in and out of bounds made it impossible to keep up those delightful walks home with boys who went in the same direction as oneself. There was no longer that hurried appeal to 'wait for me at five o'clock' as one passed a friend in the helter-skelter of reaching the class-room, when the five minutes' bell had stopped and the clock was already chiming three. It was not etiquette among the boarders of the four Houses to walk home with day-boys except in a large and amorphous company of both. It was impossible to go to tea with day-boys on Saturday afternoons without special leave both from the Housemaster and from the captain of the House. A boarder was tied down mercilessly to athletics, particularly to rowing, which was the pride of the Houses and was exalted by them above every other branch of sport. Michael, as a promising light-weight, had to swim, every Saturday, until he could pass the swimming test at the Paddington Baths, when he became a member of the rowing club, in order to cox the House four. It did not add to his satisfaction with life, when by his alleged bad steering Wheeler's House was beaten by Marlowe's House coxed by the objectionable Buckley, now on the Modern Side and, as a result of his capable handling of the ropes likely to be cox of the School Eight in the race against Dulford from Putney Bridge to Hammersmith. The Christmas holidays were a dismal business in Mr. Wheeler's empty barracks. To be sure, Mrs. Wheeler made herself as plumply agreeable as she could; but the boredom of it all was exasperating and was only sustained by reading every volume that Henty had ever written. Four weeks never dragged so endlessly, even in the glooms of Carlington Road under Nurse's rule. The Lent term with its persistent rowing practice on the muddy Thames was almost as bad as the holidays. Michael hated the barges that bore down upon him and the watermen who pulled across the bows of his boat. He hated the mudlarks by the river-side who jeered as he followed the crew into the School boathouse, and he loathed the walk home with the older boys who talked incessantly of their own affairs. Nor did the culminating disaster of the defeat by Marlowe's House mitigate his lot. When the Lent term was over, to his great disappointment, some domestic trouble made it impossible for Michael to spend the Easter holidays with Alan, so that instead of three weeks to weld again that friendship in April wanderings, in finding an early white-throat's nest in the front of May, and in all the long imagined delights of spring, Michael was left again with Mr. and Mrs. Wheeler to spend a month of rain at a bleak golf-resort, where he was only kept from an unvoiced misery by reading 'Brother takes the hand of brother' in Longfellow's Psalm of Life, melting thereat into a flood of tears that relieved his lonely oppression.

Even the summer term was a bondage with its incessant fagging for balls, while the lords of the House practised assiduously at the nets. He and Alan walked together sometimes during the 'quarter' and held on to the stray threads of their friendship that still resisted the exacting knife of the House's etiquette; but it became increasingly difficult under the stress of boarding-school existence. Indeed, it was only the knowledge that this summer term would end the miserable time and that Alan was catching up to Michael's class which supported the two friends through their exile. Michael was savagely jealous when he saw Alan leaving the School at five o'clock arm in arm with another boy. He used to sulk for a week afterwards, avoiding Alan in the 'quarter' and ostentatiously burying himself in a group of boarders. And if Alan would affectionately catch him up when he was alone, Michael would turn on him and with bitter taunts suggest that Alan's condescension was unnecessary. In School itself Michael was bored by his sojourn both in the Middle Fourth and in the Upper Fourth B. The Cicero and the Thucydides were vilely dull; all the dullest books of the Æneid were carefully chosen, while Mr. Marjoribanks and Mr. Gale were both very dull teachers. At the end of the summer examinations, Michael found himself at the bottom of the Upper Fourth B in Classics, in Drawing and in English. However, the knowledge that next term would now inevitably find him and Alan in the same class, meeting again as equals, as day-boys gloriously free, sustained him through a thunderous interview with Dr. Brownjohn. He emerged from the Doctor's study in a confusion of abusive epithets to find Alan loyally waiting for him by the great plaster cast of the Laocoön.

"Damn old Brownjohn," growled Michael. "I think he's the damnedest old beast that ever lived. I do hate him."

"Oh, bother him," cried Alan, dancing with excitement. "Look here, I say, at this telegram. It's just arrived. The porter was frightfully sick at having to give me a telegram. He is a sidy swine. What *do* you think? My uncle is going to marry Miss Carthew?"

"Get out," scoffed Michael, whose brain, overwhelmed by the pealing thunders of his late interview, refused to register any more shocks.

"No, really. Read this."

Michael took the piece of paper and read the news. But he was still under the influence of a bad year, and instead of dancing with Alan to the tune of his excitement, grumbled:

"Well, why didn't Miss Carthew send a telegram to me? I think she might have. I believe this is all bally rot."

Alan's face changed, changed indeed to an expression of such absolute disappointment that Michael was touched and, forgetting all that he had endured, thrust his arm into Alan's arm and murmured:

"By Jove, old Alan, it is rather decent, isn't it?"

When Michael reached the House, he found a letter from Miss Carthew, which consoled him for that bad year and made him still more penitent for his late ungraciousness towards Alan.

COBBLE PLACE,
July 27.

My dear old Michael,

You will be tremendously surprized to hear that I am going to marry Captain Ross. I fancy I can hear you say 'What rot, I don't believe it!' But I am, and of course you can understand how gloriously happy I feel, for you know how much you liked him. Poor old boy, I'm afraid you've had a horrid time all this year and I wish I hadn't been so stupid as to get ill, but never mind, it's over now and Captain Ross and I are coming up to London to fetch you and Alan down here to spend the whole of the holidays and make the wedding a great success. May, Joan and Nancy and my mother all send their very best love and Nancy says she's looking forward to your new ties (I don't know what obscure jest of hers this is) and also to hear of your engagement (silly girl!). I shall see you on Wednesday and you're going to have splendid holidays, I can promise you. Your mother writes to say that she is coming back to live at home in September, so there'll be no more boarding-school for you. Stella wrote to me from Germany and I hear from Frau Weingardt that everybody prophesies a triumphant career for her, so don't snub her when she comes back for her holidays in the autumn. Just be as nice as you can, and you can be very nice if you like. Will you? Now, dear old boy, my best love till we meet on Wednesday.

Your loving
Maud Carthew.

Then indeed Michael felt that life was the finest thing conceivable, and in a burst of affectionate duty wrote a long letter to Stella, giving with every detail an account of how Wheeler's beat Marlowe's at cricket, including the running-out of that beast Buckley by Michael amidst the plaudits of his House. Next morning Alan told him that his mother was frightfully keen for Michael to stay with them at Richmond, until his Uncle Ken and Miss Carthew arrived; and so Michael by special leave from Mr. Wheeler left the House a day or two before the others and had the exquisite pleasure of travelling up with Alan by the District Railway to Hammersmith Broadway for a few mornings, and of walking arm in arm with Alan through the School gates. Mrs. Merivale was as pretty as ever, almost as pretty as his own beautiful mother, and Mr. Merivale entertained Michael and Alan with his conjuring tricks and his phonograph and his ridiculous puns. Even when they reached the gate in a summer shower and ran past the sweet-smelling rose trees in the garden, Mr. Merivale shouted from the front door 'Hallo, here come the Weterans,' but when he had been severely punched for so disgraceful a joke, he was flatly impenitent and made half a dozen more puns immediately afterwards. In a day or two Miss Carthew and Captain Ross arrived, and after they had spent long mysterious days shopping in town, Michael and Alan and Miss Carthew and Captain Ross travelled down to Hampshire—the jolliest railway party that was ever known.

Nothing at Basingstead Minor seemed to have changed in five years, from the dun pony to the phloxes in the garden, from the fantail pigeons to the gardener who fed the pigs. Michael spent all the first few hours in rapid renewals of friendship with scenery and animals, dragging Alan at his heels and even suggesting about ten minutes before the gong would sound for dinner that they should bunk round and borrow the key of the tower on the hill. He and Alan slept up in the roof in a delightful impromptu of a room with uneven bare floor and sloping ceiling and above their beds a trap-door into an apple loft. There were at least half a dozen windows with every possible aspect to the neat high road and the stable-yard and the sun-dyed garden and the tall hills beyond. August was a blaze of blue and green and gold that year, but everybody at Cobble Place was busy getting ready for the wedding and Michael and Alan had the countryside to themselves. Their chief enterprize was the exploration of the sources of the stream in a canoe and a fixed endeavour to reach Basingstead Major by water. Early in the morning they would set out, well equipped with scarlet cushions and butterfly-nets and poison-bottles and sandwiches and stone bottles of ginger beer and various illustrated papers and Duke's Cameo cigarettes. Michael now paid fivepence for ten instead of a penny for five cigarettes: he also had a pipe of elegantly tenuous shape, which was knocked out so often that it looked quite old, although it was scarcely coloured at all by tobacco smoke. Nowadays he did not bother to chew highly scented sweets after smoking, because Captain Ross smoked so much that all the blame of suspicious odours could be laid on him.

Those were halcyon days on that swift Hampshire river. Michael and Alan would have to paddle hard all the morning scarcely making any progress against the stream. Every opportunity to moor the canoe was taken advantage of; and the number of Marsh Fritillaries that were sacrificed to justify a landing in rich water-meadows was enormous.

"Never mind," Michael used to say, "they'll do for swaps."

Through the dazzling weather the kingfishers with wings of blue fire would travel up and down the stream. The harvest was at its height and in unseen meadows sounded the throb of the reaper and binder, while close at hand above the splash and gurgle of the rhythmic paddles could be heard the munching of cattle. To left and right of the urgent boat darted the silver companies of dace, and deep in brown embayed pools swam the fat nebulous forms of chub. Sometimes the stream, narrowing where a large tree-trunk had fallen, gushed by their prow and called for every muscle to stand out, for every inch to be fought, for every blade of grass to be clutched before the canoe won a way through. Sometimes the stream widened to purling rapids and scarcely would even a canoe float upon the diamonded rivulets and tumbling pebbles and silting silver sand, so that Michael and Alan would have to disembark and drag the boat to deeper water. Quickly the morning went by, long before the source of the stream was found, long before even the village of Basingstead Major was reached. Some fathomless millpool would hold Michael and Alan with its hollow waterfall and overarching trees and gigantic pike. Here grew, dipping down to the water, sprays of dewberries, and here, remote even from twittering warblers and the distant harvest cries, Michael and Alan drowsed away the afternoon. They scarcely spoke, for they were too well contented with the languorous weather. Sometimes one of them would clothe a dream with a boy's slang, and that was all. Then, when the harvesters had long gone home and when the last cow was stalled, and when the rabbits were scampering by the edge of the sloping woodlands, Michael and Alan would unmoor their canoe and glide homeward with the stream. Through the deepening silence their boat would swing soundlessly past the purple loosestrife and the creamy meadowsweet, past the yellow loosestrife and scented rushes and the misted blue banks of cranesbill, past the figwort and the little yellow waterlilies, while always before their advance the voles plumped into the water one by one and in hawthorn bushes the wings of roosting birds fluttered. Around them on every side crept the mist in whose silver muteness they landed to gather white mushrooms. Home they would come drenched with dew, and arm in arm they would steal up the dusky garden to the rose-red lamps and twinkling golden candlelight of Cobble Place.

In the actual week before the wedding Michael and Alan were kept far too busy to explore streams. They ran from one end of Basinstead Minor to the other and back about a dozen times a day. They left instructions with various old ladies in the village at whose cottages guests were staying. They carried complicated floral messages from Mrs. Carthew to the Vicar and equally complicated floral replies from the Vicar to Mrs. Carthew. They were allowed to drive the aged dun pony to meet Mr. and Mrs. Merivale on the day before the wedding and had great jokes with Mr. Merivale because he would say that it was an underdone pony and because he would not believe that dun was spelt d-u-n. As for the wedding-day itself, it was for Michael and Alan one long message interrupted only by an argument with the cook with regard to the amount of rice they had a right to take.

Michael felt very shy at the reception and managed to avoid calling Miss Carthew Mrs. Ross; although Alan distinctly addressed her once with great boldness as Aunt Maud, for which he was violently punched in the ribs by Michael, as with stifled laughter they both rushed headlong from the room. However, they came back to hear old Major Carthew proposing the bride and bridegroom's health and plunged themselves into a corner with handkerchiefs stuffed into their mouths to listen to Captain Ross stammer an embarrassed reply. They were both much relieved when Mr. Merivale by a series of the most atrocious puns allowed their laughter to flow forth without restraint. All the guests went back to London later in the afternoon and Michael and Alan were left to the supervision of Nancy, who had promised to take them out for a day's shooting. They had a wonderful day over the flickering September stubble. Michael shot a lark by mistake and Alan wounded a land-rail; Nancy, however, redeemed the party's credit by bagging three brace of fat French partridges which, when eaten, tasted like pigeons, because the boys could not bear to wait for them to be hung even for two hours.

Michael had a conversation with Mrs. Carthew one afternoon, while they paced slowly and regularly the gay path beside the sunny red wall of the garden.

"Well, how do you like school now?" she asked. "Dear me, I must say you're greatly improved," she went on. "Really, when you came here five years ago, you were much too delicate-looking."

Michael kicked the gravel and tried to turn the trend of the conversation by admiring the plums on the wall, but Mrs. Carthew went on.

"Now you really look quite a boy. You and Alan both slouch abominably, and I cannot think why boys always walk on one side of their boots. I must say I do not like delicate boys. My own boy was always such a boy." Mrs. Carthew sighed and Michael looked very solemn.

"Well, do you like school?" she asked.

"I like holidays better," answered Michael.

"I'm delighted to hear it," Mrs. Carthew said decidedly.

"I thought last year was beastly," said Michael. "You see I was a boarder and that's rot, if you were a day-boy ever, at least I think so. Alan and me are in the same form next term. We're going to have a most frightful spree. We're going to do everything together. I expect school won't be half bad then."

"Your mother's going to be at home, isn't she?" Mrs. Carthew enquired.

"Yes. Rather," said Michael. "It will be awfully rum. She's always away, you know. I wonder why."

"I expect she likes travelling about," said Mrs. Carthew.

"Yes, I expect she does," Michael agreed. "But don't you think it's very rum that I haven't got any uncles or aunts or any relations? I do. I never meet people who say they knew my father like Alan does and like Miss—like Mrs. Ross does. Once I went with my mater to see an awfully decent chap called Lord Saxby and my name's Saxby. Do you think he's a relation? I asked the mater, but she said something about not asking silly questions."

"Humph!" said Mrs, Carthew, as she adjusted her spectacles to examine an espalier of favourite peaches. "I think you'll have to be very good to your mother," she continued after a minute's silence.

"Oh, rather," assented Michael vaguely.

"You must always remember that you have a particular responsibility, as you will be alone with her for a long time, and, no doubt, she has given up a great deal of what she most enjoys in order to stay with you. So don't think only of yourself."

"Oh, rather not," said Michael.

In his heart he felt while Mrs. Carthew was speaking a sense of remote anxiety. He could not understand why, as soon as he asked any direct questions, mystery enveloped his world. He had grown used to this in Miss Carthew's case, but Mrs. Carthew was just as unapproachable. He began to wonder if there really were some mystery about himself. He knew the habit among grown-up people of wrapping everything in a veil of uncertainty, but in his case it was so universally adopted that he began to be suspicious and determined to question his mother relentlessly, to lay conversational traps for her and thereby gain bit by bit the details of his situation. He was older now and had already heard such rumours of the real life of the world that a chimera of unpleasant possibilities was rapidly forming. Left alone, he began to speculate perpetually about himself, to brood over anxious guesses. Perhaps his father was in prison and not dead at all. Perhaps his father was in a lunatic asylum. Perhaps he himself had been a foundling laid on the doorstep long ago, belonging neither to his mother nor to anyone else. He racked his brain for light from the past to be shed upon his present perplexity, but he could recall no flaw in the care with which his ignorance had been cherished.

When Michael reached Carlington Road on a fine September afternoon and saw the window-boxes of crimson and white petunias and the sunlight streaming down upon the red-brick houses, he was glad to be home again in familiar Sixty-four. Inside it had all been re-papered and re-painted. Every room was much more beautiful and his mother was glad to see him. She took him round all the new rooms and hugged him close and was her slim and lovely self again. Actually, among many surprizes, Michael was to have the old gloomy morning-room for himself and his friends. It looked altogether different now in the chequered sunlight of the plane tree. The walls had been papered with scenes from cow-boy life. There were new cupboards and shelves full of new books and an asbestos gas fire. There were some jolly chairs and a small desk which almost invited one to compose Iambics.

"Can I really have chaps to tea every Saturday?" Michael asked, stupefied with pleasure.

"Whenever you like, dearest boy."

"By Jove, how horribly decent," said Michael.

Chapter IV: *Boyhood's Glory*

WHEN at the beginning of term a melancholy senior boy, meeting Michael in one of the corridors during the actual excitement of the move, asked him what form he was going into and heard he was on the road to Caryll's, this boy sighed, and exclaimed:

"Lucky young devil."

"Why?" asked Michael, pushing his way through the diversely flowing streams of boys who carried household gods to new class-rooms.

"Why, haven't you ever heard old Caryll is the greatest topper that ever walked?"

"I've heard he's rather a decent sort."

"Chaps have said to me—chaps who've left, I mean," explained the lantern-jawed adviser, "that the year with Caryll is the best year of all your life."

Michael looked incredulous.

"You won't think so," prophesied Lantern-jaws gloomily. "Of course you won't." Then with a sigh, that was audible above the shuffling feet along the corridors, he turned to enter a mathematical class-room where Michael caught a glimpse of trigonometrical mysteries upon a blackboard, as he himself hurried by with his armful of books towards Caryll's class-room. He hoped Alan had bagged two desks next to each other in the back row; but unfortunately this scheme was upset by Mr. Caryll's proposal that the Upper Fourth A should for the present sit in alphabetical order. There was only one unit between Michael and Alan, a persevering and freckled Jew called Levy, whose life was made a burden to him in consequence of his interposition.

Mr. Caryll was an old clergyman reputed in school traditions to be verging on ninety. Michael scarcely thought he could be so old, when he saw him walking to school with rapid little steps and a back as straight and soldierly as General Mace's. Mr. Caryll had many idiosyncrasies, amongst others a rasping cough which punctuated all his sentences and a curious habit of combining three pairs of spectacles according to his distance from the object in view. Nobody ever discovered the exact range of these spectacles; but, to reckon broadly, three pairs at once were necessary for an exercise on the desk before him and for the antics of the back row of desks only one. Mr. Caryll was so deaf, that the loudest turmoil in the back row reached him in the form of a whisper that made him intensely suspicious of cribbing; but, as he could never remember where any boy was sitting, by the time he had put on or taken off one of his pairs of glasses, the noise had opportunity to subside and the authors were able to compose their countenances for the sharp scrutiny which followed. Mr. Caryll always expected every pupil to cheat and invented various stratagems to prevent this vice. In a temper he was apparently the most cynical of men, but as his temper never lasted long enough for him to focus his vision upon the suspected person, he was in practice the blandest and most amiable of old gentlemen. He could never resist even the most obvious joke, and his form pandered shamelessly to this fondness of his, so that, when he made a pun, they would rock with laughter, stamp their feet on the floor and bang the lids of their desks to express their appreciation. This hullabaloo, which reached Mr. Caryll in the guise of a mild titter, affording him the utmost satisfaction, could be heard even in distant class-rooms, and sometimes serious mathematical masters in the throes of algebra would send polite messages to beg Mr. Caryll kindly to keep his class more quiet.

Michael and Alan often enjoyed themselves boundlessly in Mr. Caryll's form. Sometimes they would deliberately misconstrue Cicero to beget a joke, as when Michael translated 'abjectique homines' by 'cast-off men' to afford Mr. Caryll the chance of saying, "Tut-tut. The great booby's thinking of his cast-off clothing." Michael and Alan used to ask for leave to light the gas on foggy afternoons, and with an imitation of Mr. Caryll's rasping cough they would manage to extinguish one by one a whole box of matches to the immense entertainment of the Upper Fourth A. They dug pens into the diligent Levy: they stuck the lid of his desk with a row of thin gelatine lozenges in order that, when after a struggle he managed to open it, the lid should fly up and hit him a blow on the chin. They loosed blackbeetles in the middle of Greek Testament and pretended to be very much afraid while Mr. Caryll stamped upon them one by one, deriding their cowardice. They threw paper darts and paper pellets with unerring aim: they put drawing-pins in the seat of a fat and industrious German called Wertheim: they filled up all the ink-pots in the form with blotting-paper and crossed every single nib. They played xylophonic tunes with penholders on the desk's edge and carved their initials inside: they wrote their names in ink and made the inscription permanent by rubbing it over with blotting-paper. They were seized with sudden and unaccountable fits of bleeding from the nose to gain a short exeat to stand in the fresh air by the Fives Courts. They built up ramparts of dictionaries in the forefront of their desks to play noughts and crosses without detection: they soaked with ink all the chalk for the blackboard and divested Levy of his boots which they passed round the form during 'rep': they made elaborate jointed rods with foolscap to prod otherwise unassailable boys at the other end of the room and when, during the argument which followed the mutual correction by desk-neighbours of Mr. Caryll's weekly examination paper, they observed an earnest group of questioners gathered round the master's dais, they would charge into them from behind so violently that the front row, generally consisting of the more eager and laborious boys, was precipitated against Mr. Caryll's chair to the confusion of labour and eagerness. Retribution followed very seldom in the shape of impots; and even they were soon done by means of an elaborate arrangement by which six pens lashed together did six times the work of one. Sometimes Michael or Alan would be invited to move their desks out close to Mr. Caryll's dais of authority for a week's disgrace; but even this punishment included as compensation a position facing the class and therefore the opportunity to play the buffoon for its benefit. Sometimes Michael or Alan would be ejected with vituperation from the class-room to spend an hour in the corridor without. Unfortunately they were never ejected together, and anyway it was an uneasy experience on account of Dr. Brownjohn's habit of swinging round a corner and demanding a reason for the discovery of a loiterer in the corridor. The first time he appeared, it was always possible by assuming an air of intentness and by walking towards him very quickly to convey the impression of one upon an urgent errand; but when Dr. Brownjohn loomed on his return journey, it was necessary to evade his savage glance by creeping round the great cast of the Antinous that fronted the corridor. On one of these occasions Michael in his nervousness shook the statue and an insecurely dependent fig-leaf fell with a crash on to the floor. Michael nearly flung himself over the well of the main staircase in horror, but deaf Dr. Brownjohn swung past into a gloom beyond, and presently Michael was relieved by the grinning face of a compatriot beckoning permission to re-enter the class-room. Safely inside, the fall of the fig-leaf was made out by Michael to be an act of deliberate daring on his part, and when at one o'clock the form rushed out to verify the boast, his position was tremendously enhanced. The news flew round the school, and several senior boys were observed in conversation with Michael, so that he was able to swagger considerably. Also he turned up his trousers a full two inches higher and parted his hair on the right-hand side, a mode which had long attracted his ambition.

Now, indeed, were Michael and Alan in the zenith of boyhood's glory. No longer did they creep diffidently down the corridors; no longer did they dread to run the gauntlet of a Modern class lined up on either side to await the form-master's appearance. If some louts in the Modern Fourth dared to push them from side to side, as they went by, Michael and Alan would begin to fight and would shout, 'You stinking Modern beasts! Classics to the rescue!' To their rescue would pour the heroes of the Upper Fourth A. Down went the Modern textbooks of Chemistry and Physics, and ignominiously were they hacked along the corridor. Doubled up by a swinging blow from a bag stood the leader of the Moderns, grunting and gasping in his windless agony. Back to the serenity of Virgilian airs went the Upper Fourth A, with Michael and Alan arm in arm amid their escort, and most dejectedly did the Modern cads gather up their scientific textbooks; but during the 'quarter' great was the battle waged on the 'gravel'—that haunt of thumb-biting, acrimonious and uneasy factions. Michael and Alan were not yet troubled with the fevers of adolescence. They were cool and clear and joyous as the mountain torrent: for them life was a crystal of laughter, many-faceted to adventure. Theirs was now that sexless interlude before the Eton collar gave way to the 'stick up' and before the Eton jacket, trim and jaunty, was discarded for an ill-fitting suit that imitated the dull garb of a man. No longer were Michael and Alan grubby and inky: no longer did they fill their pockets with an agglomeration of messes: no longer did their hair sprout in bistre sparseness, for now Michael and Alan were vain of the golden lights and chestnut shadows, not because girls mattered, but because like Narcissus they perceived themselves in the mirror of popular admiration. Now they affected very light trousers and very broad collars and shoes and unwrinkling socks and cuffs that gleamed very white. They looked back with detestation upon the excesses of costume induced by the quadruple intrigue, and they congratulated themselves that no one of importance had beheld their lapse.

Michael and Alan were lords of Little Side football and in their treatment of the underlings stretched the prerogatives of greatness to the limit. They swaggered on to the field of play, where in combination on the left wing they brought off feats of astonishing swiftness and agility. Michael used to watch Alan seeming very fair in his black vest and poised eagerly for the ball to swing out from the half-back. Alan would take the spinning pass and bound forward into the stink-stained Modern juniors or embryo subalterns of Army C. The clumsiest of them would receive Alan's delicate hand full in his face and, as with revengeful mutterings the enemy bore down upon him, Alan would pass the ball to Michael, who with all his speed would gallop along the touch-line and score a try in the corner. Members of Big Side marked Michael and Alan as the two most promising three-quarters for Middle Side next year, and when the bell sounded at twenty minutes to three, the members of Big Side would walk with Michael and Alan towards the changing room and encourage them by flattery and genial ragging. In the lavatory, Michael and Alan would souse with water all the kids in reach, andthe kids would be duly grateful for so much acknowledgment of their existence from these stripling gods. In the changing room they would pleasantly fling the disordered clothes of trespassers near their sacred places on to the floor or kick the caps of Second-Form boys to the dusty tops of lockers, and then just as the clock was hard on three, they would saunter up the School steps and along the corridor to their class-room, where they would yawn their way through Cicero's prosy defence of Milo or his fourth denunciation of Catiline.

At home Michael much enjoyed his mother's company, although he was now in the cold dawn of affection for anything save Alan. He no longer was shocked by his mother's solicitude or demonstrativeness, fearful of offending against the rigid standards of the private school or the uncertain position of a new boy at a public school. He yielded gracefully to his mother's pleasure in his company out of a mixture of politeness and condescension; but he always felt that when he gave up for an hour the joys of the world for the cloister of domesticity, he was conferring a favour. At this period nothing troubled him at all save his position in the School and the necessity to spend every available minute with Alan. The uncertainty of his father's position which had from time to time troubled him was allayed by the zest of existence, and he never bothered to question his mother at all pertinaciously. In every way he was making a pleasant pause in his life to enjoy the new emotion of self-confidence, his distinction in football, his popularity with contemporaries and seniors and his passion for the absolute identification of Alan's behaviour with his and his own with Alan's. At home every circumstance fostered this attitude. Alone with his mother, Michael was singularly free to do as he liked, and he could always produce from the past precedents which she was unable to controvert for any whim he wished to establish as a custom. In any case, Mrs. Fane seemed to enjoy spoiling him, and Michael was no longer averse from her praise of his good looks and from the pleasure she expressed in the company of Alan and himself at a concert or matinée. Another reason for Michael's nonchalant happiness was his normality. Nowadays he looked at himself in the old wardrobe that once had power to terrify him with nocturnal creakings, and no longer did he deplore his thin arms and legs, no longer did he mark the diffidence of the sensitive small boy. Now he could at last congratulate himself upon his ability to hold his own with any of his equals whether with tongue or fist. Now, too, when he went to bed, he went to bed as serenely as a kitten, curling himself up to dream of sport with mice. Sometimes Alan on Friday night would accompany him to spend the week-end at Carlington Road, and when he did so, the neighbourhood was not allowed to be oblivious of the event. In the autumnal dusk Michael and he would practise drop-kicks and high punts in the middle of the street, until the ball had landed twice in two minutes on the same balcony to the great annoyance of the 'skivvy,' who was with debonair assurance invited to bung it down for a mere lordly 'thank you' from the offenders. Sometimes the ball would early in the afternoon strike a sun-flamed window, and with exquisite laughter Michael and Alan would retreat to Number 64, until the alarmed lady of the house was quietly within her own doors again. Another pleasant diversion with a football was to take drop-kicks from close quarters at the backs of errand-boys, especially on wet days when the ball left a spheroid of mud where it struck the body.

"Yah, you think yourselves—funny," the errand-boy would growl.

"We do. Oh, rather," Michael and Alan would reply and with smiling indifference defeat their target still more unutterably.

When dusk turned to night, Michael and Alan would wonder what to do and, after making themselves unbearable in the kitchen, they would sally out into the back-garden and execute some devilry at the expense of neighbours. They would walk along the boundary walks of the succeedant oblongs of garden that ran the whole length of the road; and it was a poor evening's sport which produced no fun anywhere. Sometimes they would detect, white in the darkness, a fox-terrier, whereat they would miaow and rustle the poplar trees and reduce the dog to a state of hysterical yapping which would be echoed in various keys by every dog within earshot. Sometimes they would observe a lighted kitchen with an unsuspicious cook hard at work upon the dinner, meditating perhaps upon a jelly or flavouring anxiously the soup. Then if the window were open Michael and Alan would take pot-shots at the dish with blobs of mould or creep down into the basement, if the window were shut, and groan and howl to the cook's pallid dismay and to the great detriment of her family's dinner. In other gardens they would fling explosive 'slap-bangs' against the wall of the house or fire a gunpowder train or throw gravel up to a lighted bath-room window. There was always some amusement to be gained at a neighbour's expense between six and seven o'clock, at which latter hour they would creep demurely home and dress for dinner, the only stipulation Mrs. Fane made with Michael in exchange for leave to ask Alan to stay with him.

At dinner in the orange glow of the dining-room, Michael and Alan would be completely charming and very conversational, as they told Mrs. Fane how they rotted old Caryll or ragged young Levy or scored two tries that afternoon. Mrs. Fane would seem to be much interested and make the most amusing mistakes and keep her son and her guest in an ecstatic risibility. After dinner they would sit for a while in the perfumed drawing-room, making themselves agreeable and useful by fetching Mrs. Fane's novel or blotting-pad or correspondence, or by pulling up an arm-chair or by extricating a footstool and drawing close the curtains. Then Michael and Alan would be inclined to fidget, until Michael announced it was time to go and swat. Mrs. Fane would smile exquisitely and say how glad she was they did not avoid their home work and remind them to come and say good night at ten o'clock sharp. Encouraged by Mrs. Fane's gracious dismissal, Michael and Alan would plunge into the basement and gain the sanctity of Michael's own room. They would elaborately lay the table for work, spreading out foolscap and notebooks and Cicero Pro Milone and Cicero In Catilinam and Thucydides IV and the green-backed Ion of Euripides. They would make exhaustive researches into the amount of work set to be shown up on Monday morning, and with a sigh they would seat themselves to begin. First of all the Greek Testament would be postponed until Sunday as a more appropriate day, and then Michael would feel an overpowering desire to smoke one cigarette before they began. This cigarette had to be smoked close to the open window, so that the smoke could be puffed outside into the raw autumnal air, while Alan kept 'cavé,' rushing to the door to listen at the slightest rumour of disturbance. When the cigarette was finished they would contemplate for a long time the work in front of them, and then Michael would say he thought it rather stupid to swat on Friday night with all Saturday and Sunday before them, and who did Alan think was the better Half-back—Rawson or Wilding? This question led to a long argument before Rawson was adjudged to be the better of the two. Then Alan would bet Michael he could not write down from memory the Nottinghamshire cricket team, and Michael would express his firm conviction that Alan could not possibly name the winners of the Oxford and Cambridge quarter-mile for the last three years. Finally they would both recur to the problem ever present, the best way to obtain two bicycles and, what was more important, the firm they would ultimately honour with their patronage. The respective merits of the Humber, the Rover, the Premier, the Quadrant, the Swift and the Sunbeam created a battleground for various opinions, and as for the tyres, it seemed impossible to decide between Palmers, Clinchers and Dunlops. In the middle of the discussion the clock in the passage would strike ten, at which Michael and Alan would yawn and dawdle their way upstairs. Perhaps the bicycle problem had a wearing effect, for Mrs. Fane would remark on their jaded appearance and hope they were not working too hard. Michael and Alan would look particularly conscious of their virtue and admit they had had a very tiring week, what with football and Cicero and Quadratic Equations; and so after affectionate good nights they would saunter up to bed. Upstairs, they would lean out of the bedroom window and watch the golden trains go by, and ponder the changing emeralds and rubies of the signal-box farther along the line: then after trying to soak a shadowy tomcat down below with water from the toilet-jug Michael and Alan would undress.

In the darkness Michael and Alan would lie side by side secure in a companionship of dreams. They murmured now their truly intimate thoughts: they spoke of their hopes and ambitions, of the Army with its glories of rank and adventure, of the Woods and Forests of India, of treasure on coral islands and fortunes in the cañons of the West. They spoke of the School Fifteen and of Alan's probable captaincy of it one day: they discussed the Upper Sixth with its legend of profound erudition: they wondered if it would be worth while for Michael to swat and be Captain of the School. They talked again of bicycles and decided to make an united effort to secure them this ensuing Christmas by compounding for one great gift any claims they possessed on birthday presents later in the year. They talked of love, and of the fools they had been to waste their enthusiasm on Dora and Winnie. They made up their minds to forswear the love of women with all its humiliations and disappointments and futilities. Through life each would be to the other enough. Girls would be for ever an intrusion between such deathless and endeared friends as they were. Michael pointed out how awkward it would be if he and Alan both loved the same girl and showed how it would ruin their twin lives and wreck their joint endeavour; while Alan agreed it would be mad to risk a separation for such froth of feminine attractiveness. The two of them vowed in the darkness to stick always together, so that whatever fate life held for either it should hold for both. They swore fidelity to their friendship in the silence and intimacy of the night; and when, rosy in the morning, they stood up straightly in the pale London sunlight, they did not regret the vows of the night, nor did they blush for their devotion, since the world conjured a long vista of them both arm in arm eternally, and in the immediate present all the adventurous charm of a Saturday's whole holiday.

If there was a First Fifteen match on the School ground, Michael and Alan honoured it with their attendance and liked nothing so well as to elbow their way through a mob of juniors in order to nod familiarly to a few members of the Fifteen. The School team that year was not so successful as its two predecessors, and Michael and Alan were often compelled to voice their disdain to the intense disgust of the juniors huddled about them. Sometimes they would hear an irreverent murmur of 'Hark at sidey Fane and sidey Merivale,' which would necessitate the punching of a number of heads to restore the disciplinary respect they demanded. On days when the School team was absent at Dulford or Tonbury or Haileybridge, Michael and Alan would scornfully glance at the Second Fifteen's desolate encounter with some other Second Fifteen, and vote that such second-rate football was bally rot. On such occasions the School ground used to seem too large and empty for cheerfulness, and the two friends would saunter round West Kensington on the chance of an adventure, ending up the afternoon by laying out money on sweets or on the fireworks now displayed in anticipation of the Fifth of November. Saturday evening would be spent in annoying the neighbours with squibs and Chinese crackers and jumping crackers and tourbillons and maroons and Roman candles and Bengal lights, while after dinner the elaborate preparations for home work would again be made with the same inadequate result.

On Sunday Michael and Alan used to brush their top-hats and button their gloves and tie their ties very carefully and, armed with sticks of sobriety and distinction, swagger to whatever church was fashionable among their friends. During the service they would wink to acquaintances and nudge each other and sing very loudly and clearly their favourite hymns, while through the dull hymns they would criticize their friends' female relations. So the week would fulfil its pleasant course until nine o'clock on Monday morning, when Michael and Alan would run all the way to school and in a fever of industry get through their home work with the united assistance of the rest of the Upper Fourth A, as one by one the diligent members arrived in Hall for a few minutes' gossip before Prayers. During Prayers, Michael and Alan would try to forecast by marking off the full stops what paragraph of Cicero they would each be called upon to construe; finally, when old Caryll named Merivale to take up the oration's thread, Michael would hold the crib on his knees and over Levy's laborious back whisper in the voice of a ghoul the meaning.

At Christmas, after interminable discussion and innumerable catalogues, the bicycles were bought, and in the Lent term with its lengthening twilights Michael and Alan devoted all their attention to bicycling, except in wet weather, when they played Fives, bagging the covered courts from small boys who had waited days for the chance of playing in them. Michael, during the Lent term, often rode back with Alan after School to spend the week-end at Richmond, and few delights were so rare as that of scorching over Barnes Common and down the Mortlake Road with its gardens all a-blow with spring flowers and, on the other bank of the river over Kew, the great spring skies keeping pace with their whirring wheels.

Yet best of all was the summer term, that glorious azure summer term of fourteen and a half, which fled by in a radiancy. Michael and Alan were still in the Upper Fourth A under Mr. Caryll: they still fooled away the hours of school, relying upon the charm of their joint personality to allay the extreme penalty of being sent up to the Headmaster for incorrigible knavery. They were Captain and Vice-Captain of the Classical Upper Fourth Second Eleven, preferring the glory of leadership to an ambiguous position in the tail of the

First Eleven. Michael and Alan were in their element during that sunburnt hour of cricket before afternoon school. They wore white felt hats, and Michael in one of his now rare flights of imagination thought that Alan in his looked like Perseus in a Flaxman drawing. Many turned to look at the two friends, as enlaced they wandered across the 'gravel' on their way to change out of flannels, Michael nut-brown and Alan rose-bloomed like a peach.

At five o'clock they would eat a rowdy tea in the School Tuckshop to the accompaniment of flying pellets of bun, after which they would change again for amber hours of cricket, until the sun made the shadow of the stumps as long as telegraph poles, and the great golden clock face in the School buildings gleamed a late hour. They would part from each other with regret to ride off in opposite directions. Michael would linger on his journey home through the mellow streets of Kensington, writing with his bicycle wheels lazy parabolas and curves in the dust of each quiet road. Twilight was not far off, the murmurous twilight of a London evening with its trancèd lovers and winking stars and street-lamps and window-panes. More and more slowly Michael would glide along, loath to desert the dreaming populations of dusk. He would turn down unfrequented corners and sail by unfamiliar terraces, aware of nothing but the languors of effortless motion. Time, passing by in a sensuous oblivion, made Michael as much a part of the nightfall as the midges that spun incessantly about his progress. Then round a corner some night-breeze would blow freshly in his face: he would suddenly realize it was growing late and, pressing hard the pedals of his bicycle, he would dart home, swift as a bird that crosses against the dying glow of the sunset.

Michael's mother was always glad to see him and always glad when he sat with her on the balcony outside the drawing-room. If he had wanted to cross-examine her he would have found an easy witness, so tranquil and so benignant that year was every night of June in London. But Michael had for the time put aside all speculation and drugged his imagination with animal exercise, allowing himself no time to think of anything but the present. He was dimly aware of trouble close at hand, when the terminal examinations should betray his idleness; but it was impossible to worry over what was now sheerly inevitable. This summer term was perfect, and why should one consider ultimate time? Even Stella's holiday from Germany had been postponed, as if there were a veritable conspiracy by circumstance to wave away the least element of disturbance. Next Saturday he and Alan were going to spend the day in Richmond Park; and when it came in its course what a day it was. The boys set out directly after breakfast and walked through the pungent bracken, chasing the deer and the dragonflies as if there were nothing to distinguish them. Down streamed the sun from the blue July heavens: but Michael and Alan clad in white went careless of the heat. They walked over the grass uphill and ran down through the cool dells of oak trees, down towards the glassy ponds to play 'ducks and drakes' in the flickering weather. They stood by the intersecting carriage-roads and mocked the perspiring travellers in their black garments. They cared for nothing but being alive in Richmond Park on a summer Saturday of London. At last, near a shadowy woodland where the grasses grew very tall, Michael and Alan, smothering the air with pollen, flung themselves down into the fragrancy and, while the bees droned about them, slept in the sun. Later in the afternoon the two friends sat on the Terrace among the old ladies and the old gentlemen, and the nurserymaids and the children's hoops. Down below, the Thames sparkled in a deep green prospect of England. An hour went by; the old ladies and the old gentlemen and the nurserymaids and the hoops faded away one by one under the darkling trees. Down below, the Thames threaded with shining curves a vast and elusive valley of azure. The Thames died away to a sheen of dusky silver: the azure deepened almost to indigo: lights flitted into ken one by one: there travelled up from the river a sound of singing, and somewhere in the houses behind a piano began to tinkle. Michael suddenly became aware that the end of the summer term was in sight. He shivered in the dewfall and put his arm round Alan's neck affectionately and intimately: only profound convention kept him from kissing his friend and by not doing so he felt vaguely that something was absent from this perfection of dusk. Something in Michael at that moment demanded emotional expression, and from afternoon school of yesterday recurred to his mind a note to some lines in the Sixth Æneid of Virgil. He remembered the lines, having by some accident learned his repetition for that day:

> *Huc omnis turba ad ripas effusa ruebat,*
> *Matres atque viri defunctaque corpora vita*
> *Magnanimum heroum, pueri innuptæque puellæ,*
> *Impositique rogis juvenes ante ora parentum;*
> *Quam multa in silvis auctumni frigore primo*
> *Lapsa cadunt folia, aut ad terram gurgite ab alto*
> *Quam multæ glomerantur aves ubi frigidus annus*
> *Trans pontum fugat et terris immittit apricis.*

Compare, said the commentator, Milton, Paradise Lost, Book I.

> *Thick as autumnal leaves that strew the brooks*
> *In Vallombrosa.*

As Michael mentally repeated the thunderous English line, a surge of melancholy caught him up to overwhelm his thoughts. In some way those words expressed what he was feeling at this moment, so that he could gain relief from the poignancy of his joy here in the darkness close to Alan with the unfathomable valley of the Thames beneath, by saying over and over again:

> *Thick as autumnal leaves that strew the brooks*
> *In Vallombrosa.*

"Damn, damn, damn, damn," cried Alan suddenly. "Exams on Monday! Damn, damn, damn, damn."

"I must go home and swat to-night," said Michael.

"So must I," sighed Alan.

"Walk with me to the station," Michael asked.

"Oh, rather," replied Alan.

Soon Michael was jolting back to Kensington in a stuffy carriage of hot Richmond merrymakers, while all the time he sat in the corner, saying over and over again:

> *Thick as autumnal leaves that strew the brooks*
> *In Vallombrosa.*

All Saturday night and all Sunday Michael worked breathlessly for those accursed examinations: but at the end of them he and Alan were bracketed equal, very near the tail of the Upper Fourth A. Dr. Brownjohn sent for each of them in turn, and each of them found the interview very trying.

"What do you mean by it?" roared the Headmaster to Michael. "What do you mean by it, you young blackguard? Um? Look at this list. Um? It's a contemptible position for a Scholar. Down here with a lump of rabbit's brains, you abominable little loafer. Um? If you aren't in the first five boys of the Lower Fifth next term, I'll kick you off the Foundation. What good are you to the School? Um? None at all."

As Dr. Brownjohn bellowed forth this statement, his mouth opened so wide that Michael instinctively shrank back as if from a crater in eruption.

"You don't come here to swagger about," growled the Headmaster. "You come here to be a credit to your school. You pestilent young jackanapes, do you suppose I haven't noticed your idleness? Um? I notice everything. Get out of my sight and take your hands out of your pockets, you insolent little lubber. Um?"

Michael left the Headmaster's room with an expression of tragic injury: in the corridor was a group of juniors.

"What the devil are you kids hanging about here for?" Michael demanded.

"All right, sidey Fane," they burbled. Michael dashed into the group and grabbed a handful of caps which he tossed into the dusty complications of the Laocoön. To their lamentations he responded by thrusting his hands deep down into his pockets and whistling 'Little DollyDaydreams, pride of Idaho.' The summer term would be over in a few days, and Michael was sorry to say good-bye to Alan, who was going to Norway with his father and mother and would therefore not be available for the whole of the holidays. Indeed, he was leaving two days before School actually broke up. Michael was wretched without Alan and brooded over the miseries of life that so soon transcended the joys. On the last day of term, he was seized with an impulse to say good-bye to Mr. Caryll, an impulse which he could not understand and was inclined to deplore. However, it was too strong for his conventions, and he loitered behind in the confusion of merry departures.

"Good-bye, sir," he said shyly.

Mr. Caryll took off two pairs of spectacles and examined Michael through the remaining pair, rasping out the familiar cough as he did so.

"Now, you great booby, what do you want?" he asked.

"Good-bye, sir," Michael said, more loudly.

"Oh, good-bye," said Mr. Caryll. "You've been a very idle boy"—cough—cough—"and I"—cough—cough—"I don't think I ever knew such an idle boy before."

"I've had a ripping time in your class, sir," said Michael.

"What do you mean?"—cough—cough—"are you trying to be impudent?" exclaimed Mr. Caryll, hastily putting on a second pair of spectacles to cope with the situation.

"No, sir. I've enjoyed being in your class. I'm sorry I was so low down in the list. Good-bye, sir."

Mr. Caryll seemed to realize at last that Michael was being sincerely complimentary, so he took off all the pairs of spectacles and beamed at him with an expression of the most profound benignity.

"Oh, well"—cough—cough—"we can't all be top"—cough—cough—"but it's a pity you should be so very low down"—cough—cough—"you're a Scholar too, which makes it much worse. Never mind. Good boy at heart"—cough—cough—"better luck in your next form"—cough—cough. "Hope you'll enjoy yourself on your holidays."

"Good-bye, sir. Thanks awfully," said Michael. He turned away from the well-loved class-room of old Caryll that still echoed with the laughter of the Upper Fourth A.

"And don't work too hard"—cough—cough, was Mr. Caryll's last joke.

In the corridor Michael caught up the lantern-jawed boy who had prophesied this year's pleasure at the beginning of last autumn.

"Just been saying good-bye to old Christmas," Michael volunteered.

"He's a topper," said Lantern-jaws. "The best old boy that ever lived. I wish I was going to be in his form again next term."

"So do I," said Michael. "We had a clinking good time. So long. Hope you'll have decent holidays."

"So long," said the lantern-jawed boy lugubriously, dropping most of his mathematical books. "Same to you."

When Michael was at home, he took a new volume of Henty into the garden and began to read. Suddenly he found he was bored by Henty. This knowledge shocked him for the moment. Then he went indoors and put For Name and Fame, or Through Afghan Passes back on the shelf. He surveyed the row of Henty's books gleaming with olivine edges, and presently he procured brown paper and with Cook's assistance wrapped up the dozen odd volumes. At the top he placed a slip of paper on which was written 'Presented to the Boys' Library by C. M. S. Fane.' Michael was now in a perplexity for literary recreation, until he remembered Don Quixote. Soon he was deep in that huge volume, out of the dull world of London among the gorges and chasms and waterfalls of Castile. Boyhood's zenith had been attained: Michael's imagination was primed for strange emotions.

Chapter V: *Incense*

STELLA came back from Germany less foreign-looking than Michael expected, and he could take a certain amount of pleasure in her company at Bournemouth. For a time they were well matched, as they walked with their mother under the pines. Once, as they passed a bunch of old ladies on a seat, Stella said to Michael:

"Did you hear what those people said?"

Michael had not heard, so Stella whispered:

"They said 'What good-looking children!' Shall we turn back and walk by them again?"

"Whatever for?" Michael demanded.

"Oh, I don't know," said Stella, flapping the big violet bows in her chestnut hair. "Only I like to hear people talking about me. I think it's interesting. I always try to hear what they say when I'm playing."

"Mother," Michael appealed, "don't you think Stella ought not to be so horribly conceited? I do."

"Darling Stella," said Mrs. Fane, "I'm afraid people spoil her. It isn't her fault."

"It must be her fault," argued Michael.

Michael remembered Miss Carthew's admonition not to snub Stella, but he could not help feeling that Miss Carthew herself would have disapproved of this open vanity. He wished that Miss Carthew were not now Mrs. Ross and far away in Edinburgh. He felt almost a responsibility with regard to Stella, a highly moral sensation of knowing better the world and its pitfalls than she could. He feared for the effect of its lure upon Stella and her vanity, and was very anxious his sister should always comport herself with credit to her only brother. In his mother's attitude Michael seemed to discern a dangerous inclination not to trouble about Stella's habit of thought. He resolved, when he and Stella were alone together, to address his young sister seriously. Stella's nonchalance alarmed him more and more deeply as he began to look back at his own life and to survey his wasted years. Michael felt he must convince Stella that earnestness was her only chance.

"You're growing very fast, Michael," said his mother one morning. "Really I think you're getting too big for Etons."

Michael critically examined himself in his mother's toilet-glass and had to admit that his sleeves looked short and that his braces showed too easily under his waistcoat. The fact that he could no longer survey his reflection calmly and that he dreaded to see Stella admire herself showed him something was wrong.

"Perhaps I'd better get a new suit," he suggested.

In his blue serge suit, wearing what the shops called a Polo or Shakespeare collar, Michael felt more at ease, although the sleeves were now as much too long as lately his old sleeves were too short. The gravity of this new suit confirmed his impression that age was stealing upon him and made him the more inclined to lecture Stella. This desire of his seemed to irritate his mother, who would protest:

"Michael, do leave poor Stella alone. I can't think why you've suddenly altered. One would think you'd got the weight of the world on your shoulders."

"Like Atlas," commented Michael gloomily.

"I don't know who it's like," said Mrs. Fane. "But it's very disagreeable for everybody round you."

"Michael always thinks he knows about everything," Stella put in spitefully.

"Oh, shut up!" growled Michael.

He was beginning to feel that his mother admired Stella more than himself, and the old jealousy of her returned. He was often reproved for being untidy and, although he was no longer inky and grubby, he did actually find that his hair refused to grow neatly and that he was growing clumsy both in manners and appearance. Stella always remained cool and exasperatingly debonair under his rebukes, whereas he felt himself growing hot and awkward. The old self-consciousness had returned and with it two warts on his finger and an intermittent spot on his chin. Also a down was visible on his face that somehow blunted his profile and made him more prone than ever to deprecate the habit of admiring oneself in a looking-glass. He felt impelled to untie Stella's violet bows whenever he caught her posing before the mirror, and as the holidays advanced he and she grew less and less well matched. The old worrying speculation about his father returned together with a wish that his mother would not dress in such gay colours. Michael admired her slimness and tallness, but he wished that men would not turn round and stare at her as she passed them. He used to stare back at the men with a set frowning face and try to impress them with his distaste for their manners; but day by day he grew more miserable about his mother, and would often seek to dissuade her from what he considered a too conspicuous hat or vivid ribbon. She used to laugh and tell him that he was a regular old 'provincial.' The opportunity for perfect confidence between Michael and his mother seemed to have slipped by, and he found it impossible now to make her talk about his father. To be sure, she no longer tried to wave aside his enquiries; but she did worse by answering 'yes' or 'no' to his questions according to her mood, never seeming to care whether she contradicted a previous statement or not.

Once, Michael asked straight out whether his father was in prison and he was relieved when his mother rippled with laughter and told him he was a stupid boy. At the same time, since he had been positively assured his father was dead, Michael felt that laughter, however convincing it were, scarcely became a widow.

"I cannot think what has happened to you, Michael. You were perfectly charming all last term and never seemed to have a moment on your hands. Now you hang about the house on these lovely fine days and mope and grumble. I do wish you could enjoy yourself as you used to."

"Well, I've got no friends down here," Michael declared. "What is there to do? I'm sick of the band, and the niggers are rotten, and Stella always wants to hang about on the pier so that people can stare at her. I wish she'd go back to her glorious Germany where everything is so wonderful."

"Why don't you read? You used to love reading," suggested Mrs. Fane.

"Oh, read!" exclaimed Michael. "There's nothing to read. I hate Henty. Always the same!"

"Well, I don't know anything about Henty, but there's Scott and Dickens and——"

"I've read all them, mother," Michael interrupted petulantly.

"Well, why don't you ask Mrs. Rewins if you can borrow a book from her, or I'll ask her, as you don't like going downstairs."

Mrs. Rewins brought up an armful of books which Michael examined dismally one by one. However, after several gilded volumes of sermons and sentimental Sunday-school prizes, he came across a tattered Newgate Calendar and Roderick Random, both of which satisfied somewhat his new craving for excitement. When he had finished these books, Mrs. Rewins invited him to explore the cupboard in her warm kitchen, and here Michael found Peregrine Pickle, Tom Jones, a volume of Bentley's Miscellany containing the serial of Jack Sheppard by Harrison Ainsworth, and What Every Woman of Forty-five ought to Know. The last work upset him very much because he found it unintelligible in parts, and where it was intelligible extremely alarming. An instinct of shamefulness made him conceal this book in a drawer, but he became very anxious to find out exactly how old his mother was. She, however, was more elusive on this point than he had ever known her, and each elaborate trap failed, even the innocent production of the table for ascertaining anybody's age in a blue sixpenny Encyclopædia: still, the Encyclopædia was not without its entertainment, and the table of diseases at the end was very instructive. Among the books which Michael had mined down in Mrs. Rewins' kitchen was The Ingoldsby Legends illustrated by Cruikshank. These he found very enthralling, for though he was already acquainted with The Jackdaw of Rheims, he now discovered many other poems still more amusing, in many of which he came across with pleasure quotations that he remembered to have heard used with much effect by Mr. Neech in the Shell. The macabre and ghostly lays did not affect him so much as the legends of the saints. These he read earnestly as he read Don Quixote, discerning less of laughter than of Gothic adventure in their fantastic pages, while his brain was fired by the heraldic pomps and ecclesiastical glories.

About this time he happened to pay a visit to Christchurch Priory and by the vaulted airs of that sanctuary he was greatly thrilled. The gargoyles and brasses and effigies of dead knights called to him mysteriously, but the inappropriate juxtaposition of an early Victorian tomb shocked him with a sense of sacrilege. He could not bear to contemplate the nautical trousers of the boy commemorated. Yet, simultaneously with his outraged decorum, he was attracted to this tomb, as if he detected in that ingenuous boy posited among sad cherubs some kinship with himself.

In bed that night Michael read The Ingoldsby Legends in a fever of enjoyment, while the shadows waved about the ceiling and walls of the seaside room in the vexed candlelight. As yet the details of the poems did not gain their full effect, because many of the words and references were not understood. He felt that knowledge was necessary before he could properly enjoy the colour of these tales. Michael had always been inclined to crystallize in one strong figure of imagination his vague impressions. Two years ago he had identified Mr. Neech with old prints, with Tom Brown's Schooldays and with shelves of calf-bound books. Now in retrospect he, without being able to explain his reason to himself, identified Mr. Neech with that statue of the trousered boy in Christchurch Priory, and not merely Mr. Neech but even The Ingoldsby Legends as well. He felt that they were both all wrong in the sanctified glooms of the Middle Ages, and yet he rejoiced to behold them there, as if somehow they were a pledge of historic continuity. Without the existence of the trousered boy Michael would scarcely have believed in the reality of those stone ladies and carved knights. The candlelight fluttered and jigged in the seaside room, while Mr. Neech, The Ingoldsby Legends and the oratories of Christchurch became more and more hopelessly confused. Michael's excited brain was formulating visions of immense cathedrals beneath whose arches pattered continually the populations of old prints: the tower of St. Mary's College, Oxford, rose, slim and lovely, against the storm-wrack of a Doré sky: Don Quixote tilted with knights-at-arms risen from the dead. Michael himself was swept along in cavalcades towards the clouds with Ivanhoe, Richard Cœur de Lion, Roderick Random and half a dozen woodcut murderers from the Newgate Calendar. Then, just as the candlelight was gasping and shimmering blue in the bowl of the candlestick, he fell asleep.

In the sunshine of the next day Michael almost wondered whether like someone in The Ingoldsby Legends he had ridden with witches on a broomstick. All the cool security of boyhood had left him; he was in a turmoil of desire for an astounding experience. He almost asked himself what he wanted so dearly; and, as he pondered, out of the past in a vision came the picture of himself staring at the boy who walked beside the incense with a silver boat. What did the Lay of St. Alois say?

This with his chasuble, this with his
rosary,
This with his incense-pot holding his
nose awry.

Michael felt a craving to go somewhere and smell that powerful odour again. He remembered how the boy had put out his tongue and he envied him such familiarity with pomps and glories.

"Are there any High Churches in Bournemouth?" he asked Mrs. Rewins. "Very high. Incense and all that, you know."

Mrs. Rewins informed him there was one church so high that some said it was practically 'Roming Catholic.'

"Where is it?" asked Michael, choking with excitement. Yet he had never before wanted to go to church. In the days of Nurse he had hated it. In the days of Miss Carthew he had only found it endurable if his friends were present. He had loathed the rustle of many women dressed in their best clothes. He had hated the throaty voices of smooth-faced clergymen. He had despised the sleek choir-boys smelling of yellow soap. Religion had been compounded of Collects, Greek Testament, Offertory Bags, varnish, qualms for the safety of one's top-hat, the pleasure of an extra large hassock, ambition to be grown up and bend over instead of kneeling down, the podgy feel of a Prayer Book, and a profound disapproval that only Eton and Winchester among public schools were mentioned in its diaphanous fumbling pages. Now religion should be an adventure. The feeling that he was embarking upon the unknown made Michael particularly reticent, and he was afraid to tell his mother that on Sunday morning he proposed to attend the service at St. Bartholomew's, lest she might suggest coming also. He did not want to be irritated by Stella's affectations and conceit, nor did he wish to notice various women turning round to study his mother's hat. In the end Michael did not go on Sunday to the church of his intention, because at the last moment he could not brace himself to mumble an excuse.

Late on the afternoon of the following day Michael walked through the gustiness of a swift-closing summer toward St. Bartholomew's, where it stood facing a stretch of sandy heather and twisted pine trees on the outskirts of Bournemouth. The sky was stained infrequently with the red of a lifeless sunset and, as Michael watched the desolation of summer's retreat, he listened sadly to the sibilant heather lisping against the flutes of the pines, while from time to time the wind drummed against the buttresses and boomed against the bulk of the church. Michael drew near the west door whose hinges and nails stood out unnaturally distinct in the last light of the sun. Abruptly on the blowy eve the church-bell began to ring, and from various roads Michael saw people approaching, their heads bent against the gale. At length he made up his mind to follow one of the groups through the churchyard and presently, while the gate rattled behind him in the wind, he reached the warm glooms within. As he took his seat and perceived the altar loaded with flowers, dazzling with lighted candles, he wondered why this should be so on a Monday night in August. The air was pungent with the smell of wax and the stale perfume of incense on stone. The congregation was scattered about in small groups and units, and the vaulted silence was continually broken by coughs and sighs and hollow footsteps. From the tower the bell rang in slow monotone, while the wind whistled and moaned and flapped and boomed as if, thought Michael, all the devils in hell were trying to break into the holy building. The windows were now scarcely luminous with the wan shadow of daylight and would indeed have been opaque as coal had the inside of the church been better lighted. But the few wavering gas-jets in the nave made all seem dark save where the chancel, empty and candle-lit, shone and sparkled in a radiancy. Something in Michael's attitude must have made a young man sitting behind lean over and ask if he wanted a Prayer Book. Michael turned quickly to see a lean and eager face.

"Yes, please. I left mine at home," he answered.

"Well, come and sit by me," said the young man.

Michael changed his place and the young man talked in a low whisper, while the bell rang its monotone upon the gusts which swept howling round the church.

"Solemn Evensong isn't until seven o'clock. It's our patronal festival, St. Bartholomew's Day—you know. We had a good Mass this morning. Every year we get more people. Do you live in Bournemouth?"

"No," whispered Michael. "I'm just here for the holidays."

"What a pity," said the stranger. "We do so want servers—you know—decent-looking servers. Our boys are so clumsy. It's not altogether their fault—the cassocks—you know—they're only in two sizes. They trip up. I'm the Ceremonarius, and I can tell you I have my work cut out. Of course I ought to have been helping to-night. But I wasn't sure I could get away from the Bank in time. I hope Wilson—that's our second thurifer—won't go wrong in the Magnificat. He usually does."

The bell stopped: there was a momentary hush for the battling wind to moan louder than ever: then the organ began to play and from the sacristy came the sound of a chanted Amen. Choristers appeared followed by two or three of the clergy, and when these had taken their places a second procession appeared, with boys in scarlet and lace and a tinkling censer and a priest in a robe of blood-red velvet patterned with dull gold.

"That's the new cope," whispered the stranger. "Fine work, isn't it?"

"Awfully decent," Michael whispered back.

"All I hope is the acolytes will remember to put out the candles immediately after the Third Collect. It's so important," said the stranger.

"I expect they will," whispered Michael encouragingly.

Then the Office began, and Michael, waiting for a spiritual experience, communed that night with the saints of God, as during the Magnificat his soul rose to divine glories on the fumes of the aspiring incense. There was a quality in the voices of the boys which expressed for him more beautifully than the full Sunday choir could have done, the pathos of human praise and the purity of his own surrender to Almighty God. The splendours of the Magnificat died away to a silence and one of the clergy stepped from his place to read the Second Lesson. As he came down the chancel steps Michael's new friend whispered:

"The censing of the altar was all right. It's really a good thing sometimes to be a spectator—you know—one sees more."

Michael nodded a vague assent. Already the voice of the lector was vibrating through the church.

In the end of the sabbath, as it began to dawn towards the first day of the week, came Mary Magdalene and the other Mary to see the sepulchre.

Michael thought to himself how he had come to St. Bartholomew's when Sunday was over. That was strange.

His countenance was like lightning and his raiment white as snow: and for fear of him the keepers did shake, and became as dead men.

"I wish that boy Wiggins wouldn't fidget with his zuchetto," Michael's friend observed.

And behold, he goeth before you into Galilee; there shall ye see him: lo, I have told you.

Michael felt an impulse to sob, as he mentally offered the best of himself to the worship of Christ, for the words of the lesson were striking on his soul like bells.

And when they saw him, they worshipped him: but some doubted.

"Now you see the other boy has started fidgeting with *his*," complained the young man.

And, lo, I am with you always, even unto the end of the world. Amen.

As the lector's retreating footsteps died away into the choir the words were burned on Michael's heart, and for the first time he sang the Nunc Dimittis with a sense of the privilege of personally addressing Almighty God. When the Creed was chanted Michael uttered his belief passionately, and while the Third Collect was being read between the exalted candles of the acolytes he wondered why never before had the words struck him with all their power against the fears and fevers of the night.

Lighten our darkness, we beseech thee, O Lord; and by thy great mercy defend us from all perils and dangers of this night, for the love of thy only Son, our Saviour, Jesus Christ. Amen.

The acolytes lowered their candles to extinguish them: then they darkened the altar while the hymn was being sung, and Michael's friend gave a sigh of relief.

"Perfectly all right," he whispered.

Michael himself was sorry to see the gradual extinction of the altar-lights; he had concentrated upon that radiance his new desire of adoration and a momentary chill fell upon him, as if the fiends without were gaining strength and fury. All dread and doubt was allayed when, after the murmured Grace of Our Lord, the congregation and the choir and the officiant knelt in a silent prayer. The wind still shrieked and thundered: the gas-jets waved uneasily above the huddled forms of the worshippers: but over all that incense-clouded gloom lay a spirit of tranquillity. Michael said the Our Father to himself and allowed his whole being to expand in a warmth of surrender. The purification of sincere prayer, voiced more by his attitude of mind than by any spoken word, made him infinitely at peace with life.

When the choir and clergy had filed out and the sacristan like an old rook came limping down the aisle to usher the congregation forth into the dark wind of Bartlemy-tide, Michael's friend said:

"Wait just a minute. I want to speak to Father Moneypenny for a moment, and then we can walk back together."

Michael nodded, and presently his friend came back from the sacristy with Father Moneypenny in cassock and biretta, looking like the photographs of clergymen that Michael remembered in Nurse's album long ago.

"So you enjoyed the Evensong?" enquired the priest. "Capital! You must come to Mass next Sunday. There will be a procession. By the way, Prout, perhaps your young friend would help us. We shall want extra torch-boys."

Mr. Prout agreed, and Michael, although he wondered what his mother would say, was greatly excited by the idea. They were standing now by the door of the church and as it opened a gust of wind burst in and whistled round the interior. Father Moneypenny shivered.

"What a night. The end of summer, I'm afraid."

He closed the door, and Michael and Mr. Prout forced their way through the gale over the wet gravel of the churchyard. The pine trees and the heather made a melancholy concert, and they were glad to reach the blown lamplight of the streets.

"Will you come round to my place?" Mr. Prout asked.

"Well, I ought to go back. My mater will be anxious," said Michael.

Mr. Prout thereupon invited him to come round to-morrow afternoon.

"I shall be back from the Bank about five. Good night. You've got my card? Bernard Prout, Esdraelon, Saxton Road. Good night. Pleased to have met you."

Mrs. Fane was surprised to hear of Michael's visit to St. Bartholomew's.

"You're getting so secretive, dearest boy. I'd no idea you were becoming interested in religion."

"Well, it is interesting," said Michael.

"Of course. I know it must be. So many people think of nothing else. And do you really want to march in the procession?"

"Yes, but don't you and Stella come," Michael said.

"Oh, I must, Michael. I'd love to see you in all those pretty clothes."

"Well, I *can* go round and see this chap Prout, can't I?" Michael asked.

"I suppose so," Mrs. Fane replied. "Of course, I don't know anything about him. Is he a gentleman?"

"Of course he's a gentleman," affirmed Michael warmly. "Besides I don't see it matters a bit whether he's a gentleman or not."

"No, of course it doesn't really, as it all has to do with religion," Mrs. Fane agreed. "Nothing is so mixed as religious society."

Saxton Road possessed no characteristic to distinguish it from many similar roads in Bournemouth. A few hydrangeas debated in sheltered corners whether they should be pink or blue, and the number of each house was subordinate to its title. The gate of Esdraelon clicked behind Michael's entrance just as the gate of Homeview or Ardagh or Glenside would have clicked. By the bay-window of the ground floor was planted a young passion-flower whose nursery label lisped against the brick-work, and whose tendrils were flattened beneath wads of nail-pierced flannel. Michael was directed upstairs to Mr. Prout's sitting-room on the first floor, where the owner was arranging the tea-cups.

"I'm so glad you were able to come," he said.

Michael looked round the room with interest, and while the tea-cake slowly cooled Mr. Prout discussed with enthusiasm his possessions.

"That's St. Bernardine of Sienna," he explained, pointing to a coloured statuette. "My patron, you know. Curious I should have been born on his day and be christened Bernard. I thought of changing my name to Bernardine, but it's so difficult at a Bank. Of course, I have a cult for St. Bernard too, but I never really can forgive him for opposing the Immaculate Conception. Father Moneypenny and I have great arguments on that point. I'm afraid he's a *little* bit wobbly. But absolutely sound on the Assumption. Oh, absolutely, I'm glad to say. In fact, I don't mind telling you that next year we intend to keep it as a Double of the First Class with Octave *which*, of course, it *is*. This rosary is made of olive-wood from the Garden of Gethsemane and I'm very anxious to get it blessed by the Pope. Some friends of mine are going to Rome next Easter with a Polytechnic tour, so I *may* be able to manage it. But it's difficult. The Cardinals—you know," said Mr. Prout vaguely. "They're inclined to be bitter against English Catholics. Of course, Vaughan made the mistake of his life in getting the Pope to pronounce against English Orders. I know a Roman priest told me he considered it a fatal move. However—you're waiting for your tea?"

Michael ate Mr. Prout's bread-and-butter and drank his tea, while the host hopped from trinket to trinket.

"This is a sacred amulet which belonged to one of the Macdonalds who fought at Prestonpans. I suppose you're a Jacobite? Of course, I belong to all the Legitimist Societies—the White Rose, the White Cockade, the White Carnation. Everyone. I wish I were a Scotchman, although my grandmother was a Miss Macmillan, so I've got Scotch blood. You *are* a Jacobite, aren't you?"

"Rather," said Michael as enthusiastically as his full mouth would allow him to declare.

"Of course, it's the only logical political attitude for an English Catholic to adopt," said Mr. Prout. "All this Erastianism—you know. Terrible. What's the Privy Council got to do with Vestments? Still the Episcopal appointments haven't been so bad lately. That's Lord Salisbury. Of course, we've had trouble with our Bishop. Oh, yes. He simply declines to listen to reason on the subject of Reservation for the Sick. Personally I advised Father Moneypenny not to pay any attention to him. I said the Guild of St. Wilfrid—that's our servers' guild, you know—was absolutely in favour of defiance, open defiance. But one of the churchwardens got round him. There's your Established Church. Money's what churchwardens think of—simply money. And has religion got anything to do with money? Nothing. 'Blessed are the poor.' You can't go against that, as I told Major Wilton—that's our people's warden—in the sacristy. He's a client of ours at the Bank, or I should have said a jolly sight more. I should have told him that in my opinion his attitude was simony—rank simony, and let it go at that. But I couldn't very well, and, of course, it doesn't look well for the Ceremonarius and the churchwarden to be bickering after Mass. By the way, will you help us next Sunday?"

"I'd like to," said Michael, "but I don't know anything about it."

"There'll be a rehearsal," said Mr. Prout. "And it's perfectly simple. You elevate your torch first of all at the Sanctus and then at the Consecration. And now, if you've finished your tea, I'll show you my oratory. Of course, you'll understand that I'm only in rooms here, but the landlady is a very pleasant woman. She let me plant that passion-flower in the garden. Perhaps you noticed it? The same with this oratory. It *was* a housemaid's cupboard, but it was very inconvenient—and there isn't a housemaid as a matter of fact—so I secured it. Come along."

Mr. Prout led the way on to the landing, at the end of which were two doors.

"We can't both kneel down, unless the door's open," said Mr. Prout. "But when I'm alone, I can *just* shut myself in."

He opened the oratory door as he spoke, and Michael was impressed by the appearance of it. The small window had been covered with a rice-paper design of Jesse's Rod.

"It's a bit 'Protty,'" whispered Mr. Prout. "But I thought it was better than plain squares of blue and red."

"Much better," Michael agreed.

A ledge nailed beneath the window supported two brass candlesticks and a crucifix. The reredos was an Arundel print of the Last Supper and on corner brackets on either side were statues of the Immaculate Conception and Our Lady of Victories. A miniature thurible hung on a nail and on another nail was a holy-water stoup which Michael at first thought was intended for soap. In front of the altar was a prie-dieu stacked with books of devotion. There were also blessed palms, very dusty, and a small sanctuary lamp suspended from the ceiling. Referring to this, Mr. Prout explained that really it came from the Turkish Exhibition at Earl's Court, but that he thought it would do as he had carefully exorcized it according to the use of Sarum.

"Shall we say Vespers?" suggested Mr. Prout. "You know—the Small Office of the Blessed Virgin. It won't take long. We can say Compline *too*, if you like."

"Just as you like," said Michael.

"You're sure you don't mind the door being left open? Because, you see, we can't both get in otherwise. In fact, I have to kneel sideways when I'm alone."

"Won't your landlady think it rather rum?" Michael asked.

"Good gracious, no. Why, when we have Vespers of St. Charles the Martyr, I have fellows kneeling all the way down the stairs, you know—members of the White Rose League, Bournemouth and South of England Branch."

Michael was handed a thin sky-blue book labelled *Office of the B.V.M.*

"Latin or English?" queried Mr. Prout.

"Whichever you like," said Michael.

"Well, Latin, if you don't mind. I'm anxious to learn Latin, and I find this is good practice."

"It doesn't look very good Latin," said Michael doubtfully.

"Doesn't it?" said Mr. Prout. "It ought to. It's the right version."

"I expect this is Hellenistic—I mean Romanistic—Latin," said Michael, who was proud of his momentary superiority in knowledge. "Greek Test is Hellenistic Greek."

"Do you know Greek?" asked Mr. Prout.

"A little."

Mr. Prout sighed.

When the Office was concluded, Michael promised he would attend a rehearsal of next Sunday's ceremony and, if he felt at ease, the Solemn High Mass itself. Mr. Prout, before Michael went away, lent him a book called Ritual Reason Why, and advised him to buy The Catholic Religion at One Shilling, and meanwhile to practise direct Invocation of the Saints.

At home Michael applied himself with ardour to the mastery of his religion. He wrestled with the liturgical colours; he tried to grasp the difference between Transubstantiation, Consubstantiation and the Real Presence; and he congratulated himself upon being under the immediate patronage of an Archangel. Also with Charles as his first name he felt he could fairly claim the protection of St. Charles the Martyr, though later on Mr. Prout suggested St. Charles Borromeo as a less ordinary patron. However, there was more than ritualism in Michael's new attitude, more than the passion to collect new rites and liturgies and ornaments as once he had collected the portraits of famous cricketers or silkworms or silver-paper. To be sure, it soon came to seem to him a terribly important matter whether according to the Roman sequence red were worn at Whitsuntide or whether according to Old English use white were the liturgical colour. Soon he would experience a shock of dismay on hearing that some reputed Catholic had taken the Ablutions at the wrong moment, just as once he had been irritated by ignorant people confusing Mr. W. W. Read of Surrey with Read (M.) of the same county. Beyond all this Michael sincerely tried to correct his morals and manners in the light of aspiration and faith. He experienced a revolt against impurity of any kind and was simultaneously seized with a determination to suffer Stella's conceit gladly. He really felt a deep-seated avarice for being good. He may not have distinguished between morality due to emotion and morality wrung out of intellectual assent: but he did know that the Magnificat's incense took him to a higher elation than Dora's curly head upon his shoulder, or even than Alan's bewitching company. Under the influence of faith, Michael found himself bursting with an affection for his mother such as he had not felt for a long time. Indeed Michael was in a state of love. He loved the candles on the altar, he loved his mother's beauty, he loved Stella, he loved the people on the beach and the August mornings and the zest for acquiring and devouring information upon every detail connected with the Catholic religion; and out of his love he gratified Mr. Prout by consenting to bear a torch at the Solemn High Mass on the Sunday within the octave of St. Bartholomew, Apostle and Martyr and Patron of St. Bartholomew's Church, Bournemouth.

Michael's first High Mass was an emotional experience deeper even than that windy Evensong. The church was full of people. The altar was brilliant with flowers and lights. The sacristy was crowded with boys in scarlet cassocks and slippers and zuchettos, quarrelling about their cottas and arguing about their heights. Everybody had a favourite banner which he wanted to escort and, to complicate matters still further, everybody had a favourite companion by whose side he wished to walk.

The procession was marshalled before the altar: the organ boomed through the church: the first thurifer started off, swinging his censer towards the clouded roof. After him went the cross of ebony and silver, while one by one at regular intervals between detachments of the choir the banners of the saints floated into action. Michael escorted the blue velvet banner of Our Lady, triumphant, crowned, a crescent moon beneath her feet and round about her stars and Cherubim. The procession was long enough to fill two aisles at once, and as Michael turned up the south aisle on the return to the chancel, he saw the pomp of the procession's rear—the second thurifer, Mr. Prout in a cotta bordered by lace two feet deep, the golden crucifix aloft, the acolytes with their golden candlesticks, the blood-red dalmatic and tunicle of the deacon and sub-deacon, and solemnly last of all the blood-red cope of the celebrant. Michael took no pleasure in being observed by the congregation; he was simply elated by the privilege of being able to express his desire to serve God, and during the Mass, when the Sanctus bell chimed forth, he raised his torch naturally to the pæan of the salutation. The service was long: the music was elaborate: it was back-breaking work to kneel on the chancel steps without support; but Michael welcomed the pain with pleasure. During the Elevation of the Host, as he bowed his head before the wonder of bread and wine made God, his brain reeled in an ecstasy of sublime worship. There was a silence save for the censer tinkling steadily and the low whispered words of the priest and the click of the broken wafer. The candles burned with a supernatural intensity: the boys who lately quarrelled over precedence were hushed as angels: the stillness became fearful; the cold steps burned into Michael's knees and the incense choked him. At last after an age of adoration, the plangent appeal of the Agnus Dei came with a melody that seemed the music of the sobbing world from which all tears had departed in a clarity of harmonious sound.

Before Michael left Bournemouth, Mr. Prout promised to come and see him in London, and Mr. Moneypenny said he would write to a priest who would be glad to prepare him for Confirmation. When Michael reached school again, he felt shy at meeting Alan who would talk about nothing but football and was dismayed to find Michael indifferent to the delights of playing three-quarter on Middle Side. Michael deplored Alan's failure to advance intellectually beyond mere football and the two of them temporarily lost touch with each other's ambitions. Michael now read nothing but ecclesiastical books and was greatly insulted by Mr. Viner's elementary questions. Mr. Viner was the priest to whom Mr. Moneypenny had written about Michael. He had invited him to tea and together they had settled that Michael should be confirmed early in the spring. Michael borrowed half a dozen books from Mr. Viner and returned home to make an attempt to convert the cook and the housemaid to the Catholic faith as a preliminary to converting his mother and Alan. In the end he did actually convert a boy in the Lower Fifth who for his strange beliefs suffered severely at the hands of his father, a Plymouth Brother. Michael wished that Stella had not gone back to Germany, for he felt that in her he would have had a splendid object on whom to practise his power of controversy. At Mr. Viner's house Michael met another Jacobean called Chator in whom he found a fellow-enthusiast. Chator knew of two other Jacobeans interested in Church matters, Martindale and Rigg, and the four of them founded a society called De Rebus Ecclesiasticis which met every Friday evening in Michael's room to discuss the Catholic Church in all her aspects. The discussions were often heated because Michael had violently Ultra-montane leanings, Chator was narrowly Sarum, Martindale tried to preserve a happy mean and Rigg always agreed with the last speaker. The Society De Rebus Ecclesiasticis was splendidly quixotic and gloriously unrelated to the dead present. To the quartette of members Archbishop Laud was a far more vital proposition than Archbishop Temple, the society of cavaliers was more vividly realized than the Fabian Society. As was to be expected from Michael's preoccupation with the past, he became very anxious again about his parentage. He longed to hear that in some way he was connected with Jacobite heroes and the romantic Stuarts. Mrs. Fane was no longer able to put him off with contradictions and vagueness: Michael demanded his family tree. The hymn 'Faith of our Fathers' ringing through a Notting Dale mission-hall moved him to demand his birthright of family history.

"Well, I'll tell you, Michael," said his mother at last. "Your father ought to have been the Earl of Saxby—only—something went wrong—some certificate or something."

"An Earl?" cried Michael, staggered by the splendid news. "But—but, mother, we met Lord Saxby. Who was that?"

"He's a relation. Only, please don't tell people about this, because they wouldn't understand. It's all very muddled and difficult."

"My father ought to have been Lord Saxby? Why wasn't he? Mother, was he illegitimate?"

"Michael, how can you talk like that? Of course not."

Michael blushed because his mother blushed.

"I'm sorry, mother, I thought he might have been. People are. You read about them often enough."

Michael decided that as he must not tell Chator, Martindale and Rigg the truth, he would, at any rate, join himself on to the House of Saxby collaterally. To his disappointment, he discovered that the only reference in history to an Earl of Saxby made out that particular one to be a most pestilent Roundhead. So Michael gave up being the Legitimist Earl of Saxby, and settled instead to be descended through the indiscretion of an early king from the Stuarts. Michael grew more and more ecclesiastical as time went on. He joined several Jacobite societies, and accompanied Mr. Prout on the latter's London visit to a reception at Clifford's Inn Hall in honour of the Legitimist Emperor of Byzantium. Michael was very much impressed by kissing the hand of an Emperor, and even more deeply impressed by the Scottish piper who marched up and down during the light refreshment at one shilling a head afterwards. Mr. Prout, accompanied by Michael, Chator, Martindale and Rigg, spent the Sunday of his stay in town by attending early Mass in Kensington, High Mass in Holborn, Benediction in Shoreditch and Evensong in Paddington. He also joined several more guilds, confraternities and societies and presented Michael with one hair from the five hairs he possessed of a lock of Prince Charlie's hair (authentic) before he returned to Bournemouth. This single hair was a great responsibility to Michael, until he placed it in a silver locket to wear round his neck. During that year occurred what the papers called a Crisis in the Church, and Michael and his three friends took in every week The Church Times, The Church Review, The English Churchman, Church Bells, The Record and The Rock in order to play their part in the crisis. They attended Protestant meetings to boo and hiss from the gallery or to applaud violently gentlemen on their side who rose to ask the lecturer what they supposed to be irrefutable questions. In the spring Michael made his first Confession and was confirmed. The first Confession had more effect on his imagination than the Confirmation, which in retrospect seemed chiefly a sensation of disappointment that the Bishop in view of the crisis in the Church refused to wear the mitre temptingly laid out for him by Mr. Viner. The Confession, however, was a true test of Michael's depth. Mr. Viner was by no means a priest who only thought of candles and lace. He was a gaunt and humorous man, ready to drag out from his penitents their very souls.

Michael found that first Confession an immense strain upon his truthfulness and pluck, and he made up his mind never to commit another mortal sin, so deeply did he blush in the agony of revelation. Venial faults viewed in the aggregate became appalling, and the real sins, as one by one Michael compelled himself to admit them, stabbed his self-consciousness with daggers of shame. Michael had a sense of completeness which prevented him from making a bad Confession, from gliding over his sins and telling half-truths, and having embarked upon the duties of his religion he was not going to avoid them. The Confession seemed to last for ever. Beforehand, Michael had supposed there would be only one commandment whose detailed sins would make his heart beat with the difficulty of confessing them; but when he knelt in the empty church before the severe priest, every breach of the other commandments assumed a demoniac importance. Michael thought that never before could Father Viner have listened to such a narration of human depravity from a boy of fifteen, or even from a man full grown. He half expected to see the priest rise in the middle and leave his chair in disgust. Michael felt beads of sweat trickling from his forehead: the strain grew more terrible: the crucifix before him gave him no help: the book he held fell from his fingers. Then he heard the words of absolution, tranquil as evening bells. The inessentials of his passionate religion faded away in the strength and beauty of God's acceptance of his penitence. Outside in the April sunlight Michael could have danced his exultation, before he ran home winged with the ecstasy of a light heart.

Chapter VI: *Pax*

THE Lower Fifth only knew Michael during the Autumn term. After Christmas he moved up to the Middle Fifth, and, leaving behind him, many friends, including Alan, he found himself in an industrious society concentrated upon obtaining the Oxford and Cambridge Higher Certificate for proficiency in Greek, Latin, Mathematics and either Divinity, French or History. Removed from the temptations of a merry company, Michael worked very hard indeed and kept his brain fit by argument instead of football. The prevailing attitude of himself and his contemporaries towards the present was one of profound pessimism. The scholarship of St. James' was deteriorating; there was a dearth of great English poets; novelists were not so good as once they were in the days of Dickens; the new boys were obviously inferior to their prototypes in the past; the weather was growing worse year by year; the country was plunging into an abyss. In school Michael prophesied more loudly than any of his fellow Jeremiahs, and less and less did it seem worth while in these Certificate-stifled days to seek for romance or poetry or heroism or adventure. Yet as soon as the precincts of discipline and study were left behind, Michael could extract from life full draughts of all these virtues.

Without neglecting the Oxford and Cambridge Higher Certificate he devoured voraciously every scrap of information about Catholicism which it was possible to acquire. Books were bought in tawdry repositories—Catholic Belief, The Credentials of the Catholic Church, The Garden of the Soul, The Glories of Mary by S. Alphonso Liguori, Alban Butler's Lives of the Saints, The Clifton Tracts, and on his own side of the eternal controversy, Lee's Validity of English Orders, The Alcuin Club Transactions with many other volumes. Most of all he liked to pore upon the Tourist's Church Guide, which showed with asterisks and paragraph marks and sections and daggers what churches throughout the United Kingdom possessed the five points of Incense, Lights, Vestments, Mixed Chalice and Eastward Position. He found it absorbing to compare the progress of ritual through the years.

Michael, as once he had known the ranks of the British Army from Lance-corporal to Field Marshal, could tell the hierarchy from Sexton to Pope. He knew too, as once he knew the history and uniform of Dragoons, Hussars and Lancers, the history and uniform of the religious orders—Benedictines, Cistercians, Franciscans, Dominicans (how he loved the last in their black and white habit, *Domini canes*, watchdogs of the Lord), Carmelites, Præmonstratensians, Augustinians, Servites, Gilbertines, Carthusians, Redemptorists, Capuchins, Passionists, Jesuits, Oblates of St. Charles Borromeo and the Congregation of St. Philip Neri. Michael outvied Mr. Prout in ecclesiastical possessions, and his bedroom was nearly as full as the repository from which it was stocked. There were images of St. Michael (his own patron), St. Hugh of Lincoln (patron of schoolboys) and St. James of Compostella (patron of the school), together with Our Lady of Seven Dolours, Our Lady Star of the Sea and Our Lady of Lourdes, Our Lady of Perpetual Succour, Our Lady of Victories; there were eikons, scapulars, crucifixes, candlesticks, the Holy Child of Prague, rosaries, and indeed every variety of sacred bric-à-brac. Michael slept in an oriental atmosphere, because he had formed the habit of burning during his prayers cone-shaped pastilles in a saucer. The tenuous spiral of perfumed smoke carried up his emotional apostrophes through the prosaic ceiling of the old night-nursery past the stars, beyond the Thrones and Dominations and Seraphim to God. Michael's contest with the sins of youth had become much more thrilling since he had accepted the existence of a personal fiend, and in an ecstasy of temptation he would lie in bed and defy the Devil, calling upon his patron the Archangel to descend from heaven and battle with the powers of evil in that airy arena above the coal-wharf beyond the railway lines. But the Father of Lies had many tricks with which to circumvent Michael; he would conjure up sensuous images before his antagonist; succubi materialized as pretty housemaids, feminine devils put on tights and openwork stockings to encounter him from the pages of pink weekly papers, and sometimes Satan himself would sit at the foot of his bed in the darkness and tell him tales of how other boys enjoyed themselves, arguing that it was a pity to waste his opportunities and filling his thoughts with dissolute memories. Michael would leap from his bed and pray before his crucifix, and through the darkness angels and saints would rally to his aid, until Satan slunk off with his tail between his legs, personally humiliated.

At school the fever of the examination made Michael desperate with the best intentions. He almost learned the translations of Thucydides and Sophocles, of Horace and Cicero. He knew by heart a meanly written Roman History, and no passage in Corneille could hold an invincible word. Cricket was never played that summer by the Middle Fifth; it was more useful to wander in corners of the field, murmuring continually the tables of the Kings of Judah from Maclear's sad-hued abstract of Holy Scripture. In the end Michael passed in Greek and Latin, in French and Divinity and Roman History, even in Algebra and Euclid, but the arithmetical problems of a Stockbroker, a Paper-hanger and a Housewife made all the rest of his knowledge of no account, and Michael failed to see beside his name in the school list that printed bubble which would refer him to the tribe of those who had satisfied the examiners for the Oxford and Cambridge Higher Certificate. This failure depressed Michael, not because he felt implicated in any disgrace, but because he wished very earnestly that he had not wasted so many hours of fine weather in work. He made up his mind that the mistake should never be repeated, and for the rest of his time at St. James' he resisted all set books. If Demosthenes was held necessary, Michael would read Plato, and when Cicero was set, Michael would feel bound to read Livy.

Michael looked back on the year with dissatisfaction, and wondered if school was going to become more and more boring each new term for nine more terms. The prospect was unendurably grey, and Michael felt that life was not worth living. He talked over with Mr. Viner the flatness of existence on the evening after the result of the examination was known.

"I swotted like anything," said Michael gloomily. "And what's the good? I'm sick of everything."

The priest's eyes twinkled, as he plunged deeper into his wicker arm-chair and puffed clouds of smoke towards the comfortable shelves of books.

"You want a holiday," he remarked.

"A holiday?" echoed Michael fretfully. "What's the good of a holiday with my mater at some beastly seaside place?"

"Oh, come," said the priest, smiling. "You'll be able to probe the orthodoxy of the neighbouring clergy."

"Oh, no really, it's nothing to laugh at, Mr. Viner. You've no idea how beastly it is to dawdle about in a crowd of people, and then at the end go back to another term of school. I'm sick of everything. Will you lend me Lee's Dictionary of Ecclesiastical Terms?" added Michael in a voice that contained no accent of hope.

"I'll lend you anything you like, my dear boy," said the priest, "on one condition."

"What's that?"

"Why, that you'll admit life holds a few grains of consolation."

"But it doesn't," Michael declared.

"Wait a bit, I haven't finished. I was going to say—when I tell you that we are going to keep the Assumption this August."

Michael's eyes glittered for a moment with triumph.

"By Jove, how decent." Then they grew dull again. "And I shan't be here. The rotten thing is, too, that my mater wants to go abroad. Only she says she couldn't leave me alone. But of course she could really."

"Why not stay with a friend—the voluble Chator, for instance, or Martindale, that Solomon of schoolboys, or Rigg who in Medicean days would have been already a cardinal, so admirably does he incline to all parties?"

"I can't ask myself," said Michael. "Their people would think it rum. Besides, Chator's governor has gout, and I wouldn't care to be six weeks with the other two. Oh, I do hate not being grown up."

"What about your friend Alan Merivale? I thought him a very charming youth and refreshingly unpietistic."

"He doesn't know the difference between a chasuble and a black gown," said Michael.

"Which seems to me not to matter very much ultimately," put in Mr. Viner.

"No, of course it doesn't. But if one is keen on something and somebody else isn't, it isn't much fun," Michael explained. "Besides, he can't make me out nowadays."

"Surely the incomprehensible is one of the chief charms of faith and friendship."

"And anyway he's going abroad to Switzerland—and I couldn't possibly fish for an invitation. It is rotten. Everything's always the same."

"Except in the Church of England. There you have an almost blatant variety," suggested the priest.

"You never will be serious when I want you to be," grumbled Michael.

"Oh, yes I will, and to prove it," said Mr. Viner, "I'm going to make a suggestion of unparagoned earnestness."

"What?"

"Now just let me diagnose your mental condition. You are sick of everything—Thucydides, cabbage, cricket, school, schoolfellows, certificates and life."

"Well, you needn't rag me about it," Michael interrupted.

"In the Middle Ages gentlemen in your psychical perplexity betook themselves either to the Crusades or entered a monastery. Now, why shouldn't you for these summer holidays betake yourself to a monastery? I will write to the Lord Abbot, to your lady mother, and if you consent, to the voluble Chator's lady mother, humbly pointing out and ever praying, etc., etc."

"You're not ragging?" asked Michael suspiciously. "Besides, what sort of a monastery?"

"Oh, an Anglican monastery; but at the same time Benedictines of the most unimpeachable severity. In short, why shouldn't you and Mark Chator go to Clere Abbas on the Berkshire Downs?"

"Are they strict?" enquired Michael. "You know, saying the proper offices and all that, not the Day Hours of the English Church—that rotten Anglican thing."

"Strict!" cried Mr. Viner. "Why, they're so strict that St. Benedict himself, were he to abide again on earth, would seriously consider a revision of his rules as interpreted by Dom Cuthbert Manners, O.S.B., the Lord Abbot of Clere."

"It would be awfully ripping to go there," said Michael enthusiastically.

"Well then," said Mr. Viner, "it shall be arranged. Meanwhile confer with the voluble and sacerdotal Chator on the subject."

The disappointment of the ungranted certificate, the ineffable tedium of endless school, seaside lodgings and all the weighty ills of Michael's oppressed soul vanished on that wine-gold July noon when Michael and Chator stood untrammelled by anything more than bicycles and luggage upon the platform of the little station that dreamed its trains away at the foot of the Downs.

"By Jove, we're just like pilgrims," said Michael, as his gaze followed the aspiring white road which rippled upward to green summits quivering in the haze of summer. The two boys left their luggage to be fetched later by the Abbey marketing-cart, mounted their bicycles, waved a good-bye to the friendly porter beaming among the red roses of the little station and pressed energetically their obstinate pedals. After about half a mile's ascent they jumped from their machines and walked slowly upwards until the station and clustering hamlet lay breathless below them like a vision drowned deep in a crystal lake. As they went higher a breeze sighed in the sun-parched grasses, and the lines and curves of the road intoxicated them with naked beauty.

"I like harebells almost best of any flowers," said Michael. "Do you?"

"They're awfully like bells," observed Chator.

"I wouldn't care if they weren't," said Michael. "It's only in London I want things to be like other things."

Chator looked puzzled.

"I can't exactly explain what I mean," Michael went on.

"But they make me want to cry just because they aren't like anything. You won't understand what I mean if I explain ever so much. Nobody could. But when I see flowers on a lovely road like this, I get sort of frightened whether God won't grow tired of bothering about human beings. Because really, you know, Chator, there doesn't seem much good in our being on the earth at all."

"I think that's a heresy," pronounced Chator. "I don't know which one, but I'll ask Dom Cuthbert."

"I don't care if it is heresy. I believe it. Besides, religion must be finding out things for yourself that have been found out already."

"Finding out for yourself," echoed Chator with a look of alarm. "I say, you're an absolute Protestant."

"Oh, no I'm not," contradicted Michael. "I'm a Catholic."

"But you set yourself up above the Church."

"When did I?" demanded Michael.

"Just now."

"Because I said that harebells were ripping flowers?"

"You said a lot more than that," objected Chator.

"What did I say?" Michael parried.

"Well, I can't exactly remember what you said."

"Then what's the use of saying I'm a Protestant?" cried Michael in triumph. "I think I'll play footer again next term," he added inconsequently.

"I jolly well would," Chator agreed. "You ought to have played last football term."

"Except that I like thinking," said Michael. "Which is rotten in the middle of a game. It's jolly decent going to the monastery, isn't it? I could keep walking on this road for ever without getting tired."

"We can ride again now," said Chator.

"Well, don't scorch, because we'll miss all the decent flowers if you do," said Michael.

Then silently for awhile they breasted the slighter incline of the summit.

"Only six weeks of these ripping holidays," Michael sighed. "And then damned old school again."

"Hark!" shouted Chator suddenly. "I hear the Angelus."

Both boys dismounted and listened. Somewhere, indeed, a bell was chiming, but a bell of such quality that the sound of it through the summer was like a cuckoo's song in its unrelation to place. Michael and Chator murmured their salute of the Incarnation, and perhaps for the first time Michael half realized the mysterious condescension of God. Here, high up on these downs, the Word became imaginable, a silence of wind and sunlight.

"I say, Chator," Michael began.

"What?"

"Would you mind helping me mark this place where we are?"

"Why?"

"Look here, you won't think I'm pretending? but I believe I was converted at that moment."

Chator's well-known look of alarm that always followed one of Michael's doctrinal or liturgical announcements was more profound than it had ever been before.

"Converted?" he gasped. "What to?"

"Oh, not *to* anything," said Michael. "Only different from what I was just now, and I want to mark the place."

"Do you mean—put up a cross or something?"

"No, not a cross. Because, when I was converted, I felt a sudden feeling of being frightfully alive. I'd rather put a stone and plant harebells round it. We can dig with our spanners. I like stones. They're so frightfully old, and I'd like to think, if I was ever a long way from here, of my stone and the harebells looking at it—every year new harebells and the same old stone."

"Do you know what I think you are?" enquired Chator solemnly. "I think you're a mystic."

"I never can understand what a mystic was," said Michael.

"Nobody can," said Chator encouragingly. "But lots of them were made saints all the same. I don't think you ever will be, because you do put forward the most awfully dangerous doctrines. I do think you ought to be careful about that. I do really."

Chator was spluttering under the embarrassment of his own eloquence, and Michael, delicately amused, looked at him with a quizzical smile. Chator was older than Michael, and by reason of the apoplectic earnestness of his appearance and manner, and the natural goodness of him so sincerely, if awkwardly expressed, he had a certain influence which Michael admitted to himself, however much in the public eye he might affect to patronize Chator from his own intellectual eminence. Along the road of speculation, however, Michael would not allow Chator's right to curb him, and he took a wilful pleasure in galloping ahead over the wildest, loftiest paths. To shock old Chator was Michael's delight; and he never failed to do so.

"You see," Chator spluttered, "it's not so much what you say now; nobody would pay any attention to you, and I know you don't mean half what you say; but later on you'll begin to believe in all these heretical ideas of your own. You'll end up by being an Agnostic. Oh, yes you will," he raged with torrential prophecies, as Michael leaned over the seat of his bicycle laughing consumedly. "You'll go on and on wondering this and that and improving the doctrines of the Church until you improve them right away."

"You are a funny old ass. You really are," gurgled Michael. "And what's so funny to me is that just when I had a moment of really believing you dash in with your warnings and nearly spoil it all. By Jove, did you see that Pale Clouded Yellow?" he shouted suddenly. "By Jove, I haven't seen one in England for an awful long time. I think I'll begin collecting butterflies again."

Disputes of doctrine were flung to the wind that sang in their ears as they mounted their bicycles and coasted swiftly from the bare green summits of the downs into a deep lane overshadowed by oak-trees. Soon they came to the Abbey gates, or rather to the place where the Abbey gates would one day rise in Gothic commemoration of the slow subscriptions of the faithful. At present the entrance was only marked by a stony road disappearing abruptly at the behest of a painted finger-post into verdurous solitudes. After wheeling their bicycles for about a quarter of a winding mile, the two boys came to a large open space in the wood and beheld Clere Abbey, a long low wooden building set as piously near to the overgrown foundations of old Clere Abbey as was possible.

"What a rotten shame," cried Michael, "that they can't build a decent Abbey. Never mind, I think it's going to be rather good sport here."

They walked up to the door that seemed too massive for the flimsy pile to which it gave entrance, and pealed the large bell that hung by the side. Michael was pleased to observe a grille through which peered the eyes of the monastic porter, inquisitive of the wayfarers. Then a bolt shot back, the door opened, and Michael and Chator entered the religious house.

"I'm Brother Ambrose," said the porter, a stubby man with a flat pock-marked face whose ugliness was redeemed by an expression of wonderful innocence. "Dom Cuthbert is expecting you in the Abbot's Parlour."

Michael and Chator followed Brother Ambrose through a pleasant book-lined hall into the paternal haunt where the Lord Abbot of Clere sat writing at a roll-top desk. He rose to greet the boys, who with reverence perceived him to be a tall dark angular man with glowing eyes that seemed very deeply set on either side of his great hooked nose. He could scarcely have been over thirty-five years of age, but he moved with a languid awkwardness that made him seem older. His voice was very remote and melodious as he welcomed them. Michael looked anxiously at Chator to see if he followed any precise ritual of salutation, but Dom Cuthbert solved the problem by shaking hands at once and motioning them to wicker chairs beside the empty hearth.

"Pleasant ride?" enquired Dom Cuthbert.

"Awfully decent," said Michael. "We heard the Angelus a long way off."

"A lovely bell," murmured Dom Cuthbert. "Tubular. It was given to us by the Duke of Birmingham. Come along, I'll show you the Abbey, if you're not too tired."

"Rather not," Michael and Chator declared.

The Abbot led the way into the book-lined hall.

"This is the library. You can read here as much as you like. The brethren sit here at recreation-time. This is the refectory," he went on, with distant chimings in his tone.

The two boys gazed respectfully at the bare trestle table and the raised reading-desk and the picture of St. Benedict.

"Of course we haven't much room yet," Dom Cuthbert continued. "In fact we have very little. People are very suspicious of monkery."

He smiled tolerantly, and his voice faded almost out of the refectory, as if it would soothe the harsh criticism of the world, hence infinitely remote.

"But one day"—from worldly adventure his voice came back renewed with hope— "one day, when we have some money, we shall build a real Abbey."

"This is awfully ripping though, isn't it?" observed Michael with sympathetic encouragement.

"I dare say the founder of the Order was never so well housed," agreed the Abbot.

Dom Cuthbert led them to the guest-chamber, from which opened three diminutive bedrooms.

"Your cells," the monk said. "But of course you'll feed in here," he added, indicating the small bare room in which they stood with so wide a sweep of his ample sleeve that the matchboarded ceiling soared into vast Gothic twilights and the walls were of stone. Michael was vaguely reminded of Mr. Prout and his inadequate oratory.

"The guest-brother is Dom Gilbert," continued the Abbot. "Come and see the cloisters."

They passed from the guest-room behind the main building and saw that another building formed there the second side of a quadrangle. The other two sides were still open to the hazel coppice that here encroached upon the Abbey. However, there was traceable the foundations of new buildings to complete the quadrangle, and a mass of crimson hollyhocks were shining with rubied chalices in the quiet sunlight. For all its incompleteness, this was a strangely beautiful corner of the green world.

"Are these the cloisters?" Michael asked.

"One day, one day," replied Dom Cuthbert. "A little rough at present, but before I die I'm sure there will be a mighty edifice in this wood to the glory of God and His saints."

"I'd like it best that way," said Michael. "Not all at once."

He felt an imaginative companionship with the aspirations of the Abbot.

"Now we'll visit the Chapel," said Dom Cuthbert. "We built the Chapel with our own hands of mud and stone and laths. You'll like the Chapel. Sometimes I feel quite sorry to think of leaving it for the great Abbey Church we shall one day build with the hands of workmen."

The Chapel was reached by a short cloister of primitive construction, and it was the simplest purest place of worship that Michael had ever seen. It seemed to have gathered beneath its small roof the whole of peace. On one side the hazel bushes grew so close that the windows opened on to the mysterious green heart of life. Two curtains worked with golden blazonries divided the quire from the congregation.

"This is where you'll sit," said Dom Cuthbert, pointing to two kneeling-chairs on either side of the opening into the quire. "Perhaps you'll say a prayer now for the Order. The prayers of children travel very swiftly to God."

Dom Cuthbert passed to the Abbot's stall to kneel, while Michael and Chator knelt on the chairs. When they had prayed for awhile, the Abbot took them into the sacristy and showed them the vestments and the sacred vessels of the altar, and from the sacristy door they passed into a straight woodland way.

"The Abbot's walk," said Dom Cuthbert, with a beautiful smile. "The brethren cut this wonderful path during their hours of recreation. I cannot envy any cloisters with this to walk in. How soft is the moss beneath our feet, and in Spring how loudly the birds sing here. The leaves come very early, too, and linger very late. It is a wonderful path. Now I must go and work. I have a lot of letters to write. Explore the woods and the downs and enjoy yourselves. You'll find the rules that the guests must observe pinned to the wall of the guest-room. Enjoy yourselves and be content."

The tall figure of the monk with its languid awkwardness of gait disappeared from the Abbot's walk, and the two boys, arm-in-arm, wandered off in the opposite direction.

"Everything was absolutely correct," burbled Chator. "Oh, yes, absolutely. Not at all Anglican. Perfectly correct. I'm glad. I'm really very glad. I was a bit afraid at first it might be Anglican. But it's not—oh, no, not at all."

In the guest-chamber they read the rules for guests, and discovered to their mortification that they were not expected to be present at Matins and Lauds.

"I was looking forward to getting up at two o'clock," said Michael. "Perhaps Dom Cuthbert will let us sometimes. It's really much easier to get up at two o'clock than five. Mass is at half-past five, and we must go to that."

Dom Gilbert, the guest-brother, came in with plates of bread and cheese while the boys were reading the rules, and they questioned him about going to Matins. He laughed and said they would have as much church as they wished without being quite such strict Benedictines as that. Michael was not sure whether he liked Dom Gilbert—he was such a very practical monk.

"If you go to Mass and Vespers and Compline every day," said Dom Gilbert, "you'll do very well. And please be punctual for your meals."

Michael and Chator looked injured.

"Breakfast after Mass. Bread and cheese at twelve. Cup of tea at five, if you're in. Supper at eight."

Dom Gilbert left them abruptly to eat their bread and cheese alone.

"He's rather a surly chap," grumbled Michael. "He doesn't seem to me the right one to have chosen for guest-brother at all. I had a lot I wanted to ask him. For one thing I don't know where the lav. is. I think he's a rotten guest-brother."

The afternoon passed in a walk along the wide ridge of the downs through the amber of this fine summer day. Several hares were seen and a kestrel, while Chator disposed very volubly of the claims of several Anglican clergymen to Catholicism. After tea in the hour of recreation they met the other monks, Dom Gregory the organist, Brother George and Brother William. It was not a very large monastery.

Chator found the Vespers somewhat trying to his curiosity, because owing to the interposition of the curtain he was unable to criticize the behaviour of the monks in quire. This made him very fidgety, and rather destroyed Michael's sense of peace. However, Chator restrained his ritualistic ardour very well at Compline, which in the dimness of the starlit night was a magical experience, as one by one with raised cowls the monks entered in black procession and silence absolute. Michael, where he knelt in the ante-chapel, was profoundly moved by the intimate responses and the severe Compline hymn. He liked, too, the swift departure to bed without chattering good-nights to spoil the solemnity of the last Office. Even Chator kept all conversation for the morning, and Michael felt he had never lain down upon a couch so truly sanctified, nor ever risen from one so pure as when Dom Gilbert knocked with a hammer on the door and, standing dark against the milk-white dawn, murmured 'Pax vobiscum.'

Chapter VII: *Cloven Hoofmarks*

IN the first fortnight of their stay at Clere Abbas Michael and Chator lived like vagabond hermits rejoicing in the freedom of fine weather. Mostly they went for long walks over the downs and through the woodlands of the southern slope. To the monks at recreation time they would recount their adventures with gamekeepers and contumacious farmers, their discoveries of flowers and birds and butterflies, their entertainment at remote cottage homes and the hospitalities of gipsy camps. To be sure they would often indulge in theological discussions, and sometimes, when caught by the azure-footed dusk in unfamiliar lanes, they would chant plainsong to the confusion of whatever ghostly pursuers, whether Dryads or mediæval fiends or early Victorian murderers, that seemed to dog their footsteps. So much nowadays did the unseen world mingle with the ordinary delights of youth.

"Funny thing," said Michael to Chator. "When I was a kid I used to be frightened at night—always. Then for a long time I wasn't frightened at all, and now again I have a queer feeling just after sunset, a sort of curious dampness inside me. Do you ever have it?"

"I only have it when you start me off," said Chator. "But it goes when we sing 'Te lucis ante terminum' or chant the Nicene Creed or anything holy."

"Yes, it goes with me," Michael agreed dubiously. "But if I drive it away it comes back in the middle of the night. I have all sorts of queer feelings. Sometimes I feel as if there wasn't any me at all, and I'm surprized to see a letter come addressed to me. But when I see a letter I've written, I'm still more surprized. Do you have that feeling? Then often I feel as if all we were doing or saying at a certain moment had been done or said before. Then at other times I have to hold on to a tree or hurt myself with something just to prove I'm there. And then sometimes I think nothing is impossible for me. I feel absolutely great, as if I were Shakespeare. Do you ever have that feeling?"

But Chator was either not sufficiently introspective so to resolve his moods, or else he was too simply set on his own naive religion for his personality to plunge haphazard into such spiritual currents uncharted.

The pleasantest time of the monastic week was Sunday afternoon, when Dom Cuthbert, very lank and pontifical, would lean back in the deepest wicker chair of the library to listen to various Thoughts culled by the brethren from their week's reading. The Thought he adjudged best was with a diamond pencil immortalized upon a window-pane, and the lucky discoverer derived as much satisfaction from the verdict as was compatible with Benedictine humility. Dom Cuthbert allowed Michael and Chator to share in these occasions, and he evidently enjoyed the variety of choice which displayed so nicely the characters of his flock.

One afternoon Michael chose for his excerpt Don Quixote's exclamation, "How these enchanters hate me, Sancho," with Sancho's reply, "O dismal and ill-minded enchanters."

The brethren laughed very loudly at this, for though they were English monks, and might have been considered eccentric by the Saxon world, their minds really ran on lines of sophisticated piety over platitudinous sleepers of thought. Michael blushed defiantly, and looked at Dom Cuthbert for comprehension.

"Hark at the idealist's complaint of disillusionment by the Prince of Darkness," said Dom Cuthbert, smiling.

"It's not a complaint," Michael contradicted. "It's just a remark. That's why I chose it. Besides, it gives me a satisfied feeling. Words often make me feel hungry."

The monks interrupted him with more laughter, and Michael, furiously self-conscious, left the library and went to sit alone in the stillest part of the hazel coppice.

But when he came back in the silent minutes before Vespers he read his sentence on the window-pane, and blinked half tearfully at the westering sun. He never had another Thought enshrined, because he was for ever after this trying to find sentences that would annoy Dom Gilbert, whom he suspected of leading the laughter. Visitors began to come to the Abbey now—and the two boys were much interested in the people who flitted past almost from day to day. Among them was Mr. Prout who kept up a duet of volubility with Chator from morning to night for nearly a week, at the end of which he returned to his Bournemouth bank. These discussions amused Michael most when he was able to break the rhythm of the battledores by knocking down whatever liturgical or theological shuttlecock was being used. He would put forward the most outrageous heresy as his own firm conviction, and scandalize and even alarm poor Mr. Prout, who did not at all relish dogmatic follow-my-leader and prayed for Michael's reckless soul almost as fervidly as for the confusion of the timid and malignant who annually objected to the forthcoming feast of the Assumption at St. Bartholomew's. Mr. Prout, however, was only one of a series of ritualistic young men who prattled continually of vestments and ceremonies and ornaments, until Michael began to resent their gossip and withdraw from their society into the woods, there to dream, staring up at the green and blue arch above him, of the past here in wind-stirred solitude so much the more real. Michael was a Catholic because Catholicism assured him of continuity and shrouded him with a sensuous austerity, but in these hours of revolt he found himself wishing for the old days with Alan. He was fond enough of Chator, but to Chator everything was so easy, and when one day a letter arrived to call him back to his family earlier than he expected, Michael was glad. The waning summer was stimulating his imagination with warm noons and gusty twilights; Chator's gossip broke the spell.

Michael went for solitary walks on the downs, where he loved to lie in hollows and watch the grasses fantastically large against the sky, and the bulky clouds with their slow bewitching motion. He never went to visit sentimentally the spot where stone and harebell commemorated his brief experience of faith's profundity, for he dreaded lest indifference should rob him of a perfect conception. He knew very well even already the dangerous chill familiarity of repetition. Those cloud-enchanted days of late summer made him listlessly aware of fleeting impulses, and simultaneously dignified with incommunicable richness the passivity and even emptiness of his condition. On the wide spaces of the downs he wandered luxuriously irresolute; his mind, when for a moment it goaded itself into an effort of concentration, faltered immediately, so that dead chivalries, gleaming down below in the rainy dusk of the valleys, suffered in the very instant of perception a transmutation into lamplit streets; and the wind's dull August booming made embattled drums and fanfares romantic no more than music heard in London on the way home from school. Everything came to seem impossible and intangible; Michael could not conceive that he ever was or ever would be in a class-room again, and almost immediately afterwards he would wonder whether he ever had been or ever would be anywhere else. He began to imagine himself grown up, but this was a nightmare thought, because he would either realize himself decrepit with his own young mind or outwardly the same as he was now with a mind hideously distorted by knowledge and sin. He could never achieve a consistent realization that would give him definite ambitions. He longed to make up his mind to aim at some profession, and the more he longed the more hopeless did it seem to try to fit any existing profession with the depressing idea of himself grown up. Then he would relax his whole being and let himself be once more bewitched into passivity by clouds and waving grasses.

Upon this mental state of Michael intruded one day a visitor to the Abbey. A young man with spectacles and a pear-shaped face, who wore grey flannel shirts that depressed Michael unendurably, made a determined effort to gain his confidence. The more shy that Michael became, the more earnestly did this young man press him with intimate questions about his physical well-being. For Michael it was a strange and odiously embarrassing experience. The young man, whose name was Garrod, spoke of his home in Hornsey and invited Michael to stay with him. Michael shuddered at the idea of staying in a strange suburb: strange suburbs had always seemed to him desolate, abominable and insecure. He always visualized a draughty and ill-lighted railway platform, a rickety and gloomy omnibus, countless Nonconformist chapels and infrequent policemen. Garrod spoke of his work on Sundays at a church that was daily gaining adherents, of a dissolute elder brother and an Agnostic father. Michael could have cried aloud his unwillingness to visit Garrod. But the young man was persistent; the young man was sure that Michael, from ignorance, was leading an unhealthy life. Garrod spoke of ignorance with ferocity: he trampled on it with polytechnical knowledge, and pelted it with all sorts of little books that afflicted Michael with nausea. Michael loathed Garrod, and resented his persistent instructions, his offers to solve lingering physical perplexities. For Michael Garrod defiled the country by his cockney complacency, his attacks upon public schools, his unpleasant interrogations. Michael longed for Alan that together they might rag this worm who wriggled so obscenely into the secret places of a boy's mind.

"Science is all the go nowadays," said Garrod. "And Science is what we want. Science and Religion. Some think they don't go together. Don't they? I think they do then."

"I hate science," said Michael. "Except for doctors, of course—I suppose they've got to have it," he added grudgingly. "At St. James' the Modern fellows are nearly always bounders."

"But don't you want to know what your body's made of?" demanded Garrod.

"I don't want to be told. I know quite enough for myself."

"Well, would you like to read———"

"No, I don't want to read anything," interrupted Michael.

"But have you read———"

"The only books I like," expostulated Michael, "are the books I find for myself."

"But you aren't properly educated."

"I'm at a public school," said Michael proudly.

"Yes, and public schools have got to go very soon."

"Who says so?" demanded Michael fiercely.

"We say so. The people."

"The people?" echoed Michael. "What people? Why, if public schools were done away with we shouldn't have any gentlemen."

"You're getting off of the point," said Garrod. "You don't understand what I'm driving at. You're a fellow I took a fancy to right off, as you might say. I don't want to see you ruin your health, for the want of the right word at the right moment. Oh, yes, I know."

"Look here," said Michael bluntly, "I don't want to be rude, but I don't want to talk about this any more. It makes me feel beastly."

"False modesty is the worst thing we've got to fight against," declared Garrod.

So the argument continued, while all the time the zealous young man would fling darts of information that however much Michael was unwilling to receive them generally stuck fast. Michael was relieved when Garrod passed on his way, and he vowed to himself never to run the risk of meeting him again.

The visit of Garrod opened for Michael a door to uneasy speculation. At his private school he had known the hostility of 'cads,' and later on he had been aware of the existence of 'bounders'; the cads were always easily defeated by force of arms, but this sudden attack upon his intimacy by a bounder was disquieting and difficult to deal with. He resented Garrod's iconoclasm, resented it furiously in retrospect, wishing that he had parried more icily his impudent thrusts; and he could almost have rejoiced in Garrod's reappearance that with disdain he might have wounded the fellow incurably. Yet he had a feeling that Garrod might have turned out proof against the worst weapons he knew how to use, and the memory of the 'blighter's' self-confidence was demoralizing to Michael's conception of superiority. The vision of a world populated by hostile Garrods rose up, and some of the simplicity of life vanished irredeemably, so that Michael took refuge in dreams of his own fashioning, where in a feudal world the dreamer rode at the head of mankind. Lying awake in the intense blackness of his cell, Michael troubled himself once more with his identity, wishing that he knew more about himself and his father, wishing that his mother were not growing more remote every day, wondering whether Stella over in Germany was encountering Garrods and praying hard with a sense of impotency in the darkness. He tried to make up his mind to consult Dom Cuthbert, but the lank, awkward monk, fond though he was of him, seemed unapproachable by daylight, and the idea of consulting him, still more of confessing to him, never crystallized.

These were still days bedewed with the approach of Autumn; milkwhite at morn and at noon breathless with a silver intensity that yearned upwards against an azure too ethereal, they floated sadly into night with humid, intangible draperies of mist. These were days that forbade Michael to walk afield, and that with haunting, autumnal birdsong held him in a trance. He would find himself at the day's end conscious of nothing but a remembrance of new stubble trodden mechanically with languors attendant, and it was only by a great effort that he brought himself to converse with the monks working among the harvest or for the Nativity of the Blessed Virgin to pick heavy white chrysanthemums from the stony garden of the Abbey.

Michael was the only guest staying in the Abbey on the vigil, and he sat almost in the entrance of the quire between the drawn curtains, not very much unlike the devout figure of some youthful donor in an old Italian picture, sombre against the blazing Vespers beyond. Michael was always hoping for a direct manifestation from above to reward the effort of faith, although he continually reproved himself for this desire and flouted his weakness. He used to gaze into the candles until they actually did seem to burn with angelic eyes that made his heart leap in expectation of the sign awaited; but soon fancy would betray him, and they would become candles again merely flickering.

On this September dusk there were crimson shadows of sunset deepening to purple in the corners of the chapel; the candles were very bright; the brethren in the stalls sang with austere fervour; the figure of Dom Cuthbert veiled from awkwardness by the heavy white cope moved before the altar during the censing of the Magnificat with a majesty that filled the small quire; the thurible tinkled its perfumed harmonies; and above the contentment of the ensuing hush blackbirds were heard in the garden or seen slipping to and fro like shadows across the windows.

Michael at this moment realized that there was a seventh monk in the quire, and wondered vaguely how he had failed to notice this new-comer before. Immediately after being made aware of his presence he caught the stranger's eye, and blushed so deeply that to cover his confusion he turned over the pages of a psalter. Curiosity made him look up again, but the new monk was devoutly wrapped in contemplation, nor did Michael catch his eye again during the Office. At supper he enquired about the new-comer of Dom Gilbert, who reproved him for inquisitiveness, but told him he was called Brother Aloysius. Again at Compline Michael caught his glance, and for a long time that night in the darkness he saw the eyes of Brother Aloysius gleaming very blue.

On the next day Michael, wandering by the edge of the hazel coppice, came upon Brother Aloysius with deep-stained mouth and hands gathering blackberries.

"Who are you?" asked the monk. "You gave me a very funny look at Vespers."

Michael thought this was an extremely unusual way for a monk, even a new monk, to speak, and hesitated a moment before he explained who he was.

"I suppose you can help me pick blackberries. I suppose that isn't against the rules."

"I often help the brothers," said Michael simply. "But I don't much care for picking blackberries. Still, I don't mind helping you."

Michael had an impulse to leave Brother Aloysius, but his self-consciousness prevented him from acting on it, and he kept the picker company in silence while the blackberries dropped lusciously into the basket.

"Feel my hand," said Brother Aloysius suddenly. "It's as hot as hell."

This time Michael stared in frank astonishment.

"Well, you needn't look so frightened," said the monk. "You don't look so very good yourself."

"Well, of course I'm not good," said Michael. "Only I think it's funny for a monk to swear. You don't mind my saying so, do you?"

"I don't mind. I don't mind anything," said Brother Aloysius.

Tension succeeded this statement, a tension that Michael longed to break; but he could do no more than continue to pick the blackberries.

"I suppose you wonder why I'm a monk?" demanded Brother Aloysius.

Michael looked at his questioner's pale face, at the uncomfortable eyes gleaming blue, at the full stained mouth and the long feverish hands dyed with purple juice.

"Why are you?" he asked.

"Well, I thought I'd try if anything could make me feel good, and then you looked at me in Chapel and set me off again."

"I set you off?" stammered Michael.

"Yes, you with your big girl's eyes, just like a girl I used to live with. Oh, you needn't look so proper. I expect you've often thought about girls. I did at your age. Three months with girls, three months with priests. Girls and priests—that's my life. When I was tired of women, I became religious, and when I was tired of Church, I took to women. It was a priest told me to come here to see if this would cure me, and now, damn you, you come into Chapel and stare and set me thinking of the Seven Sisters Road on that wet night I saw her last. That's where she lives, and you look exactly like her. God! you're the image of her. You might almost be her ghost incarnate."

Brother Aloysius caught hold of Michael's arm and spoke through clenched teeth. In Michael's struggle to free himself the basket of blackberries was upset, and they trod the spilt fruit into the grass. Michael broke away finally and gasped angrily:

"Look here, I'm not going to stay here. You're mad."

He ran from the monk into the depths of the wood, not stopping until he reached a silent glade. Here on the moss he sat panting, horrified. Yet when he came to compose the sentences in which he should tell Dom Cuthbert of his experience with the new monk, he found himself wishing that he had stayed to hear more. He actually enjoyed in retrospect the humiliation of the man, and his heart beat with the excitement of hearing more. Slowly he turned to seek again Brother Aloysius.

"You may as well tell me some more, now you've begun," said Michael.

For three or four days Michael was always in the company of Brother Aloysius, plying him with questions that sounded abominable to himself, when he remembered with what indignation he had rejected Garrod's offer of knowledge. Brother Aloysius spared no blushes, whether of fiery shame or furtive desire, and piece by piece Michael learned the fabric of vice. He was informed coldly of facts whose existence he had hitherto put down to his own most solitary and most intimate imaginations. Every vague evil that came wickedly before sleep was now made real with concrete examples; the vilest ideas, that hitherto he had considered peculiar to himself and perhaps a few more sadly tempted dreamers tossing through the vulnerable hours of the night, were commonplace to Brother Aloysius, whose soul was twisted, whose mind was debased to such an extent that he could boast of his delight in making the very priest writhe and wince in the Confessional.

Conversations with Brother Aloysius were sufficiently thrilling journeys, and Michael was always ready to follow his footsteps as one might follow a noctambulatory cat. The Seven Sisters Road was the scene of most of his adventures, if adventures they could be called, these dissolute pilgrimages. Michael came to know this street as one comes to know the street of a familiar dream. He walked along it in lavender sunrises watching the crenellated horizon of housetops; he sauntered through it slowly on dripping midnights, and on foggy November afternoons he speculated upon the windows with their aqueous sheen of incandescent gas. On summer dusks he pushed his way through the fetid population that thronged it, smelling the odour of stale fruit exposed for sale, and on sad grey Sabbaths he saw the ill-corseted servant girls treading down the heels of their ugly boots, and plush-clad children who continually dropped Sunday-school books in the mud.

And not only was Michael cognizant of the sordid street's exterior. He heard the creak of bells by blistered doors, he tripped over mats in narrow gloomy passages and felt his way up stale rickety stairs. Michael knew many rooms in this street of dreams: but they were all much alike with their muslin and patchouli, their aspidistras and yellowing photographs. The ribbed pianos tintinnabulated harshly with songs cut from the squalid sheets of Sunday papers: in unseen basements children whined, while on the mantelpiece garish vases rattled to the vibration of traffic.

Michael was also aware of the emotional crises that occur in the Seven Sisters Road, from the muttered curses of the old street-walkers with their crape bonnets cocked awry and their draggled musty skirts to Brother Aloysius himself shaken with excess of sin in colloquy with a ghostly voice upon a late winter dawn.

"A ghost?" he echoed incredulously.

"It's true. I heard a voice telling me to go back. And when I went back, there she was sitting in the arm-chair with the antimacassar round her shoulders because it was cold, and the carving-knife across her knees, waiting up to do for the fellow that was keeping her. I reckon it was God sent me back to save her."

Even Michael in his vicious mood could not tolerate this hysterical blasphemy, and he scoffed at the supernatural explanation. But Brother Aloysius did not care whether he was believed or not. He himself was sufficient audience to himself, ready to applaud and condemn with equal exaggeration of feeling.

After a week of self-revelation Brother Aloysius suddenly had spiritual qualms about his behaviour, and announced to Michael that he must go to Confession and free himself from the oppressive responsibility of his sin. Michael did not like the thought of Dom Cuthbert being aware of the way in which his last days at the monastery had been spent, and hoped that Brother Aloysius would confess in as general a manner as possible. Yet even so he feared that the perspicacious Abbot would guess the partner of his penitent, and, notwithstanding the sacred impersonality of the Confessional, regard Michael with an involuntary disgust. However, the confession, with all its attendant pangs of self-reproach, passed over, and Michael was unable to detect the slightest alteration in Dom Cuthbert's attitude towards him. But he avoided Brother Aloysius so carefully during the remainder of his stay, that it was impossible to test the Abbot's knowledge as directly as he could have wished.

The night before Michael was to leave the monastery, a great gale blew from the south-west and kept him wide awake hour after hour until the bell for Matins. He felt that on this his last night it would be in order for him to attend the Office. So he dressed quickly and hurried through the wind-swept corridor into the Chapel. Here, in a severity of long droning psalms, he tried to purge his mind of all it had acquired from the shamelessness of Brother Aloysius. He was so far successful that he could look Dom Cuthbert fearlessly in the face when he bade him good-bye next day, and as he coasted over the downs through the calm September sunlight, he to himself seemed like the country washed by the serene radiance of the tempest's aftermath.

Chapter VIII: *Mirrors*

MICHAEL somehow felt shy when he heard his mother's voice telling him to come into her room. He had run upstairs and knocked excitedly at her door before the shyness overwhelmed him, but it was too late not to enter, and he sat down to give her the account of his holidays. Rather dull it seemed, and robbed of all vitality by the barrier which both his mother and he hastened to erect between themselves.

"Well, dear, did you enjoy yourself at this Monastery?"

"Oh, rather."

"Is the—what do you call him?—the head monk a nice man?"

"Oh, yes, awfully decent."

"And your friend Chator, did he enjoy himself?"

"Oh, rather. Only he had to go before me. Did you enjoy yourself abroad, mother?"

"Very much, dear, thank you. We had lovely weather all the time."

"We had awfully ripping weather too."

"Have you got everything ready for school in the morning?"

"There's nothing much to get. I suppose I'll go into Cray's—the Upper Fifth. Do you want me now, mother?"

"No, dear, I have one or two letters to write."

"I think I'll go round and see if Chator's home yet. You don't mind?"

"Don't be late for dinner."

"Oh, no, rather not."

Going downstairs from his mother's room, Michael had half an impulse to turn back and confide in her the real account of his holidays. But on reflection he protested to himself that his mother looked upon him as immaculate, and he felt unwilling to disturb by such a revolutionary step the approved tranquillities of maternal ignorance.

Mr. Cray, his new form-master, was a man of distinct personality, and possessed a considerable amount of educative ability; but unfortunately for Michael the zest of classics had withered in his heart after his disappointment over the Oxford and Cambridge Certificate. Therefore Mr. Cray with his bright archæology and chatty scholarship bored Michael more profoundly than any of his masters so far had bored him. Mr. Cray resented this attitude very bitterly, being used to keenness in his form, and Michael's dreary indolence, which often came nearer to insolence, irritated him. As for the plodding, inky sycophants who fawned upon Mr. Cray's informativeness, Michael regarded them with horror and contempt. He sat surrounded by the butts and bugbears of his school-life. All the boys whose existence he had deplored seemed to have clambered arduously into the Upper Fifth just to enrage him with the sight of their industrious propinquity. There they sat with their scraggy wrists protruding from shrinking coat-sleeves, with ambitious noses glued to their books, with pens and pencils neatly disposed for demonstrative annotation, and nearly all of them conscious of having figured in the school-list with the printed bubble of the Oxford and Cambridge Higher Certificate beside their names. Contemplating them in the mass, Michael scarcely knew how he would endure another dusty year of school.

"And now we come to the question of the Homeric gate—the Homeric gate, Fane, when you can condescend to our level," said Mr. Cray severely.

"I'm listening, sir," said Michael wearily.

"Of course the earliest type of gate was without hinges—without hinges, Fane! Very much like your attention, Fane!"

Several sycophants giggled at this, and Michael, gazing very earnestly at Mr. Cray's benign but somewhat dirty bald head, took a bloody revenge upon those in reach of his javelin of quadruple penholders.

"For Monday," said Mr. Cray, when he had done with listening to the intelligent advice of his favourite pupils on the subject of gates ancient and modern, "for Monday the essay will be on Patriotism."

Michael groaned audibly.

"Isn't there an alternative subject, sir?" he gloomily enquired.

"Does Fane dislike abstractions?" said Mr. Cray. "Curious! Well, if Fane wishes for an alternative subject, of course Fane must be obeyed. The alternative subject will be An Examination into the Fundamental Doctrines of Hegelian Idealism. Does that suit Fane?"

"Very well indeed," said Michael, who had never heard of Hegel until that moment, but vowed to himself that somehow between this muggy Friday afternoon and next Monday morning he would conquer the fellow's opinions. As a matter of fact, the essay proved perfectly easy with the assistance of The Popular Encyclopedia, though Mr. Cray called it a piece of impudence and looked almost baleful when Michael showed it up.

From this atmosphere of complacent effort Michael withdrew one afternoon to consult Father Viner about his future. Underneath the desire for practical advice was a desire to talk about himself, and Michael was disappointed on arriving at Father Viner's rooms to hear thathe was out. However, learning that there was a prospect of his speedy return, he came in at the landlady's suggestion to amuse himself with a book while he waited.

Wandering round the big bay-windowed room with its odour of tobacco and books, and casting a careless glance at Father Viner's desk, Michael caught sight of his own name in the middle of a neatly written letter on the top of a pile of others. He could not resist taking a longer glance to see the address and verify the allusion to himself, and with this longer glance curiosity conquered so completely the prejudice against prying into other people's correspondence that Michael, breathing nervously under the dread of interruption, took up the letter and read it right through. It was in his present mood of anxiety about himself very absorbing.

CLERE ABBEY,
Michael Mass.

PAX ✠

Dear Brother,

I have been intending to write to you about young Michael Fane ever since he left us, and your letter of enquiry has had the effect of bringing me up to the point.

I hardly know what to tell you. He's a curious youth, very lovable, and with enough brains to make one wish that he might have a vocation for the priesthood. At the same time I noticed while he was with us, especially after the admirable Chator departed, an overwhelming languor which I very much deplored.

He spent much of his time with a very bad hat indeed, whom I have just sent away from Clere. If you ever come across Mr. Henry Meats, be careful of him. Arbuthnot of St. Aidan's, Holloway, sent him to me. You know Arbuthnot's expansive (and for his friends expensive) Christianity. This last effort of his was a snorter, a soft, nasty, hysterical, little blob of rice. I ought to have seen through the fellow before I did. Heaven knows I get enough of the tag-rag of the Movement trying to be taken on at Clere. I suppose the monastic life will always make an imperishable appeal to the worst, and, thank God, some of the best. I mention this fellow to you because I'm afraid he and Michael may meet again, and I don't at all like the idea of their acquaintanceship progressing, especially as it was unluckily begun beneath a religious roof. So keep an eye on Mr. Henry Meats. He's really bad.

Another fellow I don't recommend for Michael is Percy Garrod. Not that I think there is much danger in that direction, for I fancy Michael was very cold with him. Percy is a decent, honest, hard-working, common ass, with a deep respect for the Pope and the Polytechnic. He's a trifle zealous, however, with bastard information about physical science, and not at all the person I should choose to lecture Michael on the complications of adolescence.

We are getting on fairly well at Clere, but it's hard work trying to make this country believe there is the slightest necessity for the contemplative life. I hope all goes well with you and your work.

Yours affectionately in Xt.,
Cuthbert Manners, O.S.B.

Poor Michael. His will be a difficult position one day. I feel on re-reading this letter that I've told you nothing you don't already know. But he's one of those elusive boys who have lived within themselves too much and too long.

Michael put this letter back where he had found it, and wondered how much of the contents would be discussed by Father Viner. He was glad that Brother Aloysius had vanished, because Brother Aloysius had become like a bad dream with which he was unwilling in the future to renew acquaintance. On his own character Dom Cuthbert had not succeeded in throwing very much light—at any rate not in this letter. Father Viner came in to interrupt Michael's meditations, and began at once to discuss the letter.

"The Lord Abbot of Clere thinks you're a dreamer," he began abruptly.

"Does he, Mr. Viner?" echoed Michael, who somehow could never bring himself to the point of addressing the priest as 'Father.' Shyness always overcame his will.

"What do you dream about, young Joseph?"

"Oh, I only think about a good many things, and wonder what I'm going to be and all that," Michael replied. "I don't want to go into the Indian Civil Service or anything with exams. I'm sick of exams. What I most want to do is to get away from school. I'm sick of school, and the fellows in the Upper Fifth are a greasy crowd of swats always sucking up to Cray."

"And who is the gentleman with the crustacean name that attracts these barnacles?"

"Cray? Oh, he's my form-master, and tries to be funny."

"So do I, Michael," confessed Mr. Viner.

"Oh, well, that's different. I'm not bound to listen to you, if I don't want to. But I have to listen to Cray for eighteen hours every week, and he hates me because I won't take notes for his beastly essays. I think I'll ask my mater if I can't leave school after this term."

"And then what would you do?"

"Oh, I don't know. I could settle when I'd left."

"What about Oxford?"

"Well, I could go to Oxford later on."

"I don't think you could quite so easily as you think. Anyway, you'd much better go to Oxford straight from school."

"Eight more terms before I leave. Phew!" Michael groaned. "It's such a terrible waste of time, and I know Oxford's ripping."

"Perhaps something will come along to interest you. And always, dear boy, don't forget you have your religion."

"Yes, I know," said Michael. "But at the Abbey I met some people who were supposed to be religious, and they were pretty good rotters."

The priest looked at him and seemed inclined to let Michael elaborate this topic, but almost immediately he dismissed it with a commonplace.

"Oh, well," Michael sighed, "I suppose something will happen soon to buck me up. I hope so. Perhaps the Kensitites will start making rows in churches again," he went on hopefully. "Will you lend me the Apocryphal Gospels? We're going to have a discussion about them at the De Rebus Ecclesiasticis."

"Oh, the society hasn't broken up?" enquired Mr. Viner.

"Rather not. Only everybody's changed rather. Chator's become frightfully Roman. He was Sarum last term, and he thinks I'm frightfully heretical, only of course I say a lot I don't mean just to rag him. I say, by the way, who wrote 'In a Garden'?"

"It sounds a very general title," commented Mr. Viner, with a smile.

"Well, it's some poem or other."

"Swinburne wrote a poem in the Second Series of Poems and Ballads called 'A Forsaken Garden.' Is that what you mean?"

"Perhaps. Is it a famous poem?"

"Yes, I should say it was distinctly."

"Well, that must be it. Cray tried to be funny about it to-day in form, and said to me, 'Good heavens, haven't you read "In a Garden"?' And I said I'd never heard of it. And then he said in his funny way to the class, 'I suppose you've all read it.' And none of them had, which made him look rather an ass. So he said we'd better read it by next week."

"I can lend you my Swinburne. Only take care of it," said Mr. Viner. "It's a wonderful poem."

In a coign of the cliff between lowland and highland,

At the sea-down's edge between windward

>   *and lee,*
>   *Walled round with rocks as an inland island,*
>   *The ghost of a garden fronts the sea.*

"I say," exclaimed Michael eagerly, "I never knew Swinburne was a really great poet. And fancy, he's alive now."

"Alive, and living at Putney," said Mr. Viner.

"And yet he wrote what you've just said!"

"He wrote that, and many other things too. He wrote:

> *Before the beginning of years*
>   *There came to the making of man*
>   *Time, with a gift of tears;*
>   *Grief, with a glass that ran;*
>   *Pleasure, with pain for leaven,*
>   *Summer, with flowers that fell;*
>   *Remembrance fallen from heaven,*
>   *And madness risen from hell.*"

"Good Lord!" sighed Michael. "And he's in Putney at this very moment."

Michael went home clasping close the black volume, and in his room that night, while the gas jet flamed excitably in defiance of rule, he read almost right through the Second Series of Poems and Ballads. It was midnight when he turned down the gas and sank feverishly into bed. For a long while he was saying to himself isolated lines: *'The wet skies harden, the gates are barred on the summer side.' 'The rose-red acacia that mocks the rose.' 'Sleep, and if life was bitter to thee, brother.' 'For whom all winds are quiet as the sun, all waters as the shore.'*

In school on Monday morning Mr. Cray, to Michael's regret, did not allude to the command that his class should read 'In a Garden.' Michael was desperately anxious at once to tell him how much he had loved the poem and to remind him of the real title, 'A Forsaken Garden.' At last he could bear it no longer and went up flushed with enthusiasm to Mr. Cray's desk, nominally to enquire into an alleged mistake in his Latin Prose, but actually to inform Mr. Cray of his delight in Swinburne. When the grammatical blunder had been discussed, Michael said with as much nonchalance as he could assume:

"I read that poem, sir. I think it's ripping."

"What poem?" repeated Mr. Cray vaguely. "Oh, yes, 'Enoch Arden.'"

"'Enoch Arden,'" stammered Michael. "I thought you said 'In a Garden.' I read 'A Forsaken Garden' by Swinburne."

Mr. Cray put on his most patronizing manner.

"My poor Fane, have you never heard of Enoch Arden? Perhaps you've never even heard of Tennyson?"

"But Swinburne's good, isn't he, sir?"

"Swinburne is very well," said Mr. Cray. "Oh, yes, Swinburne will do, if you like rose-jam. But I don't recommend Swinburne for you, Fane."

Then Mr. Cray addressed his class:

"Did you all read 'Enoch Arden'?"

"Yes, sir," twittered the Upper Fifth.

"Fane, however, with that independence of judgment which distinguishes his Latin Prose from, let us say, the prose of Cicero, preferred to read 'A Forsaken Garden' by one Swinburne."

The Upper Fifth giggled dutifully.

"Perhaps Fane will recite to us his discovery," said Mr. Cray, scratching his scurfy head with the gnawed end of a penholder.

Michael blushed resentfully, and walked back to his desk.

"No?" said Mr. Cray with an affectation of great surprise.

Then he and the Upper Fifth, contented with their superiority, began to chew and rend some tough Greek particles which ultimately became digestible enough to be assimilated by the Upper Fifth; while Mr. Cray himself purred over his cubs, looking not very unlike a mangy old lioness.

"Eight more terms," groaned Michael to himself.

Mr. Cray was not so blind to his pupils' need for mild intellectual excitement, however much he might scorn the easy emotions of Swinburne. He really grew lyrical over Homeric difficulties, and even spoke enthusiastically of Mr. Mackail's translation of the Georgics; but always he managed to conceal the nobility of his theme beneath a mass of what he called 'minor points.' He would create his own rubbish heap and invite the Upper Fifth to scratch in it for pearls. One day a question arose as to the exact meaning of οὐλοχύται in Homer. Michael would have been perfectly content to believe that it meant 'whole barleycorns,' until Mr. Cray suggested that it might be equivalent to the Latin 'mola,' meaning 'grain coarsely ground.' An exhausting discussion followed, illustrated by examples from every sort of writer, all of which had to be taken down in notes in anticipation of a still more exhausting essay on the subject.

"The meal may be trite," said Mr. Cray, "but not the subject," he added, chuckling. "However, I have only touched the fringe of it: you will find the arguments fully set forth in Buttmann's Lexilogus. Who possesses that invaluable work?"

Nobody in the Upper Fifth possessed it, but all anxiously made a note of it, in order to acquire it over the counter of the Book Room downstairs.

"No use," said Mr. Cray. "Buttmann's Lexilogus is now out of print."

Michael pricked up at this. The phrase leant a curious flavour of Romance to the dull book.

"No doubt, however, you will be able to obtain it second-hand," added Mr. Cray.

The notion of tracking down Buttmann's Lexilogus possessed the Upper Fifth. Eagerly after school the diligent ones discussed ways and means. Parties were formed, almost one might say expeditions, to rescue the valuable work from oblivion. Michael stood contemptuously aside from the buzz of self-conscious effort round him, although he had made up his own mind to be one of the first to obtain the book. Levy, however, secured the first copy for fourpence in Farringdon Street, earning for his sharpness much praise. Another boy bought one for three shillings and sixpence in Paddington, the price one would expect to pay, if not a Levy; and there were rumours of a copy in Kensington High Street. To Michael the mart of London from earliest youth had been Hammersmith Broadway, and thither he hurried, hopeful of discovering Buttmann's dingy Lexilogus, for the purchase of which he had thoughtfully begged a sovereign from his mother. Michael did not greatly covet Buttmann, but he was sure that the surplus from three shillings and sixpence, possibly even from fourpence, would be very welcome.

He found at last in a turning off Hammersmith Broadway a wonderful bookshop, whose rooms upon rooms leading into one another were all lined and loaded with every kind of book. The proprietor soon found a copy of Buttmann, which he sold to Michael for half a crown, leaving him with fifteen shillings for himself, since he decided that it would be as well to return his mother at least half a crown from her sovereign. The purchase completed, Michael began to wander round the shop, taking down a book here, a book there, dipping into them from the top of a ladder, sniffing them, clapping their covers together to drive away the dust, and altogether thoroughly enjoying himself, while the daylight slowly faded and street-lamps came winking into ken outside. At last, just as the shop-boy was putting up the shutters, Michael discovered a volume bound in half-morocco of a crude gay blue, that proved on inspection to contain the complete poetical works of Algernon Charles Swinburne, for the sum of seventeen shillings and sixpence.

What was now left of his golden sovereign that should have bought so much beside Buttmann's brown and musty Lexilogus?

Michael approached the proprietor with the volume in his hand.

"How much?" he asked, with a queer choking sensation, a throbbing excitement, for he had never before even imagined the expenditure of seventeen shillings and sixpence on one book.

"What's this?" said the proprietor, putting on his spectacles. "Oh, yes, Swinburne—pirated American edition. Seventeen shillings and sixpence."

"Couldn't you take less?" asked Michael, with a vague hope that he might rescue a shilling for his mother, if not for cigarettes.

"Take less?" repeated the bookseller. "Good gracious, young man, do you know what you'd have to pay for Swinburne's stuff separate? Something like seven or eight pounds, and then they'd be all in different volumes. Whereas here you've got—lemme see—Atalanta in Calydon, Chastelard, Poems and Ballads, Songs before Sunrise, Bothwell, Tristram of Lyonesse, Songs of Two Nations, and heaven knows what not. I call seventeen shillings and sixpence very cheap for what you might almost call a man's life-work. Shall I wrap it up?"

"Yes, please," said Michael, gasping with the effect of the plunge.

But when that night he read

Swallow, my sister, O fair swift swallow,

he forgot all about the cost.

The more of Swinburne that Michael read, the more impatient he grew of school. The boredom of Mr. Cray's class became stupendous; and Michael, searching for some way to avoid it, decided to give up Classics and apply for admission to the History Sixth, which was a small association of boys who had drifted into this appendix for the purpose of defeating the ordinary rules of promotion. For instance, when the Captain of the School Eleven had not attained the privileged Sixth, he was often allowed to enter the History Sixth, in order that he might achieve the intellectual dignity which consorted with his athletic prowess.

Michael had for some time envied the leisure of the History Sixth, with its general air of slackness and its form-master, Mr. Kirkham, who, on account of holding many administrative positions important to the athletic life of the school, was so often absent from his class-room. He now racked his brains for an excuse to achieve the idle bliss of these charmed few. Finally he persuaded his mother to write to the Headmaster and apply for his admission, on the grounds of the greater utility of History in his future profession.

"But what are you going to be, Michael?" asked his mother.

"I don't know, but you can say I'm going to be a barrister or something."

"Is History better for a barrister?"

"I don't know, but you can easily say you think it is."

In the end his mother wrote to Dr. Brownjohn, and one grey November afternoon the Headmaster sailed into the class-room of the Upper Fifth, extricated Michael with a roar, and marched with him up and down the dusky corridor in a ferocious discussion of the proposal.

"Why do you want to give up your Classics?" bellowed Dr. Brownjohn.

In the echoing corridor Michael's voice sounded painfully weak against his monitor's.

"I don't want to give them up, sir. Only I would like to learn History as well," he explained.

"What's the good of History?" roared the Doctor.

"I thought I'd like to learn it," said Michael.

"You shouldn't think, you infamous young sluggard."

"And I could go on reading Classics, sir, I could really."

"Bah!" shouted Dr. Brownjohn. "Impudent nonsense, you young sloth. Why didn't you get your Certificate?"

"I failed in Arithmetic, sir."

"You'll fail in your whole life, boy," prophesied Dr. Brownjohn in bull-deep accents of reproach. "Aren't you ashamed of yourself?"

"No, sir," said Michael. "I don't think I am, because I worked jolly hard."

"Worked, you abominable little loafer? You've never worked in your life. You could be the finest scholar in the school, and you're merely a coruscation of slatternly, slipshod paste. Bah! What do you expect to do when you leave school? Um?"

"I want to go to Oxford."

"Then get the Balliol Scholarship."

"I don't want to be at Balliol," said Michael.

"Then get the major scholarship at Trinity, Cambridge."

"I don't intend to go to Cambridge," said Michael.

"Good heavens, boy," roared Dr. Brownjohn, "are you trying to arrange your own career?"

"No, sir," said Michael. "But I want to go to St. Mary's, Oxford."

"Then get a scholarship at St. Mary's."

"But I don't want to be a Scholar of any college. I want to go up as a Commoner."

The veins on Dr. Brownjohn's forehead swelled with wrath, astonishment and dismay.

"Get out of my sight," he thundered. "Get back into your class-room. I've done with you; I take no more interest in you. You're here to earn glory for your school, you're here to gain a scholarship, not to air your own opinions. Get out of my sight, you young scoundrel. How dare you argue with me? You shan't go into the History Sixth! You shall stew in your own obstinate juice in the Upper Fifth until I choose to move you out of it. Do you hear? Go back into your class-room. I'll write to your mother. She's an idiotic woman, and you're a slovenly, idle, good-for-nothing cub."

Overwhelmed with failure and very sensitive to the inquisitive glances of his classmates, Michael sat down in his own desk again as unobtrusively as he could.

Michael's peace of mind was not increased by the consciousness of Mr. Cray's knowledge of his appeal to withdraw from the Upper Fifth, and he became exposed to a large amount of sarcasm in allusion to his expressed inclination towards history. He was continually referred to as an authority on Constitutions; he was invited to bring forward comparisons from more modern times to help the elucidation of the Syracusan expedition or the Delian Confederacy.

All that Michael gained from Mr. Cray was a passion for second-hand books—the latest and most fervid of all his collecting hobbies.

One wintry evening in Elson's Bookshop at Hammersmith he was enjoying himself on the top of a ladder, when he became aware of an interested gaze directed at himself over the dull-gilt edges of a large and expensive work on Greek sculpture. The face that so regarded him was at once fascinating and repulsive. The glittering blue eyes full of laughter were immediately attractive, but something in the pointed ears and curled-back lips, something in the peculiarly white fingers faintly pencilled about the knuckles with fine black hairs, and after a moment something cruel in the bright blue eyes themselves restrained him from an answering smile.

"What is the book, Hyacinthus?" asked the stranger, and his voice was so winning and so melodious in the shadowy bookshop that Michael immediately fell into the easiest of conversations.

"Fond of books?" asked the stranger. "Oh, by the way, my name is Wilmot, Arthur Wilmot."

Something in Wilmot's manner made Michael suppose that he ought to be familiar with the name, and he tried to recall it.

"What's your name?" the stranger went on.

Michael told his name, and also his school, and before very long a good deal about himself.

"I live near you," said Mr. Wilmot. "We'll walk along presently. I'd like you to dine with me one night soon. When?"

"Oh, any time," said Michael, trying to speak as if invitations to dinner occurred to him three or four times a day.

"Here's my card," said the stranger. "You'd better show it to your mother—so that she'll know it's all right. I'm a writer, you know."

"Oh, yes," Michael vaguely agreed.

"I don't suppose you've seen any of my stuff. I don't publish much. Sometimes I read my poems to Interior people."

Michael looked puzzled.

"Interior is my name for the people who understand. So few do. I should say you'd be sympathetic. You look sympathetic. You remind me of those exquisite boys who in scarlet hose run delicately with beakers of wine or stand in groups about the corners of old Florentine pictures."

Michael tried to look severe, and yet, after the Upper Fifth, even so direct and embarrassing a compliment was slightly pleasant.

"Shall we go along? To-night the Hammersmith Road is full of mystery. But, first, shall I not buy you a book—some exquisite book full of strange perfumes and passionate courtly gestures? And so you are at school? How wonderful to be at school! How Sicilian! Strange youth, you should have been sung by Theocritus, or, better, been crowned with myrtle by some wonderful unknown Greek, some perfect blossom of the Anthology."

Michael laughed rather foolishly. There seemed nothing else to do.

"Won't you smoke? These Chian cigarettes in their diaphanous paper of mildest mauve would suit your oddly remote, your curiously shy glance. You had better not smoke so near to the savage confines of St. James' School? How ascetic! How stringent! What book shall I buy for you, O greatly to be envied dreamer of Sicilian dreams? Shall I buy you Mademoiselle de Maupin, so that all her rococo soul may dance with gilded limbs across your vision? Or shall I buy you A Rebours, and teach you to live? And yet I think neither would suit you perfectly. So here is a volume of Pater—Imaginary Portraits. You will like to read of Denys l'Auxerrois. One day I myself will write an imaginary portrait of you, wherein your secret, sidelong smile will reveal to the world the whole art of youth."

"But really—thanks very much," stammered Michael, who was beginning to suspect the stranger of madness—"it's awfully kind of you, but, really, I think I'd rather not."

"Do not be proud," said Mr. Wilmot. "Pride is for the pure in heart, and you are surely not pure in heart. Or are you? Are you indeed like one of those wonderful white statues of antiquity, unaware of the soul with all its maladies?"

In the end, so urgent was Mr. Wilmot, Michael accepted the volume of Pater, and walked with the stranger through the foggy night. Somehow the conversation was so destructive of all experience that, as Michael and his new friend went by the school-gates and perceived beyond the vast bulk of St. James' looming, Michael felt himself a stranger to it all, as if he never again would with a crowd of companions surge out from afternoon school. The stranger came as far as the corner of Carlington Road with Michael.

"I will write to your mother and ask her to let you dine with me one night next week. You interest me so much."

Mr. Wilmot waved a pontifical good-bye and vanished in the direction of Kensington.

At home Michael told his mother of the adventure. She looked a little doubtful at his account of Mr. Wilmot.

"Oh, he's all right, really, Mother. Only, you know, a little peculiar. But then he's a poet."

Next day came a letter from Mr. Wilmot.

205 EDWARDES SQUARE, W.
November.

Dear Mrs. Fane,

I must apologize for inviting your son to dinner so unceremoniously. But he made a great appeal to me, sitting on the top of a ladder in Elson's Bookshop. I have a library, in which he may enjoy himself whenever he likes. Meanwhile, may he come to dinner with me on Friday next? Mr. Johnstone, the Member for West Kensington, is coming with his nephew who may be dull without Michael. Michael tells me he thinks of becoming an ecclesiastical lawyer. In that case Johnstone will be particularly useful, and can give him some hints. He's a personal friend of old Dr. Brownjohn. With many apologies for my 'impertinence,'

Yours very truly,
Arthur Wilmot.

"This is a perfectly sensible letter," said Mrs. Fane.

"Perhaps I thought he was funnier than he really was. Does he say anything else except about me sitting on the top of a ladder?"

Somehow Michael was disappointed to hear that this was all.

Chapter IX: *The Yellow Age*

DINNER with Mr. Arthur Wilmot occupied most of Michael's thoughts for a week. He was mainly concerned about his costume, and he was strenuously importunate for a tail-coat. Mrs. Fane, however, was sure that a dinner-jacket would better become his youthfulness. Then arose the question of stick-up collars. Michael pointed out that very soon he would be sixteen, and that here was a fine opportunity to leave behind the Polo or Shakespeare collar.

"You're growing up so quickly, dearest boy," sighed his mother.

Michael was anxious to have one of the new double collars.

"But don't they look rather *outré*?" protested Mrs. Fane.

"Well, Abercrombie, the Secretary of the Fifteen, wears one," observed Michael.

"Have your own way, dear," said Mrs. Fane gently.

Two or three days before the dinner-party Michael braved everything and wore one of the new double collars to school. Its extravagant advent among the discreet neckwear of the Upper Fifth caused a sensation. Mr. Cray himself looked curiously once or twice at Michael, who assumed in consequence a particularly nonchalant air, and lounged over his desk even more than usual.

"Are you going on the stage, Fane?" enquired Mr. Cray finally, exasperated by Michael's indolent construing.

"Not that I know of," said Michael.

"I wasn't sure whether that collar was part of your get-up as an eccentric comedian."

The Upper Fifth released its well-worn laugh, and Michael scowled at his master.

However, he endured the sarcasm of the first two days and still wore the new collars, vowing to himself that presently he would make fresh attacks upon the convention of school attire, since apparently he was able thereby to irritate old Cray.

After all, the dinner-party was not so exciting as he had hoped from the sample of his new friend's conversation. To be sure he was able to smoke as much as he liked, and drink as much champagne as he knew how without warning headshakes; but Mr. Johnstone, the Member for West Kensington, was a moon-faced bore, and his nephew turned out to be a lank nonentity on the despised Modern side. Mr. Johnstone talked a good deal about the Catholic movement, which somehow during the last few weeks was ceasing to interest Michael so much as formerly. Michael himself ascribed this apostasy to his perusal, ladder-high, of Zola's novel Lourdes with its damaging assaults upon Christian credulity. The Member of Parliament seemed to Michael, after his psychical adventures of the past few months, curiously dull and antique, and he evidently considered Michael affected. However, he encouraged the idea of ecclesiastical law, and promised to talk to Dr. Brownjohn about Michael's release from the thraldom of Classics. As for the nephew, he seemed to be able to do nothing but stretch the muscles of his chicken-like neck and ask continually whether Michael was going to join the Field Club that some obscure Modern Lower Master was in travail with at the moment. He also invited Michael to join a bicycling club that apparently met at Surbiton every other Saturday afternoon. Mr. Wilmot contented himself with silence and the care of his guests' entertainment.

Finally the Member for West Kensington with his crudely jointed nephew departed into the fog, and Mr. Wilmot, with an exaggerated sigh, shut the front door.

"I must be going too," said Michael grudgingly.

"My dear boy, the evening has scarcely begun," objected Mr. Wilmot. "Come upstairs to my library, and tell me all about your opinions, and whether you do not think that everything is an affectation."

They went up together.

"Every year I redecorate this room," Mr. Wilmot explained. "Last year it was apple-green set out with cherry-red. Now I am become a mysterious peacock-blue, for lately I have felt terribly old. How well this uncertain tint suits your fresh languor."

Michael admired the dusky blue chamber with the plain mirrors of tarnished gilt, the gleaming books and exotic engravings, and the heterogeneous finery faintly effeminate. He buried himself in a deep embroidered chair, with an ebony box of cigarettes at his feet, while Mr. Wilmot, after a myriad mincing preliminaries, sought out various highly coloured bottles of liqueurs.

"This is a jolly ripping room," sighed Michael.

"It represents a year's moods," said Mr. Wilmot.

"And then will you change it?" asked Michael.

"Perhaps. The most subtly painted serpent casts ultimately its slough. Creme-de-Menthe?"

"Yes, please," said Michael, who would have accepted anything in his present receptive condition.

"And what do you think of life?" enquired Mr. Wilmot, taking his place on a divan opposite Michael. "Do you mind if I smoke my Jicky-scented hookah?" he added.

"Not at all," said Michael. "These cigarettes are jolly ripping. I think life at school is frightfully dull—except, of course, when one goes out. Only I don't often."

"Dull?" repeated Mr. Wilmot. "Listen to the amazing cruelty of youth, that finds even his adventurous Sicilian existence dull."

"Well, it is," said Michael. "I think I used to like it, but nowadays everything gets fearfully stale almost at once."

"Already your life has been lived?" queried Mr. Wilmot very anxiously.

"Well, not exactly," Michael replied, with a quick glance towards his host to make sure he was not joking. "I expect that when I leave school I shall get interested again. Only just lately I've given up everything. First I was keen on Footer, and then I got keen on Ragging, and then I got keen on Work even (this was confessed apologetically), and just lately I've been keen on the Church—only now I find that's pretty stale."

"The Church!" echoed Mr. Wilmot. "How wonderful! The dim Gothic glooms, the sombre hues of stained glass, the incense-wreathèd acolytes, the muttering priests, the bedizened banners and altars and images. Ah, elusive and particoloured vision that once was mine!"

"Then I got keen on Swinburne," said Michael.

"You advance along the well-worn path of the Interior and Elect," said Mr. Wilmot.

"I'm still keen on Swinburne, but he makes me feel hopeless. Sad and hopeless," said Michael.

"Under the weight of sin?" asked Mr. Wilmot.

"Not exactly—because he seems to have done everything and——"

"You'd like to?"

"Yes, I would," said Michael. "Only one can't live like a Roman Emperor at a public school. What I hate is the way everybody thinks you ought to be interested in things that aren't really interesting at all. What people can't understand about me is that I *could* be keener than anybody about things schoolmasters and that kind don't think right or at any rate important. I don't mean to say I want to be dissipated, but——"

"Dissipated?" echoed Mr. Wilmot, raising his eyebrows.

"Well, you know what I mean," blushed Michael.

"Dissipation is a condition of extreme old age. I might be dissipated, not you," said Mr. Wilmot. "Why not say wanton? How much more beautiful, how much more intense a word."

"But wanton sounds so beastly affected," said Michael. "As if it was taken out of the Bible. And you aren't so very old. Not more than thirty."

"I think what you're trying to say is that, under your present mode of life, you find self-expression impossible. Let me diagnose your symptoms."

Michael leaned forward eagerly at this proposal. Nothing was so entertaining to his egoism just now as diagnosis. Moreover, Mr. Wilmot seemed inclined to take him more seriously than Mr. Viner, or, indeed, any of his spiritual directors so far. Mr. Wilmot prepared himself for the lecture by lighting a very long cigarette wrapped in brittle fawn-coloured paper, whose spirals of smoke Michael followed upward to their ultimate evanescence, as if indeed they typified with their tenuous plumes and convolutions the intricate discourse that begot them.

"In a sense, my dear boy, your charm has waned—the faerie charm, that is, which wraps in heedless silver armour the perfect boyhood of man. You are at present a queer sort of mythical animal whom we for want of a better term call 'adolescent.' Intercourse with anything but your own self shocks both you and the world with a sense of extravagance, as if a centaur pursued a nymph or fought with a hero. The soul—or what we call the soul—is struggling in the bondage of your unformed body. Lately you had no soul, you were ethereal and cold, yet withal in some remote way passionate, like your own boy's voice. Now the silly sun is melting the snow, and what was a little while since crystalline clear virginity is beginning to trickle down towards a headlong course, carrying with it the soiled accumulation of the years to float insignificantly into the wide river of manhood. But I am really being almost intolerably allegorical—or is it metaphorical?"

"Still, I think I understand what you mean," Michael said encouragingly.

"Thrown back upon your own resources, it is not surprizing that you attempt to allay your own sense of your own incongruity by seeking for its analogy in the decorative excitements of religion or poetry. Love would supply the solution, but you are still too immature for love. And if you do fall in love, you will sigh for some ample and unattainable matron rather than the slim, shy girl that would better become your pastoral graces. At present you lack all sense of proportion. You are only aware of your awkwardness. Your corners have not yet been, as they say, knocked off. You are still somewhat proud of their Gothic angularity. You feel at home in the tropic dawns of Swinburne's poetry, in the ceremonious exaggerations of Mass, because neither of these conditions of thought and behaviour allow you to become depressed over your oddity, to see yourself crawling with bedraggled wings from the cocoon of mechanical education. The licentious ingenuity of Martial, Petronius and Apuleius with their nightmare comedies and obscene phantasmagoria, Lucian, that *boulevardier* of Olympic glades, all these could allow you to feel yourself more at home than does Virgil with his peaceful hexameters or the cold relentless narrations of Thucydides."

"Yes, that's all very well," objected Michael. "But other chaps seem to get on all right without being bored by ordinary things."

"Already spurning the gifts of Apollo, contemptuous of Artemis, ignorant of Bacchus and Aphrodite, you are bent low before Pallas Athene. Foolish child, do not pray for wisdom in this overwise thin-faced time of ours. Rather demand of the gods folly, and drive ever furiously your temperament like a chariot before you."

"I met an odd sort of chap the other day," Michael said thoughtfully. "A monk he was, as a matter of fact—who told me a skit of things—you know—about a bad life. It's funny, though I hate ugly things and common things, he gave me a feeling that I'd like to go right away from everything and live in one of those horrible streets that you pass in an omnibus when the main road is up. Perhaps you don't understand what I mean?"

Mr. Wilmot's eyes glittered through the haze of smoke.

"Why shouldn't I understand? Squalor is the Parthenope of the true Romantic. You'll find it in all the poets you love best—if not in their poetry, certainly in their lives. Even romantic critics are not without temptation. One day you shall read of Hazlitt and Sainte-Beuve. And now, dear boy, here is my library which holds as many secrets as the Spintrian books of Elephantis, long ago lost and purified by the sea. I am what the wise world would call about to corrupt your mind, and yet I believe that for one who like you must some day make trial of the uttermost corruption, I am prescribing more wisely than Chiron, that pigheaded or rather horse-bodied old prototype of all schoolmasters, who sent his hero pupils one after another into the world, proof against nothing but a few spear-thrusts. I offer you better than fencing-bouts and wrestling-matches. I offer you a good library. Read every day and all night, and when you are a man full grown, you will smile at the excesses of your contemporaries, at their divorces and disgraces. You will stand aloof like a second Aurelius, coining austere aphorisms andmocking the weakness of your unlearned fellows. Why are priests generally so inept in the confessional? Because they learn their knowledge of life from, a frowsy volume of Moral Theology that in the most utterly barbarous Latin emits an abstract of humanity's immeasurable vice. In the same way most young men encounter wickedness in some sudden shock of depravity from which they retire blushing and mumbling, 'Who'd have thought it!' ' Who'd have thought it!' they cry, and are immediately empanelled on a jury.

"Not so you, O more subtle youth, with the large deep eyes and secret sidelong smile.

"There on my shelves are all the ages. I have spoken to you of Petronius, of Lucian and Apuleius. There is Suetonius, with his incredibly improper tales that show how beastliness takes root and flowers from the deposited muck of a gossip's mind. There is Tacitus, ever willing to sacrifice decency to antithesis, and Ausonius, whose ribald verses are like monkish recreation; yet he had withal a pretty currency of honest silver Latin, Christian though he was. You must read your Latin authors well, for, since you must be decadent, it is better to decay from a good source. And neglect not the Middle Ages. You will glide most easily into them from the witches and robbers of Apuleius. You will read Boccaccio, whose tales are intaglios carved with exquisitely licentious and Lilliputian scenes. Neither forget Villon, whose light ladies seem ever to move elusively in close-cut gowns of cloth-of-gold and incredibly tall steeple-hats. But even with Villon the world becomes complicated, and you will soon reach the temperamental entanglements of the nineteenth century, for you may avoid the coarse, the beery and besotted obviousness of the Georgian age.

"But I like the eighteenth century almost best of all," protested Michael.

"Then cure yourself of that most lamentable and most démodé taste, or I shall presently believe that you read a page or two of Boswell's Life of Johnson every morning, while the water is running into your bath. You can never be a true decadent, treading delicately over the garnered perfection of the world's art, if you really admire and enjoy the eighteenth century."

Michael, however, looked very doubtful over his demanded apostasy.

"But, never mind," Mr. Wilmot went on. "When you have read Barbey d'Aurevilly and Baudelaire, Mallarmé, Verlaine, Catulle Mendès and Verhaeren, when the Parnassians and Symbolists have illuminated you, and you become an Interior person, when Aubrey Beardsley and Felicien Rops have printed their fierce debauchery upon your imagination, then you will be glad you have forsaken the eighteenth century. How crude is the actual number eighteen, how far from the passionate mystery of seventeen or the tired wisdom of nineteen! O wonderful nineteenth century, in whose grey humid dusk you and I are lucky enough to live!"

"But what about the twentieth century?" asked Michael.

Mr. Wilmot started.

"Listen, and I will tell you my intention. Two more years have yet to run before that garish and hideous date, prophetic of all that is bright and new and abominably raw. But I shall have fled, how I know not; haply mandragora will lure my weary mind to rest. I think I should like to die as La Gioconda was painted, listening to flute-players in a curtained alcove; or you, Michael, shall read to me some diabolic and funereal song of Baudelaire, so that I may fearfully pass away."

Michael, sitting in the dim room of peacock-blue made tremendously nocturnal by the heavy smoke of all the cigarettes, did not much care for the turn the conversation of Mr. Wilmot had taken. It had been interesting enough, while the discussion applied directly to himself; but all this vague effusion of learning meant very little to him. At the same time, there was an undeniable eccentricity in a member of the Upper Fifth sitting thus in fantastic communion with a figure completely outside the imagination of Mr. Cray or any of his inky groundlings. Michael began to feel a contemptuous pity for his fellows now buried in bedclothes, hot and heavy with Ciceronian sentences and pious preparation. He began to believe that if he wished to keep pace with this new friendship, he must acquire something of Mr. Wilmot's heightened air. And however mad he might seem, there stood the books, and there stood the cigarettes for Michael's pleasure. It was all very exciting, and it would not have been possible to say that before he met Wilmot.

The friendship progressed through the rest of the autumn-term, and Michael drifted farther away from the normal life of the school than even his incursion into Catholicism had taken him. That phase of his development had penetrated deeper than any other, and from time to time Michael knew bitter repentances and made grim resolutions. From time to time letters would arrive from Dom Cuthbert asking him down to Clere Abbey; Mr. Viner, too, would question him narrowly about his new set of friends, and Michael's replies never seemed perfectly satisfactory to the shrewd priest.

It was by his costume more than by anything else that Michael expressed at first his sense of emancipation. He took to coming to school in vivid bow-ties that raised Mr. Cray's most sarcastic comments.

"The sooner you go to the History Sixth, Fane, and take that loathsome ribbon with you, the better for us all. Where did you get it? Out of the housemaid's trunk, one would say, by its appearance."

"It happens to be a tie," said Michael with insolence in his tone.

"Oh, it happens to be a tie, does it? Well, it also happens to be an excellent rule of St. James' School that all boys, however clever, wear dark suits and black ties. There also happens to be an excellent cure for pretentious and flamboyant youths who disregard this rule. There happens to be a play by one Euripides called the Alcestis. I suggest you write me out the first two hundred lines of it."

Michael's next encounter was with Mr. Viner, on the occasion of his producing in the priest's pipe-seasoned sitting-room a handkerchief inordinately perfumed with an Eastern scent lately discovered by Wilmot.

"Good heavens, Michael, what Piccadilly breezes are you wafting into my respectable and sacerdotal apartment?"

"I rather like scent," explained Michael lamely.

"Well, I don't, so, for goodness' sake don't bring any more of it in here. Pah! Phew! It's worse than a Lenten address at a fashionable church. Really, you know, these people you're in with now are not at all good for you, Michael."

"They're more interesting than any of the chaps at school."

"Are they? There used to be a saying in my undergraduate days, 'Distrust a freshman that's always seen with third-year men.' No doubt the inference is often unjust, but still the proverb remains."

"Ah, but these people aren't at school with me," Michael observed.

"No, I wish they were. They might be licked into better shape, if they were," retorted the priest.

"I think you're awfully down on Wilmot just because I didn't meet him in some churchy set. If it comes to that, I met some much bigger rotters than him at Clere."

"My dear Michael," argued Father Viner, "the last place I should have been surprized to see Master Wilmot would be in a churchy set. Don't forget that if religion is a saving grace, religiosity is a constitutional weakness. Can't you understand that a priest like myself who has taken the average course, public-school, 'varsity, and theological college, meets a thundering lot of Wilmots by the way? My dear fellow, many of my best friends, many of the priests you've met in my rooms, were once upon a time every bit as decadent as the lilified Wilmot. They took it like scarlet fever or chicken-pox, and feel all the more secure now for having had it. Decadence, as our friend knows it, is only a new-fangled name for green-sickness. It's a healthy enough mental condition for the young, but it's confoundedly dangerous for the grown-up. The first pretty girl that looks his way cures it in a boy, if he's a normal decent boy. I shouldn't offer any objection to your behaviour, if you were being decadent with Mark Chator or Martindale or Rigg. Good heavens, the senior curate at the best East-end Mission, when he was at Oxford, used to walk down the High leading a lobster on a silver chain, and even that wasn't original, for he stole the poor little fantastic idea from some precious French poet. But that senior curate is a very fine fellow to-day. No, no, this fellow Wilmot and all his set are very bad company for you, and I do not like your being decadent with these half-baked fancy-cakes."

Michael, however, would not admit that Mr. Viner was right, and frequented the dangerous peacock-blue room in Edwardes Square more than ever. He took Chator there amongst others, and was immensely gratified to be solemnly warned at the end of the visit that he was playing with Hell-fire. This seemed to him an interesting and original pastime, and he hinted to solemn, simple, spluttering old Chator of more truly Satanic mysteries.

After Christmas Michael had his way and was moved into the History Sixth, mainly owing to the intervention of the Member for West Kensington. The History Sixth was presided over by Mr. Kirkham, whose nominal aim in life was the amelioration of Jacobean athletics. From the fact that he wore an M.C.C. ribbon round his straw hat, and an Oxford University Authentic tie, it is probable that the legend of his former skill at cricket was justified. In reality he was much more interested in Liberalism than anything else, and persistently read Blue Books, under-lining the dramatic moments of Royal Commissions and chewing his moustache through pages of dialogue hostile to his opinions. A rumour sped round the school that he had been invited to stand for Parliament, a rumour which Michael, on the strength of dining with the Member for West Kensington, flatly contradicted.

The History Sixth class-room was a pleasant place, the only class-room in the school that ever saw the sun. Its windows looked out on the great green expanse of the school ground, where during the deserted hours of work the solitary roller moved sedately and ancient women weeded the pitches.

There were only seven boys in the History Sixth. There was Strang, the Captain of the Eleven, who lounged through the dull Lent term and seemed, as he spread his bulk over the small desk, like a half-finished statue to which still adhered a fragment of uncarved stone. There was Terry, the Vice-Captain of the Fifteen and most dapper half-back that ever cursed forwards. He spent his time trying to persuade Strang to take an interest in Noughts and Crosses. There was beak-nosed Thomson who had gained an Exhibition at Selwyn College, Cambridge, and dark-eyed Mallock, whose father wrote columnar letters to The Times. Burnaby, who shocked Michael very much by prophesying that a certain H. G. Wells, now writing about Martian invasions, was the coming man, and Railton, a weedy and disconsolate recluse, made up with Michael himself the class-list.

There was an atmosphere of rest about the History Sixth, a leisured dignity that contrasted very delightfully with the spectacled industry of the Upper Fifth. To begin with, Mr, Kirkham was always ten minutes after every other master in entering his class-room. This habit allowed the members of his form to stroll gracefully along the corridors and watch one by one the cavernous doors of other class-rooms absorb their victims. Michael would often go out of his way to pass Mr. Cray's room, in order to see with a luxurious sense of relief the intellectual convicts of the Upper Fifth hurrying to their prison. Many other conventions of school-life were slackened in the History Sixth. A slight eccentricity of attire was not considered unbecoming in what was, at any rate in its own opinion, a faintly literary society. The room was always open between morning and afternoon school, and it was not an uncommon sight to see members of the form reading novels in tip-tilted chairs. Most of the home work was set a week in advance, which did away with the unpleasant necessity of speculating on the 'construe' or hurriedly cribbing with a hastily peppered variety of mistakes the composition of one's neighbour. Much of the work was simple reading, and as for the essays, by a legal fiction they were always written during the three hours devoted to Mathematics. Tradition forbade any member of the History Sixth to take Mathematics seriously, and Mr. Gaskell, the overworked Mathematical master, was not inclined to break this tradition. He used to write out a problem or two on the blackboard for the sake of appearances, and then settle down to the correction of his more serious pupils' work, while the History Sixth devoted themselves to their more serious work. One of the great social earthquakes that occasionally devastate all precedent occurred when Mr. Gaskell was away with influenza, and his substitute, an earnest young novice, tried to make Strang and Terry do a Quadratic Equation.

"But, sir, we never do Mathematics."

"Well, what are you here for?" asked the novice. "What am *I* here for?"

"We don't know," replied the History Sixth in unison; and the vendetta that followed the complaint of their behaviour to Mr. Kirkham made the novice's mastership a burden to him during Mr. Gaskell's illness. Enraged conservatism called for reprisals, until Mr. Kirkham pointed out with a felicity acquired from long perusal of Parliamentary humour, "You are Jacobeans, not Jacobins," and with this mild joke quenched the feud.

The effect of his transference to the History Sixth made Michael more decadent than ever, for the atmosphere of his new class encouraged him along the orchidaceous path pointed out by Arthur Wilmot. He was not now decadent from any feeling of opposition to established things, but he was decadent from conviction of the inherent rightness of such a state. At first the phase had manifested itself in outward signs, a little absurdly; now his actual point of view was veering into accord with the externals.

Sunday was a day at Edwardes Square from which Michael returned almost phosphorescent with decay. Sunday was the day on which Mr. Wilmot gathered from all over London specimens of corruption that fascinated Michael with their exotic and elaborate behaviour. Nothing seemed worth while in such an assembly except a novel affectation. Everything was a pose. It was a pose to be effeminate in speech and gesture; it was a pose to drink absinthe; it was a pose to worship the devil; it was a pose to buy attenuated volumes of verse at an unnatural price, for the sake of owning a sonnet that was left out in the ordinary edition; it was a pose to admire pictures that to Michael at first were more like wallpapers than pictures; it was really a pose to live at all. Conversation at these delicate entertainments was like the conversations overheard in the anterooms of private asylums. Everyone was very willowy in his movements, whether he were smoking or drinking or looking for a box of matches. Michael attempted to be willowy at school once, but gave it up on being asked if he had fleas.

One of the main charms at first of these Sunday afternoon gatherings was the way in which, one after another, every one of the guests would take Michael aside and explain how different he (the guest) was from all the rest of humanity. Michael was flattered, and used to become very intense and look very soul-searching, and interject sympathetic exclamations until he discovered that the confidant usually proceeded to another corner of the room to entrust someone else with his innermost heart. He became cynical after a while, especially when he found that the principal points of difference from the rest of the world were identical in every one of the numerous guests who sought his counsel and his sympathy.

However, he never became cynical enough to distrust the whole school of thought and admit that Father Viner's contempt was justifiable. If ever he had any doubts, he was consoled by assuring himself that at any rate these new friends were very artistic, and how important it was to be artistic no one could realize who was not at school.

Under the pressure of his insistent temperament, Michael found his collection of statuettes and ecclesiastical bric-à-brac very depressing. As a youth of the Florentine Renaissance he could not congratulate himself upon his room, which was much too much unlike either a Carpaccio interior or an Aubrey Beardsley bedroom. Between these two his ambition wavered.

One by one the statuettes were moved to the top of a wardrobe where for a while they huddled, a dusty and devoted crowd, until one by one they met martyrdom at the hands of the housemaid. In their place appeared Della Robbia reliefs and terra-cotta statuettes of this or that famous Greek youth. The muscular and tearful pictures of Guido Reni, the bland insipidities of Bouguereau soon followed the statuettes, meeting a comparable martyrdom by being hung in the servants' bedroom. The walls of Michael's room were papered with a brown paper, which was intended to be very artistic, but was really merely sad. It was lightened, however, by various daring pictures in black and red that after only a very short regard really did take shape as scenes of Montmartre. There were landscapes of the Sussex downs, with a slight atmosphere of Japan and landscapes of Japan that were not at all like Japan, but none the less beautiful for that. The books of devotion were banished to the company of superannuated Latin and Greek textbooks on the lower shelf of a cupboard in the morning-room, whose upper shelf was stacked with tinned fruits. Incense was still burnt, not as once to induce prayers to ascend, but to stupefy Michael with scent and warmth into an imitation of a drug-taker's listless paradise. This condition was accentuated by erecting over the head of his bed a canopy of faded green satin, which gave him acute æsthetic pleasure, until one night it collapsed upon him in the middle of the night. Every piece of upholstery in the room was covered with art linens that with the marching years had ousted the art muslins of Michael's childhood. He also covered with squares of the same material the gas brackets, pushing them back against the wall and relying for light upon candles only. Notwithstanding Wilmot's talk about literature, the influence of Wilmot's friends was too strong, and Michael could not resist the deckle-edges of negligible poets. As these were expensive, Michael's library lacked scope, and he himself, reflecting his pastime, came to believe in the bitterness and sweetness and bitter-sweetness of the plaintive sinners who printed so elegantly on such permanent paper the versification of their irregularity.

Irregularity was now being subjected to Michael's process of idealistic alchemy, and since his conception of irregularity was essentially romantic, and since he shrank from sentiment, he was able to save himself, when presently all this decoration fell to pieces, and revealed naked unpleasantness. Nothing in his present phase had yet moved him so actually as his brief encounter with Brother Aloysius. That glimpse of a fearful and vital underworld had been to him romantic without trappings; it was a glimpse into an underworld to which one day he might descend, since it asked no sighing for the vanished joys of the past, for the rose-gardens of Rome. He began to play with the idea of departing suddenly from his present life and entering the spectral reality of the Seven Sisters Road, treading whatever raffish raddled pavement knew the hollow steps of a city's prowlers. Going home on Sunday nights from the perfumed house in Edwardes Square and passing quickly and apprehensively figures that materialized in a circle of lamplight, he would contrast their existence with what remained in his senses of stale cigarette-smoke and self-conscious airs and attitudes. Yet the very picture he conjured of the possibility that haunted him made him the more anxious to substitute for the stark descent to hell the Sicilian or Satanic affectations of the luxurious mimes who postured against a background of art. Much of the talk at Edwardes Square concerned itself with the pastoral side of school-life, and Michael found himself being cross-questioned by elderly faun-like men who had a conception of an English public-school that was more Oriental than correct. Michael vainly tried to dispel these illusions, which made him resentful and for the moment crudely normal. He felt towards them much as he felt towards Garrod's attempt to cure his ignorance at Clere. These were excellent fellows from whom to accept a cigarette or sometimes even an invitation to lunch at a Soho restaurant, but when they presumed upon his condescension and dared to include in their tainted outlook himself as a personal factor, Michael shrivelled with a virginal disdain.

Unreasonably to the others, Michael did not object very much to Wilmot's oracular addresses on the delights of youth. He felt that so much of Wilmot was in the mere word, and he admired so frankly his embroideries of any subject, and above all he liked Wilmot so much personally, that he listened to him, and was even so far influenced by him as to try to read into the commonplace of a summer term all that Wilmot would suggest.

"O fortunate shepherd, to whom will you pipe to-morrow, or what slim and agile companion will you crown for his prowess? O lucky youth, able to drowse in the tempered sunlight that the elm-trees give, while your friend splendidly cool in his white flannels bats and bowls for your delight!"

"But I haven't got any particular friend that I can watch," objected Michael.

"One day you will terribly regret the privileges of your pastoral life."

"Do you really think I am not getting all I can out of school?" demanded Michael.

"I'm sure you're not," said Wilmot.

Michael began to trouble himself over Wilmot's warning, and also he began to look back with sentimental regret to what had really been his happiest time, his friendship with Alan. Pride kept him from approaching Alan with nothing to offer for nearly two years' indifference. There had been no quarrel. They had merely gradually drifted apart, yet it was with a deep pang of remorse that one day he realized in passing the dusty Upper Fifth that Alan was now wrestling with that imprisonment. Michael racked his brains to think of some way by which he and Alan might come together in their old amity, their perfect fellowship. He sought some way that would make it natural and inevitable, but no way presented itself. He could, so deep was his sudden regret, have stifled his own pride and deliberately invited Alan to be friends; he would even have risked a repulse; but with the renewal of his longing for the friendship came a renewal of the old sympathy and utter comprehension of Alan's most secret moods, and Michael realized that his old friend would be too shy to accept this strange, inexplicable revival, unless it were renewed, as it was begun, by careless, artless intercourse.

The immediate result of this looking back to an earlier period was to arouse in Michael an interest in boys younger than himself, and through his idealism to endow them with a conscious joy of life which he fell to envying. He had a desire to warn them of the enchantment under whose benign and dulcet influence they lived, to warn them that soon the lovely spell would be broken, and bid them make the most of their stripling time. Continually he was seeing boys in the lower forms whose friendship blooming like two flowers on a spray shed a fragrance so poignant that tears came springing to his eyes. He began to imagine himself very old, to feel that by some unkind gift of temperament he had nothing left to live for. It chanced that summer term the History Sixth learned for repetition the Odes of Keats, and in the Ode on a Grecian Urn Michael found the expression of his mood:

Fair youth, beneath the trees, thou canst not leave
    Thy song, nor ever can those trees be bare;
        Bold Lover, never, never canst thou kiss,
    Though winning near the goal—yet, do not grieve;
        She cannot fade, though thou hast not thy bliss,
    For ever wilt thou love, and she be fair!

These lines were learnt in June, and for Michael they enshrined immortally his yearning. Never had the fugitive summer glided so fast, since never before had he sat in contemplation of its flight. Until this moment he had been one with the season's joy like a bird or a sunbeam, but now for the first time he had the opportunity of regarding the empty field during the hours of school, and of populating it with the merry ghosts of the year with Caryll. All through schooltime the mowing-machine hummed its low harmony of perishable minutes and wasted sunlight. The green field was scattered with the wickets of games in progress that stood luminously in golden trios, so brightly did the sunny weather enhance their wood. The scoring-board of the principal match stared like a stopped clock with the record of the last breathless run, and as if to mock the stillness from a distant corner came a sound of batting, where at the nets the two professionals practised idly. A bluebottle buzzed upon the window-pane; pigeons flapped from pinnacle to pinnacle of the chapel; sparrows cheeped on a persistent note; pens scratched paper; Mr. Kirkham turned a Blue Book's page at regular intervals.

    Ah, happy, happy boughs! that cannot shed
    Your leaves, nor ever bid the Spring adieu;
        And, happy melodist, unwearied
        For ever piping songs for ever new.

Thus for him would the trancèd scene for ever survive.

The History Sixth were for the purposes of cricket linked to the Classical Lower Sixth, but Michael did not play that term. Instead, a strayed reveller, he would move from game to game of the Junior School, hearing the shrill encouragement and pondering the rose-red agility of a Classical lower form, in triumph over minor Moderns. Michael was continually trying to perceive successors to himself and Alan, and he would often enter into shy colloquy with the juniors, who were awed by his solemn smile, and shuffled uneasily from leg to leg.

Two boys whom Michael finally determined should stand as types of Alan and him gradually emerged from the white throng of Lower School cricket. One of them was indeed very like Alan, and had the same freckled smile. With this pair Michael became intimate, as one becomes intimate with two puppies. He would pet and scold them, encourage them to be successful in their sport, and rebuke them for failure. They perhaps found him entertaining, and were certainly proud to be seen in conversation with him, for though Michael himself was not an athletic hero, he was the companion of heroes, and round him clung the shining mirage of their immortality.

Then one day, unknown to Michael, these two boys became involved in a scandal; the inquisition of a great public school pinned them down desperately struggling, miserably afraid; the rumour of their expulsion went callously round the gossiping ranks of their fellows. Michael was informed of their disgrace by dark-eyed Mallock whose father wrote columnar letters to The Times. Michael said bitter things to the complacent Mallock and offered with serious want of dignity for a member of the leisurely and cultivated History Sixth, to punch Mallock's damned head.

Mallock said sneeringly that he supposed Michael sympathized with the little beasts. Michael replied that he merely sympathized with them because he was profoundly sure that it was a pack of lies.

"You'd better go and tell the Old Man that, because they say he's going to expel them to-day."

Michael turned pale with fury.

"I damned well will go, and when I come back I'll ram you upside down in the Tuck Shop butter-tub."

Mallock flushed under the ignominy of this threat, and muttered his conviction that Michael was talking through his hat. Just then Mr. Kirkham entered the class-room, and Michael immediately went up to him and asked if he might go and speak to the Headmaster.

Mr. Kirkham stared with amazement, and his voice, which always seemed to hesitate whether it should come out through his mouth or his nose, on this occasion never came out at all, but stayed in the roof of Mr. Kirkham's mouth.

"Can I, sir?" Michael repeated.

"I suppose you can," said Mr. Kirkham.

The class followed Michael's exit with wide eyes; even the phlegmatic Strang was so deeply moved that he sat upright in his chair and tapped his head to indicate midsummer madness.

Outside in the echoing corridor, where the plaster casts looked coldly down, Michael wrestled with his leaping heart, forcing it into tranquillity so that he could grapple with the situation he had created for himself. By the Laocoön he paused. Immediately beyond was the sombre doorway of the Head's room. As he paused on the threshold two ridiculous thoughts came to him—that Lessing's Laocoön was one of the set books for the English Literature prize, and that he would rather be struggling in the coils of that huge stone snake than standing thus invertebrate before this portentous door.

Then Michael tapped. There was no answer but a dull buzz of voices. Again Michael tapped and, beating down his heart, turned the handle that seemed as he held it to swell to pumpkin size in his grasp. Slowly he pushed the door before him, expecting to hear a bellowed summons to appear, and wondering whether he could escape unknown to his class-room if his nerve failed him even now. Then he heard the sound of tears, and indignation drove him onwards, drove him so urgently that actually he slammed the great door behind him, and made the intent company aware of his presence.

"What do *you* want?" shouted Dr. Brownjohn. "Can't you see I'm busy?"

"I want to speak to you, sir." The words actually seemed to come from his mouth winged with flames, such a volcano was Michael now.

"I'm busy. Go outside and wait," roared the Headmaster.

Michael paused to regard the scene—the two boys sobbing with painful regular intake of breath, oblivious of him; the witnesses, a sheepish crew; the school-porter waiting for his prey; old Mr. Caryll coughing nervously and apparently on the verge of tears himself; the odious Paul Pry of a Secretary nibbling his pen; and in the background other masters waiting with favourable or damning testimony.

The drama of gloating authority shook Michael to the very foundation of his being, and he came rapidly into the middle of the room, came right up to the Headmaster, until he felt engulfed in the black silk gown, and at last said slowly and with simple conviction:

"I think you're all making a mistake."

When he had spoken Michael could have kicked himself for not shouting furiously the torrid denunciations which had come surging up for utterance. Then he immediately began to talk again, to his own great surprise, calmly and very reasonably.

"I know these kids—these two boys, I mean—quite well. It's impossible for any of this to be true. I've seen them a lot this term—practically every day. Really, sir, you'll make a terrible mistake if you expel them. They're awfully decent little chaps. They are really, sir. Of course they're too frightened now to say anything for themselves. It's not fair for everybody to be set at them like this."

Michael looked despairingly at the masters assembled.

"And these other boys who've been brought in to tell what they know. Why, they're frightened too. They'd say anything. Why don't you, why don't you——"

Michael looked round in despair, stammered, broke down, and then to his own eternal chagrin burst into tears. He moved hastily over to the window, striving to pull himself together, seeing through an overpowering blur the great green field in the garish sunlight. Yet his tears, shameful to him, may have turned the scale, for one by one the masters came forward with eager testimony of good; and with every word of praise the tears rushed faster and faster to Michael's eyes. Then he heard old Caryll's rasping cough and broken benignant sentences, which with all their memories lulled his emotion to quietude again.

"Hope you'll bring it in non probatum, Headmaster"—cough—cough—"good boys both "—cough—cough—"sure it's a mistake—Fane's a good boy too—idle young rascal—but a good heart"—cough—cough—"had him under me for a year—know him well——"

Dr. Brownjohn, with a most voluminous wave, dismissed the matter. Everyone, even the Paul Pry of a Secretary, went out of the room, and as the door closed Michael heard Mr. Caryll addressing the victims.

"Now then, don't cry any more, you young boobies."

Michael's thoughts followed them upstairs to the jolly class-room, and he almost smiled at the imagination of Mr. Caryll's entrance and the multitudinous jokes that would demonstrate his relief at his pupils' rescue. Michael recovered from his dream to find the Headmaster speaking to him in his most rumbling bass.

"I don't know why I allowed you to interfere in this disgraceful affair, boy. Um?"

"No, sir," Michael agreed.

"But since you are here, I will take the opportunity of warning you that the company you keep is very vile."

Michael looked apprehensive.

"If you think nothing is known of your habits out of school, you are much mistaken. I will not have any boy at my school frequenting the house of that deboshed nincompoop Wilmot."

Dr. Brownjohn's voice was now so deep that it vibrated in the pit of Michael's stomach like the diapason of the school organ.

"Give up that detestable association of mental impostors and be a boy again. You have disappointed me during the whole of your career; but you're a winning boy. Um? Go back to your work."

Michael left the august room with resolves swaying in his brain, wondering what he could do to repay the Old Man. It was too late to take a very high place in the summer examinations. Yet somehow, so passionate was his gratitude, he managed to come out third.

Michael never told his mother about his adventure, but in the reaction against Wilmot and all that partook of decadence, and in his pleasure at having done something, however clumsily, he felt a great wish to include his mother in his emotion of universal love.

"Where are we going these holidays?" he asked.

"I thought perhaps you'd like to stay at your monastery again," said Mrs. Fane. "I was thinking of going abroad."

Michael's face fell, and his mother was solicitously penitent.

"My dearest boy, I never dreamed you would want to be with me. You've always gone out on Sundays."

"I know, I'm sorry, I won't again," Michael assured her.

"And I've made my arrangements now. I wish I'd known. But why shouldn't you go and see Stella? It seems a pity that you and she should grow up so much apart."

"Well, I will, if you like," said Michael.

"Dearest boy, what has happened to you? You are so agreeable," exclaimed Mrs. Fane.

In the end it was arranged that Michael should accompany Mr. Viner on his holiday in France, and afterwards stay with Stella with a family at Compiègne for the rest of the time. Michael went to see his mother off at Charing Cross before he joined Mr. Viner.

"Darling Michael," she murmured as the train began to move slowly forward. "You're looking so well and happy—just like you were two years ago. Just like——"

The rest of the comparison was lost in the noise of the speeding train.

Chapter X: *Stella*

MICHAEL spent a charming fortnight with Father Viner in Amiens, Chartres and Rouen. The early Masses to which they went along the cool, empty streets of the morning, and the shadowy, candle-lit Benedictions from which they came home through the deepening dusk gave to Michael at least a profound hope, if not the astonishing faith of his first religious experience. Sitting with the priest at the open window of their inn, while down below the footsteps of the wayfarers were pattering like leaves, Michael recaptured some of that emotion of universal love which with sacramental force had filled his heart during the wonder of transition from boyhood to adolescence. He did not wish to know more about these people than could be told by the sound of their progress so light, so casual, so essentially becoming to the sapphirine small world in which they hurried to and fro. The passion of hope overwhelmed Michael's imagination with a beauty that was perfectly expressed by the unseen busy populations of a city's waning twilight. Love, birth, death, greed, ambition, all humanity's stress of thought and effort, were merged in a murmurous contentment of footfalls and faint-heard voices. Michael supposed that somehow to God the universe must sound much as this tall street of Rouen sounded now to him at his inn window, and he realized for the first time how God must love the world. Later, the twilight and voices and footfalls would fade together into night, and through long star-scattered silences Michael would brood with a rapture that became more than hope, if less than faith with restless, fiery heart. Then clocks would strike sonorously; the golden window-panes would waver and expire; Mr. Viner would tap his pipe upon the sill; and Michael and he would follow their own great shadows up into bedrooms noisy in the night-wind and prophetic of sleep's immense freedom, until with the slanting beams of dawn Michael would wake and at Mass time seek to enchain with prayers indomitable dreams.

The gravity of Michael's demeanour suited the grey town in which he sojourned, and though Mr. Viner used to teaze him about his saintly exterior, the priest seemed to enjoy his company.

"But don't look so solemn when you meet your sister, or she'll think you're sighing for a niche in Chartres Cathedral, which for a young lady emancipated from Germany would be a most distressing thought."

"I'm enjoying myself," said Michael earnestly.

"My dear old chap, I'm not questioning that for a moment, and personally I find your attitude consorts very admirably with the mood in which these northern towns of France always throw me," said Mr. Viner.

The fortnight came to an end, and to commemorate this chastening interlude of a confidence and a calm whose impermanence Michael half dreaded, half desired, he bought a pair of old candlesticks for the Notting Dale Mission. Michael derived a tremendous consolation from this purchase, for he felt that, even if in the future he should be powerless to revive this healing time, its austere hours would be immortalized, mirrored somehow in the candlesticks' bases as durably as if engraved upon a Grecian urn. There was in this impulse nothing more sentimental than in his erection last year of the small cairn to celebrate a fleeting moment of faith on the Berkshire downs.

Stella was already settled in the bosom of the French family when Michael reached Compiègne, and as he drove towards the Pension he began for the first time to wonder what his sister would be like after these two years. He was inclined to suppose that she would be a problem, and he already felt qualms about the behaviour of her projected suddenly like this from Germany into an atmosphere of romance. For Michael, France always stood out as typically romantic to his fancy. Spain and Italy were not within his realization as yet, and Germany he conceived of as a series of towns filled with the noise of piano-scales and hoarse gutturals. He hoped that Stella was not even now plunged into a girlish love-affair with one of the idle young Frenchmen who haunted so amorously the sunshine of this gay land. He even began to rehearse, as his carriage jolted along the cobbled embankment of the Oise, a particularly scathing scene in which he coldly denounced the importunate lover, while Stella stood abashed by fraternal indignation. Then he reflected that after all Stella was only fifteen and, as he remembered her, too much wrapped up in a zest for public appreciation to be very susceptible of private admiration. Moreover, he knew that most of her time was occupied by piano-practice. An emotion of pride in his accomplished sister displaced the pessimism of his first thoughts. He took pleasure in the imagination of her swaying the whole Pension by her miraculous execution, and he began to build up the picture of his entrance upon the last crashing chords of a sonata, when after the applause had ceased he would modestly step forward as the brother of this paragon.

The carriage was now bowling comfortably along a wide tree-shaded avenue bordered on either side by stretches of greenery which were dappled with children and nursemaids and sedate little girls with bobbing pigtails. Michael wondered if Stella was making a discreet promenade with the ladies of the family, half hoped she was, that he might reach the Pension before her and gracefully welcome her, as she, somewhat flustered by being late for his arrival, hurried up the front-door steps. Then, just as he was wondering whether there would or would not be front-door steps to the Pension, the cab drew up by a house with a green verandah and front-garden geranium-dyed to right and left of a vivid gravel path. Michael perceived, with a certain disapproval, that the verandah sheltered various ladies in wicker chairs. He disliked the notion of carrying up his bag in the range of their cool criticism, nor did he relish the conversation that would have to be embarked upon with the neat maid already hurrying to meet him. But most contrary to his preconceived idea of arrival was the affectionate ambush laid for him by Stella just when he was trying to remember whether 'chambre' were masculine or feminine. Yet, even as he felt Stella's dewy lips on his, and her slim fingers round his neck, he reproached himself for his silly shyness, although he could only say:

"Hullo, look out for my collar."

Stella laughed ripplingly.

"Oh, Michael," she cried, "I'm most frightfully glad to see you, you darling old Michael."

Michael looked much alarmed at the amazing facility of her affectionate greeting, and vaguely thought how much easier existence must be to a girl who never seemed to be hampered by any feeling of what people within earshot would think of her. Yet almost immediately Stella herself relapsed into shyness at the prospect of introducing Michael to the family, and it was only the perfectly accomplished courtesy of Madame Regnier which saved Michael from summarily making up his mind that these holidays were going to be a most ghastly failure.

The business of unpacking composed his feelings slightly, and a tap at his door, followed by Stella's silvery demand to come in, gave him a thrill of companionship. He suddenly realized, too, that he and his sister had corresponded frequently during their absence, and that this queer shyness at meeting her in person was really absurd. Stella, wandering round the room with his ties on her arm, gave Michael real pleasure, and she for her part seemed highly delighted at the privilege of superintending his unpacking.

He noted with a sentimental fondness that she still hummed, and he was very much impressed by the flowers which she had arranged in the cool corners of the pleasant room. On her appearance, too, as she hung over the rail of his bed chatting to him gaily, he congratulated himself. He liked the big apple-green bows in her chestnut hair; he liked her slim white hands and large eyes; and he wondered if her smile were like his, and hoped it was, since it was certainly very subtle and attractive.

"What sort of people hang out in this place?" he asked.

"Oh, nice people," Stella assured him. "Madame Regnier is a darling, and she loves my playing, and Monsieur is fearfully nice, with a grey beard. We always play billiards in the evening, and drink cassis. It's lovely. There are three darling old ladies, widows I think. They sit and listen to me playing, and when I've finished pay me all sorts of compliments, which sound so pretty in French. One of them said I was 'ravissante.'"

"Are there any kids?" asked Michael.

Stella said there were no kids, and Michael sighed his relief.

"Do you practise much?"

"Oh, no, I'm having a holiday, I only practise three hours a day."

"How much?" asked Michael. "Good Lord, do you call that a holiday?"

"Why, you silly old thing, of course it is," rippled Stella.

Presently it was time for déjeuner, and they sat down to eat in a room, of shaded sunlight, watching the green jalousies that glowed like beryls, and listening to a canary's song. Michael was introduced to Madame Graves, Madame Lamarque and Madame Charpentier, the three old widows who lived at the Pension, and who all looked strangely alike, with their faces and hands of aged ivory and their ruffles and wristbands starched to the semblance of fretted white coral. They ate mincingly in contrast to M. Regnier who, guarded by a very large napkin, pitchforked his food into his mouth with noisy recklessness. Later in the mellow August afternoon Michael and he walked solemnly round the town together, and Michael wondered if he had ever before raised his hat so many times.

After dinner, when the coffee and cassis had been drunk, Madame Regnier invited Stella to play to them. Dusk was falling in the florid French drawing-room, but so rich was the approach of darkness that no lamps brooded with rosy orbs, and only a lighted candle on either side of Stella stabbed the gloom in which the listeners leaned quietly back against the tropic tapestries of their chairs, without trying to occupy themselves with books or crochet-work.

Michael sat by the scented window, watching the stars twinkle, it almost seemed, in tune with the vibrant melodies that Stella rang out. In the bewitching candlelight the keyboard trembled and shimmered like water to a low wind. Deep in the shadow the three old ladies sat in a waxen ecstasy, so still that Michael wondered whether they were alive. He did not know whose tunes they were that Stella played; he did not know what dreams they wove for the old ladies, whether of spangled opera-house or ball; he did not care, being content to watch the lissome hands that from time to time went dancing away on either side from the curve of Stella's straight back, whether to play with raindrops in the treble or marshal thunders from the bass. The candlelight sprayed her flowing chestnut hair with a golden mist that might have been an aureole over which the apple-green bows floated unsubstantial like amazing moths.

Michael continually tried to shape his ideas to the inspiration of the music, but every image that rose battling for expression lost itself in a peerless stupefaction.

Then suddenly Stella stopped playing, and the enchantment was dispelled by murmurous praise and entering lamplight. Stella, slim as a fountain, stood upright in the centre of the drawing-room and, like a fountain, swayed now this way, now that, to catch the compliments so dear to her. Michael wished the three old ladies would not appeal to him to endorse their so perfectly phrased enthusiasm, and grew very conscious of the gradual decline of 'oui' into 'wee' as he supported their laudation. He was glad when M. Regnier proposed a game of billiards, and glad to see that Stella could romp, romp so heartily indeed that once or twice he had to check a whispered rebuke.

But later on when he said good night to her outside his bedroom, he had an impulse to hug her close for the unimaginable artistry of this little sister.

Michael and Stella went out next day to explore the forest of Compiègne. They wandered away from the geometrical forest roads into high glades and noble chases; they speculated upon the whereabouts of the wild-boars that were hunted often, and therefore really did exist; they lay deep in the bracken utterly remote in the ardent emerald light, utterly quiet save for the thrum of insects rising and falling. In this intimate seclusion Michael found it easy enough to talk to Stella. Somehow her face, magnified by the proportions of the surroundingvegetation, scarcely seemed to belong to her, and Michael had a sensation of a fairy fellowship, as he felt himself being absorbed into her wide and strangely magical eyes. Seen like this they were as overwhelmingly beautiful as two flowers, holding mysteries of colour and form that could never be revealed save thus in an abandonment of contemplation.

"Why do you stare at me, Michael?" she asked.

"Because I think it's funny to realize that you and I are as nearly as it's possible to be the same person, and yet we're as different from each other as we are from the rest of people. I wonder, if you didn't know I was your brother, and I didn't know you were my sister, if we should have a sort of—what's the word?—intuition about it? For instance, you can play the piano, and I can't even understand the feeling of being able to play the piano. I wish we knew our father. It must be interesting to have a father and a mother, and see what part of one comes from each."

"I always think father and mother weren't married," said Stella.

Michael blushed hotly, taken utterly aback.

"I say, my dear girl, don't say things like that. That's a frightful thing to say."

"Why?"

"Why? Why, because people would be horrified to hear a little girl talking like that," Michael explained.

"Oh, I thought you meant they'd be shocked to think of people not being married."

"I say, really, you know, Stella, you ought to be careful. I wouldn't have thought you even knew that people sometimes—very seldom, though, mind—don't get married."

"You funny old boy," rippled Stella. "You must think I'm a sort of doll just wound up to play the piano. If I didn't know that much after going to Germany, why—oh, Michael, I do think you're funny."

"I was afraid these beastly foreigners would spoil you," muttered Michael.

"It's not the foreigners. It's myself."

"Stella!"

"Well, I'm fifteen and a half."

"I thought girls were innocent," said Michael with disillusion in his tone.

"Girls grow older quicker than boys."

"But I mean always innocent," persisted Michael. "I don't mean all girls, of course. But—well—a girl like you."

"Very innocent girls are usually very stupid girls," Stella asserted.

Michael made a resolution to watch his sister's behaviour when she came back to London next year to make her first public appearance at a concert. For the moment, feeling overmatched, he changed the trend of his reproof.

"Well, even if you do talk about people not being married, I think it's rotten to talk about mother like that."

"You stupid old thing, as if I should do it with anyone but you, and I only talked about her to you because you look so sort of cosy and confidential in these ferns."

"They're not ferns—they're bracken. If I thought such a thing was possible," declared Michael, "I believe I'd go mad. I don't think I could ever again speak to anybody I knew."

"Why not, if they didn't know?"

"How like a girl! Stella, you make me feel uncomfortable, you do really."

Stella stretched her full length in the luxurious greenery.

"Well, mother never seems unhappy."

"Exactly," said Michael eagerly. "Therefore, what you think can't possibly be true. If it were, she'd always look miserable."

"Well, then who *was* our father?"

"Don't ask me," said Michael gloomily. "I believe he's in prison—or perhaps he's in an asylum, or deformed."

Stella shuddered.

"Michael, what a perfectly horrible idea. Deformed!"

"Well, wouldn't you sooner he were deformed than that you were—than that—than the other idea?" Michael stammered.

"No, I wouldn't," Stella cried. "I'd much, much, much rather that mother was never married."

Michael tried to drag his mind towards the comprehension of this unnatural sentiment, but the longer he regarded it the worse it seemed, and with intense irony he observed to Stella:

"I suppose you'll be telling me next that you're in love."

"I'm not in love just at the moment," said Stella blandly.

"Do you mean to say you have been in love?"

"A good deal," she admitted.

Michael leaped to his feet, and looked down on her recumbent in the bracken.

"But only in a stupid schoolgirly way?" he gasped.

"Yes, I suppose it was," Stella paused. "But it was fearfully thrilling all the same—especially in duets."

"Duets?"

"I used to read ahead, and watch where our hands would come together, and then the notes used to get quite slippery with excitement."

"Look here," Michael demanded, drawing himself up, "are you trying to be funny?"

"No," Stella declared, rising to confront Michael. "He was one of my masters. He was only about thirty, and he was killed in Switzerland by an avalanche."

Michael was staggered by the confession of this shocking and precocious child, as one after another his chimeras rose up to leer at him triumphantly.

"And did he make love to you? Did he try to kiss you?" Michael choked out.

"Oh, no," said Stella. "That would have spoilt it all."

Michael sighed under a faint lightening of his load, and Stella came up to him engagingly to slip her arm into his.

"Don't be angry with me, Michael, because I have wanted so dreadfully to be great friends with you and tell you all my secrets. I want to tell you what I think about when I'm playing; and, Michael, you oughtn't to be angry with me, because you were simply just made to be told secrets. That's why I played so well last night. I was telling you a secret all the time."

"Do you know what it is, Stella?" said Michael, with a certain awe in his voice. "I believe our father is in an asylum, and I believe you and I are both mad—not raving mad, of course—but slightly mad."

"All geniuses are," said Stella earnestly.

"But we aren't geniuses."

"I am," murmured Stella in a strangely quiet little voice that sounded in Michael's ears like the song of a furtive melodious bird.

"Are you?" he whispered, half frightened by this assertion, delivered under huge overarching trees in the burning silence of the forest. "Who told you so?"

"I told myself so. And when I tell myself something very solemnly, I can't be anything but myself, and I must be speaking the truth."

"But even if you're a genius—and I suppose you might be—I'm not a genius. I'm clever, but I'm not a genius."

"No, but you're the nearest person to being me, and if you're not a genius, I think you can understand. Oh, Michael," Stella cried, clasping his arm to her heart, "you do understand, because you never laughed when I told you I was a genius. I've told lots of girl-friends, and they laugh and say I'm conceited."

"Well, you are," said Michael, feeling bound not to lose the opportunity of impressing Stella with disapproval as well as comprehension.

"I know I am. But I must be to go on being myself. Oh, you darling brother, you do understand me. I've longed for someone to understand me. Mother's only proud of me."

"I'm not at all proud of you," said Michael crushingly.

"I don't want you to be. If you were proud of me, you'd think I belonged to you, and I don't ever want to belong to anybody."

"I shouldn't think you ever would," said Michael encouragingly, as they paced the sensuous mossy path in a rapture of avowals. "I should think you'd frighten anybody except me. But why do you fall in love, then?"

"Oh, because I want to make people die with despair."

"Great Scott, you are an unearthly kid."

"Oh, I'm glad I'm unearthly," said Stella. "I'd like to be a sort of Undine. I think I am. I don't think I've got a soul, because when I play I go rushing out into the darkness to look for my soul, and the better I play the nearer I get."

Michael stopped beneath an oak-tree and surveyed this extraordinary sister of his.

"Well, I always thought I was a mystic, but, good Lord, you're fifty times as much of a mystic as I am," he exclaimed with depressed conviction.

Suddenly Stella gave a loud scream.

"What on earth are you yelling at?" said Michael.

"Oh, Michael, look—a most enormous animal. Oh, look, oh, let me get up a tree. Oh, help me up. Push me up this tree."

"It's a wild-boar," declared Michael in a tone of astonished interest.

Stella screamed louder than ever and clung to Michael, sobbing. The boar, however, went on its way, routing among the herbage.

"Well, you may be a genius," said Michael, "but you're an awful little funk."

"But I was frightened."

"Wild-boars aren't dangerous except when they're being hunted," Michael asserted positively.

Stella soon became calm under the influence of her brother's equanimity. Arm-in-arm they sauntered back towards Compiègne, and so for a month of serene weather they sauntered every day, and every day Michael pondered more and more deeply the mystery of woman. He was sorry to say good-bye to Stella when she went back to Germany, and longed for the breathless hour of her first concert, wishful that all his life he might stand between her and the world, the blundering wild-boar of a world.

Chapter XI: *Action and Reaction*

ALMOST before the confusion of a new term had subsided, Michael put his name down to play football again, and it was something in the nature of an occasion when in the first sweltering Middle-side game he scored six tries. Already his contemporaries had forgotten that he was once a fleet and promising three-quarter, so that his resurrection was regarded as an authentic apparition, startling in its unexpectedness. Michael was the only person not much surprized when he was invited by Abercrombie to play as substitute for one of the Seniors absent from a Big-side trial. Yet even Michael was surprized when in the opening match between Classics and Moderns he read his name on the notice-board as sixteenth man; and when, through the continued illness of the first choice, he actually found himself walking on to the field between the black lines of spectators, he was greatly content. Yet the finest thrill of all came when in the line-out he found himself on the left wing with Alan, with Alan not very unlike the old Alan even now in the coveted Tyrian vest of the Classical First Fifteen.

Into that game Michael poured all he felt of savage detestation for everything that the Modern side stood for. Not an opponent was collared that did not in his falling agony take on the likeness of Percy Garrod; not a Modern half-back was hurled into touch who was not in Michael's imagination insolent with damnably destructive theories of life. It was exhilarating, it was superb, it was ineffable, the joy of seeing Alan hand off a Modern bounder and swing the ball out low to him crouching vigilant upon the left. It was intoxicating, it was divine to catch the ball, and with zigzag leap and plunge to tear wildly on towards the Modern goal, to hear the Classical lower boys shriek their high-voiced thrilling exhortations, to hear the maledictions of the enemy ricochetting from a force of speed that spun its own stability. Back went the ball to Alan, shouting with flushed face on his right, just as one of the Modern three-quarters, with iron grip round Michael's faltering knees, fetched him crashing down.

"Good pass," cried the delighted Classical boys, and "Well run, sir, well run, sir!" they roared as Alan whizzed the ball along to the dapper, the elusive, the incomparable Terry.

"Go in, yourself," they prayed, as Terry like a chamois bounded straight at the despairing full-back, then with a gasp that triumphed over the vibrant hush, checked himself, and in one peerless spring breasted the shoulders of the back to come thudding down upon the turf with a glorious try.

Now the game swayed desperately, and with Alan ever beside him Michael lived through every heroic fight of man. They were at Thermopylae, stemming the Persian charges with hack and thrust and sweeping cut; they were at Platea with Aristides and Pausanias, vowing death rather than subjugation; the body of Terry beneath a weight of Modern forwards, crying, "Let me up, you stinkers!" was fought for as long ago beneath the walls of Troy the battle raged about the body of Patroclus. And when the game was over, when the Moderns had been defeated for the first time in four resentful years of scientific domination, when the Classical Fifteen proudly strode from the field, immortal in muddied Tyrian, it was easy enough to walk across the gravel arm-in-arm with Alan and, while still the noise of the contest and the cries of the onlookers echoed in their ears, it was easy to span the icy floes of two drifting years in one moment of careless, artless intercourse.

"You'll get your Second Fifteen colours," said Alan confidently.

"Not this year," Michael thought.

"You'll get your Third Fifteen cap for a snip."

"Yes, I ought to get that," Michael agreed.

"Well, that's damned good, considering you haven't played for two years," Alan vowed.

And as he spoke Michael wondered if Alan had ever wished for his company in the many stressful games from which he had been absent.

Michael now became one of that group of happy immortals in the entrance-hall, whose attitudes of noble ease graced the hot-water pipes below the 'board' on which the news of the school fluctuated daily. This society, to which nothing gave admission but a profound sense of one's own right to enter it, varied from time to time only in details. As a whole composition it was immutable, as permanent, as decorative and as appropriate as the frieze of the Parthenon. From twenty minutes past nine until twenty-seven minutes past nine, from twenty-five minutes past eleven until twenty-eight minutes past eleven, from ten minutes to three until two minutes to three the heroes of the school met in a large familiarity whose Olympian laughter awed the fearful small boy that flitted uneasily past and chilled the slouching senior that rashly paused to examine the notices in assertion of an unearned right. Even masters entering through the swinging doors seemed glad to pass beyond the range of the heroes' patronizing contemplation.

Michael found a pedestal here, and soon idealized the heedless stupidity of these immortals into a Lacedemonian rigour which seemed to him very fine. He accepted their unimaginative standards, their coarseness, their brutality as virtues, and in them he saw the consummation of all that England should cherish. He successfully destroyed a legend that he was clever, and though at first he found it difficult to combat the suspicion of æsthetic proclivities and religious eccentricity, even of poetic ambitions which overshadowed his first welcome, he was at last able to get these condoned as a blemish upon an otherwise diverting personality with a tongue nimble enough to make heroes guffaw. Moreover, he was a friend of Alan, who with his slim disdain and perfectly stoic bearing was irreproachable, and since Michael frankly admired his new friends, and since he imparted just enough fantasy to their stolid fellowship to lend it a faint distinction, he was very soon allowed to preserve a flavour of oddity, and became in time arbiter of whatever elegance they could claim. Michael on his side was most anxious to conform to every prejudice of the Olympians, esteeming their stolidity far above his own natural demeanour, envious too of their profoundly ordinary point of view and their commonplace expression of it.

Upon this assembly descended the news of war with the Transvaal, and for three months at least Michael shared in the febrile elation and arrogance and complacent outlook of the average Englishman. The Olympians recalled from early schooldays the forms of heroes who were even now gazetted to regiments on their way to the front, and who but a little while ago had lounged against these very hot-water pipes. Sandhurst and Woolwich candidates lamented their ill-luck in being born too young, and consoled themselves with proclaiming that after all the war was so easy that scarcely were they missing anything at all. Then came the first low rumble of defeat, the first tremulous breath of doubt.

Word went round that meetings were being held to stop the war, and wrathfully the heroes mounted a London Road Car omnibus, snatched the Union Jack from its socket, and surged into Hammersmith Town Hall to yell and hoot at the farouche Irishmen and dirty Socialists who were mouthing their hatred of the war and exulting in the unlucky capture of two regiments. The School Cadet Corps could not accept the mass of recruits that demanded to be enrolled. Drums were bought by subscription, and in the armoury down under the School tattoo and rataplan voiced the martial spirit of St. James'.

One day Alan brought back the news that his Uncle Kenneth was ordered to the front, that he would sail from Southampton in a few days. Leave was granted Alan to go and say good-bye, and in the patriotic fervour that now burned even in the hearts of schoolmasters, Michael was accorded leave to accompany him.

They travelled down to Southampton on a wet, windy November day, proud to think as they sat opposite one another in the gloomy railway-carriage that in some way since this summons they were both more intimately connected with the war.

In a dreary Southampton hotel they met Mrs. Ross, and Michael thought that she was very beautiful and very brave waiting in the chilly fly-blown dining-room of the hotel. Three years of marriage scarcely seemed to have altered his dear Miss Carthew; yet there was a dignity, a carven stillness that Michael had never associated with the figure of his governess, or perhaps it was that now he was older, more capable of appreciating the noble lines of this woman.

It gave Michael a sentimental pang to watch Mrs. Ross presiding over their lunch as she had in the past presided over so many lunches. They spoke hardly at all of Captain Ross's departure, but they talked of Nancy, and how well she was doing as secretary to Lord Perham, of Mrs. Carthew, still among the roses and plums of Cobble Place, and of a hundred jolly bygone events. Mrs. Ross was greatly interested to hear of Stella, and greatly amused by Michael's arrangement of her future.

Then Captain Ross came in, and after a few jokes, which fell very flat in the bleak dining-room—perhaps because the two boys were in awe of this soldier going away to the wars, or perhaps because they knew that there was indeed nothing to joke about—said:

"The regiment comes in by the 2.45. We shall embark at once. What's the time now?"

Everyone, even the mournful waiter, stared up at the wall. It was two o'clock.

"Half an hour before I need go down to the station," said Captain Ross, and then he began to whistle very quietly. The wind was getting more boisterous, and the rain rattled on the windows as if, without, a menacing hand flung gravel for a signal.

"Can you two boys amuse yourselves for a little while?" asked Captain Ross.

"Oh, rather," said Michael and Alan.

"I've just one or two things I wanted to say to you, dear," said Captain Ross, turning to his wife. They left the dining-room together. Michael and Alan sat silently at the table, crumbling bread and making patterns in the salt-cellar. They could hear the gaunt clock ticking away on the stained wall above them. From time to time far-off bugles sounded above the tossing wind. So they sat for twenty solemn minutes. Then the husband and wife came back. The bill was paid; the door of the hotel swung back; the porter said 'Good luck, sir,' very solemnly, and in a minute they were walking down the street towards the railway-station through the wind and rain.

"I'll see you on the dock in a moment," said Captain Ross. "You'd better take a cab down and wait under cover."

Thence onwards for an hour or more all was noise, excitement and bustle in contrast to the brooding, ominous calm of the dingy hotel. Regiments were marching down to the docks; bands were playing; there were drums and bugles, shouts of command, clatter of horses, the occasional rumble of a gun-carriage, enquiries, the sobbing of children and women, oaths, the hooting of sirens, a steam-engine's whistle, and at last, above everything else, was heard the wail of approaching pipes.

Nearer and nearer swirled the maddening, gladdening, heart-rending tune they played; the Kintail Highlanders were coming; they swung into view; they halted, company after company of them; there were shouts of command very close; suddenly Michael found his hand clenched and saw Captain Ross's grey eyes smiling good-bye; Alan's sleeve seemed to have a loose thread that wanted biting off; the sirens of the great transport trumpeted angrily and, resounding through the sinking hearts of those who were not going, robbed them of whatever pluck was left. Everywhere in view sister, mother, and wife were held for a moment by those they loved. The last man was aboard; the gangway was hauled up; the screw pounded the water; the ship began to glide away from the dock with slow, sickening inevitableness. Upon the air danced handkerchiefs, feeble fluttering envoys of the passionate farewells they flung to the wind. Spellbound, intolerably powerless, the watchers on shore waved and waved; smaller grew the faces leaning over the rail; smaller and smaller, until at last they were unrecognizable to those left behind; and now the handkerchiefs were waved in a new fever of energy as if with the fading of the faces there had fallen upon the assembly a fresh communal grief, a grief that, no longer regarding personal heartbreaks, frantically pursued the great graceful ship herself whose prow was straining for the open sea. Still, though now scarcely even were human forms discernible upon the decks, the handkerchiefs jigged on for horribly mechanic gestures, as if those who waved them were become automatons through sorrow.

Glad of the musty peace of a railway-carriage after the tears and confusion of the docks, Michael and Alan and Mrs. Ross spoke very little on the journey back to London.

"Aren't you going to stay the night with us at Richmond?" Alan asked.

"No, I must get down to Cobble Place. My large son has already gone there with his nurse."

"Your son?" exclaimed Michael. "Oh, of course, I forgot."

So Alan and he put Mrs. Ross into her train and rode back together on an omnibus, proud citizens of an Empire whose inspiration they had lately beheld in action.

Next morning the Olympians on their frieze were considerably impressed by Michael's account of the stirring scene at Southampton.

"Oh, the war will be over almost at once. We're not taking any risks. We're sending out enough men to conquer more than the Transvaal," said the heroes wisely.

But soon there came the news of fresh defeats, and when in the middle of January school reassembled there were actually figures missing from the familiar composition itself. Actually contemporary heroes had left, had enlisted in the Volunteers and Yeomanry, were even now waiting for orders and meantime self-consciously wandering round the school-grounds in militant khaki. Sandhurst and Woolwich candidates passed with incredible ease; boys were coming to school in mourning; Old Jacobeans died bravely, and their deaths were recorded in the school magazine; one Old Jacobean gained the Victoria Cross, and everyone walked from prayers very proudly upon that day.

Michael was still conventionally patriotic, but sometimes with the progress of the war a doubt would creep into his mind whether this increasing blazonry of a country's emotion were so fine as once he had thought it, whether England were losing some of her self-control under reverses, and, worst of all, whether in her victories she were becoming blatant. He remembered how he had been sickened by the accounts of American hysteria during the war with Spain, whose weaker cause, true to his earliest inclinations, he had been compelled to champion. And now when the tide was turning in England's favour, when every other boy came to school wearing a khaki tie quartered with blue or red and some of them even came tricked out with Union Jack waistcoats, when the wearing of a British general's head on a button and the hissing of Kruger's name at a pantomime were signs of high emotion, when many wastrels of his acquaintance had uniforms, and when the patriotism of their friends consisted of making these undignified supernumeraries drunk, Michael began to wonder whether war conducted by a democracy had ever been much more than a circus for the populace.

And when one bleak morning in early spring he read in a fatal column that Captain Kenneth Ross had been killed in action, his smouldering resentment blazed out, and as he hurried to school with sickened heart and eyes in a mist of welling tears, he could have cursed everyone of the rosetted patriots for whose vainglory such a death paid the price. Alan, as he expected, was not at school, and Michael spent a restless, miserable morning. He hated the idea of discussing the news with his friends of the hot-water pipes, and when one by one the unimaginative, flaccid comments flowed easily forth upon an event that was too great for them even to hear, much less to speak of, Michael's rage burst forth:

"For God's sake, you asses, don't talk so much. I'm sick of this war. I'm sick of reading that a lot of decent chaps have died for nothing, because it is for nothing, if this country is never again going to be able to stand defeat or victory. War isn't anything to admire in itself. All the good of war is what it makes of the people who fight, and what it makes of the people who stay at home."

The Olympians roared with laughter, and congratulated Michael on his humorous oration.

"Can't you see that I'm serious? that it is important to be gentlemen?" Michael shouted.

"Who says we aren't gentlemen?" demanded a very vapid, but slightly bellicose hero.

"Nobody says *you* aren't a gentleman, you ass; at least nobody says you eat peas with a knife, but, my God, if you think it's decent to wear that damned awful button in your coat when fellows are being killed every day for you, for your pleasure, for your profit, for your existence, all I can say is I don't."

Michael felt that the climax of this speech was somewhat weak, and he relapsed into silence, biting his nails with the unexpressed rage of limp words.

"You might as well say that the School oughtn't to cheer at a football match," said Abercrombie the Captain.

"I would say so, if I thought that all the cheerers never expected and never even intended to play themselves. That's why professional football is so rotten."

"You were damned glad to get your Third Fifteen cap," Abercrombie pointed out gruffly.

The laugh that followed this rebuke from the mightiest of the immortals goaded Michael into much more than he had intended to say when he began his unlucky tirade.

"Oh, was I?" he sneered. "That's just where you're quite wrong, because, as a matter of fact, I don't intend to play football any more, if School Footer is simply to be a show for a lot of wasters. I'm not going to exert myself like an acrobat in a circus, if it all means nothing."

The heroes regarded Michael with surprize and distaste; they shrank from him coldly as if his unreasonable outburst in some way involved their honour. They laughed uncomfortably, each one hiding himself behind another's shoulders, as if they mocked a madman. The bell for school rang, and the heroes left him. Michael, still enraged, went back to his class-room. Then he wondered if Alan would hate him for having made his uncle's death an occasion for this breach of a school's code of manners. He supposed sadly that Alan would not understand any more than the others what he felt. He cursed himself for having let these ordinary, obvious, fat-headed fools impose upon his imagination, as to lead him to consider them worthy of his respect. He had wasted three months in this society; he had thought he was happy and had congratulated himself upon at last finding school endurable. School was a prison, such as it always had been. He was seventeen and a schoolboy. It was ignominious. At one o'clock he waited for nobody, but walked quickly home to lunch, still fuming with the loss of his self-control and, as he looked back on the scene, of his dignity.

His mother came down to lunch with signs of a morning's tears, and Michael looked at her in astonishment. He had not supposed that she would be much affected by the death of Captain Ross, and he enquired if she had been writing to Mrs. Ross.

"No, dear," said Mrs. Fane. "Why should I have written to Mrs. Ross this morning?"

"Didn't you see in the paper?" Michael asked.

"See what?"

"That Captain Ross was killed in action."

"Oh, no," gasped his mother, white and shuddering. "Oh, Michael, how horrible, and on the same day."

"The same day as what?"

Mrs. Fane looked at her son for a moment very intently, as if she were minded to tell him something. Then the parlour-maid came into the room, and she seemed to change her mind, and finally said in perfectly controlled accents:

"The same day as the announcement is made that—that your old friend Lord Saxby has raised a troop of horse—Saxby's horse. He is going to Africa almost at once."

"Another gentleman going to be killed for the sake of these rowdy swine at home!" said Michael savagely.

"Michael! What do you mean? Don't you admire a man for—for trying to do something for his country?"

"It depends on the country," Michael answered, "If you think it's worth while doing anything for what England is now, I don't. I wouldn't raise a finger, if London were to be invaded to-morrow."

"I don't understand you, dearest boy. You're talking rather like a Radical, and rather like old Conservative gentlemen I remember as a girl. It's such a strange mixture. I don't think you quite understand what you're saying."

"I understand perfectly what I'm saying," Michael contradicted.

"Well, then I don't think you ought to talk like that. I don't think it's kind or considerate to me and, after you've just heard about Captain Ross's death, I think it's irreverent. And I thought you attached so much importance to reverence," Mrs. Fane added in a complaining tone.

Michael was vexed by his mother's failure to understand his point of view, and became harder and more perverse every minute.

"Lord Saxby would be shocked to hear you talking like this, shocked and horrified," she went on.

"I'm very sorry for hurting Lord Saxby's feelings," said Michael with elaborate sarcasm. "But really I don't see that it matters much to him what I think."

"He wants to see you before he sails," said Mrs. Fane.

"To see me? Why?" gasped Michael. "Why on earth should he want to see me?"

"Well, he's—he's in a way the head of our family."

"He's not taken much interest in me up to the present. It's rather odd he should want to see me now when he's going away."

"Michael, don't be so bitter and horrid. Lord Saxby's so kind, and he—and he—might never come back."

"Dearest mother," said Michael, "I think you're a little unreasonable. Why should I go and meet a man now, and perhaps grow to like him—and then say good-bye to him, perhaps for ever?"

"Michael, do not talk like that. You are selfish and brutal. You've grown up to be perfectly heartless, although you can be charming. I think you'd better not see Lord Saxby. He'd be ashamed of you."

Michael rose in irritation.

"My dear mother, what on earth business is it of Lord Saxby's how I behave? I don't understand what you mean by being ashamed of me. I have lived all these years, and I've seen Lord Saxby once. He sent me some Siamese stamps and some soldiers. I dare say he's a splendid chap. I know I liked him terrifically, when I was a kid, and if he's killed I shall be sorry—I shall be more than sorry—I shall be angry, furious that for the sake of these insufferable rowdies another decent chap is going to risk his life."

Mrs. Fane put out her hand to stop Michael's flowing tirade, but he paid no attention, talking away less to her than to himself. Indeed, long before he had finished, she made no pretence of listening, but merely sat crying quietly.

"I've been thinking a good deal lately about this war," Michael declared. "I'm beginning to doubt whether it's a just war, whether we didn't simply set out on it for brag and money. I'm not sure that I want to see the Boers conquered. They're a small independent nation, and they have old-fashioned ideas and they're narrow-minded Bible-worshippers, but there's something noble about them, something much nobler than there is in these rotten adventurers who go out to fight them. Of course, I don't mean by that people like Captain Ross or Lord Saxby. They're gentlemen. They go either because it's their duty or because they think it's their duty. And they're the ones that get killed. You don't hear of these swaggerers in khaki being killed. I haven't heard yet of many of them even going to the front at all. Oh, mother, I am fed up with the rotten core of everything that looks so fine on the outside."

Mrs. Fane was now crying loud enough to make Michael stop in sudden embarrassment.

"I say, mother, don't cry. I expect I've been talking nonsense," he softly told her.

"I don't know where you get these views. I was always so proud of you. I thought you were charming and mysterious, and you're simply vulgar!"

"Vulgar?" echoed Michael in dismay.

Mrs. Fane nodded vehemently.

"Oh, well, if I'm vulgar, I'll go."

Michael hurried to the door.

"Where are you going?" asked his mother in alarm.

"Oh, Lord, only to school. That's what makes a scene like this so funny. After I've worked myself up and made you angry——"

"Not angry, dear. Only grieved," interrupted his mother.

"You were more than grieved when you said I was vulgar. At least I hope you were. But, after it's all over, I go trotting off like a good little boy to school—to school—to school. Oh, mother, what is the good of expecting me to believe in the finest fellows in the world being killed, while I'm still at school? What's the good of making me more wretched, more discontented, more alive to my own futile existence by asking me now, when he's going away, to make friends with Lord Saxby? Oh, darling mother, can't you realize that I'm no longer a little boy who wants to clap his hands at the sight of a red coat? Let me kiss you, mother, I'm sorry I was vulgar, but I've minded so dreadfully about Captain Ross, and it's all for nothing."

Mrs. Fane let herself be petted by her son, but she did not again ask Michael to see Lord Saxby before he went away to the war.

Alan was still absent at afternoon school, and Michael, disdaining his place in the heroic group, passed quickly into the class-room and read in Alison of Salamanca and Albuera and of the storming of Badajoz, wondering what had happened to his country since those famous dates. He supposed that then was the nation's zenith, for from what he could make out of the Crimean War, that had been as little creditable to England as this miserable business of the present.

In the afternoon Michael thought he would walk over to Notting Dale and see Mr. Viner—perhaps he would understand some of his indignation—and this evening when all was quiet he must write to Mrs. Ross. On his way down the Kensington Road he met Wilmot, whom he had not seen since the summer, for luckily about the time of the row Wilmot had been going abroad and was only lately back. He recognized Wilmot's fanciful walk from a distance, and nearly crossed over to the opposite pavement to avoid meeting him; but on second thoughts decided he would like to hear a fresh opinion of the war.

"Why, here's a delightful meeting," said Wilmot, "I have been wondering why you didn't come round to see me. You got my cards?"

"Oh, yes, rather," said Michael.

"I have been in Greece and Italy. I wish you had been with me. I thought of you, as I sat in the ruined rose-gardens of Paestum. You've no idea how well those columns of honey-coloured Travertine would become you, Michael. But I'm so glad to see that you have not yet clothed yourself in khaki. This toy war is so utterly absurd. I feel as if I were living in a Christmas bazaar. How dreadfully these puttees and haversacks debase even the most beautiful figures. What is a haversack? It sounds so Lenten, so eloquent of mortification. I have discovered some charming Cyprian cigarettes. Do come and let me watch you enjoy them. How young you look, and yet how old!"

"I'm feeling very fit," said Michael loftily.

"How abruptly informative you are! What has happened to you?"

"I'm thinking about this war."

"Good gracious," cried Wilmot in mincing amazement. "What an odd subject. Soon you will be telling me that by moonlight you brood upon the Albert Memorial. But perhaps your mind is full of trophies. Perhaps you are picturing to yourself in Piccadilly a second column of Trajan displacing the amorous and acrobatic Cupid who now presides over the painted throng. Come with me some evening to the Long Bar at the Criterion, and while the Maori-like barmaids titter in their *dévergondage*, we will select the victorious site and picture to ourselves the Boer commanders chained like hairy Scythians to the chariot of whatever absurd general chooses to accept the triumph awarded to him by our legislative *bourgeoisie*."

"I think I must be getting on," said Michael.

"How urgent! You speak like Phaeton or Icarus, and pray remember the calamities that befell them. But seriously, when are you coming to see me?"

"Oh, I'm rather busy," said Michael briefly.

Wilmot looked at him curiously with his glittering eyes for a moment. Then he spoke again:

"Farewell, Narcissus. Have you learnt that I was but a shallow pool in which to watch your reflection? Did I flatter you too much or not enough? Who shall say? But you know I'm always your friend, and when this love-affair is done, I shall always be interested to hear the legend of it told movingly when and where you will, but perhaps best of all in October when the full moon lies like a huge apricot upon the chimneys of the town. Farewell, Narcissus. Does she display your graces very clearly?"

"I'm not in love with anybody, if that's what you mean," said Michael.

"No? But you are on the margin of a strange pool, and soon you will be peeping over the bulrushes to stare at yourself again."

Then Mr. Wilmot, making his pontifical and undulatory adieu, passed on.

"Silly ass!" said Michael to himself. "And he always thinks he knows everything."

Michael turned out of the noisy main road into the sylvan urbanity of Holland Walk. A haze of tender diaphanous green clung to the boles of the smirched elms, softening the sooty decay that made their antiquity so grotesque and so dishonourable. Michael sat down for a while on a bench, inhaling the immemorial perfume of a London spring and listening to the loud courtship of the blackbirds in the ragged shrubberies that lined the railings of Holland Park. He was not made any the more content with himself by this effluence of revivified effort that impregnated the air around him. He was out of harmony with every impulse of the season, and felt just as tightly fettered now as long ago he used to feel on waits by this same line of blackened trees with Nurse to quell his lightest step towards freedom. Where was Nurse now? The pungent odour of privet blown along a dying wind of March was quick with old memories of forbidden hiding-places, and he looked up, half expectant of her mummified shape peering after his straying steps round the gnarled and blackened trunk of the nearest elm. Michael rose quickly and went on his way towards Notting Dale. This Holland Walk had always been a haunted spot, not at all a place to hearten one, especially where at the top it converged to a silent passage between wooden palings whose twinkling interstices and exudations of green slime had always been queerly sinister. Even now Michael was glad when he could hear again the noise of traffic in the Bayswater Road. As he walked on towards Mr. Viner's house he gave rein to fanciful moralizings upon these two great roads on either side of the Park that ran a parallel course, but never met. How foreign it all seemed on this side with unfamiliar green omnibuses instead of red, with never even a well-known beggar or pavement-artist. The very sky had an alien look, seeming vaster somehow than the circumscribed clouds of Kensington. Perhaps after all the people of this intolerably surprising city were not so much to be blamed for their behaviour during a period of war. They had nothing to hold them together, to teach them to endure and enjoy, to suffer and rejoice in company. These great main roads sweeping West and East with multitudinous chimney-pots between were symbolic of the whole muddle of existence.

"But what do I want?" Michael asked himself so loudly that an errand-boy stayed his whistling and stared after him until he turned the corner.

"I don't know," he muttered in the face of a fussy little woman, who jumped aside to let him pass.

Soon he was deep in one of Mr. Viner's arm-chairs and, without waiting even to produce one of the attenuated pipes he still affected, exclaimed with desolating conviction:

"I'm absolutely sick of everything!"

"What, again?" said the priest, smiling.

"It's this war."

"You're not thinking of enlisting in the Imperial Yeomanry?"

"Oh, no, but a friend of mine—Alan Merivale's uncle—has been killed. It seems all wrong."

"My dear old chap," said Mr. Viner earnestly, "I'm sorry for you."

"Oh, it isn't me you've got to pity," Michael cried. "I'd be glad of his death. It's the finest death a fellow can have. But there's nothing fine about it, when one sees these gibbering blockheads shouting and yelling about nothing. I don't know what's the matter with England."

"Is England any worse than the rest of the world?" asked Mr. Viner.

"All this wearing of buttons and khaki ties!" Michael groaned.

"But that's the only way the man in the street can show his devotion. You don't object to ritualism, do you? You cross yourself and bow down. The church has colours and lights and incense. Do all these dishonour Our Lord's death?"

"That's different," said Michael. "And anyway I don't know that the comparison is much good to me now. I think I've lost my faith. I am sorry to shock you, Mr. Viner."

"You don't shock me at all, my dear boy."

"Don't I?" said Michael in slightly disappointed tones.

"You forget that a priest is more difficult to shock than anyone on earth."

"I like the way you take yourself as a typical priest. Very few of them are like you."

"Come, that's rather a stupid remark, I think," said Mr. Viner coldly.

"Is it? I'm sorry. It doesn't seem to worry you very much that I've lost my faith," Michael went on in an aggrieved voice.

"No, because I don't think you have. I've got a high enough opinion of you to believe that if you really had lost your faith, you wouldn't plunge comfortably down into one of my arm-chairs and give me the information in the same sort of tone you'd tell me you'd forgotten to bring back a book I'd lent you."

"I know you always find it very difficult to take me seriously," Michael grumbled. "I suppose that's the right method with people like me."

"I thought you'd come up to talk about the South African War. If I'd known the war was so near home, I shouldn't have been so frivolous," said the priest. His eyes were so merry in the leaping firelight that Michael was compelled against his will to smile.

"Of course, you make me laugh at the time and I forget how serious I meant to be when I arrived, and it's not until I'm at home again that I realize I'm no nearer to what I wanted to say than when I came up," protested Michael.

"I'm not the unsympathetic boor you'd make me out," Mr. Viner said.

"Oh, I perfectly understand that all this heart-searching becomes a nuisance. But honestly, Mr. Viner, I think I've done nothing long enough."

"Then you do want to enlist?" said the priest quickly.

"Why must 'doing' mean only one thing nowadays? Surely South Africa hasn't got a monopoly of whatever's being done," Michael argued. "No, I don't want to enlist," he went on. "And I don't want to go into a monastery, and I'm not sure that I really even want to go to church again."

"Give up going for a bit," advised the priest.

Michael jumped up from the chair and walked over to the bay-window, through which came a discordant sound of children playing in the street outside.

"It's impossible to be serious with you. I suppose you're fed up with people like me," Michael complained. "I know I'm moody and irritating, but I've got a lot to grumble about. I don't seem to have any natural inclination for any profession. I'm not a musical genius like my young sister. That's pretty galling, you know, really. After all, girls can get along better than boys without any special gifts, and she simply shines compared with me. I have no father. I've no idea who I was, where I came from, what I'm going to be. I keep on trying to be optimistic and think everything is good and beautiful, and then almost at once it turns out bad and ugly."

"Has your religion really turned out bad and ugly?" asked the priest gently.

"Not right through, but here and there, yes."

"The religion itself or the people who profess it?" Mr. Viner persisted.

"Doesn't it amount to the same thing ultimately?" Michael parried. "But leave out religion for the moment, and consider this war. The only justification for such a war is the moral effect it has on the nations engaged. Now, I ask you, do you sincerely believe there has been a trace of any purifying influence since we started waving Union Jacks last September? It's no good; we simply have not got it in us to stand defeat or victory. At any rate, if the Boers win, it will mean the preservation of something. Whereas if we win, we shall just destroy everything."

"Michael, what do you think is the important thing for this country at this moment?" Mr. Viner asked.

"Well, I suppose I still think it is that the people—the great mass of the nation, that is—should be happier and better. No, I don't think that's it at all. I think the important thing is that the people should be able to use the power that's coming to them in bigger lumps every day. I'd like to think it wasn't, I'd like to believe that democracy always will be as it always has been—a self-made failure. But against my own will I can't help believing that this time democracy is going to carry everything before it. And this war is going to hurry it on. Of course it is. The masses will learn their power. They'll learn that generals can make fools of themselves, that officers can be done without, that professional soldiers can be cowards, but that simply by paying we can still win. And where's the money coming from? Why, from the class that tried to be clever and bluff the people out of their power by staging this war. Well, do you mean to tell me that it's good for a democracy, this sudden realization of their omnipotence? Look here, you think I'm an excitable young fool, but I tell you I've been pitching my ideals at a blank wall like so many empty bottles and——"

"Were they empty?" asked Mr. Viner. "Are you sure they were empty? May they not have been cruses of ointment the more precious for being broken?"

"Well, I wish I could keep one for myself," Michael said.

"My dear boy, you'll never be able to do that. You'll always be too prodigal of your ideals. I should have no qualms about your future, whatever you did meanwhile. And, do you know, I don't think I have many qualms about this England of ours, however badly she behaves sometimes. I'm glad you recognize that the people are coming into their own. I wish that *you* were glad, but you will be one day. The Catholic religion must be a popular religion. The Sabbath was made for man, you know. Catholicism is God's method of throwing bottles at a blank wall—but not empty bottles, Michael. On the whole, I would sooner that now you were a reactionary than a Dantonist. Your present attitude of mind at any rate gives you the opportunity of going forward, instead of going back; there will be plenty of ideals to take the places of those you destroy, however priceless. And the tragedy of age is not having any more bottles to throw."

During these words that came soothingly from Mr. Viner's firm lips Michael had settled himself down again in the arm-chair and lighted his pipe.

"Come, now," said the priest, "you and I have muddled through our discussion long enough, let's gossip for a change. What's Mark Chator doing?"

"I haven't seen much of him this term. He's still going to take orders. I find old Chator's eternal simplicity and goodness rather wearing. Life's pretty easy for him. I wish I could get as much out of it as easily," Michael answered.

"Well, I can't make any comment on that last remark of yours without plunging into platitudes that would make you terribly contemptuous of my struggles to avoid them. But don't despise the Chators of this world."

"Oh, I don't. I envy them. Well, I must go. Thanks awfully for putting up with me again."

Michael picked up his cap and hurried home. When he reached Carlington Road, he was inclined to tell his mother that, if she liked, he would go and visit Lord Saxby before he sailed; but when it came to the point he felt too shy to reopen the subject, and decided to let the proposal drop.

He was surprized to find that it was much easier to write to Mrs. Ross about her husband than he thought it would be. Whether this long and stormy day (he could scarcely believe that he had only read the news about Captain Ross that morning) had purged him of all complexities of emotion, he did not know; but certainly the letter was easy enough.

64 CARLINGTON ROAD.

My dear Mrs. Ross,

I can't tell you the sadness of to-day. I've thought about you most tremendously, and I think you must be gloriously proud of him. I felt angry at first, but now I feel all right. You've always been so stunning to me, and I've never thanked you. I do want to see you soon. I shall never forget saying good-bye to Captain Ross. Mother asked me to go and say good-bye to Lord Saxby. I don't suppose you ever met him. He's a sort of cousin of ours. But I did not want to spoil the memory of that day at Southampton. I haven't seen poor old Alan yet. He'll be in despair. I'm longing to see him to-morrow. This is a rotten letter, but I can't write down what I feel. I wish Stella had known Captain Ross. She would have been able to express her feelings.

With all my love,
Your affectionate
Michael.

In bed that night Michael thought what a beast he had made of himself that day, and flung the blankets feverishly away from his burnt-out self. Figures of well-loved people kept trooping through the darkness, and he longed to converse with them, inspired by the limitless eloquence of the night-time. All that he would say to Mr. Viner, to Mrs. Ross, to Alan, even to good old Chator, splashed the dark with fiery sentences. He longed to be with Stella in a cool woodland. He almost got up to go down and pour his soul out upon his mother's breast; but the fever of fatigue mocked his impulse and he fell tossing into sleep.

Chapter XII: *Alan*

MICHAEL left the house early next day that he might make sure of seeing Alan for a moment before Prayers. A snowy aggregation of cumulus sustained the empyrean upon the volume of its mighty curve and swell. The road before him stretched shining in a radiant drench of azure puddles. It was a full-bosomed morning of immense peace.

Michael rather dreaded to see Alan appear in oppressive black, and felt that anything like a costume would embarrass their meeting. But just before the second bell he came quickly up the steps dressed in his ordinary clothes, and Michael in the surging corridor gripped his arm for a moment, saying he would wait for him in the 'quarter.'

"Is your mater fearfully cut up?" he asked when they had met and were strolling together along the 'gravel.'

"I think she was," said Alan. "She's going up to Cobble Place this morning to see Aunt Maud."

"I wrote to her last night," said Michael.

"I spent nearly all yesterday in writing to her," said Alan. "I couldn't think of anything to say. Could you?"

"No, I couldn't think of very much," Michael agreed. "It seemed so unnecessary."

"I know," Alan said. "I'd really rather have come to school."

"I wish you had. I made an awful fool of myself in the morning. I got in a wax with Abercrombie and the chaps, and said I'd never play football again."

"Whatever for?"

"Oh, because I didn't think they appreciated what it meant for a chap like your Uncle Kenneth to be killed."

"Do you mean they said something rotten?" asked Alan, flushing.

"I don't think you would have thought it rotten. In fact, I think the whole row was my fault. But they seemed to take everything for granted. That's what made me so wild."

"Look here, we can't start a conversation like this just before school. Are you going home to dinner?" Alan asked.

"No, I'll have dinner down in the Tuck," said Michael, "and we can go for a walk afterwards, if you like. It's the first really decent day we've had this year."

So after a lunch of buns, cheese-cakes, fruit pastilles, and vanilla biscuits, eaten in the noisy half-light of the Tuckshop, accompanied by the usual storm of pellets, Michael and Alan set out to grapple with the situation Michael had by his own hasty behaviour created.

"The chaps seem rather sick with you," observed Alan, as they strolled arm-in-arm across the school-ground not yet populous with games.

"Well, they are such a set of sheep," Michael urged in justification of himself.

"I thought you rather liked them."

"I did at first. I do still in a way. I do when nothing matters; but that horrible line in the paper did matter most awfully, and I couldn't stick their bleating. You see, you're different. You just say nothing. That's all right. But these fools tried to say something and couldn't. I always did hate people who *tried* very obviously. That's why I like you. You're so casual and you always seem to fit."

"I don't talk, because I know if I opened my mouth I should make an ass of myself," said Alan.

"There you are, that's what I say. That's why it's possible to talk to you. You see I'm a bit mad."

"Shut up, you ass," commanded Alan, smiling.

"Oh, not very mad. And I'm not complaining. But I *am* a little bit mad. I always have been."

"Why? You haven't got a clot on your brain, have you?"

"Oh, Great Scott, no! It's purely mental, my madness."

"Well, I think you're talking tosh," said Alan firmly. "If you go on thinking you're mad, you will be mad, and then you'll be sorry. So shut up trying to horrify me, because if you really were mad I should bar you," he added coolly.

"All right," said Michael, a little subdued, as he always was, by Alan's tranquil snubs. "All right. I'm not mad, but I'm excitable."

"Well, you shouldn't be," said Alan.

"I can't help my character, can I?" Michael demanded.

"You're not a girl," Alan pointed out.

"Men have very strong emotions often," Michael argued.

"They may have them, but they don't show them. Just lately you've been holding forth about the rotten way in which everybody gets hysterical over this war. And now you're getting hysterical over yourself, which is much worse."

"Damn you, Alan, if I didn't like you so much I shouldn't listen to you," said Michael, fiercely pausing.

"Well, if I didn't like you, I shouldn't talk," answered Alan simply.

As they walked on again in silence for a while, Michael continually tried to get a perspective view of his friend, puzzling over his self-assurance, which was never offensive, and wondering how a person so much less clever than himself could possibly make him feel so humble. Alan was good-looking and well-dressed; he was essentially debonair; he was certainly in appearance the most attractive boy in the school. It always gave Michael the most acute thrill of admiration to see Alan swinging himself along so lithe and so graceful. It made him want to go up and pat Alan's shoulder and say, "You fine and lovely creature, go on walking for ever." But mere good looks were not enough to explain the influence which Alan wielded, an influence which had steadily increased during the period of their greatest devotion to each other, and had never really ceased during the period of their comparative estrangement. Yet, if Michael looked back on their joint behaviour, it had always been he who apparently led and Alan who followed.

"Do you know, old chap," said Michael suddenly, "you're a great responsibility to me."

"Thanks very much and all that," Alan answered, with a mocking bow.

"Have you ever imagined yourself the owner of some frightfully famous statue?" Michael went on earnestly.

"Why, have you?" Alan countered, with his familiar look of embarrassed persiflage.

Michael, however, kept tight hold of the thread that was guiding him through the labyrinth that led to the arcana of Alan's disposition.

"You've the same sort of responsibility," he asserted. "I always feel that if I were the owner of the Venus of Milo, though I could move her about all over the place and set her up wherever I liked, I should be responsible to her in some way. I should feel she was looking at me, and if I put her in a wrong position, I should feel ashamed of myself and half afraid of the statue."

"Are you trying to prove you're mad?" Alan enquired.

"Do be serious," Michael begged, "and tell me if you think you understand what I mean. Alan, you used to discuss everything with me when we were kids, why won't you discuss yourself now?"

Alan looked up at the sky for a moment, blinking in the sun, perhaps to hide the tremor of feeling that touched for one instant the corners of his mouth. Then he said:

"Do you remember years ago, when we were at Eastbourne and you met Uncle Kenneth for the first time, he told me at dinner not to be a showman? I've always remembered that remark of his, and I think it applies to one showing off oneself as much as to showing off other people. I think that's why I'm different from you."

Michael glanced up at this.

"You can be damned rude when you like," he murmured.

"Well, you asked me."

"So I'm a showman?" said Michael.

"Oh, for Heaven's sake don't begin to worry over it. It doesn't make any odds to me what you are. I don't think it ever would," he added simply, and in this avowal was all that Michael craved for. Under a sudden chill presentiment that before long he would test this friend of his to the last red throb of his proud heart, Michael took comfort from this declaration and asked no more for comprehension or sympathy. Those were shifting sands of feeling compared with this rock-hewn permanence of Alan. He remembered the stones upon the Berkshire downs, the stolid, unperceiving, eternal stones. Comparable to them alone stood Alan.

They had turned out of the gates of the school-ground by now, and were strolling heedless of direction through the streets of West Kensington that to Michael seemed all at once strangely alluring with their display of a sedate and cosy life. He could not recall that he had ever before been so sensitive to the atmosphere of sunlit security which was radiated by these windows with their visions of rosy babies bobbing and laughing, of demure and saucy maids, of polished bird-cages and pots of daffodils. The white steps were in tune with the billowy clouds, and the scarlet pillar-box at the corner had a friendly, human smile. It was a doll's-house world, whose dainty offer of intimate citizenship refreshed Michael's imagination like a child's picture-book.

He began to reflect that the opinions of Abercrombie and his friends round the hot-water pipes were wrought out in such surroundings as these, and he arrived gradually at a sort of compassion for them, picturing the lives of small effort that would inevitably be their portion. He perceived that they would bear the burden of existence in the future, struggling to preserve their gentility against the envy of the class beneath them and the contempt of those above. These gay little houses, half of whose charm lay in their similarity, were as near as they would ever come to any paradise of being. Michael had experienced many spasms of love for his fellow-men, and now in one of these outbursts he suddenly realized himself in sympathy with mediocrity.

"Rather jolly round here," said Alan. "I suppose a tremendous lot of chaps from the school live about here. Funny thing, if you come to think of it. Practically everybody at St. James' slides into a little house like this. A few go into the Army; a few go to the 'Varsity. But this is really the School."

Alan indicated an empty perambulator standing outside one of the houses. "Funny thing if the kid that's waiting for should be Captain of the School in another eighteen years. I wouldn't be surprized."

Alan had just expressed so much of what Michael himself was thinking that he felt entitled to put the direct question which a moment ago he had been shy of asking.

"Do you feel as if you belonged to all this?"

"No," said Alan very coolly.

"Nor do I," Michael echoed.

"And that's why it was rotten of you to give yourself away to Abercrombie and the other chaps," Alan went on severely.

"Yes, I think it was," Michael agreed.

Then they retraced their steps unconsciously, wandering along silently in the sunlight towards the school. Michael did not want to converse because he was too much elated by this walk, and the satisfying way in which Alan had lived up to his ideal of him. He began to weave a fine romance of himself and Alan going through life together in a lofty self-sufficiency from which they would condescend to every aspect of humanity. He was not sure whether Alan would condescend so far and so widely as himself, and he was not sure whether he wanted him to, whether it would not always be a relief to be aware of Alan as a cold supernal sanctuary from the vulgar struggles in which he foresaw his own frequent immersion. Meanwhile he must make it easy for Alan by apologizing to Abercrombie and the rest for his ridiculous passion of yesterday. He did not wish to imperil Alan's superb aloofness by involving him in the acrimonious and undignified defence of a friend. There should be no more outbreaks. So much Michael vowed to his loyalty. However, the apology must be made quickly—if possible, this afternoon before school—and as they entered the school-ground again, Michael looked up at the clock, and said:

"Do you mind if I bunk on? I've something I must do before the bell goes."

Alan shook his head.

To Abercrombie and the other immortals Michael came up quickly and breathlessly.

"I say, you chaps, I'm sorry I made such an ass of myself yesterday; I felt chippy over that friend of mine being killed."

"That's all right, old bangabout," said Abercrombie cordially, and the chorus guffawed their forgiveness. They did more. They called him 'Bangs' thereafter, commemorating, as schoolboys use, with an affectionate nickname their esteem.

The next day a letter came for Michael from Mrs. Ross, and impressed with all the clarity of writing much of what he had dimly reached out for in his friendship with Alan. He read the letter first hurriedly on his way to school in the morning; but he read it a second and third time along those serene and intimate streets where he and Alan had walked the day before.

COBBLE PLACE,
March, 1900.

My dearest Michael,

You and Alan are the only people to whom I can bear to write to-day. I am grieving most for my young son, because he will have to grow up without his father's splendid example always before him. I won't write of my own sorrow. I could not.

My husband, as you know, was very devoted to you and Alan, and he had been quite worried (and so had I) that you and he seemed to have grown away from one another. It was a moment of true delight to him, when he read a long letter from dear old Alan describing his gladness at playing football again with you. Alan expresses himself much less eloquently than you do, but he is as deeply fond of you as I know you are of him. His letters are full of you and your cleverness and popularity; and I pray that all your lives you will pull together for the good. Kenneth used always to admire you both so much for your ability to 'cope with a situation.' He was shot, as you know, leading his men (who adored him) into action. Ah, how I wish he could lead his own little son into action. You and Alan will have that responsibility now.

It is sweet of you to thank me for being so 'stunning' to you. It wasn't very difficult. But you know how high my hopes have always been and always will be for you, and I know that you will never disappoint me. There may come times which with your restless, sensitive temperament you will find very hard to bear. Always remember that you have a friend in me. I have suffered very much, and suffering makes the heart yearn to comfort others. Be very chivalrous always, and remember that of all your ideals your mother should be the highest. I hope that you'll be able to come and stay with us soon after Easter. God bless you, dear boy, and thank you very much for your expression of the sorrow I know you share with me.

Your loving
Maud Ross.

I wonder if you remember how you used to love Don Quixote as a child. Will you always be a Don Quixote, however much people may laugh? It really means just being a gentleman.

Chapter XIII: *Sentiment*

BACK once more upon his pedestal in the frieze, Michael devoted himself to enjoying, while still they were important to his life, the conversation and opinions of the immortals. He gave up worrying about the war and yielded himself entirely either to the blandishments of his seniority in the school or of dreams about himself at Oxford, now within sight of attainment. Four more terms of school would set him free, and he had ambitions to get into the Fifteen in his last year. He would then be able to look back with satisfaction to the accomplishment of something. He actually threw himself into the rowdiest vanguard of Mafeking's celebrators, and accepted the occasion as an excuse to make a noise without being compelled to make the noise alone. These Bacchanalia of patriotism were very amusing, and perhaps it was a good thing for the populace to be merry; moreover, since he now had Alan to idealize, he could afford to let his high thoughts of England's duty and England's honour become a little less stringent.

He spent much time with Alan in discussing Oxford and in building up a most elaborate and logical scheme of their life at the University. He was anxious that Alan should leave the classical Lower Sixth, into which he had climbed somewhat hardly, and come to join him in the leisure of the History Sixth. He spoke of Strang whose Captaincy of Cricket shed such lustre on the form, of Terry whose Captaincy of Football next year would shed an equal lustre. But Alan, having found the journey to the Lower Sixth so arduous, was disinclined to be cheated of the intellectual eminence of the Upper Sixth which had been his Valhalla so long.

Michael and Alan had been looking forward to a visit to Cobble Place during the Easter holidays; but Mrs. Fane was much upset by the idea of being left alone, and Michael had to decline the invitation, which was a great disappointment. In the end he and his mother went to Bournemouth, staying rather grandly at one of the large hotels, and Michael was able to look up some old friends, including Father Moneypenny of St. Bartholomew's, Mrs. Rewins, their landlady of three years back, and Mr. Prout.

The passion-flower at Esdraelon had grown considerably, but that was the only thing which showed any signs of expansion, unless Mr. Prout's engagement to be married could be accepted as evidence of expansion. Michael thought it had a contrary effect, and whether from that cause or from his own increased age he found poor Prout sadly dull. It was depressing to hear that unpleasantness was expected at the Easter vestry that year; Michael could not recall any year in which that had not been the case. It was depressing to learn that the People's Churchwarden was still opposed to the Assumption. It was most depressing of all to be informed that Prout saw no prospect of being married for at least five years. Michael, having failed with Prout, tried to recapture the emotion of his first religious experience at St. Bartholomew's. But the church that had once seemed so inspiring now struck him as dingily and poorly designed, without any of the mystery which once had made it beautiful. He wondered if everything that formerly had appealed to his imagination were going to turn out dross, and he made an expedition to Christchurch Priory to test this idea. Here he was relieved to find himself able to recapture the perfect thrill of his first visit, and he spent a rich day wandering between the grey church and the watery meadows near by, about whose plashy levels the green rushes were springing up in the fleecy April weather.

Michael concluded that all impermanent emotions of beauty proved that it was merely the emotion which had created an illusion of beauty, and he was glad to have discovered for himself a touchstone for his æsthetic judgments in the future. He would have liked to see Alan in the cloistral glooms of the Priory, and thought how he would have enhanced with his own eternity of classic shape the knights and ladies praying there. Michael sympathized with the trousered boy whom Flaxman, contrary to every canon, might almost be said to have perpetrated. He felt slightly muddled between classic and romantic art, and could not make up his mind whether Flaxman's attempt or the mediæval sculptor's achievement were worthier of admiration. He tried to apply his own test, and came to the conclusion that Flaxman was really all wrong. He decided that he only liked the trousered boy because the figure gave him sentimental pleasure, and he was sure that true classical art was not sentimental. Finally he got himself in a complete muddle, sitting among these hollow chantries and pondering art's evaluations; so he left the Priory behind him, and went dreamily through the water-meadows under the spell of a simple beauty that needed no analysis. Oxford would be like this, he thought; a place of bells and singing streams and towers against the horizon.

He waited by a stile, watching the sky of which sunset had made a tranced archipelago set in a tideless sea. The purple islands stood out more and more distinct against the sheeted gold that lapped their indentations; then in a few moments the gold went out to primrose, the purple isles were grey as mice, and by an imperceptible breath of time became merged in a luminous green that held the young moon led downwards through the west by one great sulphur star.

This speculation of the sky made Michael late for dinner, and gave his mother an opportunity to complain of his daylong desertion of her.

"I rather wish we hadn't come to Bournemouth," said Michael. "I think it's a bad place for us to choose to come together. I remember last time we stayed here you were always criticizing me."

"I suppose Bournemouth must have a bad effect on you, dearest boy," said Mrs. Fane in her most gentle, most discouraging voice.

Michael laughed a little bitterly.

"You're wonderful at always being able to put me in the wrong," he said.

"You're sometimes not very polite, are you, nowadays? But I dare say you'll grow out of this curious manner you've lately adopted towards me."

"Was I rude?" asked Michael, quickly penitent.

"I think you were rather rude, dear," said Mrs. Fane. "Of course, I don't want you never to have an opinion of your own, and I quite realize that school has a disastrous effect on manners, but you didn't apologize very gracefully for being late for dinner, did you, dear?"

"I'm sorry. I won't ever be again," said Michael shortly.

Mrs. Fane sighed, and the meal progressed in silence. Michael, however, could never bear to sulk, and he braced himself to be pleasant.

"You ought to come over to Christchurch, mother. Shall we drive over one day?"

"Well, I'm not very fond of looking at churches," said Mrs. Fane. "But if you want to go, let us. I always like you to do everything you want."

Michael sighed at the ingenuity of his mother's method, and changed the subject to their fellow-guests.

"That's rather a pretty girl, don't you think?"

"Where, dear?" asked Mrs. Fane, putting up her lorgnette and staring hard at the wife of a clergyman sitting across the room from their table.

"No, no, mother," said Michael, beaming with pleasure at the delightful vagueness of his mother which only distressed him when it shrouded his own sensations. "The next table—the girl in pink."

"Yes, decidedly," said Mrs. Fane. "But dreadfully common. I can't think why those sort of people come to nice hotels. I suppose they read about them in railway guides."

"I don't think she's very common," said Michael.

"Well, dear, you're not quite at the best age for judging, are you?"

"Hang it, mother, I'm seventeen."

"It's terrible to think of," said Mrs. Fane. "And only such a little while ago you were the dearest baby boy. Then Stella must be sixteen," she went on. "I think it's time she came back from the Continent."

"What about her first concert?"

"Oh, I must think a lot before I settle when that is to be."

"But Stella is counting on it being very soon."

"Dear children, you're both rather impetuous," said Mrs. Fane, deprecating with the softness of her implied rebuke the quality, and in Michael at any rate for the moment quenching all ardour.

"I wonder if it's wise to let a girl be a professional musician," she continued. "Dear me, children are a great responsibility, especially when one is alone."

Here was an opportunity for Michael to revive the subject of his father, but he had now lost the cruel frankness of childhood and shrank from the directness of the personal encounter such a topic would involve. He was seized with one of his fits of shy sensitiveness, and he became suddenly so deeply embarrassed that he could scarcely even bring himself to address his mother as 'you.' He felt that he must go away by himself until he had shaken off this uncomfortable sensation. He actually felt a kind of immodesty in saying 'you' to his mother, as if in saying so much he was trespassing on the forbidden confines of her individuality. It would not endure for more than an hour or so, this fear of approach, this hyperæsthesia of contact and communication. Yet not for anything could he kiss her good night and, mumbling a few bearish excuses, he vanished as soon as dinner was over, vowing that he would cure himself of this mood by walking through the pine trees and blowy darkness of the cliffs.

As he passed through the hotel lounge, he saw the good-looking girl, whom his mother had stigmatized as common, waiting there wrapped up in a feathery cloak. He decided that he would sit down and observe her until the sister came down. He wished he knew this girl, since it would be pleasant after dinner to stroll out either upon the pier or to listen to the music in the Winter Garden in such attractive company. Michael fancied that the girl, as she walked slowly up and down the lounge, was conscious of his glances, and he felt an adventurous excitement at his heart. It would be a daring and delightful novelty to speak to her. Then the sister came down, and the two girls went out through the swinging doors of the hotel, leaving Michael depressed and lonely. Was it a trick of the lamplight, or did he really perceive her head turn outside to regard him for a moment?

During his walk along the cliffs Michael played with this idea. By the time he went to bed his mind was full of this girl, and it was certainly thrilling to come down to breakfast next morning and see what blouse she was wearing. Mrs. Fane always had breakfast in her room, so Michael was free to watch this new interest over the cricket matches in The Sportsman. He grew almost jealous of the plates and forks and cups which existed so intimately upon her table, and he derived a sentimental pleasure from the thought that nothing was more likely than that to-morrow there would be an exchange of cups between his table and hers. He conceived the idea of chipping a piece out of his own cup and watching every morning on which table it would be laid, until it reached her.

At lunch Michael, as nonchalantly as he could speak, asked his mother whether she did not think the pretty girl dressed rather well.

"Very provincial," Mrs. Fane judged.

"But prettily, I think," persisted Michael. "And she wears a different dress every day."

"Do you want to know her?" asked Mrs. Fane.

"Oh, mother, of course not," said Michael, blushing hotly.

"I dare say they're very pleasant people," Mrs. Fane remarked. "I'll speak to them after lunch, and tell them how anxious you are to make their acquaintance."

"I say, mother," Michael protested. "Oh, no, don't, mother. I really don't want to know them."

Mrs. Fane smiled at him, and told him not to be a foolish boy. After lunch, in her own gracious and distinguished manner which Michael always admired, Mrs. Fane spoke to the two sisters and presently beckoned to Michael who crossed the room, feeling rather as if he were going in to bat first for his side.

"I don't think I know your name," said Mrs. Fane to the elder sister.

"McDonnell—Norah McDonnell, and this is my sister Kathleen."

"Scotch?" asked Mrs. Fane vaguely and pleasantly.

"No, Irish," contradicted the younger sister. "At least by extraction. McDonnell is an Irish name. But we live in Burton-on-Trent. Father and mother are coming down later on."

She spoke with the jerky speech of the Midlands, and Michael rather wished she did not come from Burton-on-Trent, not on his own account, but because his mother would be able to point out to him how right she had been about their provincialism.

"Are you going anywhere this evening?" Michael managed to ask at last.

"I suppose we shall go on the pier. We usually go on the pier. Eh, but it's rather dull in Bournemouth. I like Llandudno better. Llandudno's fine," said the elder Miss McDonnell with fervour.

Mrs. Fane came to the rescue of an awkward conversation by asking the Miss McDonnells if they would take pity on her son and invite him to accompany them. And so it was arranged.

"Happy, Michael?" asked his mother when the ladies, with many smiles, had withdrawn to their rooms.

"Yes. I'm all right," said Michael. "Only I rather wish you hadn't asked them so obviously. It made me feel rather a fool."

"Dearest boy, they were delighted at the idea of your company. They seem quite nice people too. Only, as I said, very provincial. Older, too, than I thought at first."

Michael asked how old his mother thought they were, and she supposed them to be about twenty-seven and thirty. Michael was inclined to protest against this high estimate, but since he had spoken to the Miss McDonnells, he felt that after all his mother might be right.

In the evening his new friends came down to dinner much enwrapped in feathers, and Michael thought that Kathleen looked very beautiful in the crimson lamplight of the dinner-table.

"How smart you are, Michael, to-night!" said Mrs. Fane.

"Oh, well, I thought as I'd got my dinner-jacket down here I might as well put it on. I say, mother, I think I'll get a tail-coat. Couldn't I have one made here?"

"Isn't that collar rather tight?" asked Mrs. Fane anxiously. "And it seems dreadfully tall."

"I like tall collars with evening dress," said Michael severely.

"You know best, dear, but you look perfectly miserable."

"It's only because my chin is a bit sore after shaving."

"Do you have to shave often?" enquired Mrs. Fane, tenderly horrified.

"Rather often," said Michael. "About once a week now."

"She has pretty hands, your lady love," said Mrs. Fane, suddenly looking across to the McDonnells' table.

"I say, mother, for goodness' sake mind. She'll hear you," whispered Michael.

"Oh, Michael dear, don't be so foolishly self-conscious."

After dinner Michael retired to his room, and came down again smoking a cigarette. Mrs. Fane made a little *moue* of surprise.

"I say, mother, don't keep on calling attention to everything I do. You know I've smoked for ages."

"Yes, but not so very publicly, dear boy."

"Well, you don't mind, do you? I must begin some time," said Michael.

"Michael, don't be cross with me. You're so deliciously amusing, and so much too nice for those absurd women," Mrs. Fane laughed.

Just then the Miss McDonnells appeared on the staircase, and Michael frowned at his mother not to say any more about them.

It was a fairly successful evening. The elder Miss McDonnell bored Michael rather with a long account of why her father had left Ireland, and what a blow it had been to him to open a large hotel in Burton-on-Trent. He was also somewhat fatigued by the catalogue of Mr. McDonnell's virtues, of his wit and courage and good looks and shrewdness.

"He has a really old-fashioned sense of humour," said Miss McDonnell. "But then, of course, he's Irish. He's accounted quite the cleverest man in Burton, but then, being Irish, that's not to be wondered at."

Michael wished she would not say 'wondered' as if it were 'wandered,' and indeed he was beginning to think that Miss McDonnell was a great trial, when he suddenly discovered that by letting his arm hang very loosely from his shoulder it was possible without the slightest hint of intention occasionally to touch Kathleen's hand as they walked along. The careful calculation that this proceeding demanded occupied his mind so fully that he was able to give mechanical assents to Miss McDonnell's praise of her father, and apparently at the same time impress her with his own intelligence.

As the evening progressed Michael slightly increased the number of times he tapped Kathleen's hand with his, and after about an hour's promenade of the pier he was doing a steady three taps a minute. He now began to speculate whether Kathleen was aware of these taps, and from time to time he would glance round at her over his shoulder, hopeful of catching her eyes.

"Are you admiring my sister's brooch?" asked Miss McDonnell. "Eh, I think it's grand. Don't you?"

Kathleen giggled lightly at this, and asked her sister how she could, and then Michael with a boldness that on reflection made him catch his breath at the imagination of it, said that while he was admiring Miss Kathleen's brooch he was admiring her eyes still more.

"Oh, Mr. Fane. How can you!" exclaimed Kathleen.

"Well, he's got good taste, I'm sure," said Miss McDonnell. "But, there, after all, what can you expect from an Irish girl? All Irish girls have fine eyes."

When Michael went to bed he felt that on the whole he had acquitted himself that first evening with considerable success, and as he fell asleep he dreamed triumphantly of a daring to-morrow.

It was an April day, whose deeps of azure sky made the diverse foliage of spring burn in one ardent green. Such a day spread out before his windows set Michael on fire for its commemoration, and he made up his mind to propose a long bicycling expedition to the two Miss McDonnells. He wished that it were not necessary to invite the elder sister, but not even this April morning could embolden him so far as to ask Kathleen alone. Mrs. Fane smilingly approved of his proposal, but suggested that on such a warm day it would be wiser not to start until after lunch. So it was arranged, and Michael thoroughly enjoyed the consciousness of escorting these girls out of Bournemouth on their trim bicycles. Indeed, he enjoyed his position so much that he continually looked in the shop-windows, as they rode past, to observe the effect and was so much charmed by the result that he crossed in front of Miss McDonnell, and upset her and her bicycle in the middle of the town.

"Eh, that's a nuisance," said Miss McDonnell, surveying bent handlebars and inner tyre swelling like a toy balloon along the rim. "That was quite a mishap," she added, shaking the dust from her skirt.

Michael was in despair over his clumsiness, especially when Miss Kathleen McDonnell remarked that there went the ride she'd been looking forward to all day.

"Well, you two go on an I'll walk back," Miss McDonnell offered.

"Oh, but I can easily hire another machine," said Michael.

"No. I'll go back. I've grazed my knee a bit badly."

Michael was so much perturbed to hear this that without thinking he anxiously asked to be allowed to look, and wished that the drain by which he was standing would swallow him up when he realized by Kathleen's giggling what he had said.

"It's all right," said Miss McDonnell kindly. "There's no need to worry. I hope you'll have a pleasant ride."

"I say, it's really awfully ripping of you to be so jolly good-tempered about it," Michael exclaimed. "Are you sure I can't do anything?"

"No, you can just put my bicycle in the shop along there, and I'll take the tram back. Mind and enjoy yourselves, and don't be late."

The equable Miss McDonnell then left her sister and Michael to their own devices.

They rode along in alert silence until they left Branksome behind them and came into hedgerows, where an insect earned Michael's cordial gratitude by invading his eye. He jumped off his bicycle immediately and called for Kathleen's aid, and as he stood in the quiet lane with the girl's face close to his and her hand brushing his cheeks, Michael felt himself to be indeed a favourite of fortune.

"There it is, Mr. Fane," said Miss Kathleen McDonnell. And, though he tried to be sceptical for a while of the insect's discovery, he was bound to admit the evidence of the handkerchief.

"Thanks awfully," said Michael. "And I say, I wish you wouldn't call me Mr. Fane. You know my Christian name."

"Oh, but I'd feel shy to call you Michael," said Miss McDonnell.

"Not if I called you Kathleen," Michael suggested, and felt inclined to shake his own hand in congratulation of his own magnificent daring.

"Well, I must say one thing. You don't waste much time. I think you're a bit of a flirt, you know," said Kathleen.

"A flirt," Michael echoed. "Oh, I say, do you really think so?"

"I'm afraid I do," murmured Kathleen. "Shall we go on again?"

They rode along in renewed silence for several miles, and then they suddenly came upon Poole Harbour lying below them, washed in the tremulous golden airs of the afternoon.

"I say, how ripping!" cried Michael, leaping from his machine and flinging it away from him against a bank of vivid grass. "We must sit down here for a bit."

"It is pretty," said Kathleen. "It's almost like a picture."

"I'm glad you're fond of beautiful things," said Michael earnestly.

"Well, one can't help it, can one?" sighed Kathleen.

"Some people can," said Michael darkly. "There's rather a good place to sit over there," he added, pointing to a broken gate that marked the entrance to an oak wood, and he faintly touched the sleeve of Kathleen's blouse to guide her towards the chosen spot.

Then they sat leaning against the gate, she idly plucking sun-faded primroses, he brooding upon the nearness of her hand. In such universal placidity it could not be wrong to hold that hand wasting itself amid small energies. Without looking into her eyes, without turning his gaze from the great tranquil water before him, Michael took her hand in his so lightly that save for the pulsing of his heart he scarcely knew he held it. So he sat breathless, enduring pins and needles, tolerating the uncertain pilgrimage of ants rather than move an inch and break the yielding spell which made her his.

"Are you holding my hand?" she asked, after they had sat a long while pensively.

"I suppose I am," said Michael. Then he turned and with full-blooded cheeks and swimming eyes met unabashed Kathleen's demure and faintly mocking glance.

"Do you think you ought to?" she enquired.

"I haven't thought anything about that," said Michael. "I simply thought I wanted to."

"You're rather old for your age," she went on, with an inflection of teazing surprize in her soft voice. "How old are you?"

"Seventeen," said Michael simply.

"Goodness!" cried Kathleen, withdrawing her hand suddenly. "And I wonder how old you think I am?"

"I suppose you're about twenty-five."

Kathleen got up and said in a brisk voice that destroyed all Michael's bravery, "Come, let's be getting back. Norah will be thinking I'm lost."

Just when they were nearing the outskirts of Branksome, Kathleen dismounted suddenly and said:

"I suppose you'll be surprized when I tell you I'm engaged to be married?"

"Are you?" faltered Michael; and the road swam before him.

"At least I'm only engaged secretly, because my fiancé is poor. He's coming down soon. I'd like you to meet him."

"I should like to meet him very much," said Michael politely.

"You won't tell anybody what I've told you?"

"Good Lord, no. Perhaps I might be of some use," said Michael. "You know, in arranging meetings."

"Eh, you're a nice boy," exclaimed Kathleen suddenly.

And Michael was not perfectly sure whether he thought himself a hero or a martyr.

Mrs. Fane was very much diverted by Michael's account of Miss McDonnell's accident, and teazed him gaily about Kathleen. Michael would assume an expression of mystery, as if indeed he had been entrusted with the dark secrets of a young woman's mind; but the more mysterious he looked the more his mother laughed. In his own heart he cultivated assiduously his devotion, and regretted most poignantly that each new blouse and each chosen evening-dress was not for him. He used to watch Kathleen at dinner, and depress himself with the imagination of her spirit roaming out over the broad Midlands to meet her lover. He never made the effort to conjure up the lover, but preferred to picture him and Kathleen gathering like vague shapes upon the immeasurable territories of the soul.

Then one morning Kathleen took him aside after breakfast to question his steadfastness.

"Were you in earnest about what you said?" she asked.

"Of course I was," Michael affirmed.

"He's come down. He's staying in rooms. Why don't you ask me to go out for a bicycle ride?"

"Well, will you?" Michael dutifully invited.

"I'm so excited," said Kathleen, fluttering off to tell her sister of this engagement to go riding with Michael.

In about half an hour they stood outside the small red-brick house which cabined the bold spirit of Michael's depressed fancies.

"You'll come in and say 'how do you do'?" suggested Kathleen.

"I suppose I'd better," Michael agreed.

They entered together the little efflorescent parlour of the house.

"This is my fiancé—Mr. Walter Trimble," Kathleen proudly announced.

"Pleased to meet you," said Mr. Trimble. "Kath tells me you're on to do us a good turn."

Michael looked at Mr. Trimble, resolutely anxious to find in him the creator of Kathleen's noble destiny. He saw a thick-set young man in a splendidly fitting, but ill-cut blue serge suit; he saw a dark moustache of silky luxuriance growing amid regular features; in fact, he saw someone that might have stepped from one of the grandiose frames of that efflorescent little room. But he was Kathleen's choice, and Michael refused to let himself feel at all disappointed.

"I think it's bad luck not to be able to marry, if one wants to," said Michael deeply.

"You're right," Mr. Trimble agreed. "That's why I want Kath here to marry me first and tell her dad afterwards."

"I only wish I dared," sighed Kathleen. "Well, if we're going to have our walk, we'd better be getting along. Will I meet you by the side-gate into the Winter Garden at a quarter to one?"

"Right-o," said Michael.

"I wonder if you'd lend Mr. Trimble your bicycle?"

"Of course," said Michael.

"Because we could get out of the town a bit," suggested Kathleen. "And that's always pleasanter."

Michael spent a dull morning in wandering about Bournemouth, while Kathleen and her Trimble probably rode along the same road he and she had gone a few days back. He tried to console himself with thoughts of self-sacrifice, and he took a morbid delight in the imagination of the pleasure he had made possible for others. But undeniably his own morning was dreary, and not even could Swinburne's canorous Triumph of Time do much more than echo somewhat sadly through the resonant emptiness of his self-constructed prison, whose windows opened on to a sentimental if circumscribed view of unattainable sweetness.

Michael sat on a bench in a sophisticated pine-grove and, having lighted a cigarette, put out the match with his sighing exhalation of *'O love, my love, and no love for me.'* It was wonderful to Michael how perfectly Swinburne expressed his despair. *'O love, my love, had you loved but me.'* And why had she not loved him? Why did she prefer Trimble? Did Trimble ever read Swinburne? Could Trimble sit like this smoking calmly a cigarette and breathing out deathless lines of love's despair? Michael began to feel a little sorry for Kathleen, almost as sorry for her as he felt for himself. Soon the Easter holidays would be over, and he would go back to school. He began to wonder whether he would wear the marks of suffering on his countenance, and whether his friends would eye him curiously, asking themselves in whispers what man this was that came among them with so sad and noble an expression of resignation. As Michael thought of Trimble and Kathleen meeting in Burton-on-Trent and daily growing nearer to each other in love, he became certain that his grief would indeed be manifest. He pictured himself sitting in the sunlit serene class-room of the History Sixth, a listless figure of despair, an object of wondering, whispering compassion. And so his life would lose itself in a monotone of discontent. Grey distances of time presented themselves to him with a terrible menace of loneliness; the future was worse than ever, a barren waste whose horizon would never darken to the silhouette of Kathleen coming towards him with open arms. Never would he hold her hand again; never would he touch those lips at all; never would he even know what dresses she wore in summer. *'O love, my love, and no love for me.'*

When Michael met Kathleen by the side-gate of the Winter Gardens, and received his bicycle back from Trimble, he suddenly wondered whether Kathleen had told her betrothed that another had held her hand. Michael rather hoped she had, and that the news of it had made Trimble jealous. Trimble, however, seemed particularly pleased with himself, and invited Michael to spend the afternoon with him, which Michael promised to do, if his mother did not want his company.

"Well, did you have a decent morning?" Michael enquired of Kathleen, as together they rode towards their hotel.

"Oh, we had a grand time; we sat down where you and me sat the other day."

Michael nearly mounted the pavement at this news, and looked very gloomy.

"What's the matter?" Kathleen pursued. "You're not put out, are you?"

"Oh, no, not at all," said Michael sardonically. "All the same, I think you might have turned off and gone another road. I sat and thought of you all the morning. But I don't mind really," he added, remembering that at any rate for Kathleen he must remain that chivalrous and selfless being which had been created by the loan of a bicycle. "I'm glad you enjoyed yourself. I always want you to be happy. All my life I shall want that."

Michael was surprised to find how much more eloquent he was in the throes of disappointment than he had ever been through the prompting of passion. He wished that the hotel were not already in sight, for he felt that he could easily say much more about his renunciation, and indeed he made up his mind to do so at the first opportunity. In the afternoon he told his mother he was going to pay a visit to Father Moneypenny. He did not tell her about Trimble, because he feared her teazing; although he tried to deceive himself that the lie was due to his loyalty to Kathleen.

"What shall we do?" asked Trimble. "Shall we toddle round to the Shades and have a drink?"

"Just as you like," Michael said.

"Well, I'm on for a drink. It's easier to talk down at the Shades than in here."

Michael wondered why, but he accepted a cigar, and with Trimble sought the speech-compelling Shades.

"It's like this," Trimble began, when they were seated on the worn leather of the corner lounge. "I took a fancy to you right off. Eh, I'm from the North, and I may be a bit blunt, but by gum I liked you, and that's how it is. Yes. I'm going to talk to you the same as I might to my own brother, only I haven't got one."

Michael looked a little apprehensive of the sack of confidences that would presently be emptied over his head, and, seeking perhaps to turn Trimble from his intention, asked him to guess his age.

"Well, I suppose you're anything from twenty-two to twenty-three."

Michael choked over his lemon-and-dash before he announced grimly that he was seventeen.

"Get out," said Trimble sceptically. "You're more than that. Seventeen? Eh, I wouldn't have thought it. Never mind, I said I was going to tell you. And by gum I will, if you say next you haven't been weaned."

Michael resented the freedom of this expression and knitted his eyebrows in momentary distaste.

"It's like this," Mr. Trimble began again, "I made up my mind to-day that Kath's the lass for me. Now am I right? That's what I want to ask you. Am I right?"

"I suppose if you're in love with her and she's in love with you, yes," said Michael.

"Well, she is. Now you wouldn't think she was passionate, would you? You'd say she was a bit of ice, wouldn't you? Well, by gum, I tell you, lad, she's a furnace. Would you believe that?" Mr. Trimble leaned back triumphantly.

Michael did not know what comment to make on this information, and took another sip of his lemon-and-dash.

"Well, now what I say is—and I'm not a chap who's flung round a great deal with the girls—what I say is," Trimble went on, banging the marble table before him, "it's not fair on a lass to play around like this, and so I've made up my mind to marry her. Am I right? By gum, lad, I know I'm right."

"I think you are," said Michael solemnly. "And I think you're awfully lucky."

"Lucky?" echoed Trimble, "I'm lucky enough, if it wasn't for her domned old father. The lass is fine, but him—well, if I was to tell you what he is, you'd say I was using language. So it's like this. I want Kath to marry me down here. I'll get the license. I've saved up a hundred pounds. I'm earning two hundred a year now. Am I right?"

"Perfectly right," said Michael earnestly, who, now that Trimble was showing himself to possess real fervour of soul, was ready to support him, even at the cost of his own suffering. He envied Trimble his freedom from the trammels of education, which for such a long while would prevent himself from taking such a step as marriage by license. Indeed, Michael scarcely thought he ever would take such a step now, since it was unlikely that anyone with Kathleen's attraction would lure him on to such a deed.

Trimble's determination certainly went a long way to excuse the failings of his outer person in Michael's eyes, and indeed, as he pledged him a stirrup-cup of lemon-and-dash, Trimble and Young Lochinvar were not seriously distinct in Michael's imaginative anticipation of the exploit.

So all day and every day for ten days Michael presumably spent his time with Kathleen, notwithstanding Mrs. Fane's tenderly malicious teazing, notwithstanding the elder Miss McDonnell's growing chill, and notwithstanding several very pointed questions from the interfering old spinsters and knitters in the sun of the hotel-gardens. That actually he spent his time alone in watching slow-handed clocks creep on towards a quarter to one or a quarter to five or a quarter to seven, filled Michael daily more full with the spiritual rewards of his sacrifice. He had never known before the luxury of grief, and he had no idea what a variety of becoming attitudes could be wrought of sadness, and not merely attitudes, but veritable dramas. One of the most heroically poignant of these was founded on the moment when Kathleen should ask him to be godfather to her first-born. "No, no," Michael would exclaim. "Don't ask me to do that. I have suffered enough." And Kathleen would remorsefully and silently steal from the dusky room a-flicker with sad firelight, leaving Michael a prey to his own noble thoughts. There was another drama scarcely less moving, in which the first-born died, and Michael, on hearing the news, took the night express to Burton in order to speak words of hope above the little duplicate of Trimble now for ever still in his cradle. Sometimes in the more expansive moments of Michael's celibacy Trimble and Kathleen would lose all their money, and Michael, again taking the night express to Burton-on-Trent, would offer to adopt about half a dozen duplicates of Trimble.

Finally the morning of the marriage arrived, and Michael, feeling that this was an excellent opportunity to have the first of his dramas staged in reality, declined to be present. His refusal was a little less dramatic than he had intended, because Kathleen was too much excited by her own reckless behaviour to act up. While Michael waited for the ceremony's conclusion, he began a poem called 'Renunciation.' Unfortunately the marriage service was very much faster than his Muse, and he never got farther than half the opening line, '*If I renounce.*' Michael, however, ascribed his failure to a little girl who would persist in bouncing a tennis ball near his seat in the gardens.

The wedding was only concluded just in time, because Mr. and Mrs. McDonnell arrived on the following day and Michael's expeditions with Kathleen were immediately forbidden. Possibly the equable Miss McDonnell had been faintly alarmed for her sister's good name. At any rate she had certainly been annoyed by her continuous neglect.

Michael, however, had a long interview with Trimble, and managed to warn Kathleen that her husband was going to present himself after dinner. Trimble and he had thought this was more likely to suit Mr. McDonnell's digestion than an after-breakfast confession. Michael expressed himself perfectly willing to take all the blame, and privately made up his mind that if Mr. McDonnell tried to be 'too funny,' he would summon his mother to 'polish him off' with the vision of her manifest superiority.

Somewhat to Michael's chagrin his share in the matter was overlooked by Mr. McDonnell, and the oration he had prepared to quell the long-lipped Irish father was never delivered. Whatever scenes of domestic strife occurred, occurred without Michael's assistance, and he was not a little dismayed to be told by Kathleen in the morning that all had passed off well, but that in the circumstances her father had thought they had better leave Bournemouth at once.

"You're going?" stammered Michael.

"Yes. We must be getting back. It's all been so sudden, and Walter's coming into the business, and oh, I'm as happy as the day is long." Michael watched them all depart, and after a few brave good-byes and three flutters from Kathleen's handkerchief turned sadly back into the large, unfriendly hotel. He knew the number of Kathleen's room, and in an access of despair that was, however, not so overwhelming as to preclude all self-consciousness, he wandered down the corridor and peeped into the late haunt of his love. The floor was littered with tissue paper, broken cardboard-boxes, empty toilet-bottles, and all the disarray of departure. Michael caught his breath at the sudden revelation of this abandoned room's appeal. Here was the end of Kathleen's maidenhood; here still lingered the allurement of her presence; but Trimble could never see this last virginal abode, this elusive shrine that Michael wished he could hire for sentimental meditations. Along the corridor came the sound of a dustpan. He looked round hastily for one souvenir of Kathleen, and perceived still moist from her last quick ablution a piece of soap. He seized it quickly and surrendered the room to the destructive personality of the housemaid.

"Well, dear," asked Mrs. Fane at lunch, "did your lady love give you anything to commemorate your help? Darling Michael, you must have made a most delicious knight-errant."

"Oh, no, she didn't give me anything," said Michael. "Why should she?"

Then he blushed, thinking of the soap that was even now enshrined in a drawer and scenting his handkerchiefs and ties. He wondered if Alan would understand the imperishable effluence from that slim cenotaph of soap.

Chapter XIV: *Arabesque*

IN the air of the Easter holidays that year there must have been something unusually amorous even for April, for when Michael came back to school he found that most of his friends and contemporaries had been wounded by love's darts. Alan, to be sure, returned unscathed, but as he had been resting in the comparatively cloistral seclusion of Cobble Place, Michael did not count his whole heart much honour to anything except his lack of opportunity. Everybody else had come back in possession of girls; some even had acquired photographs. There was talk of gloves and handkerchiefs, of flowers and fans, but nobody, as far as Michael could cautiously ascertain, had thought of soap; and he congratulated himself upon his relic. Also, apparently, all his friends in their pursuit of Eastertide nymphs had been successful, and he began to take credit to himself for being unlucky. His refusal (to this already had come Kathleen's suddenly withdrawn hand) gave him a peculiar interest, and those of his friends in whom he confided looked at him with awe, and listened respectfully to his legend of despair.

Beneath the hawthorns on the golden afternoons and lingering topaz eves of May, Michael would wait for Alan to finish his game of cricket, and between lazily applauded strokes and catches he would tell the tale of Kathleen to his fellows:

"I asked her to wait for me. Of course she was older than me. I said I was ready to marry her when I was twenty-one, but there was another chap, a decent fellow, devilish handsome, too. He was frightfully rich, and so she agreed to elope with him. I helped them no end. I told her father he simply must not attempt to interfere. But, of course, I was frightfully cut up—oh, absolutely knocked out. We're all of us unlucky in love in our family. My sister was in love with an Austrian who was killed by an avalanche. I don't suppose I shall ever be in love again. They say you never really fall in love more than once in your life.

I feel a good deal older this term. I suppose I look ... oh, well hit indeed—run it out, and again, sir, and again ...!"

So Michael would break off the tale of his love, until one of his listeners would seek to learn more of passion's frets and fevers.

"But, Bangs, what about the day she eloped? What did you do?"

"I wrote poetry," Michael would answer.

"Great Scott, that's a bit of a swat, isn't it?"

"Yes, it's a bit difficult," Michael would agree. "Only, of course, I only write *vers libre*. No rhymes or anything."

And then an argument would arise as to whether poetry without rhymes could fairly be called poetry at all. This argument, or another like it, would last until the cricket stopped, when Michael and his fellows would stroll into the pavilion and examine the scoring-book or criticize the conduct of the game.

It was a pleasant time, that summer term, and life moved on very equably for Michael, notwithstanding his Eastertide heartbreak. Alan caused him a little trouble by his indifference to anything but cricket, and one Sunday, when May had deepened into June, Michael took him to task for his attitude. Alan had asked Michael over to Richmond for the week-end, and the two of them had punted down the river towards Kew. They had moored their boat under a weeping willow about the time when the bells for church, begin to chime across the level water-meadows.

"Alan, aren't you ever going to fall in love?" Michael began.

"Why should I?" Alan countered in his usual way.

"I don't know. I think it's time you did," said Michael. "You've no idea how much older it makes you feel. And I suppose you don't want to remain a kid for ever. Because, you know, old chap, you are an awful kid beside me."

"Thanks very much," said Alan. "I believe you're exactly one month older, as a matter of fact."

"Yes, in actual time," said Michael earnestly. "But in experience I'm years older than you."

"That must be why you're such a rotten field," commented Alan. "After forty the joints get stiff."

"Oh, chuck being funny," said Michael severely. "I'm in earnest. Now you know as well as I do that last term and the term before I was miserable. Well, look at me now. I'm absolutely happy."

"I thought you were so frightfully depressed," said Alan, twinkling. "I thought you'd had an unlucky love affair. It seems to take you differently from the way it takes most people."

"Oh, of course, I *was* miserable," Michael explained. "But now I'm happy in her happiness. That's love."

Alan burst out laughing, and Michael observed that if he intended to receive his confidences in such a flippant way, he would in future take care to be more secretive.

"I'm showing you what a lot I care about you," Michael went on in tones of deepest injury, "by telling you about myself. I think it's rather rotten of you to laugh."

"But you've told everybody," Alan pointed out.

Michael took another tack, and explained to Alan that he wanted the spur of his companionship in everything.

"It would be so ripping if we were both in love," he sighed. "Honestly, Alan, don't you feel I'm much more developed since last term? I say, you played awfully well yesterday against Dulford Second. If you go on improving at the rate you are now, I don't see why you shouldn't get your Blue at Oxford. By Jove, you know, in eighteen months we shall be at Oxford. Are you keen?"

"Frightfully keen," said Alan. "Especially if I haven't got to be in love all the time."

"I'm not going to argue with you any more," Michael announced. "But you're making a jolly big mistake. Still, of course, I do understand about your cricket, and I dare say love might make you a bit boss-eyed. Perhaps when footer begins again next term, I shall get over this perpetual longing I have for Kathleen. You've no idea how awful I felt when she said she loved Trimble. He was rather a bounder too, but of course I had to help them. I say, Alan, do you remember Dora and Winnie?"

"Rather," said Alan, smiling. "We made pretty good asses of ourselves over them. Do you remember how fed up Nancy got?"

So, very easily the conversation drifted into reminiscences of earlier days, until the sky was quilted with rose-tipped pearly clouds. Then they swung a Japanese lantern in the prow and worked up-stream towards Richmond clustering dark against the west, while an ivory moon shimmered on the dying azure of the day behind.

Throughout June the image of Kathleen became gradually fainter and fainter with each materialization that Michael evoked. Then one evening before dinner he found that the maid had forgotten to put a fresh cake of soap in the dish. It was a question of ringing the bell or of callously using Kathleen's commemorative tablet. Michael went to his drawer and, as he slowly washed his hands, he washed from his mind the few insignificant outlines of Kathleen that were printed there. The soap was Trèfle Incarnat, and somewhat cynically Michael relished the savour of it, and even made up his mind to buy a full fat cake when this one should be finished. Kathleen, however, even in the fragrant moment of her annihilation, had her revenge, for Michael experienced a return of the old restlessness and discontent that was not mitigated by Alan's increasing preoccupation with cricket. He did not complain of this, for he respected the quest of School Colours, and was proud for Alan. At the same time something must be done to while away these warm summer evenings until at Basingstead Minor, where his mother had delightfully agreed to take a cottage for the summer, he and Alan could revive old days at Cobble Place.

One evening Michael went out about nine o'clock to post a letter and, finding the evening velvety and calm, strolled on through the enticing streets of twilight. The violet shadows in which the white caps and aprons of gossiping maids took on a moth-like immaterial beauty, the gliding, enraptured lovers, the scent of freshly watered flower-boxes, the stars winking between the chimney-pots, and all the drowsy alertness of a fine London dusk drew him on to turn each new corner as it arrived, until he saw the sky stained with dull gold from the reflection of the lively crater of the Earl's Court Exhibition, and heard over the vague intervening noises music that was sometimes clearly melodious, sometimes a mere confusion of spasmodic sound.

Michael suddenly thought he would like to spend his evening at the Exhibition, and wondered to himself why he had never thought of going there casually like this, why always he had considered it necessary to devote a hot afternoon and flurried evening to its exploitation. By the entrance he met a fellow-Jacobean, one Drake, whose accentuated mannishness, however disagreeable in the proximity of the school, might be valuable at the Exhibition. Michael therefore accepted his boisterous greeting pleasantly enough, and they passed through the turnstiles together.

"I'll introduce you to a smart girl, if you like," Drake offered, as they paused undecided between the attractions of two portions of the Exhibition. "She sells Turkish Delight by the Cave of the Four Winds. Very O.T., my boy," Drake went on.

"Do you mean——" Michael began.

"What? Rather," said Drake. "I've been home to her place."

"No joking?" Michael asked.

"Yes," affirmed Drake with a triumphant inhalation of sibilant breath.

"Rather lucky, wasn't it?" Michael asked. "I mean to say, it was rather lucky to meet her."

"She might take you home," suggested Drake, examining Michael critically.

"But I mightn't like her," Michael expostulated.

"Good Lord," exclaimed Drake, struck by a point of view that was obviously dismaying in its novelty, "you don't mean to say you'd bother about that, if you could?"

"Well, I rather think I should," Michael admitted. "I think I'd want to be in love."

"You are an extraordinary chap," said Drake. "Now if I were dead nuts on a girl, the last thing I'd think of would be that."

They walked along silently, each one pondering the other's incomprehensibleness, until they came to the stall presided over by Miss Mabel Bannerman, who in Michael's opinion bore a curious resemblance to the Turkish Delight she sold. With the knowledge of her he had obtained from Drake, Michael regarded Miss Bannerman very much as he would have looked at an animal in the Zoological Gardens with whose habits he had formed a previous acquaintanceship through a book of natural history. He tried to perceive beyond her sachet-like hands and watery blue eyes and spongy hair and full-blown breast the fascination which had made her her man's common property. Then he looked at Drake, and came to the conclusion that the problem was not worth the difficulty of solution.

"I think I'll be getting back," said Michael awkwardly.

"Why, it's not ten," gasped Drake. "Don't be an ass. Mabel gets out at eleven, and we can take her home. Can't we, Mabel?"

"Sauce!" Mabel archly snapped.

This savoury monosyllable disposed of Michael's hesitation, and, as the personality of Mabel cloyed him with a sudden nausea like her own Turkish Delight, he left her to Drake without another word and went home to bed.

The night was hot and drew Michael from vain attempts at sleep to the open window where, as he sat thinking, a strange visionary survey of the evening, a survey that he himself could scarcely account for, was conjured up. He had not been aware at the time of much more than Drake and the Turkish Delight stall. Now he realized that he too craved for a Mabel, not a peony of a woman who could be flaunted like a vulgar button-hole, but a more shy, a more subtle creature, yet conquerable. Then, as Michael stared out over the housetops at the brooding pavilion of sky which enclosed the hectic city, he began to recall the numberless glances, the countless attitudes, all the sensuous phantasmagoria of the Exhibition's population. He remembered a slim hand, a slanting eye, lips translucent in a burst of light. He caught at scents that, always fugitive, were now utterly incommunicable; he trembled at the remembrance of some contact in a crowd that had been at once divinely intimate and unendurably remote. The illusion of all the city's sleepers calling to him became more and more vivid under each stifling breath of the night. Somewhere beneath that sable diadem of chimney-tops she lay, that lovely girl of his desire. He would not picture her too clearly lest he should destroy the charm of this amazing omnipotence of longing. He would be content to enfold the imagination of her, and at dawn let her slip from his arms like a cloud. He would sit all the night time at his window, aware of kisses. Was this the emotion that prompted poets to their verses? Michael broke his trance to search for paper and pencil, and wrote ecstatically.

In the morning, when he read what he had written, he hastily tore it up, and made up his mind that the Earl's Court Exhibition would feed his fire more satisfactorily than bad verses. Half a guinea would buy a season-ticket, and July should be a pageant of sensations.

Every night Michael went to Earl's Court, and here a hundred brilliant but evanescent flames were kindled in his heart, just as in the Exhibition gardens every night for three hours the fairy-lamps spangled the edge of the paths in threads of many-tinted lights. Michael always went alone, because he did not desire any but his own discoveries to reward his excited speculation. At first he merely enjoyed the sensation of the slow stream of people that continually went up and down, or strolled backwards and forwards, or circled round the bandstand that was set out like a great gaudy coronet upon the parterres of lobelias and geraniums and calceolarias that with nightfall came to seem brocaded cushions.

It was a time profitable with a thousand reflections, this crowded hour of the promenade. There was always the mesmeric sighing of silk skirts and the ceaseless murmur of conversation; there was the noise of the band and the tapping of canes; there was, in fact, a regularity of sound that was as infinitely soothing as breaking waves or a wind-ruffled wood. There were the sudden provocative glances which flashed as impersonally as precious stones, and yet lanced forth a thrill that no faceted gem could give. There were hands whose white knuckles, as they rippled over Michael's hands in some momentary pressure of the throng, gave him a sense of being an instrument upon which a chord had been clearly struck. There were strands of hair that floated against his cheeks with a strange, but exquisitely elusive intimacy of communication. It was all very intoxicating and very sensuous; but the spell crept over him as imperceptibly as if he were merely yielding himself to the influence of a beautiful landscape, as if he were lotus-eating in a solitude created by numbers.

Michael, however, was not content to dream away in a crowd these passionate nights of July; and after a while he set out to find adventures in the great bazaar of the Exhibition, wandering through the golden corridors and arcades with a queer sense of suppressed expectancy. So many fantastic trades were carried on here, that it was natural to endow the girls behind the counters with a more romantic life than that of ordinary and anæmic shop-assistants. Even Miss Mabel Bannerman amid her Turkish Delight came to seem less crude in such surroundings, and Michael once or twice had thoughts of prosecuting his acquaintanceship; for as yet he had not been able to bring himself to converse with any of the numerous girls, so much more attractive than Mabel, who were haunting him with their suggestion of a strange potentiality.

Michael wandered on past the palmists who went in and out of their tapestried tents; past the physiognomists and phrenologists and graphologists; past the vendors of scents and silver; past the languid women who spread out their golden rugs from Samarcand; past the Oriental shops fuming with odorous pastilles, where lamps encrusted in deep-hued jewels of glass glimmered richly; past that slant-eyed cigarette-seller with the crimson fez crowning her dark hair.

July was nearing its end; the holidays were in sight; and still Michael had got no farther with his ambitions; still at the last moment he would pass on and neglect some perfect opportunity for speech. He used to rail at his cowardice, and repeat to himself all his academic knowledge of frail womanhood. He even took the trouble to consult the Ars Amatoria, and was so much impressed by Ovid's prescription for behaviour at a circus that he determined to follow his advice. To put his theory into practice, Michael selected a booth where seals performed for humanity at sixpence a head. But all his resolutions ended in sitting mildly amused by the entertainment in a condition of absolute decorum.

School broke up with the usual explosion of self-congratulatory rhetoric from which Michael, owing to his Exhibition ticket, failed to emerge with any calf-bound souvenir of intellectual achievement. He minded this less than his own pusillanimous behaviour on the brink of experience. It made him desperate to think that in two days he would be at Basingstead with his mother and Alan and Mrs. Ross, utterly remote even from the pretence of temptation.

"Dearest Michael, you really must get your things together," expostulated Mrs. Fane, when he announced his intention of going round to the Exhibition as usual on the night before they were to leave town.

"Well, mother, I can pack when I come in, and I do want to get all I can out of this 'season.' You see it will be absolutely wasted for August and half September."

"Michael," said Mrs. Fane suddenly, "you're not keeping anything from me?"

"Good gracious, no. What makes you ask?" Michael demanded, blushing.

"I was afraid that perhaps some horrid girl might have got hold of you," said Mrs. Fane.

"Why, would you mind very much?" asked Michael, with a curious hopefulness that his mother would pursue the subject, as if by so doing she would give him an opportunity of regarding himself and his behaviour objectively.

"I don't know that I should mind very much," said Mrs. Fane, "if I thought you were quite certain not to do anything foolish." Then she seemed to correct the laxity of her point of view, and substituted, "anything that you might regret."

"What could I regret?" asked Michael, seeking to drive his mother on to the rocks of frankness.

"Surely you know what better than I can tell you. Don't you?" The note of interrogation caught the wind, and Mrs. Fane sailed off on the starboard tack.

"But as long as you're not keeping anything from me," she went on, "I don't mind. So go out, dear child, and enjoy yourself by all means. But don't be very late."

"I never am," said Michael quickly, and a little resentfully as he thought of his very decorous homecomings.

"I know you're not. You're really a very dear fellow," his mother murmured, now safe in port.

So at nine o'clock as usual Michael passed through the turnstiles and began his feverish progress across the Exhibition grounds, trying as he had never tried before to screw himself up to the pitch of the experience he craved.

He was standing by one of the entrances to the Court of Marvels, struggling with his self-consciousness and egging himself on to be bold on this his last night, when he heard himself accosted as Mr. Michael Fane. He looked round and saw a man whom he instantly recognized, but for the moment could not name.

"It is Mr. Michael Fane?" the stranger asked. "You don't remember me? I met you at Clere Abbey."

"Brother Aloysius!" Michael exclaimed, and as he uttered the high-sounding religious appellation he almost laughed at the incongruity of it in connection with this slightly overdressed and dissolute-looking person he so entitled.

"Well, not exactly, old chap. At least not in this get-up. Meats is my name."

"Oh, yes," said Michael vaguely. There seemed no other comment on such a name, and Mr. Meats himself appeared sensitive to the implication of uncertainty, for he made haste to put Michael at ease by commenting on its oddity.

"I suppose you're thinking it's a damned funny exchange for Brother Aloysius. But a fellow can't help his name, and that's a fact."

"You've left the Abbey then?" enquired Michael.

"Oh Lord, yes. Soon after you went. It was no place for me. Manners, O.S.B., gave me the push pretty quick. And I don't blame him. Well, what are you doing? Have a drink? Or have you got to meet your best girl? My, you've grown since I saw you last. Quite the Johnny nowadays. But I spotted you all right. Something about your eyes that would be very hard to forget."

Michael thought that if it came to unforgettable eyes, the eyes of Mr. Meats would stand as much chance of perpetual remembrance as any, since their unholy light would surely set any heart beating with the breathless imagination of sheer wickedness.

"Yes, I have got funny eyes, haven't I?" said Meats in complacent realization of Michael's thoughts. And as he spoke he seemed consciously to exercise their vile charm, so that his irises kindled slowly with lambent blue flames.

"Come on, let's have this drink," urged Meats, and he led the way to a scattered group of green tables. They sat down, and Michael ordered a lemon-squash.

"Very good drink too," commented Meats. "I think I'll have the same, Rosie," he said to the girl who served them.

"Do you know that girl?" Michael asked.

"Used to. About three years ago. She's gone off though," said Meats indifferently.

Michael, to hide his astonishment at the contemptuous suggestion of damaged goods, enquired what Meats had been doing since he left the Monastery.

"Want to know?" asked Meats.

Michael assured him that he did.

"You're rather interested in me, aren't you? Well, I can tell you a few things and that's a fact. I don't suppose that there's anybody in London who could tell you more. But you might be shocked."

"Oh, shut up!" scoffed Michael, blushing with indignation.

Then began the shameless narration of the late Brother Aloysius, whom various attainments had enabled to gain an equal profit from religion and vice. Sometimes as Michael listened to the adventures he was reminded of Benvenuto Cellini or Casanova, but almost immediately the comparison would be shattered by a sudden sanctimonious blasphemy which he found nauseating. Moreover, he disliked the sly procurer that continually leered through the man's personality.

"You seem to have done a lot of dirty work for other people," Michael bluntly observed at last.

"My dear old chap," replied Meats, "of course I have. You see, in this world there are lots of people who can always square their own consciences, if the worst of what they want to do is done for them behind the scenes as it were. You never yet heard a man confess that he ruined a girl. Now, did you? Why, I've heard the most shocking out-and-outers anyone could wish to meet brag that they've done everything, and then turn up their eyes and thank God they've always respected real purity. Well, I never respected anything or anybody. And why should I? I never had a chance. Who was my mother? A servant. Who was my father? A minister, a Nonconformist minister in Wales. And what did the old tyke do? Why, he took the case to court and swore my mother was out for blackmail. So she went to prison, and he came smirking home behind the village band; and all the old women in the place hung out Union Jacks to show they believed in him. And then his wife gave a party."

Michael looked horrified and felt horrified at this revelation of vileness, and yet, all the time he was listening, through some grotesquery of his nerves he was aware of thinking to himself the jingle of Little Bo-peep.

"Ah, that's touched you up, hasn't it?" said Meats, eagerly leaning forward. "But wait a bit. What did my mother do when she came out? Went on the streets. Do you hear? On the streets, and mark you, she was a servant, a common village servant, none of your flash Empire goods. Oh, no, she never knew what it was like to go up the river on a Sunday afternoon. And she drank. Well, of course she drank. Gin was as near as she ever got to paradise. And where was I brought up? Not among the buttercups, my friend, you may lay on that. No, I was down underneath, underneath, underneath where a chap like you will never go because you're a gentleman. And so, though, of course, you're never likely to ruin a girl, you'll always have your fun. Why shouldn't you? Being a nicely brought-up young gentleman, it's your birthright."

"But how on earth did you ever become a monk?" asked Michael, anxious to divert the conversation away from himself.

"Well, it does sound a bit improbable, I must say. I was recommended there by a priest—a nice chap called Arbuthnot who'd believe a chimney-sweep was a miller. But Manners was very sharp on to me, and I was very sharp on to Manners. Picking blackberries and emptying slops! What a game! I came with a character and left without one. Probationer was what they called me. Silly mug was what I called myself."

"You seem to know a lot of priests," said Michael.

"Oh, I've been in with parsons since I was at Sunday-school. Well, don't look so surprised. You don't suppose my mother wanted me hanging round all the afternoon! Now I very soon found out that one can always get round a High Church slum parson, and very often a Catholic priest by turning over a new leaf and confessing. It gets them every time, and being by nature generous, it gets their pockets. That's why I gave up Dissenters and fashionable Vicars. Dissenters want more than they give, and fashionable Vicars are too clever. That's why they become fashionable Vicars, I suppose," said Meats pensively.

"But you couldn't go on taking in even priests for ever," Michael objected.

"Ah, now I'll tell you something. I do feel religious sometimes," Meats declared solemnly. "And I do really want to lead a new life. But it doesn't last. It's like love. Never mind, perhaps I'll be lucky enough to die when I'm working off a religious stretch. I give you my word, Fane, that often in these fits I've felt like committing suicide just to cheat the devil. Would you believe that?"

"I don't think you're as bad as you make out," said Michael sententiously.

"Oh, yes, I am," smiled the other. "I'm rotten bad. But I reckon the first man I meet in hell will be my father, and if it's possible to hurt anyone down there more than they're being hurt already, I'll do it. But look here, I shall get the hump with this blooming conversation you've started me off on. Come along, drink up and have another, and tell us something about yourself."

"Oh, there's nothing to tell," Michael sighed. "My existence is pretty dull after yours."

"I suppose it is," said Meats, as if struck by a new thought. "Everything has its compensations, as they say."

"Frightfully dull," Michael vowed. "Why, here am I still at school! You know I wouldn't half mind going down underneath, as you call it, for a while. I believe I'd like it."

"If you knew you could get up again all right," commented Meats.

"Oh, of course," Michael answered. "I don't suppose Æneas would have cared much about going down to hell, if he hadn't been sure he could come up again quite safely."

"Well, I don't know your friend with the Jewish name," said Meats. "But I'll lay he didn't come out much wiser than he went in if he knew he could get out all right by pressing a button and taking the first lift up."

"Oh, well, I was only speaking figuratively," Michael explained.

"So was I. The same here, and many of them, old chap," retorted Meats enigmatically.

"Ah, you don't think I'm in earnest. You think I'm fooling," Michael complained.

"Oh, yes, I think you'd like to take a peep without letting go of Nurse's apron," sneered Meats.

"Well, perhaps one day you'll see me underneath," Michael almost threatened.

"No offence, old chap," said Meats cordially. "It's no good my giving you an address because it won't last, but London isn't very big, and we'll run up against one another again, that's a cert. Now I've got to toddle off and meet a girl."

"Have you?" asked Michael, and his enquiry was tinged with a faint longing that the other noticed at once.

"Jealous?" enquired Meats. "Why, look at all the girls round about you. It's up to you not to feel lonely."

"I know," said Michael fretfully. "But how the deuce can I tell whether they want me to talk to them?"

Meats laughed shrilly.

"What are you afraid of? Leading some innocent lamb astray?"

Again to Michael occurred the ridiculous rhyme of Bo-peep. So insistent was it that he could scarcely refrain from humming it aloud.

"Of course I'm not afraid of that," he protested. "But how am I to tell they won't think me a brute?"

"What would it matter if they did?" asked Meats.

"Well, I should feel a fool."

"Oh, dear. You're very young, aren't you?"

"It's nothing to do with being young," Michael asserted. "I simply don't want to be a cad."

"Somebody else is to be the cad first and then it's all right, eh?" chuckled Meats. "But it's a shame to teaze a nice chap like you. I dare say Daisy'll have a friend with her."

"Is Daisy the girl you're going to see?"

"You've guessed my secret," said Meats. "Come on, I'll introduce you."

As Michael rose to follow Meats, he felt that he was like Faust with Mephistopheles. But Faust had asked for his youth back again. Michael only demanded the courage not to waste youth while it was his to enjoy. He felt that his situation was essentially different from the other, and he hesitated no longer.

The next half-hour passed in a whirl. Michael was conscious of a slim brunette in black and scarlet, and of a fairy-like figure by her side in a dress of shimmering blue; he was conscious too of a voice insinuating, softly metallic, and of fingers that touched his wrist as lightly as silk. There were whispers and laughters and sudden sweeping embarrassments. There was a horrible sense of publicity, of curious mocking eyes that watched his progress. There was an overwhelming knowledge of money burning in his pocket, of money hard and round and powerful. There were hot waves of remorse and the thought of his heart hammering him on to be brave. A cabman leaned over from his box like a gargoyle. A key clicked.

Then, it seemed a century afterwards, Carlington Road stretched dim, austere, forbidding to Michael's ingress. A policeman's deep salutation sounded portentously reproachful. The bloom of dawn was on the windows. The flames in the street-lamps were pale as primroses. At his own house Michael saw the red and amber sparrows in their crude blue vegetation horribly garish against the lighted entrance-hall. The Salve printed funereally upon the mat was the utterance of blackest irony. He hastily turned down the gas, and the stairs caught a chill unreality from the creeping dawn. The balustrade stuck to his parched hands; the stairs creaked grotesquely to his breathless ascent. His mother stood like a ghost in her doorway.

"Michael, how dreadfully late you are."

"Am I?" said Michael. "I suppose it is rather late. I met a fellow I know."

He spoke petulantly to conceal his agitation, and his one thought was to avoid kissing her before he went up to his own room.

"It's all right about my packing," he murmured hastily. "In the morning I shall have time. I'm sorry I woke you. Good night."

He had passed; and he looked back compassionately, as she faded in her rosy and indefinite loveliness away to her room.

Then, with the patterns of foulard ties crawling like insects before his strained eyes, with collars coiling and uncoiling like mainsprings, with all his clothes in one large intolerable muddle, Michael pressed the cold sheets to his forehead and tried to imagine that to-morrow he would be in the country.

Chapter XV: Grey Eyes

AS Michael sat opposite to his mother in the railway-carriage on the following morning, he found it hard indeed to realize that an ocean did not stretch between them. He did not feel ashamed; he had no tremors for the straightforward regard; he had no uneasy sensation that possibly even now his mother was perplexing herself on account of his action. He simply felt that he had suffered a profound change and that his action of yesterday called for a readjustment of his entire standpoint. Or rather, he felt that having since yesterday travelled so far and lived so violently, he could now only meet his mother as a friend from whom one has been long parted and whose mental progress during many years must be gradually apprehended.

"Why do you look at me with such a puzzled expression, Michael?" asked Mrs. Fane. "Is my hat crooked?"

Michael assured her that nothing was the matter with her hat.

"Do you want to ask me something?" persisted Mrs. Fane.

Michael shook his head and smiled, wondering whether he did really wish to ask her a question, whether he would be relieved to know what attitude she would adopt towards his adventure. With so stirring a word did he enhance what otherwise would have seemed base. His mother evidently was aware of a tension in this ridiculously circumscribed railway-carriage. Would it be released if he were to inform her frankly of what had happened, or would such an admission be an indiscretion from which their relationship would never recover? After all she was his mother, and there must positively exist in her inmost self the power of understanding what he had done. Some part of the impulse which had actuated his behaviour would surely find a root in the heart of the handsome woman who travelled with such becoming repose on the seat opposite to him. He forgot to bother about himself in this sudden new pleasure of observation that seemed to endow him with undreamed-of opportunities of distraction and, what was more important, with a stable sense of his own individuality. How young his mother looked! Until now he had taken her youth for granted, but she must be nearly forty. It was scarcely credible that this tall slim creature with the proud, upcurving mouth and lustrous grey eyes was his own mother. He thought of his friends' homes that were presided over by dumpy women in black silk with greying hair. Even Alan's mother, astonishingly pretty though she was, seemed in the picture he conjured of her to look faded beside his own.

And while he was pondering his mother's beauty, the train reached the station at which they must alight for Basingstead. There was Alan in white flannels on the platform, there too was Mrs. Ross; and as she greeted his mother Michael's thoughts went back to the day he saw these two come together at Carlington Road, and by their gracious encounter drive away the shadow of Nurse.

"I vote we walk," said Alan. "Mrs. Fane and Aunt Maud can drive in the pony-chaise, and then your luggage can all come up at once in the cart."

So it was arranged, and as Michael watched his mother and Mrs. Ross drive off, he was strangely reminded of a picture that he had once dearly loved, a picture by Flaxman of Hera and Athene driving down from Olympus to help the Greeks. Λευκώλενος Ἥρη—that was his mother, and γλαυκῶπις Ἀθήνη—that was Mrs. Ross. He could actually remember the line in the Iliad that told of the gates of heaven, where the Hours keep watch, opening for the goddesses' descent—αὐτόμαται δέ πύλαι μύκοον οὐρανοι ἅς ἔχον Ὧραι. At the same time for all his high quotations, Michael could not help smiling at the dolefully senescent dun pony being compared to the golden steeds of Hera or at the pleasant old porter who hastened to throw open the white gate of the station-drive serving as a substitute for the Hours.

The country air was still sweet between the hazel hedgerows, although the grass was drouthy and the scabious blooms were already grey with dust. Nothing for Michael could have been more charged with immemorial perfume than this long walk at July's end. It held the very quintessence of holiday airs through all the marching years of boyhood. It was haunted by the memory of all the glad anticipations of six weeks' freedom that time after time had succeeded the turmoil of breaking up for the August holidays. The yellow amoret swinging from the tallest shoot of the hedge was the companion of how many summer walks. The acrid smell of nettles by the roadside was prophetic of how many pastoral days. The butterflies, brown and white and tortoiseshell, that danced away to right and left over the green bushes, to what winding paths did they not summon. And surely Alan gave a final grace to this first walk of the holidays. Surely he crystallized all hopes, all memories, all delights of the past in a perfection of present joy.

Yet Michael, as he walked beside him, could only think of Alan as a beautiful inanimate object for whom perception did not exist. Inanimate, however, was scarcely the word to describe one who was so very definitely alive: Michael racked his invention to discover a suitable label for Alan, but he could not find the word. With a shock of misgiving he asked himself whether he had outgrown their friendship, and partly to test, but chiefly to allay his dread, he took Alan's arm with a gesture of almost fierce possession. He was relieved to find that Alan's touch was still primed with consolation, that companionship with him still soothed the turbulence of his own spirit reaching out to grasp what could never be expressed in words, and therefore could never be grasped. Michael was seized with a longing to urge Alan to grow up more quickly, to make haste lest he should be left behind by his adventurous friend. Michael remembered how he used to dread being moved up, hating to leave Alan in a class below him, how he had deliberately dallied to allow Alan to overtake him. But idleness in school-work was not the same as idleness in experience of life, and unless Alan would quickly grow up, he knew that he must soon leave him irremediably behind. It was distressing to reflect that Alan would be shocked by the confidence which he longed to impose upon him, and it was disquieting to realize that these last summer holidays of school, however complete with the quiet contentment of familiar pleasures, would for himself grow slowly irksome with deferred excitement.

But as the green miles slowly unfolded themselves, as the dauntless yellow amoret still swung from a lissome stem, as Alan spoke of the river and the grey tower on the hill, Michael saw the fretful colours of the Exhibition grow dim; and when dreaming in the haze of the slumberous afternoon they perceived the village and heard the mysterious murmur of human tranquillity, Michael's heart overflowed with gratitude for the sight of Alan by his side. Then the church-clock that struck a timeless hour sounded for him one of those moments whose significance would resist eternally whatever lying experience should endeavour to assail the truth which had made of one flashing scene a revelation.

Michael was ineffably refreshed by his vision of the imperishable substance of human friendship, and he could not but jeer at himself now for having a little while back put Alan into the domain of objects inanimate.

"There's your cottage," said Alan. "It's practically next door to Cobble Place. Rather decent, eh?"

Michael could not say how decent he thought it, nor how decent he thought Alan.

"I vote we go up the river after tea," he suggested.

"Rather," said Alan. "I expect you'll come round to tea with us. Don't be long unpacking."

"I shan't, you bet," said Michael.

Nor was he, and after a few minutes he and his mother were sitting in the drawing-room at Cobble Place, eating a tea that must have been very nearly the same as an unforgettable tea of nine years ago. Mrs. Carthew did not seem quite so old; nor indeed did anybody, and as for Joan and May Carthew, they were still girls. Yet even when he and Alan had stayed down here for the wedding only four years ago, Michael had always been conscious of everybody's age. And now he was curiously aware of everybody's youth. He supposed vaguely that all this change of outlook was due to his own remarkable precocity and rapid advance; but nevertheless he still ate with all the heartiness of childhood.

After tea Mrs. Ross with much tact took up Michael by himself to see her son and, spared the necessity of comment, Michael solemnly regarded the fair-haired boy of two who was squeaking an india-rubber horse for his mother's benefit.

"O you attractive son of mine," Mrs. Ross sighed in a whisper.

"He's an awfully sporting kid," Michael said.

Then he suddenly remembered that he had not seen Mrs. Ross since her husband was killed. Yet from this chintz-hung room whose casements were flooded with the amber of the westering sun, how far off seemed fatal Africa. He remembered also that to this very same gay room he had long ago gone with Miss Carthew after tea, that here in a ribboned bed he had first heard the news of her coming to live at 64 Carlington Road.

"We must have a long talk together soon," said Mrs. Ross, seeming to divine his thoughts. "But I expect you're anxious to revive old memories and visit old haunts with Alan. I'm going to stay here and talk to Kenneth while Nurse has her tea."

Michael lingered for a moment in the doorway to watch the two. Then he said abruptly, breathlessly:

"Mrs. Ross, I think painters and sculptors are lucky fellows. I'd like to paint you now. I wish one could understand the way people look, when one's young. But I'm just beginning to realize how lucky I was when you came to us. And yet I used to be ashamed of having a governess. Still, I believe I did appreciate you, even when I was eight."

Then he fled, and to cover his retreat sang out loudly for Alan all the way downstairs.

"I say, Aunt Enid wants to talk to you," said Alan.

"Aunt Enid?" Michael echoed.

"Mrs. Carthew," Alan explained.

"I vote we go for a walk afterwards, don't you?" Michael suggested.

"Rather," said Alan. "I'll shout for you, when I think you've jawed long enough."

Michael found Mrs. Carthew in her sun-coloured garden, cutting down the withering lupins whose silky seed-pods were strewn all about the paths.

"Can you spare ten minutes for an old friend?" asked Mrs. Carthew.

Michael thought how tremendously wise she looked, and lest he should be held to be staring unduly, he bent down to sweep together the shimmering seed-pods, while Mrs. Carthew snipped away, talking in sentences that matched the quick snickasnack of her weapon.

"I must say you've grown up into an attractive youth. Let me see, you must be seventeen and a half. I suppose you think yourself a man now? Dear me, these lupins should have been cut back a fortnight ago. And now I have destroyed a hollyhock. Tut-tut, I'm getting very blind. What did you think of Maud's son? A healthy rosy child, and not at all amenable to discipline, I'm glad to say. Well, are you enjoying school?"

The old lady paused with her scissors gaping, and looked shrewdly at Michael.

"I'm getting rather fed up with it," Michael admitted. "It goes on for such a long time. It wasn't so bad this term, though."

Then he remembered that whatever pleasures had mitigated the exasperation of school last term were decidedly unscholastic, and he blushed.

"I simply loathed it for a time," he added.

"Alan informs me he acquired his first eleven cap this term and will be in the first fifteen as Lord Treasurer or something," Mrs. Carthew went on. "Naturally he must enjoy this shower of honours. Alan is decidedly typical of the better class of unthinking young Englishman. He is pleasant to look at—a little colt-like perhaps, but that will soon wear off. My own dear boy was very like him, and Maud's dear husband was much the same. You, I'm afraid, think too much, Michael."

"Oh, no, I don't think very much," said Michael, disclaiming philosophy, and greatly afraid that Mrs. Carthew was supposing him a prig.

"You needn't be ashamed of thinking," she said. "After all, the amount you think now won't seriously disorganize the world. But you seem to me old for your age, much older than Alan for instance, and though your conversation with me at any rate is not mature, nevertheless you convey somehow an impression of maturity that I cannot quite account for."

Michael could not understand why, when for the first time he was confronted with somebody who gave his precocity its due, he was unable to discuss it eagerly and voluminously, why he should half resent being considered older than Alan.

"Don't look so cross with me," Mrs. Carthew commanded. "I am an old woman, and I have a perfect right to say what I please to you. Besides, you and I have had many conversations, and I take a great interest in you. What are you going to be?"

"Well, that's what I can't find out," said Michael desperately. "I know what I'm not going to be, and that's all."

"That's a good deal, I think," said Mrs. Carthew. "Pray tell me what professions you have condemned."

"I'm not going into the Army. I'm not going into the Civil Service. I'm not going to be a doctor or a lawyer."

"Or a parson?" asked Mrs. Carthew, crunching through so many lupin stalks at once that they fell with a rattle on to the path.

"Well, I have thought about being a parson," Michael slowly granted. "But I don't think parsons ought to marry."

"Good gracious," exclaimed Mrs. Carthew, "you're surely not engaged?"

"Oh, no," said Michael; but he felt extremely flattered by the imputation. "Still, I might want to be."

"Then you're in love," decided Mrs. Carthew. "No wonder you look so careworn. I suppose she's nearly thirty and has promised to wait until you come of age. I can picture her. If I had my stick with me I could draw her on the gravel. A melon stuck on a bell-glass, I'll be bound."

"I'm not in love, and if I were in love," said Michael with dignity, "I certainly shouldn't be in love with anyone like that. But I could be in love at any moment, and so I don't think I shall be a parson."

"You've got plenty of time," said Mrs, Carthew. "Alan says you're going to Oxford next year."

Michael's heart leapt,—next year had never before seemed so imminent.

"I suppose you'll say that I'm an ignorant and foolish old woman, if I attempt to give you advice about Oxford; but I gave you advice once about school, and I'll do the same again. To begin with, I think you'll find having been to St. James' a handicap. I have an old friend, the wife of a don, who assures me that many of the boys who go up from your school suffer at Oxford from their selfish incubation by Dr. Brownjohn. They're fit for killing too soon. In fact, they have been forced."

"Ah, but I saw that for myself," said Michael. "I had a row with Brownjohn about my future."

"How delighted I am to hear that!" said Mrs. Carthew. "I think that I'll cut back the delphiniums also. Then you're not going in for a scholarship?"

"No," said Michael. "I don't want to be hampered, and I think my mother's got plenty of money. But Alan's going to get a scholarship."

"Yes, that is unfortunately necessary," said Mrs. Carthew. "Still, Alan is sufficiently typical of the public-school spirit—an odious expression yet always unavoidable—to carry off the burden. If you were poor, I should advise you to buy overcoats. Three smart overcoats are an equipment for a poor man. But I needn't dwell on social ruses in your case. Remember that going to Oxford is like going to school. Be normal and inconspicuous at first; and when you have established yourself as an utterly undistinguished young creature, you can career into whatever absurdities of thought, action or attire you will. In your first year establish your sanity; in your second year display your charm; and in your third year do whatever you like. Now there is Alan calling, and we'll leave the paths strewn with these cut stalks as a Memento Mori to the gardener. What a charming woman your mother is. She has that exquisite vagueness which when allied with good breeding is perfectly irresistible, at any rate to a practical and worldly old woman like me. But then I've had an immense amount of time in which to tidy up. Pleasant hours to you down here. It's delightful to hear about the place the sound of boys laughing and shouting."

Michael left Mrs. Carthew, rather undecided as to what exactly she thought of him or Alan or anybody else. As he walked over the lawn that went sloping down to the stream, he experienced a revulsion from the interest he took in listening to what people thought about him, and he now began to feel an almost morbid sensitiveness to the opinion of others. This destroyed some of the peace which he had sought and cherished down here in the country. He began to wonder if that wise old lady had been laughing at him, whether all she said had been an implied criticism of his attitude towards existence. Her praise must have been grave irony; her endorsement of his behaviour had been disguised reproof. She really admired Alan, and had only been trying as gently as possible to make him come into line with her nephew. He himself must seem to her eccentric, undignified, a flamboyant sort of creature whom she pitied and whose errors she wished to remedy. Michael was mortified by his retrospect of the conversation, and felt inclined when he saw Alan to make an excuse and retire from his society, until his self-esteem had recovered from the rebuke that had lately been inflicted. Indeed, it called for a great effort on Michael's part to embark in the canoe with his paragon and sit face to face without betraying the wound that was damaging his own sense of personality.

"You had a very long jaw with Aunt Enid," said Alan. "I thought you were never coming. She polished me off in about three minutes."

Michael looked darkly at Alan for a moment before he asked with ungracious accentuation what on earth Alan and Mrs. Carthew had talked about.

"She was rather down on me," said Alan. "I think she must have thought I was putting on side about getting my Eleven."

Michael was greatly relieved to hear this, and his brow cleared as he enquired what was wrong.

"Well, I can't remember her exact words," Alan went on. "But she said I must be careful not to grow up into a strong silent Englishman, because their day was done. She practically told me I was rather an ass, and pretended to be fearfully surprised when she heard I was going to try for a scholarship at Oxford. She was squashing slugs all the time she was talking, and I could do nothing but look a bigger fool than ever and count the slugs. I ventured to remark once that most people thought it was a good thing to be keen on games, and she said half the world was composed of fools which accounted for the preponderation—I mean preponderance—of pink on the map. She said it always looked like an advertizement of successful fox-hunting. And when I carefully pointed out that I'd never all my life had a chance to hunt, she said 'More's the pity,' I couldn't make out what she was driving at; so, feeling rather a worm, I shot off as soon as I could. What did she say to you?"

"Oh, nothing much," said Michael triumphantly. "She's a rum old girl, but rather decent."

"She's too clever for me," said Alan, shaking his head. "It's like batting to a pro."

Then from the complexities of feminine judgment, the conversation glided easily like the canoe towards a discussion of the umpire's decision last term in giving Alan out l.b.w. to a ball that pitched at least two feet away from the off stump.

"It was rotten," said Alan fervidly.

"It was putrid," Michael agreed.

To avoid the difficulty of a first night in a strange cottage, Mrs. Fane and Michael had supper at Cobble Place; and after a jolly evening spent in looking for pencils to play games that nobody could ever recollect in all their rich perfection of potential incidents, Michael and Mrs. Fane walked with leisurely paces back to Woodbine Cottage through a sweet-savoured moonless night.

Michael enjoyed the intimate good night beneath so small a roof, and wished that Stella were with them. He lay awake, reading from each in turn of the tower of books he had erected by his bedside to fortify himself against sleeplessness. It was a queer enough mixture—Swinburne, Keats, Matthew Arnold, Robinson Crusoe, Half-hours with the Mystics, Tom Brown's Schooldays, Daudet's Sappho, the second volume of The Savoy, The Green Carnation, Holy Living and Dying; and as each time he changed his mind and took another volume, on the gabled ceiling the monstrous shadow that was himself filled him with a dreadful uncertainty. After an hour or so, he went to sit by the low window, leaning out and seeming to hear the dark world revolve in its course. Stars shook themselves clear from great rustling trees, and were in time enmeshed by others. The waning moon came up behind a rounded hill. A breeze fluttered down the dusty road, and was silent.

Michael fell to wondering whether he could ever bring himself in tune with these slow progressions of nature, whether he could renounce after one haggard spell of experience the mazy stir of transitory emotions that danced always beyond this dream. An Half-hour with St. John of the Cross made him ask himself whether this were the dark night of the soul through which he was passing. But he had never travelled yet, nor was he travelling now. He was simply sitting quiescent, allowing himself to be passed. These calm and stately figures of humanity whom he admired in their seclusion had only reached it after long strife. Mrs. Carthew had lost a husband and a son, had seen her daughter leave her house as a governess. Joan and May had for many years sunk their hopes in tending their mother. Nancy was away earning money, and would be entitled to retire here one day. Mrs. Ross had endured himself and Stella for several years, had married and lost her husband, and had borne a child. All these had won their timeless repose and their serene uncloying ease. They were not fossils, but perdurable images of stone. And his mother, she was—he stopped his reverie. Of his mother he knew nothing. Outside the dust stirred in the road fretfully; a malaise was in the night air. Michael shivered and went back to bed, and as he turned to blow out his candle he saw above him huge and menacing his own shadow. A cock crowed.

"Silly ass," muttered Michael, "he thinks it's already morning," and turning over after a dreamless sleep he found it was morning. So he rose and dressed himself serenely for a long sunburnt day.

On his way up the road to call for Alan he met the postman, who in answer to his enquiries handed him a letter from South Africa stamped all over with mysterious official abbreviations. He took it up to his mother curiously.

At lunch he asked her about the news from the war.

"Yes, dear, I had a letter," she murmured.

"From Lord Saxby, I suppose?"

"Yes, dear."

"Anything interesting?" Michael persisted.

"Oh, no, it's only about marches and not being able to wash properly."

"I thought it might be interesting," Michael speculated.

"No, dear. It wouldn't interest you," said Mrs. Fane in her tone of gentle discouragement.

"I don't want to be inquisitive," said Michael resentfully.

"No, dear, I'm sure you don't," his mother softly agreed.

The holidays ran their pastoral course of sun and rain, of clouds and winds, until the last week arrived with September in her most majestic mood of flawless halcyon. These were days that more than any hitherto enhanced for Michael the reverence he felt for the household of Cobble Place. These were days when Mrs. Carthew stepped wisely along her flowery enclosure, pondering the plums and peaches on the warm walls that in a transcendency of mellow sunlight almost took on the texture of living sunburnt flesh. These were days when Joan and May Carthew went down the village street with great bunches of Michaelmas daisies, of phloxes and Japanese anemones, or sat beneath the mulberry tree, sewing in the bee-drowsed air.

At the foot of the hill beyond the stream was a straggling wind-frayed apple-orchard, fresh pasturage for lambs in spring, and now in September a jolly haunt for the young son of Mrs. Ross. Here one afternoon, when Alan was away at Basingstead Major playing the last cricket match of the year, Michael plunged down in the grass beside her.

They sat for a while in silence, and Mrs. Ross seemed to Michael to be waiting for him to speak first, as if by her own attitude of mute expectation she could lure him on to express himself more openly than by direct question and shy answer. He felt the air pregnant with confidences, and kept urging himself on to begin the statement and revelation of his character, sure that whatever he desired to ask must be asked now while he was perhaps for the last time liable to this grave woman's influence, conscious of the security of goodness, envious of the maternity of peace. This grey-eyed woman seemed to sit above him like a proud eagle, careless of homage, never to be caught, never to be tamed, a figure for worship and inspiration. Michael wondered why all the women who awed him had grey eyes. Blue eyes fired his senses, striking sparks and kindling answering flames from his own blue eyes. Brown eyes left him indifferent. But grey eyes absorbed his very being, whether they were lustrous and violet-shaded like his mother's and Stella's, or whether, like Mrs. Ross's, they were soft as grey sea-water that in a moment could change to the iron-bound rocks they were so near.

Still Michael did not speak, but watched Mrs. Ross solemnly hand back to the rosy child sitting beside her in the grass the fallen apples that he would always fling from him exuberantly, panting the while at laughter's highest pitch.

"I wonder if I ever laughed like that," said Michael.

"You were a very serious little boy, when I first knew you," Mrs. Ross told him.

"I must have been rather depressing," Michael sighed.

"No, indeed you were not, dear Michael," she answered. "You had much too much personality."

"Have I now?" Michael asked sharply.

"Yes, of course you have."

"Well, what gives it to me?"

"Surely personality is something that is born with one. Personality can't be made," said Mrs. Ross.

"You don't think experience has got anything to do with it?" Michael pressed.

"I think experience makes the setting, and according to the experience the personality is perfected or debased, but nothing can destroy personality, not even death," she murmured, far away for a moment from this orchard.

"Which would you say had the stronger personality—Alan or I?" asked Michael.

"I should say you had," said Mrs. Ross. "Or at any rate you have a personality that will affect a larger number of people, either favourably or unfavourably."

"But Alan influences me more than I influence him," Michael argued.

"That may be," Mrs. Ross admitted. "Though I think your influence over Alan is very strong in this way. I think Alan is always very eager to see you at your best, and probably as your friendship goes on he will be more solicitous for you than for himself. I should say that he would be likely to sink himself in you. I wonder if you realize what a passionately loyal soul he is."

Michael flushed with pleasure at this appreciation of his friend, and his ambition went flying over to Basingstead Major to inspire Alan to bat his best. Then he burst forth in praise of him; he spoke of his changelessness, his freedom from moods, his candour and toleration and modesty.

"But the terrible thing is," said Michael suddenly, "that I always feel that without noticing it I shall one day leave Alan behind."

"But when you turn back, you'll find him just the same, don't forget; and you may be glad that he did not come with you. You may be glad that from his slowness you can find an indication of the road that I'm sure you yourself will one day try to take. Alan will travel by it all his life. You'll travel by it ultimately. Alan will never really appreciate its beauty. You will. That will be your recompense for what you suffer before you find it."

Mrs. Ross, as if to conceal emotion, turned quickly to romp with her son. Then she looked at Michael:

"And haven't you already once or twice left Alan behind?"

Suddenly to Michael her grey eyes seemed accusing.

"Yes, I suppose I have," he granted. "But isn't that the reason why my personality affects more people than his? You said just now that experience was only the setting, but I'm sure in my case it's more than a mere setting."

And even as he spoke all his experience seemed to cloud his brow, knitting and lining it with perplexed wrinkles.

"Mrs. Ross, you won't think me very rude if I say you always remind me of Pallas Athene? You always have, you know. At first it was just a vague outward resemblance, because you're tall and sort of cool-looking, and I really think your nose is rather Greek, if you don't mind my saying so."

"Oh, Michael," Mrs. Ross smiled. "I think you're even more unalterable than Alan. I seem to see you as a little boy again, when you talk like that."

Michael, however, was too keen on the scent of his comparison to be put off by smiles, and he went on eagerly:

"Now I realize that you actually are like Athene. You're one of those people who seem to have sprung into the world fully armed. I can't imagine that you were ever young."

Mrs. Ross laughed outright at this.

"Wait a minute," cried Michael. "Or ever old for that matter. And you know all about me. No, you needn't shake your head like that. Because you do."

Young Kenneth was so much roused by Michael's triumphant asseverations that he began to shout and kick in delighted tune and fling the apples from him with a vigour that he had never yet reached.

"You know," Michael continued breathlessly, while the boy on the grass gurgled his endorsement of every word. "You know that I'm old for my age, that I've already done things that other chaps at school only whisper about."

He stopped suddenly, for the grey eyes had become like rocks, and though the baby still panted ecstatically, there fell a chill.

"I'm very sorry to hear it," said Mrs. Ross.

"Well, why did you lead me on to confide in you?" said Michael sullenly. "I thought you would sympathize."

"Michael, I apologize," she said, melting. "I didn't mean to hurt your feelings. I dare say—ah, Michael, you see how easily all my shining armour falls to pieces."

"Another broken bottle," Michael muttered.

He got up abruptly and, though there were tears in his eyes, she could not win him back.

"Dear old boy, do tell me. Don't make the mistake of going back into yourself, because I failed you for a moment."

Mrs. Ross held out her hand, but Michael walked away.

"You don't understand," he turned to say. "You couldn't understand. And I don't want you to be able to understand. You mustn't think I'm sulking, or being rude, and really I'd rather you didn't understand. That boy of yours won't ever want you to understand. I don't think he'll ever do anything that isn't perfectly comprehensible."

"Michael," said Mrs. Ross, "don't be so bitter. You'll be sorry soon."

"Soon?" asked Michael fiercely. "Soon? Why soon? What's going to happen to make me sorry soon? Something is going to happen. I know. I feel it."

He fled through the wind-frayed orchard up the hill-side. With his back against the tower called Grogg's Folly he looked over four counties and vowed he would go heedless of everything that stood between him and experience. He would deny himself nothing; he would prove to the hilt everything.

"I must know," he wrung out of himself. "Everything that has happened must have happened for some reason. I will believe that. I can't believe in God, until I can believe in myself. And how can I believe in myself yet?"

The four counties under September's munificence mocked him with their calm.

"I know that all these people at Cobble Place are all right," he groaned. "I know that, just as I know Virgil is a great poet. But I never knew Virgil was great until I read Swinburne. Oh, I want to be calm and splendid and proud of myself, but I want to understand life while I'm alive. I want to believe in immortality, but in case I never can be convinced of it, I want to be convinced of something. Everything seems to be tumbling down nowadays. What's so absurd is that nobody can understand anybody else, let alone the universe. Mrs. Ross can understand why I like Alan, but she can't understand why I want love. Viner can understand why I get depressed, but he can't understand why I can't be cured immediately. Wilmot could understand why I wanted to read his rotten books, but he can't understand why the South African War upset me. And so on with everybody. I'm determined to understand everybody," Michael vowed, "even if I can't have faith," he sighed to the four counties.

Chapter XVI: *Blue Eyes*

MICHAEL managed to avoid during the rest of the week any reference, direct or indirect, to his interrupted conversation with Mrs. Ross, though he fancied a reproachfulness in her manner towards him, especially at the moment of saying good-bye. He was not therefore much surprised to receive a letter from her soon after he was back in Carlington Road.

COBBLE PLACE,
September 18th.

My dear Michael,

I have blamed myself entirely for what happened the other day. I should have been honoured by your confidence, and I cannot think why a wretched old-fashioned priggishness should have shown itself just when I least wished it would. I confess I was shocked for a moment, and perhaps I horridly imagined more than you meant to imply. If I had paused to think, I should have known that your desire to confide in me was alone enough to prove that you were fully conscious of the effect of anything you may have done. And after all in any sin—forgive me if I'm using too strong a word under a misapprehension—it is the effect which counts most deeply.

I'm inclined to think that in all you do through life, you will chiefly have to think of the effect of it on other people. I believe that you yourself are one of those characters that never radically deteriorate. This is rather a dangerous statement to make to anyone so young as you are. But I'm sure you are wise enough not to use it in justification of any wrong impulse. Do always remember, my dear boy, that however unscathed you feel yourself to be, you must never assume that to be the case with anyone else. I am really dreadfully distressed to think that by my own want of sympathy on a crucial occasion I have had to try to put into a letter what could only have been hammered out in a long talk. And we did hammer out something the other day. Or am I too optimistic? Write to me some time and reassure me a little, for I'm truly worried about you, and so indignant with my stupid self. Best love from us all,

Your affectionate
Maud Ross.

Michael merely pondered this letter coldly. He was still under the influence of the disappointment, and when he answered Mrs. Ross he answered her without regard to any wound he might inflict.

64 CARLINGTON ROAD,
Sunday.

Dear Mrs. Ross,

Please don't bother any more about it. I ought to have known better. I don't think it was such a very crucial occasion. The weather is frightfully hot, and I don't feel much like playing footer this term. I'm reading Dante, not in Italian, of course. London is as near the Inferno as anything, I should think. It's horribly hot. Excuse this short letter, but I've nothing to say.

Yours affectionately,
Michael.

Mrs. Ross made one more brief attempt to recapture him, but Michael put her off with the most superficial gossip of school-life, and she did not try again. He meant to play football, notwithstanding the hot weather, but finding that his boots were worn out, he continually put off buying another pair and let himself drift into October before he began. Then he hurt his leg, and had to stop for a while. This spoiled his faint chance for the First Fifteen, and in the end he gave up football altogether without much regret.

Games were a great impediment after all, when October's thin blue skies and sheen of pearl-soft airs led him on to dream along the autumnal streets. Sometimes he would wander by himself through the groves of Hyde Park and Kensington Gardens, or on some secluded green chair he would sit reading Verlaine, while continuously about him the slow leaves of the great planes swooped and fluttered down ambiguously like silent birds.

One Saturday afternoon he was sitting thus, when through the silver fog that on every side wrought the ultimate dissolution of the view Michael saw the slim figure of a girl walking among the trees. His mind was gay with Verlaine's delicate and fantastic songs, and this slim girl, as she moved wraith-like over the ground marbled with fallen leaves, seemed to express the cadence of the verse which had been sighing across the printed page.

The girl with downcast glance walked on, seeming to follow her path softly as one might follow through embroidery a thread of silk, and as she drew nearer to Michael out of the fog's enchantment she lost none of her indefinite charm; but she seemed still exquisite and silver-dewed. There was no one else in sight, and now already Michael could hear the lisping of her steps; then a breath of air among the tree-tops more remote sent floating, swaying, fluttering about her a flight of leaves. She paused, startled by the sudden shower, and at that moment the down-going autumnal sun glanced wanly through the glades and lighted her gossamer-gold hair with kindred gleams. The girl resumed her dreaming progress, and Michael now frankly stared in a rapture. She was dressed in deepest green box-cloth, and the heavy folds that clung to that lissome form made her ankles behind great pompons of black silk seem astonishingly slender. One hand was masked by a small muff of astrakhan; the other curled behind to gather close her skirt. Her hair tied back with a black bow sprayed her tall neck with its beaten gold. She came along downcast until she was within a few feet of Michael; then she looked at him. He smiled, and her mouth when she answered him with answering smile was like a flower whose petals have been faintly stirred. Indeed, it was scarcely a smile, scarcely more than a tremor, but her eyes deepened suddenly, and Michael drawn into their dusky blue exclaimed simply:

"I say, I've been watching you for a long time."

"I don't think you ought to talk to me like this in Kensington Gardens. Why, there's not a soul in sight. And I oughtn't to let you talk."

Her voice was low with a provocative indolence of tone, and while she spoke her lips scarcely moved, so that their shape was never for an instant lost, and the words seemed to escape like unwilling fugitives.

"What are you reading?" she idly asked, tapping Michael's book with her muff.

"Verlaine."

"French?"

He nodded, and she pouted in delicious disapproval of his learned choice.

"Fancy reading French unless you've got to."

"But I enjoy these poems," Michael declared. "As a matter of fact you're just like them. At least you were when I saw you first in the distance. Now you're more real somehow."

Her gaze had wandered during his comparison and Michael, a little hurt by her inattention, asked if she were expecting somebody.

"Oh, no. I just came out for a walk. I get a headache if I stay in all the afternoon. Now I must go on. Good-bye."

She scattered with a light kick the little heap of leaves that during their conversation she had been amassing, and with a half-mocking wave of her muff prepared to leave him.

"I say, don't tear off," Michael begged. "Where do you live?"

"Oh, a long way from here," she said.

"But where?"

"West Kensington."

"So do I," cried Michael, thinking to himself that all the gods of luck and love were fighting on his side this afternoon. "We'll walk home together."

"Shall we?" murmured the girl, poised on bent toes as if she were minded to flee from him in a breath.

"Oh, we must," vowed Michael.

"But I mustn't dawdle," she protested.

"Of course not," he affirmed with almost an inflexion of puritanical rigour.

"You're leaving your book, stupid," she laughed, as he rose to take his place by her side.

"I wouldn't have minded, because all that's in that book is in you," he declared. "I think I'll leave it behind for a lark."

She ran back lightly and opened it to see whether his name were on the front page.

"Michael Fane," she murmured. "What does 'ex libris' mean?" Yet even as she asked the question her concentration failed, and she seemed not to hear his answer.

"You didn't really want to know, you funny girl," said Michael.

"Know what?" she echoed, blinking round at him over her shoulder as they walked on.

"The meaning of 'ex libris.'"

"But I found out your name," she challenged. "And you don't know mine."

"What is it?" Michael dutifully asked.

"I don't think I'll tell you."

"Ah, do."

"Well, then, it's Lily—and I've got a sister called Doris."

"How old are you?"

"How old do you think?"

"Seventeen?" Michael hazarded.

She nodded. It was on the tip of his tongue to claim kinship on the score of their similar years, but discretion defeated honesty, and he said aloofly, gazing up at the sky:

"I'm nineteen and a half."

She told him more as they mingled with the crowds in Kensington High Street, that her mother was Mrs. Haden, who recited in public sometimes, that her sister Doris wanted to go on the stage, and that they lived in Trelawny Road.

"I know Trelawny Road," Michael interjected, and in the gathering crowds she was perforce closer to him, so that he was fain to guide her gently past the glittering shops, immensely conscious of the texture of her dress. They emerged into wider, emptier pavements, and the wind came chilly down from Camden Hill, so that she held her muff against her cheek, framing its faint rose. Twilight drew them closer, and Michael wishful of an even less frequented pavement suggested they should cross the road by Holland Park. A moment she paused while a scarlet omnibus clattered past, then she ran swiftly to where the trees overhung the railings. It was exhilarating to follow her over the wooden road that answered to his footsteps like castanets, and as he caught up with her to fondle her bent arm. Their walk died away to a saunter, while the street-lamps beamed upon them with longer intervals of dark between each succeeding lampshine. More slowly still they moved towards West Kensington and parting. Her arm was twined round his like ivy, and their two hands came together like leaves. At last the turning she must take appeared on the other side of the road, and again she ran and again he caught her arm. But this time it was still warm with long contact and divinely familiar, since but for a moment had it been relinquished. The dim side-street enfolded them, and no dismaying passers-by startled their intercourse.

"But soon it will be Trelawny Road," she whispered.

"Then kiss me quickly," said Michael. "Lily, you must."

It was in the midmost gloom between two lamps that they kissed first.

"Lily, once again."

"No, no," she whispered.

"But you're mine," he called exultantly. "You are. You know you are."

"Perhaps," she whispered, but even as his arms drew her towards him, she slipped from his embrace, laughed very low and sweet, bounded forward, waved her muff, ran swiftly to the next lamp-post, paused and blew him kisses, then vanished round the corner of her road.

But a long time ago they had said they would meet to-morrow, and as Michael stood in a maze all the clocks in the world ding-donged in his ears the hour of their tryst.

There was only one thing to do for the expression of his joy, and that was to run as hard as he could. So he ran, and when he saw two coal-holes, he would jump from one to the other, rejoicing in the ring of their metal covers. And all the time out of breath he kept saying, "I'm in love, in love, in love."

Every passer-by into whose eyes he looked seemed to have the most beautiful expression; every poor man seemed to demand that he should stay awhile from his own joy to comfort him. The lamp-posts bloomed like tropic flowers, swaying and nodding languorously. Every house took on a look of the most unutterable completeness; the horses galloped like Arabian barbs; policemen expanded like beneficent genii; errand boys whistled like nightingales; all familiarity was enchanted, and seven-leagued boots took him forward as easily as if he travelled a world subdued to the effortless transitions of sleep. Carlington Road stretched before him bright, kindly, beckoning to his ingress. Against the lighted entrance-hall of Number 64 Michael saw the red and amber sparrows like humming-birds, ruby-throated, topaz-winged. The parlour-maid's cap and apron were of snow, and the banisters of sandalwood.

Michael went to bed early that he might meet her in dreams, but still for a long time he sat by his window peering at the tawny moon, while at intervals trains went quickly past sparkling and swift as lighted fuses. The scent of the leaves lying in the gardens all along Carlington Road was vital with the airs from which she had been evoked that afternoon, and his only regret was that his bedroom looked out on precisely the opposite direction from that where now she was sleeping. Then he himself became envious of sleep, and undressed quickly like one who stands hot-footed by a lake's edge, eager for the water's cool.

Michael met Lily next day by the dusky corner of a street whose gradual loss of outline he had watched occur through a patient hour. It was not that Lily was late, but that Michael was so early. Yet in his present mood of elation he could enjoy communion even with bricks and mortar. He used every guileful ruse to cheat time of his determined moment. He would walk along with closed eyes for ten paces and with open eyes for ten paces, the convention with himself, almost the wager, being that Lily should appear while his eyes were closed. It would have been truly disappointing had she swung round the corner while his eyes were open. But as it still lacked half an hour of her appointment, there was not much fear of that. Then, as really her time drew near, a tenser game was played, by which Lily was to appear when his left foot was advanced. This match between odd and even lasted until in all its straightness of perfect division six o'clock was inscribed upon his watch. No other hour could so well have suited her form.

Now began the best game of all, since it was played less with himself than with fortune. Michael went to the next turning, and, hiding himself from the view of Trelawny Road, only allowed himself to peep at each decade. At a hundred and sixty-three he said "She's in sight," one hundred and sixty-four, "She's coming." The century was eliminated, too cumbersome for his fiery enumeration. Sixty-five, "I know she is." Sixty-six, sixty-seven, sixty-eight, sixty-nine! One hundred and seventy was said slowly with an exquisite dragging deliberation. Then Michael could look, and there she was with muff signalling through the azure mists of twilight.

"I say, I told mother about you," murmured Lily. "And she said, 'Why didn't you ask him to come in to tea?' But of course she doesn't know I'm meeting you this evening. I'm supposed to be going to church."

Michael's heart leaped at the thought that soon he would be able to see her in her own home among her own belongings, so that in future no conjured picture of her would be incomplete.

"Rather decent of your mother," he said.

"Oh, well, she's got to be very easy-going and all that, though of course she doesn't like us to get talked about. What shall we do now?"

"Walk about, I suppose," said Michael. "Unless we get on top of a bus and ride somewhere? Why not ride up to Hammersmith Broadway and then walk along the towing-path?"

They found a seat full in the frore wind's face, but yet the ride was all too short, and almost by the time Michael had finished securing the waterproof rug in which they sat incapable of movement, so tightly were they braced in, it was time to undo it again and dismount. While the church bells were ringing, they crossed Hammersmith Suspension

Bridge ethereal in the creeping river-mist and faintly motionable like a ship at anchor. Then they wandered by the river that lapped the dead reeds and gurgled along the base of the shelving clay bank. The wind drearily stirred the osier-beds, and from time to time the dull tread of indefinite passing forms was heard upon the sodden path. Michael could feel the humid fog lying upon Lily's sleeve, and when he drew her cheek to his own it was bedewed with the falling night. But when their lips met, the moisture and October chill were all consumed, and like a burning rose she flamed upon his vision. Words to express his adoration tumbled around him like nightmare speech, evasive, mocking, grotesquely inadequate.

"There are no words to say how much I love to hold you, Lily," he complained. "It's like holding a flower. And even in the dark I can see your eyes."

"I can't see yours," she murmured, and therefore nestled closer, "I like you to kiss me," she sighed.

"Oh, why do you?" Michael asked. "Why me?"

"You're nice," she less than whispered.

"Lily, I do love you."

And Michael bit his lip at the close of "love" for the sweet pain of making the foolish word more powerful, more long.

"What a funny husky voice," she murmured in her own deep indolent tones.

"Do you like me to call you 'darling' or 'dearest' best?" he asked.

"Both."

"Ah, but which do you like best?"

To Michael the two words were like melodies which he had lately learned to play. Indeed, they seemed to him his own melodies never played before, and he was eager for Lily to pronounce judgment.

"Why do you ask questions?" she wondered.

"Say 'dearest' to me," Michael begged.

"No, no," she blushed against his heart.

"But say which you like best," he urged. "Darling or dearest?"

"Well, darling," she pouted.

"You've said it," cried Michael rapturously. "Now you can say it of your own accord. Oh, Lily, say it when you kiss me."

"But supposing I never kiss you ever again?" asked Lily, pulling away from his arms. "And besides we must go back."

"Well, we needn't hurry."

"Not if you come at once," she agreed.

One more kiss, one more gliding dreaming walk, one more pause to bid the river farewell from the towering bridge, one more wrestle with the waterproof-rug, one more slow lingering and then suddenly swift escaping finger, one more wave of the muff, one last aerial salutation, and she was gone till Wednesday.

Michael was left alone between the tall thin houses of Kensington, but beneath his feet he seemed to feel the world swing round through space; and all the tall thin houses, all the fluted lamp-posts, all the clustering chimney-pots reeled about him in the ecstasy of his aroused existence.

Chapter XVII: Lily

WHEN Michael came into the dining-room after he had left Lily, his mother said: "Dearest boy, what have you been doing? Your eyes are shining like stars."

Here was the opportunity to tell her about Lily, but Michael could not avail himself of it. These last two days seemed as yet too incomplete for revelation. Somehow he felt that he was creating a work of art, and that to tell his mother of conception or progress would be to spoil the perfection of his impulse. There was only one person on earth to whom he could confide this cataclysmic experience, and that was Alan. He and Alan had dreamed enough together in the past to make him unashamed to announce at last his foothold on reality. But supposing Alan were to laugh, as he had laughed over the absurdity of Kathleen? Such a reception of his news would ruin their friendship; and yet if their friendship could not endure the tale of true love, was it not already ruined? He must tell Alan, at whatever cost.

And where should he tell him? Such a secret must not be lightly entrusted. Time and place must come harmoniously, befalling with that rare felicity which salutes the inevitable hours of a human life.

"Mother," said Michael, "would you mind if I stayed the night over at Richmond?"

"To-night?" Mrs. Fane echoed in astonishment.

"Well, perhaps not to-night," conceded Michael unwillingly. "But to-morrow night?"

"To-morrow night by all means," Mrs. Fane agreed.

"Nothing has happened?" she asked anxiously. "You seem so flushed and strange."

"I'm just the same as usual," Michael declared. "It's hot in this room. I think I'll take a short walk."

"But you've been out all the afternoon," Mrs. Fane protested.

"Oh, well, I've nothing to do at home."

"You're not feverish?"

"No, no, mother," Michael affirmed, disengaging his parched hand from her solicitous touch. "But you know I often feel restless."

She released him, tenderly smiling; and for one moment he nearly threw himself down beside her, covetous of childhood's petting. But the impulse spent itself before he acted upon it, and soon he was wandering towards Trelawny Road. How empty the corner of it looked, how stark and melancholy soared the grey houses guarding its consecrated entrance, how solitary shone the lamp-posts, and how sadly echoed the footsteps of people going home. Yet only three hours ago they had met on this very flagstone that must almost have palpitated to the pressure of her shoes.

Michael walked on until he stood opposite her house. There was a light in the bay-window by the front door; perhaps she would come out to post a letter. O breathless thought! Surely he heard the sound of a turning handle. Ah, why had he not begged her to draw aside the blind at a fixed time that he could be cured of his longing by the vision of her darling form against the pane? How bitter was the irony of her sitting behind that brooding window-pane, unconscious of him. Two days must crawl past before she would meet him again, before he would touch her hand, look actually into her eyes, watch every quiver and curve of her mouth. Places would be enriched with the sight of her, while he ached with the torment of love. School must drag through ten intolerable hours; he must chatter with people unaware of her; and she must live two days apart from his life, two days whose irresponsible minutes and loveless occupations made him burn with jealousy of time itself.

Suddenly the door of Lily's house opened, and Michael felt the blood course through his body, flooding his heart, swaying his very soul. There was a voice in the glimmering hall, but not her voice. Nor was it her form that hurried down the steps. It was only the infinitely fortunate maidservant whose progress to the letter-box he watched with a sickening disappointment. There went one who every day could see Lily. Every morning she was privileged to wake her from her rose-fired sleep. Every night she could gossip with her outside the magical door of her room. Lily must sometimes descend into the kitchen, and there they must talk. And yet the idiotic creature was staring curiously at some unutterably dull policeman, and wasting moments she did not appreciate. Then a leaping thought came to Michael, that if she wasted enough time Lily might look round the front-door in search of her. But too soon for such an event the maidservant pattered back; the door slammed; and only the window-panes of dull gold brooded immutably. How long before Lily went up to bed? And did she sleep in a room that fronted the road? Michael could bear it no longer and turned away from the exasperation of her withheld presence; and he made up his mind that he must know every detail of her daily life before he again came sighing ineffectively like this in the night-time.

Michael was vexed to find that he could not even conjure Lily to his side in sleep, but that even there he must be surrounded by the tiresome people of ordinary life. However, there was always a delicious moment, just before he lost complete consciousness, when the image of her dissolved and materialized elusively above the nebulous confines of semi-reality; while always at the very instant of awakening he was aware of her moth-winged kisses trembling upon the first liquid flash of daylight.

In the 'quarter' Michael suggested to Alan that he should come back to Richmond with him, and when Alan looked a little astonished at this Monday night proposal, he explained that he had a lot to talk over.

"I nearly came over at nine o'clock last night," Michael announced.

Alan seemed to realize that it must indeed be something of importance and could scarcely wait for the time when they should be fast alone and primed for confidences.

After dinner Michael proposed a walk up Richmond Hill, and without any appearance of strategy managed to persuade Alan to rest awhile on one of the seats along the Terrace. In this late autumnal time there was no view of the Thames gleaming beneath the sorcery of a summer night. There was nothing now but a vast airiness of mist damascening the blades of light with which the street-lamps pierced the darkness.

"Pretty wet," said Alan distastefully patting the seat.

"We needn't stay long, but it's rather ripping, don't you think?" Michael urged. "Alan, do you remember once we sat here on a night before exams at the end of a summer term?"

"Yes, but it was a jolly sight warmer than it is now," said Alan.

"I know. We were in 'whites,'" said Michael pensively. "Alan, I'm in love. I am really. You mustn't laugh. I was a fool over that first girl, but now I am in love. Alan, she's only seventeen, and she has hair the colour of that rather thick honey you get at chemists. Only it isn't thick, but as foamy as a lemon-sponge. And her mouth is truly a bow and her voice is gloriously deep and exciting, and her eyes are the most extraordinary blue—as blue as ink in a bottle when you hold it up to the light—and her chin is in two pieces rather like yours, and her ankles—well—her ankles are absolutely divine. The extraordinary luck is that she loves me, and I want you to meet her. I'm describing her very accurately like this because I don't want you to think I'm raving or quoting poetry. You see, you don't appreciate poetry, or I could describe her much better."

"I do appreciate poetry," protested Alan.

"Oh, I know you like Kipling and Adam Lindsay Gordon, but I mean real poetry. Well, I'm not going to argue about that. But, Alan, you must be sympathetic and believe that I really am in love. She has a sister called Doris. I haven't met her yet, but she's sure to be lovely, and I think you ought to fall in love with her. Now wouldn't that be splendid? Alan, you do believe I'm in love this time?"

Michael paused anxiously.

"I suppose you must be," said Alan slowly.

"And you're glad?" asked Michael a little wistfully.

"What's going to happen?" Alan wondered.

"Well, of course not much can happen just now. Not much can happen while one is still at school," Michael went on. "But don't let's talk about what is going to be. Let's talk about what is now."

Alan looked at him reproachfully.

"You used to enjoy talking about the future."

"Because it used always to be more interesting," Michael explained.

Alan rose from the seat and taking Michael's arm drew him down the hill.

"And will you come and meet her sister?" Michael asked.

"I expect so," said Alan.

"Hurrah!" cried the lover.

"I suppose this means the end of football, the end of cricket, in fact the end of school as far as you're concerned," Alan complained. "I wish you'd waited a little."

"I told you I was years older than you," Michael pointed out, involuntarily making excuses.

"Only because you would encourage yourself to think so. Well, I hope everything will go well. I hope you won't take it into your head to think you've got to marry her immediately, or any rot like that."

"Don't be an ass," said Michael.

"Well, you're such an impulsive devil. By Jove, the fellow that first called you 'Bangs' was a bit of a spotter."

"It was Abercrombie," Michael reminded him.

"I should think that was the only clever thing he ever did in his life," said Alan.

"Why, I thought you considered him no end of a good man."

"He was a good forward and a good deep field," Alan granted. "But that doesn't make him Shakespeare."

Thence onwards war, or rather sport the schoolboys' substitute, ousted love from the conversation, and very soon solo whist with Mr. and Mrs. Merivale disposed of both.

On Tuesday night Michael in a fever of enthusiasm for Wednesday's approach wrote a letter to Stella.

64 CARLINGTON ROAD,
October, 1900.

My dear Stella,

After this you needn't grouse about my letters being dull, and you can consider yourself jolly honoured because I'm writing to tell you that I'm in love. Her name is Lily Haden. Only, of course, please don't go shouting this all over Germany, and don't write a gushing letter to mother, who doesn't know anything about it. I shouldn't tell you if you were in London, and don't write back and tell me that you're in love with some long-haired dancing-master or one-eyed banjo-player, because I know *now what love is, and it's nothing like what you think it is.*

Lily is fair—not just fair like a doll, but frightfully *fair. In fact, her hair is like bubbling champagne, I met her in Kensington Gardens. It was truly romantic, not a silly, giggling, gone-on-a-girl sort of meeting. I hope you're getting on with your music. I shall introduce Lily to you just before your first concert, and then if you can't play, well, you never will. You might write me a letter and say what you think of my news. Not a gushing letter, of course, but as sensible as you can make it.*

Your loving brother,
Michael.

Michael had meant to say much more to Stella, but ink and paper seemed to violate the secluded airs in which Lily had her being. However, Stella would understand by his writing at all that he was in deadly earnest, and she was unearthly enough to supply what was missing from his account.

Meanwhile to-morrow was Wednesday, the mate of Saturday and certainly of all the days in the week his second favourite. Monday, of course, was vile. Tuesday was colourless. Thursday was nearly as bad as Monday. Friday was irksome and only a little less insipid than Tuesday. Sunday had many disadvantages. Saturday was without doubt the best day, and Wednesday was next best, for though it was not a half-holiday, as long ago it had been at Randell House, still it had never quite lost its suggestion of holiday. Wednesday—the very word said slowly had a rich individuality. Wednesday—how promptly it sprang to the lips for any occasion of festivity that did not require full-blown reckless Saturday. Monday was dull red. Tuesday was cream-coloured. Thursday was dingy purple. Friday was a harsh scarlet, but Wednesday was vivid apple-green, or was it a clear cool blue? One or the other.

So, tantalizing himself by not allowing a single thought of Lily while he was undressing, Michael achieved bed very easily. Here all trivialities were dismissed, and like one who falls asleep when a star is shining through his window-pane Michael fell asleep, with Lily radiant above the horizon.

It was rather a disappointing Wednesday, for Lily said she could not stay out more than a minute, since her mother was indoors and would wonder what she was doing. However on Saturday she would see Michael again, and announce to her mother that she was going to see him, so that on Sunday Michael could be invited to tea.

"And then if mother likes you, why, you can often come in," Lily pointed out. "That is, if you want to."

"Saturday," sighed Michael.

"Well, don't spoil the few minutes we've got by being miserable."

"But I can't kiss you."

"Think how much nicer it will be when we can kiss," said Lily philosophically.

"I don't believe you care a damn whether we kiss or not," said Michael.

"Don't I?" murmured Lily, quickly touching his hand and as quickly withdrawing it to the prison of the muff.

"Ah, do you, Lily?" Michael throbbed out.

"Of course. Now I must go. Good-bye. Don't forget Saturday in the Gardens, where we met last time. Good-bye, good-bye, good-bye!" She was running from him backwards, forbidding with a wave his sudden step towards her. "No, if you dare to move, I shan't meet you on Saturday. Be good, be good."

By her corner she paused, stood on tiptoe for one provocative instant, blew a kiss, laughed her elfin laugh and vanished more swift than any Ariel.

"Damn!" cried Michael sorely, and forthwith set out to walk round West Kensington at five miles an hour, until his chagrin, his disappointment and his heartsick emptiness were conquered, or at any rate sufficiently humbled to make him secure against unmanly tears.

When Saturday finally did arrive, Michael did not sit reading Verlaine, but wandered from tree-trunk to tree-trunk like Orlando in despair. Then Lily came at last sedately, and brought the good news that to-morrow Michael should come to tea at her house.

"But where does your mother think we met?" he asked in perplexity.

"Oh, I told her it was in Kensington Gardens," said Lily carelessly.

"But doesn't she think I must be an awful bounder?"

"Why, you silly, I told her you were at St. James' School."

"But I never told you I was at school," exclaimed Michael, somewhat aghast.

"I know you didn't, and you never told me that you weren't eighteen yet."

"I am in a month or two," said Michael. "But, good Lord, who have you been talking to?"

"Ah, that's the greatest secret in the world," laughed Lily.

"Oh, no, do tell me."

"Well, I know a boy called Drake who knows you."

"That beast!" cried Michael.

"I think he's quite a nice boy. He lives next door to us and——"

Michael kicked angrily the dead leaves lying about his feet, and almost choked with astonished fury.

"Why, my dear girl, he's absolutely barred. He's as unpopular as anybody I know. I hope you won't discuss me with that hulking brute. What the deuce right has he got to tell you anything about me?"

"Because I asked him, and you needn't look so enraged, because if you want to know why you're coming to tea, it's because I asked Arthur——"

"Who's Arthur?" growled Michael.

"Arthur Drake."

"Go on," said Michael icily.

"I shan't go on, if you look like that."

"I can't help how I look. I don't carry a glass round with me," said Michael. "So I suppose this worm Drake had the cheek to tell your mother I was all right. Drake! Wait till I see the brute on Monday morning."

"Well, if you take my advice," said Lily, "you'll be nice to him, because he's supposed to have introduced us."

"What lies! What lies!" Michael stamped.

"You told me a lie about your age," Lily retorted. "And I've told mother a lie on your account, so you needn't be so particular. And if you think you're going to make me cry, you're not."

She sat down on a seat and looked out at the bare woodland with sullen eyes.

"Has Drake ever dared to make love to you?" demanded Michael.

"That's my business," said Lily. "You've no right to ask me questions like that."

Michael looked at her so adorable even now, and suddenly throwing his dignity to the dead leaves, he sat close beside her caressingly.

"Darling Lily," he whispered, "it was my fault. I lied first. I don't care how much you talked about me. I don't care about anything but you. I'll even say Drake is a decent chap—though he really isn't even moderately decent. Lily, we had such a rotten Wednesday, and to-day ought to be perfect. Will you forgive me? Will you?"

And the quarrel was over.

"But you don't care anything about Drake?" Michael asked, when half an hour had dreamed itself away.

"Of course not," she reassured him. "Arthur likes Doris better than me."

"But he mustn't like Doris," said Michael eagerly. "At least she mustn't like him. Because I've got a friend—at least three million times as decent as Drake—who wants to be in love with Doris, or rather he will want to be when he sees her."

"Why, you haven't seen Doris yourself yet," laughed Lily.

"Oh, of course my plan may all come to nothing," Michael admitted. "But look here, I vote we don't bother about anybody else in the world but ourselves for the rest of the afternoon."

Nor did they.

"Shall I wear a top-hat to-morrow?" Michael asked even in the very poignancy of farewell. "I mean—will your mother prefer it?"

"Oh, no, the people who come to tea with us on Sunday are mostly artists and actors," decided Lily judicially.

"Do lots of people come then?" asked Michael, quickly jealous.

"A good many."

"I might as well have fallen in love with one of the Royal Family," sighed Michael in despair.

"What do you mean?"

"Well, I never can see you alone," he declared.

"Why, we've had the whole of this afternoon," she told him.

"Do you call sitting in the middle of Kensington Gardens being alone? Why, it was crammed with people," he ejaculated in disgust.

"I must go, I must go, I must go," Lily whispered and almost seemed to be preening her wings in the lamplight before she flew away.

"I say, what number is Drake's house?" Michael asked, with a consummate affectation of casual enquiry.

She told him laughingly, and in a most malicious hurry would not even linger a moment to ask him why he wanted to know. Coldly and deliberately Michael after dinner rang the bell of Drake's house.

"Is—er—Master Arthur at home?" he asked the maid.

"Master Arthur," she cried. "Someone to see you."

"Hullo, Bangs," shouted Drake, emerging effusively from a doorway.

"Oh, hullo," said Michael loftily. "I thought I'd call to see if you felt like coming out."

"Right-o," said Drake. "Wait half a tick while I tell my mater. Come in, and meet my people."

"Oh, no," said Michael. "I'm beastly untidy."

He would condescend to Drake for the sake of his love, but he did not think that love demanded the sacrifice of condescending to a possibly more expansive acquaintance with Drake's family.

"So you've met the fair Lily," Drake said, as they strolled along. "Pretty smart, what, my boy?"

"I'm going to tea with them to-morrow," Michael informed him.

"Mrs. Haden's a bit thick," said Drake confidentially. "And Doris is of a very coming-on disposition."

Michael thought of Alan and sighed; then he thought of himself listening to this and he was humiliated.

"But Lily is a bit stand-offish," said Drake. "Of course I never could stand very fair girls, myself. I say, talking of girls, there's a girl in Sherringham Road, well—she's an actress's French maid, as a matter of fact, but, my gad, if you like cayenne, you ought to come along with me, and I'll introduce you. She'll be alone now. Are you on?"

"Oh, thanks very much," said Michael. "But I must get back. Good-night, Drake."

"Well, you're a nice chap to ask a fellow to come out. Come on, don't be an ass. Her name's Marie."

"I don't care if her name's Marie or Mabel or what it is," Michael declared in exasperation. "I'm sorry. I've got to go home. Thanks for coming out."

He turned abruptly and walked off, leaving Drake to apostrophize his eccentricity and seek consolation with Marie.

On Sunday afternoon Michael, torn between a desire to arrive before the crowd of artists and actors who thronged the house and an unwillingness to obtrude upon the Sabbath lethargy of half-past three o'clock, set out with beating heart to invade Lily's home. Love made him reckless and luck rewarded him, for when he enquired for Mrs. Haden the maid told him that only Miss Lily was in.

"Who shall I say?" she asked.

"Mr. Fane."

"Step this way, please. Miss Lily's down in the morning-room."

And this so brief and so bald a colloquy danced in letters of fire across the darkling descent of the enclosed stairs down to the ground-floor.

"Someone to see you, Miss Lily."

Not Iris could have delivered a richer message.

Deep in a wicker chair by a dull red fire sat Lily with open book upon her delicate dress of lavender. The door closed; the daylight of the grey October afternoon seemed already to have fled this room. Dusky in a corner stood a great dolls' house, somewhat sad like a real house that has been left long untenanted.

"Well, now we're alone enough," murmured Lily.

He knelt beside her chair and let his head fall upon her silken shoulder.

"I'm glad you're in your own room," Michael sighed in answer.

Outside, a muffin-man went ringing through the sombre Sabbath chill; and sometimes, disturbing the monotonous railings above the area, absurd legs were seen hurrying to their social tasks. No other sign was given of a life that went on unaware of these two on whom time showered twenty golden minutes.

"Mother and Doris will be back at four," Lily said. "Is my face flushed?"

Fresh carnations would have seemed faded near her, when she looked at Michael for an answer.

"Only very slightly," he reassured her.

"Come up to the drawing-room," she commanded.

"Can I look at your dolls' house?" Michael asked.

"That old thing," said Lily scornfully.

Reverently he pulled aside the front of the battered dwelling-place, and saw the minute furniture higgledy-piggledy.

"I wonder if anyone has ever thought of burning an old dolls' house," said Michael thoughtfully. "It would be rather a rag. I've got an old toy fire-engine somewhere at home."

"You baby," said Lily.

"Well, it depresses me to see that dolls' house all disused and upside down and no good any more. My kiddy sister gave hers to a hospital. What a pity I never thought of burning that," sighed Michael regretfully. "I say, some time we must explore this room. It reminds me of all sorts of things."

"What sort of things?" asked Lily indifferently.

"Oh, being a kid."

"Well, I don't want to be reminded of that," said Lily. "I wish I was older than I am."

"Oh, so do I," said Michael. "I don't want to be a kid again."

Upstairs in the drawing-room it was still fairly light, but the backs of the grey houses opposite and the groups of ghostly trees that filmed the leaden air seemed to call for curtains to be drawn across the contemplation of their melancholy. Yet before they sat down by the crackling fire, Michael and Lily stood with their cheeks against the cold window-panes in a luxury of bodeful silence.

"No, you're not to sit so close now," Lily ordained, when by a joint impulse they turned to inhabit the room in which they had been standing. Michael saw a large photograph album and seized it.

"No, you're not to look in that," Lily cried.

"Why not?" he asked, holding it high above his head.

"Because I don't want you to," said Lily. "Put it down."

"I want to see if there are any photographs of you when you were a kid."

"Well, I don't want you to see them," Lily persisted.

In the middle of a struggle for possession of the album, Mrs. Haden and Doris came in, and Michael felt rather foolish.

"What a dreadfully noisy girl you are, Lily," said Mrs. Haden. "And is this your friend Mr. Fane? How d'ye do?"

"I'm afraid it was my fault," said Michael. "I was trying to bag the photograph album."

"Oh, Lily hates anyone to see that picture of her," Doris interposed. "She's so conceited, and just because——"

"Shut up, you beast," cried Lily.

"Her legs——"

"Doris!" interposed Mrs. Haden. "You must remember you're grown up now."

"Mother, can't I burn the photograph?" said Lily.

"No, she's not to, mother," Doris interrupted. "She's not to, is she? You jealous thing. You'd love to burn it because it's good of me."

"Well, really," said Mrs. Haden, "what Mr. Fane can be thinking of you two girls, I shouldn't like to guess."

The quarrel over the album died down as easily as it had begun, and the entrance of the tea adjusted the conversation to a less excited plane.

Mrs. Haden was a woman whom Michael could not help liking for her open breezy manner and a certain large-handed toleration which suited her loud deep voice. But he was inclined to deprecate her obviously dyed hair and the plentifulness of pink powder; nor could he at first detect in her any likeness to Lily who, though Mrs. Haden persistently reproached her as a noisy girl, stood for Michael as the slim embodiment of a subtle and easy tranquillity. Gradually, however, during the afternoon he perceived slight resemblances between the mother and daughter that showed them vaguely alike, as much alike at any rate as an elk and a roedeer.

Doris Haden was much less fair than Lily, though she could only have been called dark in comparison with her sister. She had a high complexion, wide almond-shaped eyes of a very mutable hazel, and a ripe, sanguine mouth. She was dressed in a coat and skirt of crushed-strawberry frieze, whose cool folds seemed to enhance her slightly exotic air. Michael could not help doubting whether she and Alan were perfectly suited to one another. He could not imagine that she would not care for him, but he wondered about Alan's feelings; and Drake's overnight description stuck unpleasantly in his mind with a sensation of disloyalty to Lily whose sister after all Doris was.

They were not left very long without visitors, for one by one young men came in with a self-possession and an assumption of familiarity that Michael resented very much, and all the more deeply because he felt himself at a disadvantage. He wondered if Lily were despising him, and wished that she would not catch hold of these detestable young men by the lapels of their coats, or submit to their throaty persiflage. Once when the most absolutely self-possessed of all, a tall thin creature with black fuzzy hair and stilted joints, pulled Lily on to his knee to talk to him, Michael nearly dived through the window in a fury of resentment.

All these young men seemed to him to revel in their bad taste, and their conversation, half-theatrical, half-artistic, was of a character that he could not enter into. Mrs. Haden's loud laugh rang out over the clatter of tea-cups; Doris walked about the room smoking a cigarette and humming songs; Lily moved from group to group with a nonchalance that seriously perturbed Michael, who retired more and more deeply behind a spreading palm in the darkest corner of the room. Yet he could not tear himself away from the fascination of watching Lily's grace; he could not surrender her to these marionettes of vulgar fashion; he could not go coldly out into the Sabbath night without the consolation of first hustling these intruders before him.

The afternoon drew on to real dusk; the gas was lighted; songs were sung and music was played. All these young men seemed accomplished performers of insignificant arts. Mrs.

Haden recited, and in this drawing-room her heightened air and accentuated voice made Michael blush. Doris went upstairs for a moment and presently came down in a Spanish dancing-dress, in which she swayed about and rattled castanets and banged a tambourine, while the young men sat round and applauded through the smoke of their cigarettes. These cigarettes began to affect Michael's nerves. Wherever he looked he could see their flattened corpses occupying nooks. They were in the flower-pots; they littered the grate; they were strewn on brass ash-trays; and even here and there on uninflammable and level spots they stood up like little rakish mummies slowly and acridly cremating themselves. Michael wondered uneasily what Lily was going to do to entertain these voracious listeners. He hoped she would not debase her beauty by dancing on the hearthrug like her sister. In the end, Lily was persuaded to sing, and her voice very low and sweet singing some bygone coon song, was tremendously applauded.

Supper-time drew on, and at last the parlour-maid came in and enquired with a martyred air how many she should lay for.

"You must all stay to supper," cried Mrs. Haden in deafening hospitality. "Everybody. Mr. Fane, you'll stay, won't you?"

"Oh, thanks very much," said Michael shyly, and wished that these confounded young men would not all look at him as if they had perceived him suddenly for the first time. Everybody seemed as a matter of course to help to get supper ready, and Michael found himself being bumped about and handed plates and knives and glasses and salad-bowls. Even at supper he found himself as far as it was possible to be from Lily, and he thought that never in his life had food tasted so absolutely of nothing. But the evening came to an end, and Michael was consoled for his purgatory by Mrs. Haden's invitation to call whenever he liked. In the hall too Lily came out to see him off, and he besought her anxiously to assure him truthfully that to all these young men she was indifferent.

"Of course, I don't care for any of them. Why, you silly, they all think I'm still a little girl."

Then since a friendly draught had closed the drawing-room door, she kissed him; and he forgot all that had happened before, and sailed home on thoughts that carried him high above the iron-bound sadness of the Sunday night.

Some time early in the week came a letter from Stella in answer to his, and when Michael read it he wished that Stella would come home, since only she seemed to appreciate what love meant. Yet Stella was even younger than Lily.

STUTTGART,
Sunday.

Darling Michael,

I'm writing a sonata about Lily. It's not very good unfortunately, so you'll never be able to hear it. But after all, as you don't understand music, perhaps I will let you hear it. I wish you had told me more about Lily. I think she's lucky. You must be simply a perfect person to be in love with. Most boys are so silly. That's why only men of at least thirty attract me. But of course if I could find someone younger who would be content to love me and not mind whether I loved him, I should prefer that. You say I don't know what love is. How silly you are, Michael. Now isn't it thrilling to take Lily's hand? I do know what love is. But don't look shocked, because if you can still look shocked, you don't know what love is. Don't forget I'm seventeen next month, and don't forget I'm a girl as well as Lily. Lily is a good name for her, if she is very fair. I expect she really has cendré hair. I hope she's rather tall and delicate-looking. I hope she's a violin sort of girl, or like those notes half-way up the treble. It must have been perfect when you met her. I can just imagine you, especially if you like October as much as I do. Did the leaves come falling down all round you, when you kissed her? Oh, Michael, it must have been enchanting. I want to come back soon, soon, soon, and see this Lily of yours. Will she like me? Is she fond of music?

I must have my first concert next summer. Mother must not put me off. Why doesn't she let me come home now? There's some reason for it, I believe. Thank goodness, you'll have left school soon. You must be sick of it, especially since you've fallen in love.

I think of you meeting Lily when I play Schumann, and when I play Chopin I think of you walking about underneath her window, and when I play Beethoven I think of you kissing her.

Darling Michael, I love you more than ever. Be interested in me still, because I'm not interested in anybody but you, except, of course, myself and my music.

Oh, do bring Lily to my first concert, and I'll see you two alone of all the people in the Hall and play you so close together that you'll nearly faint. Now you think I'm gushing, I suppose, so I'll shut up.

With a most tremendous amount of love,

Your delightful sister,
Stella.

"I wonder if she ought to write like that," said Michael to himself. "Oh, well, I don't see why she shouldn't."

Certainly as one grew older a sister became a most valuable property.

Chapter XVIII: *Eighteen Years Old*

TO Michael it seemed almost incredible that school should be able to continue as the great background against which his love stood out like a delicate scene carved by the artist's caprice in an obscure corner of a strenuous and heroic decoration. Michael was hardly less conscious of school on Lily's account, and in class he dreamed neither more nor less than formerly; but his dreams partook more of ecstasy than those nebulous pictures inspired by the ambitions and ideals and books of youth's progress. Nevertheless in the most ultimate refinement of meditation school weighed down his spirit. It is true that games had finally departed from the realm of his consideration, but equally with games much extravagance of intellect and many morbid pleasures had gone out of cultivation. Balancing loss with gain, he found himself at the close of his last autumn term with a surer foothold on the rock-hewn foundations of truth.

Michael called truth whatever of emotion or action or reaction or reason or contemplation survived the destruction he was dealing out to the litter of idols that were beginning to encumber his passage, many of which he thought he had already destroyed when he had merely covered them with a new coat of gilt. During this period he began to enjoy Wordsworth, to whom he came by way of Matthew Arnold, like a wayfarer who crosses green fields and finds that mountains are faint upon the horizon. A successful lover, as he called himself, he began to despise anything in his reading of poetry that could not measure its power with the great commonplaces of human thought.

The Christmas holidays came as a relief from the burden of spending so much of his time in an atmosphere from which he was sure he had drained the last draught of health-giving breath. Michael no longer regarded, save in a contemptuous aside, the microcosm of school; the pleasures of seniority had staled; the whole business was now a tedious sort of mental quarantine. If he had not had Lily to occupy his leisure, he would have expired of restless inanition; and he wondered that the world went on allowing youth's load of education to be encumbered by a dead-weight of superfluous information. Alan, for instance, had managed to obtain a scholarship some time in late December, and would henceforth devote himself to meditating on cricket for one term and playing it hard for another term. It would be nine months before he went to Oxford, and for nine months he would live in a state of mental catalepsy fed despairingly by the masters of the Upper Sixth with the few poor last facts they could scrape together from their own time-impoverished store. Michael, in view of Alan's necessity for gaining this scholarship, had never tried to lure him towards Doris and a share in his own fortune. But he resolved that during the following term he would do his best to galvanize Alan out of the catalepsy that he woefully foresaw was imminent.

Meanwhile the Christmas holidays were here, and Michael on their first night vowed all their leisure to Lily.

There was time now for expeditions farther afield than Kensington Gardens, which in winter seemed to have lost some of their pastoral air. The naked trees no longer veiled the houses, and the city with its dingy railings and dingy people and mud-splashed omnibuses was always an intrusion. Moreover, fellow-Jacobeans used to haunt their privacy; and often when it was foggy in London, out in the country there was winter sunlight.

These were days whose clarity and silence seemed to call for love's fearless analysis, and under a sky of turquoise so faintly blue that scarcely even at the zenith could it survive the silver dazzle of the low January sun, Michael and Lily would swing from Barnet into Finchley with Michael talking all the way.

"Why do you love me?" he would flash.

"Because I do."

"Oh, can't you think of any better reason than that?"

"Because—because—oh, Michael, I don't want to think of reasons," Lily would declare.

"You *are* determined to marry me?" Michael would flash again.

"Yes, some day."

"You don't think you'll fall in love with anybody else?"

"I don't suppose so."

"Only suppose?" Michael would echo on a fierce pause.

"Well, no, I won't."

"You promise?"

"Yes, yes, I promise," Lily would pout.

Then the rhythm of their walk would be renewed, and arm-in-arm they would travel on, until the next foolish perplexity demanded solution. Twilight would often find them still on the road, and when some lofty avenue engulphed their path, the uneasy warmth of the overarching trees would draw them very close, while hushed endearments took them slowly into lampshine.

When the dripping January rains came down, Michael spent many afternoons in the morning-room of Lily's house. Here, subject only to Doris's exaggerated hesitation to enter, Michael would build up for himself and Lily the indissoluble ties of a childhood that, though actually it was spent in ignorance of each other's existence, possessed many links of sentimental communion.

For instance, on the wall hung Cherry Ripe—the same girl in white frock and pink sash who nearly fourteen years ago had conjured for Michael the first hazy intimations of romance. Here she hung, staring down at them as demurely if not quite so sheerly beautiful as of old. Lily observed that the picture was not unlike Doris at the same age, and Michael felt at once that such a resemblance gave it a permanent value. Certainly his etchings of Montmartre and views of the Sussex Downs would never be hallowed by the associations that made sacred this oleograph of a Christmas Annual.

There were the picture-books of Randolph Caldecott tattered identically with his own, and Michael pointed out to Lily that often they must have sat by the fire reading the same verse at the same moment. Was not this thought almost as fine as the actual knowledge of each other's daily life would have been? There were other books whose pages, scrawled and dog-eared, were softened by innumerable porings to the texture of Japanese fairy-books. In a condition practically indistinguishable all of these could be found both in Carlington Road and Trelawny Road.

There were the mutilated games that commemorated Christmas after Christmas of the past. Here was the pack of Happy Families with Mrs. Chip now a widow, Mr. Block the Barber a widower, and the two young Grits grotesque orphans of the grocery. There were Ludo and Lotto and Tiddledy-Winks whose counters, though terribly depleted, were still eloquent with the undetermined squabbles and favourite colours of childhood.

Michael was glad that Lily should spring like a lovely ghost from the dust of familiar and forgotten relics. It had been romantic to snatch her on a dying cadence of Verlaine out of the opalescent vistas of October trees; but his perdurable love for her rested on these immemorial affections whose history they shared.

Lily herself was not so sensitive to this aroma of the past as Michael. She was indeed apt to consider his enthusiasm a little foolish, and would wonder why he dragged from the depths of untidy cupboards so much rubbish that only owed its preservation to the general carelessness of the household. Lily cared very little either for the past or the future, and though she was inclined to envy Doris her dancing-lessons and likelihood of appearing some time next year on the stage, she did not seem really to desire any activity of career for herself. This was a relief to Michael, who frankly feared what the stage might wreak upon their love.

"But I wish you'd read a little more," he protested. "You like such rotten books."

"I feel lazy when I'm not with you," she explained. "And, anyway, I hate reading."

"Do you think of me all the time I'm away from you?" Michael asked.

Lily told him she thought of nothing else, and his pride in her admission led him to excuse her laziness, and even made him encourage it. There was, however, about the atmosphere of Lily's home a laxity which would have overcome more forcible exhortations than Michael's. He was too much in love with Lily's kisses to do more than vaguely criticize her surroundings. He did not like Mrs. Haden's pink powder, but nevertheless the pink powder made him less sensitive than he might have been to Mrs. Haden's opinion of his daily visits and his long unchaperoned expeditions with Lily. The general laxity tended to obscure his own outlook, and he had no desire to state even to himself his intentions. He felt himself tremendously old when he thought of kisses, but when he tried to visualize Lily and himself even four years hence, he felt hopelessly young. Mrs. Haden evidently regarded him as a boy, and since that fact seemed to relieve her of the slightest anxiety, Michael had no desire to impress upon her his precocity. The only bann that Mrs. Haden laid on his intercourse with Lily was her refusal to allow him to take her out alone at night, but she had no objection to him escorting Doris and Lily together to the theatre; nor did she oppose Michael's plan to celebrate the last night of the holidays by inviting Alan to make a quartette for the Drury Lane pantomime. Alan had only just come back from skating in Switzerland with his father, and he could not refuse to join Michael's party, although he said he was "off girls" at the moment.

"You always are," Michael protested.

"And I'm not going to fall in love, even to please you," Alan added.

"All right," Michael protested. "Just because you've been freezing yourself to death all the holidays, you needn't come back and throw cold water over me."

They all dined with Mrs. Haden, and Michael could not help laughing to see how seriously and how shyly Alan took the harum-scarum feast at which, between every course, one of the girls would rush upstairs to fetch down a fan or a handkerchief or a ribbon.

"I think your friend is charming," said Mrs. Haden loudly, when she and Michael were alone for a minute in the final confusion of not being late. Michael wondered why something in her tone made him resent this compliment. But there was no opportunity to puzzle over his momentary distaste, because it was time to start for the occupation of the box which Mrs. Haden had been given by one of her friends.

"I vote we drive home in two hansoms," suggested Michael as they stood in the vestibule when the pantomime was over.

Alan looked at him quickly and made a grimace. But Michael was determined to enjoy Lily's company during a long uninterrupted drive, and at the same time to give Alan the opportunity of finding out whether he could possibly attach himself to Doris.

Michael's own drive enthralled him. The hot theatre and the glittering performance had made Lily exquisitely tired and languorous, and Michael thought she had never surrendered herself so breathlessly before, that never before had her flowerlike kisses been so intangible and her eyes so drowsily passionate. Lulled by the regularity of the motion, Lily lay along his bended arm as if asleep, and, as he held her, Michael's sense of responsibility became more and more dreamily indistinct. The sensuousness of her abandonment drugged all but the sweet present and the poignant ecstasy of possession.

"I adore you," he whispered. "Lily, are you asleep? Lily! Lily, you are asleep, asleep in my arms, you lovely girl. Can you hear me talking to you?"

She stirred in his embrace like a ruffling bird; she sighed and threw a fevered hand upon his shoulder.

"Michael, why do you make me love you so?" she murmured, and fell again into her warm trance.

"Are you speaking to me from dreams?" he whispered. "Lily, you almost frighten me. I don't think I knew I loved you so much. The whole world seems to be galloping past. Wake up, wake up. We're nearly home."

She stretched herself in a rebellious shudder against consciousness and looked at Michael wide-eyed.

"I thought you were going to faint or something," he said.

Hardly another word they spoke, but sat upright staring before them at the oncoming lamp-posts. Soon Trelawny Road was reached, and in that last good night was a sense of nearness that never before had Michael imagined.

By her house they waited for a minute in the empty street, silent, hand-in-hand, until the other cab swung round the corner. Alan and Michael watched the two girls disappear through the flickering doorway, and then they strolled back towards Carlington Road, where Alan was spending the night.

"Well?" asked Michael. "What do you think of Lily?"

"I think she's very pretty."

"And Doris?"

"I didn't care very much for her really," said Alan apologetically, "She's pretty, not so pretty as Lily, of course; but, I say, Michael, I suppose you'll be offended, but I'd better ask right out ... who are they?"

"The Hadens?"

"Yes. I thought Mrs. Haden rather awful. What's Mr. Haden? or isn't there a Mr. Haden?"

"I believe he's in Burmah," said Michael.

"Burmah?"

"Why shouldn't he be?"

"No reason at all," Alan admitted, "but ... well ... I thought there was something funny about that family."

"You think everything's funny that's just a little bit different from the deadly average," said Michael. "What exactly was funny, may I ask?"

"I don't think Mrs. Haden is a lady, for one thing," Alan blurted out.

"I do," said Michael shortly, "And, anyway, if she weren't, I don't see that that makes any difference to me and Lily."

"But what are you going to do?" Alan asked. "Do you think you're going to marry her?"

"Some day. Life isn't a cricket-match, you know," said Michael sententiously. "You can't set your field just as you would like to have it at the moment."

"You know best what's good for you," Alan sighed.

"Yes ... I think I do. I think it's better to live than to stagnate as you're doing."

"What does your mother say?" Alan asked.

"I haven't told her anything about Lily."

"No, because you're not in earnest. And if you're in earnest, Lily isn't."

"What the devil do you know about her?" Michael angrily demanded.

"I know enough to see you're both behaving like a couple of reckless kids," Alan retorted.

"Damn you!" cried Michael in exasperation. "I wish to god you wouldn't try to interfere with what doesn't after all concern you very much."

"You insisted on introducing me," Alan pointed out.

"Because I thought it would be a rag if we were both in love with sisters. But you're turning into a machine. Since you've swotted up into the Upper Sixth, you've turned into a very good imitation of the prigs you associate with. Everybody isn't like you. Some people develop.... I could have been just like you if I had cared to be. I could have been Captain of the School and Scholar of Balliol with my nose ground down to εἰ and ἐάν, hammering out tenth-rate Latin lyrics and reading Theocritus with the amusing parts left out. But what's the good of arguing with you? You're perfectly content and you think you can be as priggish as you like, as long as you conceal it by making fifty runs in the Dulford match. I suppose you consider my behaviour unwholesome at eighteen. Well, I dare say it is by your standards. But are your standards worth anything? I doubt it. I think they're fine up to a point. I'm perfectly willing to admit that we behaved like a pair of little blighters with those girls at Eastbourne. But this is something altogether different."

"We shall see," said Alan simply. "I'm not going to quarrel with you. So shut up."

Michael walked along in silence, angry with himself for having caused this ill-feeling by his obstinacy in making an unsuitable introduction, and angry with Alan because he would accentuate by his attitude the mistake.

By the steps of his house Michael stopped and looked at Alan severely.

"This is the last time I shall attempt to cure you," he announced.

"All right," said Alan with perfect equanimity. "You can do anything you like but quarrel. You needn't talk to me or look at me or think about me until you want to. I shall feel a bit bored, of course, but, oh, my dear old chap, do get over this love-sickness soon."

"This isn't like that silly affair at Bournemouth last Easter," Michael challenged.

"I know that, my dear chap. I wish it was."

With the subject of love finally sealed between him and Alan, Michael receded farther and farther from the world of school. He condescended indeed to occupy a distinguished position by the hot-water pipes of the entrance-hall, where his aloofness and ability to judge men and gods made him a popular, if slightly incomprehensible, figure. Towards all the masters he emanated a compassion which he really felt very deeply. Those whom he liked he conversed with as equals; those whom he disliked he talked to as inferiors. But he pitied both sections. In class he was polite, but somewhat remote, though he missed very few opportunities of implicitly deriding the Liberal views of Mr. Kirkham. The whole school with its ant-like energy, whose ultimate object and obvious result were alike inscrutable to Michael, just idly amused him, and he reserved for Lily all his zest in life.

The Lent term passed away with parsimonious February sunlight, with March lying grey upon the houses until it proclaimed itself suddenly in a booming London gale. The Easter holidays arrived, and Mrs. Fane determined to go to Germany and see Stella. Would Michael come? Michael pleaded many disturbed plans of cricket-practice; of Matriculation at St. Mary's College, Oxford; of working for the English Literature Prize; of anything indeed but his desire to see with Lily April break to May. In the end he had his own way, and Mrs. Fane went to the continent without his escort.

Lily was never eager for the discussions and the contingencies and the doubts of love; in all their walks it had been Michael who flashed the questions, she who let slip her answers. The strange fatigue of spring made much less difference to her than to him, and however insistent he was for her kisses, she never denied him. Michael tried to feel that the acquiescence of the hard, the reasonable, the intellectual side of him to April's passionate indulgence merely showed that he was more surely and more sanely growing deeper in love with Lily every day. Sometimes he had slight tremors of malaise, a sensation of weakening fibres, and dim stirrings of responsibility; but too strong for them was his heart's-ease, too precious was Lily's rose-bloomed grace of submission. The more sharply imminent her form became upon his thought, the more surely deathless did he suppose his love. Michael's mind was always framing moments in eternity, and of all these moments the sight of her lying upon the vivid grass, the slim, the pastoral, the fair immortal girl stood unparagoned by any. There was no landscape that Lily did not make more inevitably composed. There was no place of which she did not become tutelary, whether she lay among the primroses that starred the steep brown banks of woodland or whether she fronted the great sunshine of the open country; but most of all when she sat in cowslips, looking over arched knees at the wind.

Michael fell into the way of talking to her as if he were playing upon Dorian pipes the tale of his love:

"I must buy you a ring, Lily. What ring shall I buy for you? Rings are all so dull. Perhaps your hands would look wrong with a ring, unless I could find a star-sapphire set in silver. I thought you were lovely in autumn, but I think you are more lovely in spring. How the days are going by; it will soon be May. Lily, if you had the choice of everything in the world, what would you choose?"

"I would choose to do nothing."

"If you had the choice of all the people in the world, would you choose me?"

"Yes. Of course."

"Lily, you make me curiously lazy. I want never again to do anything but sit in the sun with you. Why can't we stay like this for ever?"

"I shouldn't mind."

"I wish that you could be turned into a primrose, and that I could be turned into a hazel-bush looking down at you for ever. Or I wish you could be a cowslip and I could be a plume of grass. Lily, why is it that the longer I know you, the less you say?"

"You talk enough for both," said Lily.

"I talk less to you than to anyone. I really only want to look at you, you lovely thing."

But the Easter holidays were almost over, and Michael had to go to Oxford for his Matriculation. On their last long day together, Lily and he went to Hampton Court and dreamed the sad time away. When twilight was falling Michael said he had a sovereign to spend on whatever they liked best to do. Why should they not have dinner on a balcony over the river, and after dinner drive all the way home in a hansom cab?

So they sat grandly on the chilly balcony and had dinner, until Lily in her thin frock was cold.

"But never mind," said Michael. "I'll hold you close to me all the way to London."

They found their driver and told him where to go. The man was very much pleased to think he had a fare all the way to London, and asked Michael if he wanted to drive fast.

"No, rather slow, if anything," said Michael.

The fragrant miles went slowly past, and all the way they drove between the white orchards, and all the way like a spray of bloom Lily was his. Past the orchards they went, past the twinkling roadside houses, past the gates where the shadows of lovers fell across the road, past the breaking limes and lilac, past the tulips stiff and dark in the moonlight, through the high narrow street of Brentford, past Kew Bridge and the slow trams with their dim people nodding, through Chiswick and into Hammersmith where a piano-organ was playing and the golden streets were noisy. It was Doris who opened the door.

"Eleven o'clock," she said. "Mother's rather angry."

"You'd better not come in," said Lily to Michael. "She'll be all right again by next week, when you come back."

"Oh, no, I'll come in," he insisted. "I'd rather explain why we're so late."

"It's no use arguing with mother when she's unreasonable," said Lily. "I shall go up to bed; I don't want to have a row."

"That's right," Doris sneered. "Always take the shortest and easiest way. You are a coward."

"Oh, shut up," said Lily, and without another word went upstairs.

"You've spoilt her," said Doris. "Well, are you going to see mother? She isn't in a very pleasant mood, I warn you."

"She's never been angry before," said Michael hopelessly.

"Well, she has really," Doris explained. "Only she's vented it on me."

"I say, I'm awfully sorry. I had no idea—" Michael began.

"Oh, don't apologize," said Doris. "I'm used to it. Thank god, I'm going on the stage next year; and then Lily and mother will be able to squabble to their heart's content."

Mrs. Haden was sitting in what was called The Cosy Corner; and she treated Michael's entrance with exaggerated politeness.

"Won't you sit down? It's rather late, but do sit down."

All the time she was speaking the plate-rack above The Cosy Corner was catching the back of her hair, and Michael wondered how long it would be before she noticed this.

"Really, I think it's very wrong of you to bring my daughter home at this hour," Mrs. Haden clattered. "I'm sure nobody likes young people to enjoy themselves more than I do. But eleven o'clock! Where is Lily now?"

"Gone to bed," said Doris, who seized the opportunity to depart also.

"I'm awfully sorry, Mrs. Haden," said Michael awkwardly "But as it was my last night, I suggested driving back from Hampton Court. It was all my fault; I do hope you won't be angry with Lily."

"But I am angry with Lily," said Mrs. Haden. "Very angry. She's old enough to know better, and you're old enough to know better. How will people think I'm bringing up my daughters, if they return at midnight with young men in hansoms? I never heard of such a thing. You're presuming on your age. You've no business to compromise a girl like this."

"Compromise?" stammered Michael.

"None of the young people but you has ever ventured to behave like this," Mrs. Haden went on with sharply metallic voice. "Not one of them. And, goodness knows, every Sunday the house is full of them."

"But they don't come to see Lily," Michael pointed out. "They come to see you."

"Are you trying to be rude to me?" Mrs. Haden asked.

"No, no," Michael assured her. "And, honestly, Mrs. Haden, I didn't think you minded me taking Lily out."

"But what's going to happen?" Mrs. Haden demanded.

"Well—I—I suppose I want to marry Lily."

Michael wondered if this statement sounded as absurd to Mrs. Haden as it sounded to himself.

"What nonsense!" she snapped. "What utter nonsense! A schoolboy talking such nonsense. Marriage indeed! You know as well as I do that you've never thought about such a step."

"But I have," said Michael. "Very often, as it happens."

"Then you mustn't go out with Lily again. Why, it's worse than I thought. I'm horrified."

"Do you mean I'm never to come here again?" Michael asked in despair.

"Come occasionally," said Mrs. Haden. "But only occasionally."

"All right. Thanks," said Michael, feeling stunned by this unexpected rebuke. "Good night, Mrs. Haden."

In the hall he found Doris.

"Well?" she asked.

"Your mother says I'm only to come occasionally."

"Oh, that won't last," said Doris encouragingly.

"Yes, but I'm not sure that she isn't right," said Michael. "Oh, Doris, damn. I wish I couldn't always see other people's point of view."

"Mother often has fits of violent morality," said Doris. "And then we always catch it. But really they don't last."

"Doris, you don't understand. It isn't your mother's disapproval I'm worrying over. It's myself. Lily might have waited to say good-night," Michael murmured miserably.

But straight upon his complaint he saw Lily leaning over from the landing above and blowing kisses, and he felt more calm.

"Don't worry too much about Lily," whispered Doris, as she held the door open for him.

"Why?"

"I shouldn't, that's all," she said enigmatically, and closed the door very gently.

At the time Michael was not conscious of any deep impression made by the visit to Oxford for his Matriculation; he was too much worried by the puzzle of his future conduct with regard to Lily. He felt dull in the rooms where he spent two nights alone; he felt shy among the forty or fifty boys from other public-schools; he was glad to go back to London. Vaguely the tall grey tower remained in his mind, and vaguely the cool Gothic seemed to offer a shelter from the problems of behaviour, but that was all.

When he returned, the torment of Lily's desired presence became more acute. His mother wrote to say that she would not be back for three days, and the only consolation was the hint that most probably Stella would come back with her.

Meanwhile this was Saturday, and school did not begin until Tuesday. Time after time Michael set out towards Trelawny Road; time after time he checked himself and fought his way home again. Mrs. Haden had been right; he had behaved badly. Lily was too young to bear the burden of their passionate love. And was she happy without him? Was she sighing for him? Or would she forget him and resume an existence undisturbed by him? But the thought of wasted time, of her hours again unoccupied, of her footsteps walking to places ignorant of him was intolerable.

Sunday came round, and Michael thought that he would fling himself into the stream of callers; but the idea of doing so became humiliating, and instead he circled drearily round the neighbouring roads, circled in wide curves, and sometimes even swooped into the forbidden diameter of Trelawny Road. But always before he could bring himself to pass her very door, he would turn back into his circle and the melancholy Sabbath sunlight of May.

Twilight no more entranced him, and the lovers leaning over to one another languorously in their endearments, moving with intertwined arms and measured steps between the wine-dark houses, annoyed him with their fatuous complacency and their bland eyes. He wanted her, his slim and silent Lily, who blossomed in the night-time like a flower. Her wrists were cool as porcelain and the contact of her form swaying to his progress was light as silk. Everyone else had their contentment, and he must endure wretchedly without the visible expression of his beauty. It was not yet too late to see her; and Michael circled nearer to Trelawny Road. This time he came to Lily's house; he paused within sound of laughter upon the easeful step; and then again he turned away and walked furiously on through the empty Sabbath streets.

In his room, when it was now too late to think of calling, Michael laughed at himself for being so sensitive to Mrs. Haden's reproaches. He told himself that all she said was due to the irritation of the moment, that to-morrow he must go again as if nothing had happened, that people had no right to interfere between lovers. But then, in all its florid bulk, St. James' School rose up, and Michael admitted to himself that to the world he was merely a foolish schoolboy. He, the dauntless lover, must be chained to a desk for five hours every day. A boy and girl affair! Michael ground his teeth with exasperation. He must simply prove by renouncing for a term his part in Lily's life that he was a schoolboy by an accident of time. A man is as old as he feels! He would see Lily once more, and tell her that for the sake of their ultimate happiness, he would give her up for the term of his bondage. Other great and romantic lovers had done the same; they may not have gone to school, but they had accepted menial tasks for the sake of their love.

Yet in the very middle of the night when the thickest darkness seemed to stifle self-deception, Michael knew that he had bowed to authority so easily because his conscience had already told him what Mrs. Haden so crudely hinted. When he was independent of school it would be different. Michael made up his mind that the utmost magnanimity would be possible, if he could see Lily once to tell her of his resolution. But on the next day Lily was out, and Mrs. Haden talked to him instead.

"I've forbidden Lily to go out with you alone," she said. "And I would prefer that you only came here when I am in the house."

"I was going to suggest that I shouldn't come at all until July—until after I had left school, in fact," answered Michael.

"Perhaps that would be best. Then you and Lily will be more sensible."

"Good-bye," said Michael hurriedly, for he felt that he must get out of this stifling room, away from this overwhelming woman with her loud voice and dyed hair and worldly-wise morality. Then he had a sudden conception of himself as part of a scene, perceiving himself in the rôle of the banished lover nobly renouncing all. "I won't write to her. I won't make any attempt to see her," he offered.

"You'll understand," said Mrs. Haden, "that I'm afraid of—that I think," she corrected, "it is quite likely that Lily is just as bad for you as you are for Lily. But of course the real reason I feel I ought to interfere is on account of what people say. If Mr. Haden were not in Burmah ... it would be different."

Michael pitied himself profoundly for the rest of that day; but after a long luxury of noble grief the image of Lily came to agitate and disconcert his acquiescence, and the insurgent fevers of love goaded his solitude.

Mrs. Fane and Stella returned during the first week of school. The great Steinway Grand that came laboriously in through the unsashed window of the third story gave Michael, as it lay like a boulder over Carlington Road, a wonderful sense of Stella's establishment at home. Stella's music-room was next to his bedroom, and when in her nightgown she came to practise in the six o'clock sunshine Michael thought her music seemed the very voice of day. So joyously did the rills and ripples and fountains of her harmony rouse him from sleep that he refrained from criticizing her apparel, and sat contented in the sunlight to listen.

Suddenly Stella wheeled round and said:

"Do tell me about Lily."

"Well, there's been rather a row," Michael began. "You see, I took her to Hampton Court and we drove...." Michael stopped, and for the first time he obtained a cold clear view of his behaviour, when he found he was hesitating to tell Stella lest he might set her a bad example.

"Go on," she urged. "Don't stop."

"Well, we were rather late. But of course it was the first time, and I hope you won't think you can drive back at eleven o'clock with somebody because I did once—only once."

"Why, was there any harm in it?" asked Stella quickly, and, as if to allay Michael's fear by so direct a question, one hand went trilling in scale towards the airy unrealities of the treble.

"No, of course there was no harm in it," said Michael.

"Then why shouldn't I drive back at eleven o'clock if I wanted to?" asked Stella, striking elfin discords as she spoke.

"It's a question of what people think," said Michael, falling back upon Mrs. Haden's line of defence.

"Bother people!" cried Stella, and immediately she put them in their place somewhere very far down in the bass.

"Well, anyway," said Michael, "I understood what Mrs. Haden meant, and I've agreed not to see Lily until after I leave school."

"And then?"

"Well, then I shall see her," said Michael.

"And drive back at eleven o'clock in hansoms?"

"Not unless I can be engaged," Michael surrendered to convention.

"And don't you mind?"

"Of course I mind," he confessed gloomily.

"Why did you agree, then?" Stella asked.

"I had to think about Lily, just as I should have to think about you," he challenged.

"Darling Michael, I love you dreadfully, but I really should not pay the least little tiny bit of attention to you—or anybody else, if that's any consolation," she added. "As it happens, I've never yet met anybody with whom I'd care to drive about in a hansom at eleven o'clock, but if I did, three o'clock in the morning would be the same as three o'clock in the afternoon."

"Stella, you ought not to talk like that," Michael said earnestly. "You don't realize what people would suppose. And really I don't think you ought to practise in your nightgown."

"Oh, Michael, if I practised in my chemise, I shouldn't expect you to mind."

"Stella! Really, you know!"

"Listen," she said, swinging away from him back to the keyboard. "This is the Lily Sonata."

Michael listened, and as he listened he could not help owning to himself that in her white nightgown, straight-backed against the shimmering ebony instrument, little indeed would matter very much among those dancing black and white notes.

"Or in nothing at all," said Stella, stopping suddenly.

Then she ran across to Michael and, after kissing him on the top of his head, waltzed very slowly out of the room.

But not even Stella could for long take away from Michael the torment of Lily's withheld presence. As a month went by, the image of her gained in elusive beauty, and the desire to see became a madness. He tried to evade his promise by haunting the places she would be likely to frequent, but he never saw her. He wondered if she could be in London, and he nearly wrote to ask. There was no consolation to be gained from books; there was no sentiment to be culled from the spots they had known together. He wanted herself, her fragility, her swooning kisses, herself, herself. She was the consummation of idyllic life, the life he longed for, the passionate life of beauty expressed in her. Stella had her music; Alan had his cricket; Mrs. Ross had her son; and he must have Lily. How damnable were these silver nights of June, how their fragrance musk-like even here in London fretted him with the imagination of wasted beauty. These summer nights demanded love; they enraged him with their uselessness.

"Isn't Chopin wonderful?" cried Stella. "Just when the window-boxes are dripping and the earth's warm and damp and the air is all turning into velvet."

"Oh, very wonderful," said Michael bitterly.

And he would go out on the dreaming balcony and, looking down on the motionless lamps, he would hear the murmur and rustle of people. But he was starving amid this rich plenitude of colour and scent; he was idle upon these maddening, these music-haunted, these royal nights that mocked his surrender.

And in the silent heart of the night when the sheets were fibrous and the mattress was jagged, when the pillow seared him and his eyes were like sand, what resolutions he made to carry her away from Kensington; but in the morning how coldly impossible it was to do so at eighteen.

One afternoon coming out of school, Michael met Drake.

"Hullo!" said Drake. "How's the fair Lily? I haven't seen you around lately."

"Haven't you?" said Michael. "No, I haven't been round so much lately."

He spoke as if he had suddenly noticed he had forgotten something.

"I asked her about you—over the garden-wall; so don't get jealous," Drake said with his look of wise rakishness. "And she didn't seem particularly keen on helping out the conversation. So I supposed you'd had a quarrel. Funny girl, Lily," Drake went on. "I suppose she's all right when you know her. Why don't you come in to my place?"

"Thanks," said Michael.

He felt that fate had given him this opportunity. He had not sought it. He might be able to speak to Lily, and if he could, he would ask her to meet him, and promises could go to the devil. He determined that no more of summer's treasure should be wasted.

He had a thrill in Drake's dull drawing-room from the sense of nearness to Lily, and from the looking-glass room it was back to back with the more vital drawing-room next door.

Michael could hardly bear to look out of the window into the oblong gardens; two months away from Lily made almost unendurable the thought that in one tremulous instant he might be imparadised in the vision of her reality.

"Hullo! She's there," said Drake from the window. "With another chap."

Michael with thudding heart and flaming cheeks stood close to Drake.

"Naughty girl!" said Drake. "She's flirting."

"I don't think she was," said Michael, but, even as he spoke, the knowledge that she was tore him to pieces.

Chapter XIX: *Parents*

THE brazen sun lighted savagely the barren streets, as Michael left Trelawny Road behind him. His hopeless footsteps rasped upon the pavement. His humiliation was complete. Not even was his personality strong enough to retain the love of a girl for six weeks. Yet he experienced a morbid sympathy with Lily, so unutterably beneath the rest of mankind was he already inclined to estimate himself. Stella opened wide her grey eyes when she greeted his pale disheartened return.

"Feeling ill?" she asked.

"I'm feeling a worthless brute," said Michael, plunging into a dejected acquiescence in the worst that could be said about him.

"Tell me," whispered Stella. "Ah, do."

"I've found out that Lily is quite ready to flirt with anybody. With anybody!"

"What a beastly girl!" Stella flamed.

"Well, you can't expect her to remain true to a creature like me," said Michael, declaring his self-abasement.

"A creature like you?" cried Stella. "Why, Michael, how can you be so absurd? If you speak of yourself like that, I shall begin to think you *are* 'a creature' as you call yourself. Ah, no, but you're not, Michael. It's this Lily who is the creature. Oh, don't I know her, the insipid puss! A silly little doll that lets everybody pull her about. I hate weak girls. How I despise them!"

"But you despise boys, Stella," Michael reminded her. "And this chap she was flirting with was much older than me. Perhaps Lily is like you, and prefers older men."

Michael had no heart left even to maintain his stand against Stella's alarming opinions and prejudices so frankly expressed.

"Like me," Stella cried, stamping her foot. "Like me! How dare you compare her with me? I'm not a doll. Do you think anyone has ever dared to kiss me?"

"I'm sorry," said Michael. "But you talk so very daringly that I shouldn't be surprized by anything you told me. At the same time I can't help sympathizing with Lily. It must have been dull to be in love with a schoolboy—an awkward lout of eighteen."

"Michael! I will not hear you speak of yourself like that. I'm ashamed of you. How can you be so weak? Be proud. Oh, Michael, do be proud—it's the only thing on earth worth being."

Stella stood dominant before him. Her grey eyes flashed; her proud, upcurving mouth was slightly curled: her chin was like the chin of a marble goddess, and yet with that brown hair lapping her wide shoulders, with those long legs, lean-flanked and supple, she was more like some heroic boy.

"Yes, you can be proud enough," said Michael. "But you've got something to be proud of. What have I got?"

"You've got me," said Stella fiercely.

"Why, yes, I suppose I have," Michael softly agreed. "Let's talk about your first appearance."

"I was talking about it to mother when a man called Prescott came."

"Prescott?" said Michael. "I seem to have heard mother speak about him. I wonder when it was. A long time ago, though."

"Well, whoever he was," said Stella, "he brought mother bad news."

"How do you know?"

"Have you ever seen mother cry?"

"Yes, once," said Michael. "It was when I was talking through my hat about the war."

"I've never seen her cry," said Stella pensively. "Until to-day."

Michael forgot about his own distress in the thought of his mother, and he sat hushed all through the evening, while Stella played in the darkness. Mrs. Fane went up to her own room immediately she came in that night, and the next morning, which was Saturday, Michael listlessly took the paper out to read in the garden, while he waited for Stella to dress herself so that they could go out together and avoid the house over which seemed to impend calamity.

Opening the paper, Michael saw an obituary notice of the Earl of Saxby. He scanned the news, only half absorbing it:

"In another column will be found the details—enteric—adds another famous name to the lamentable toll of this war—the late nobleman did not go into society much of late years—formerly Captain in the Welsh Guards—born 1860—married Lady Emmeline MacDonald, daughter of the Earl of Skye, K.T.—raised corps of Mounted Infantry (Saxby's Horse)—great traveller—unfortunately no heir to the title which becomes extinct."

Michael guessed the cause of his mother's unhappiness of yesterday. He went upstairs and told Stella.

"I suppose mother was in love with him," she said.

"I suppose she was," Michael agreed. "I wish I hadn't refused to say good-bye to him. It seems rather horrible now."

Mrs. Fane had left word that she would not be home until after dinner, and Michael and Stella sat apprehensive and silent in the drawing-room. Sometimes they would toss backwards and forwards to each other reassuring words, while outside the livid evening of ochreous oppressive clouds and ashen pavements slowly dislustred into a night swollen with undelivered rain and baffled thunders.

About nine o'clock Mrs. Fane came home. She stood for a moment in the doorway of the room, palely regarding her children. She seemed undecided about something, but after a long pause she sat down between them and began to speak:

"Something has happened, dear children, that I think you ought to know about before you grow any older."

Mrs. Fane paused again and stared before her, seeming to be reaching out for strength to continue. Michael and Stella sat breathless as the air of the night. Mrs. Fane's white kid gloves fell to the floor softly like the petals of a blown rose, and as if she missed their companionship in the stress of explication, she went on more rapidly.

"Lord Saxby has died in the Transvaal of enteric fever, and I think you both ought to know that Lord Saxby was your father."

When his mother said this, the blood rushed to Michael's face and then immediately receded, so that his eyelids as they closed over his eyes to shield them from the room's suddenly intense light glowed greenly; and when he looked again anywhere save directly at his mother, his heart seemed to have been crushed between ice. The room itself went swinging up in loops out of reach of his intelligence, that vainly strove to bring it back to familiar conditions. The nightmare passed: the drawing-room regained its shape and orderly tranquillity: the story went on.

"I have often wished to tell you, Michael, in particular," said his mother, looking at him with great grey eyes whose lustrous intensity cooled his first pained sensation of shamefulness, "Years ago, when you were the dearest little boy, and when I was young and rather lonely sometimes, I longed to tell you. But it would not have been fair to weigh you down with knowledge that you certainly could not have grasped then. I thought it was kinder to escape from your questions, even when you said that your father looked like a prince."

"Did I?" Michael asked, and he fell to wondering why he had spoken and why his voice sounded so exactly the same as usual.

"You see ... of course ... I was never married to your father. You must not blame him, because he wanted to marry me always, but Lady Saxby wouldn't divorce him. I dare say she had a right to nurse her injury. She is still alive. She lives in an old Scottish castle. Your father gave up nearly all his time to me. That was why you were both alone so much. You must forgive me for that, if you can. But I knew, as time went on that we should never be married, and.... Your father only saw you once, dearest Stella, when you were very tiny. You remember, Michael, when you saw him. He loved you so much, for of course, except in name, you were his heir. He wanted to have you to live with him. He loved you."

"I suppose that's why I liked him so tremendously," said Michael.

"Did you, dearest boy?" said Mrs. Fane, and the tears were in her grey eyes. "Ah, how dear it is of you to say that."

"Mother, I can't tell you how sorry I am I never went to say good-bye. I shall never forgive myself," said Michael. "I shall never forgive myself."

"But you must. It was my fault," said his mother. "I dare say I asked you tactlessly. I was so much upset at the time that I only thought about myself."

"Why did he go?" asked Stella suddenly.

"Well, that was my fault. I was always so dreadfully worried over the way in which I had spoilt his life that when he thought he ought to go and fight for his country, I could not bear to dissuade him. You see, having no heir, he was always fretting and fretting about the extinction of his family, and he had a fancy that the last of his name should do something for his country. He had given up his country for me, and I knew that if he went to the war he would feel that he had paid the debt. I never minded so much that we weren't married, but I always minded the feeling that I had robbed him by my love. He was such a very dear fellow. He was always so good and patient, when I begged him not to see you both. That was his greatest sorrow. But it wouldn't have been fair to you, dear children. You must not blame me for that. I knew it was better that you should be brought up in ignorance. It was, wasn't it?" she asked wistfully.

"Better," Michael murmured.

"Better," Stella echoed.

Mrs. Fane stood up, and Michael beheld her tall, tragical form with a reverence he had never felt for anything.

"Children, you must forgive me," she said.

And then simply, with repose and exquisite fitness she left Michael and Stella to themselves. By the door Stella overtook her.

"Mother darling," she cried. "You know we adore you. You do, don't you?"

Mrs. Fane smiled, and Michael thought he would cherish that smile to the end of his life.

"Well?" said Michael, when Stella and he were sitting alone again.

"Of course I've known for years it was something like this," said Stella.

"I can't think why I never guessed. I ought to have guessed easily," Michael said. "But somehow one never thinks of anything like this in connection with one's own mother."

"Or sister," murmured Stella, looking up at a spot on the ceiling.

"I wish I could kick myself for not having said good-bye to him," Michael declared. "That comes of talking too much. I talked much too much then. Talking destroys action. What a beast I was. Lily and I look rather small now, don't we?" he went on. "When you think of the amount that mother must have suffered all these years, it just makes Lily and me look like illustrations in a book. It's a curious thing that this business about mother and ... Lord Saxby ought, I suppose, to make me feel more of a worm than ever, but it doesn't. Ever since the first shock, I've been feeling prouder and prouder. I can't make it out."

Then suddenly Michael flushed.

"I say, I wonder how many of our friends have known all the time? Mrs. Carthew and Mrs. Ross both know. I feel sure by what they've said. And yet I wonder if Mrs. Ross does know. She's so strict in her notions that ... I wonder ... and yet I suppose she isn't so strict as I thought she was. Perhaps I was wrong."

"What are you talking about?" Stella asked.

"Oh, something that happened at Cobble Place. It's not important enough to tell you."

"What I'm wondering," said Stella, "is what mother was like when she was my age. She didn't say anything about her family. But I suppose we can ask her some time. I'm really rather glad I'm not 'Lady Stella Fane.' It would be ridiculous for a great pianist to be 'Lady Something.'"

"You wouldn't have been Lady Stella Fane," Michael contradicted. "You would have been Lady Stella Cunningham. Cunningham was the family name. I remember reading about it all when I was interested in Legitimists."

"What are they?" Stella asked. "The opposite of illegitimate?"

Michael explained the difference, and he was glad that the word 'illegitimate' should first occur like this. The pain of its utterance seemed mitigated somehow by the explanation.

"It's an extraordinary thing," Michael began, "but, do you know, Stella, that all the agony of seeing Lily flirting seems to have died away, and I feel a sort of contempt ... for myself, I mean. Flirting sounds such a loathsome word after what we've just listened to. Alan was right, I believe. I shall have to tell Alan about all this. I wonder if it will make any difference to him. But of course it won't. Nothing makes any difference to Alan."

"It's about time I met him," said Stella.

"Why, haven't you?" Michael exclaimed. "Nor you have. Great Scott! I've been so desperately miserable over Lily that I've never asked Alan here once. Oh, I will, though."

"I say, oughtn't we to go up to mother?" said Stella.

"Would she like us to?" Michael wondered.

"Oh, yes, I'm sure she would."

"But I can't express what I feel," Michael complained. "And it will be absurd to go and stand in front of her like two dummies."

"I'll say something," Stella promised; and, "Mother," she said, "come and hear me play to you."

The music-room, with its spare and austere decoration, seemed to Michael a fit place for the quiet contemplation of the tale of love he had lately heard.

Whatever of false shame, of self-consciousness, of shock remained was driven away by Stella's triumphant music. It was as if he were sitting beneath a mountain waterfall that, graceful and unsubstantial as wind-blown tresses, was yet most incomparably strong, and wrought an ice-cold, a stern purification.

Then Stella played with healing gentleness, and Michael in the darkness kissed his mother and stole away to bed, not to dream of Lily that night, not to toss enfevered, but quietly to lie awake, devising how to show his mother that he loved her as much now as he had loved her in the dim sunlight of most early childhood.

About ten days later Mrs. Fane came to Michael and Stella with a letter.

"I want to read you something," she said. "Your father's last letter has come."

"*We are in Pretoria now, and I think the war will soon be over. But of course there's a lot to be done yet. I'm feeling seedy to-night, and I'm rather sighing for England. I wonder if I'm going to be ill. I have a presentiment that things are going wrong with me—at least not wrong, because in a way I would be glad. No, I wouldn't, that reads as if I were afraid to keep going.*

"*I keep thinking of Michael and Stella. Michael must be told soon. He must forgive me for leaving him no name. I keep thinking of those Siamese stamps he asked for when I last saw him. I wish I'd seen him again before I went. But I dare say you were right. He would have guessed who I was, and he might have gone away resentful.*"

Michael looked at his mother, and thanked her implicitly for excusing him. He was glad that his father had not known he had declined to see him.

"*I don't worry so much over Stella. If she really has the stuff in her to make the name you think she will, she does not need any name but her own. But it maddens me to think that Michael is cut out of everything. I can scarcely bear to realize that I am the last. I'm glad he's going to Oxford, and I'm very glad that he chose St. Mary's. I was only up at Christ Church a year, and St. Mary's was a much smaller college in those days. Now of course it's absolutely one of the best. Whatever Michael wants to do he will be able to do, thank God. I don't expect, from what you tell me of him, he'll choose the Service. However, he'll do what he likes. When I come back, I must see him and I shall be able to explain what will perhaps strike him at first as the injustice of his position. I dare say he'll think less hardly of me when I've told him all the circumstances. Poor old chap! I feel that I've been selfish, and yet....*

"*I wonder if I'm going to be ill. I feel rotten. But don't worry. Only, if by any chance I can't write again, will you give my love to the children, and say I hope they'll not hate the thought of me? That piano was the best Prescott could get. I hope Stella is pleased with it.*"

"Thanks awfully for reading us that," said Michael.

Chapter XX: *Music*

MRS. FANE, having momentarily lifted the veil that all these years had hidden her personality from Michael and Stella, dropped it very swiftly again. Only the greatest emotion could have given her the courage to make that avowal of her life. During the days that elapsed between the revelation and the reading of Lord Saxby's last letter, she had lived very much apart from her children, so that the spectacle of her solitary grief had been deeply impressed upon their sensibility.

Michael was reminded by her attitude of those long vigils formerly sustained by ladies of noble birth before they departed into a convent to pray, eternally remote from the world. He himself became endowed with a strange courage by the contemplation of his mother's tragical immobility. He found in her the expression of those most voiceless ideals of austere conduct that until this vision of resignation had always seemed doomed to sink broken-winged to earth. The thought of Lily in this mood became an intrusion, and he told himself that, even if it were possible to seek the sweet unrest of her presence, beneath the sombre spell of this more classic sorrow he would have shunned that lovely and romantic girl. Michael's own realization of the circumstances of his birth occupied a very small part of his thoughts. His mind was fixed upon the aspect of his mother mute and heavy-lidded from the remembrance of that soldier dead in Africa. Michael felt no outrage of fate in these events. He was glad that death should have brought to his father the contentment of his country's honour, that in the grace of reconciliation he should be healed of his thwarted life. Nor could Michael resent that news of death which could ennoble his mother with this placidity of comprehension, this staid and haughty mien of sorrow. And he was grateful, too, that death should upon his own brow dry the fever dew of passion.

But when she had read that last letter, Mrs. Fane strangely resumed her ordinary self. She was always so finely invested with dignity, so exquisitely sheathed, in her repose, Michael scarcely realized that now, after she had read the letter, the vision of her grief was once more veiled against him by that faintly discouraging, tenderly deliberate withdrawal of her personality, and that she was still as seclusive as when from his childhood she had concealed the sight of her love, living in her own rose-misted and impenetrable privacy.

It was Stella who by a sudden request first roused Michael to the realization that his mother was herself again.

"Mother," she said, "what about my first concert? The season is getting late."

"Dearest Stella," Mrs. Fane replied, "I think you can scarcely make your appearance so soon after your father's death."

"But, mother, I'm sure he wouldn't have minded. And after all very few people would know," Stella persisted.

"But I should prefer that you waited for a while," said Mrs. Fane, gently reproachful. "You forget that we are in mourning."

For Michael somehow the conventional expression seemed to disturb the divinity of his mother's carven woe. The world suddenly intervened.

"Well, I don't think I ought to wait for ever," said Stella.

"Darling child, I wonder why you should think it necessary to exaggerate so foolishly," said Mrs. Fane.

"But I'm so longing to begin," Stella went on.

"I don't know that anybody has ever suggested you shouldn't begin," Mrs. Fane observed. "But there is a difference between your recklessness and my more carefully considered plans."

"Mother, will you agree to a definite date?" Stella demanded.

"By all means, dear child, if you will try to be a little less boisterous and impetuous. For one thing, I never knew you were ready to begin at once like this."

"Oh, mother, after all these years and years of practising!" Stella protested.

"But are you ready?" Mrs. Fane enquired in soft surprise. "Really ready? Then why not this autumn? Why not October?"

"Before I go up to Oxford," said Michael quickly.

Stella was immediately and vividly alert with plans for her concert.

"I don't think any of the smaller halls. Couldn't I appear first at one of the big orchestral concerts at King's Hall? I would like to play a Concerto ... Chopin, I think, and nothing else. Then later on I could have a concert all to myself, and play Schumann, and perhaps some Brahms."

So in the end it was settled after numberless interviews, letters, fixtures, cancellations, and all the fuming impediments of art's first presentation at the court of the world.

The affairs and arrangements connected with Stella's career seemed to Michael the proper distraction for his mother and sister during his last two or three weeks of school, before they could leave London. Mrs. Fane had suggested they should go to Switzerland in August, staying at Lucerne, so that Stella would not be hindered in her steady practice.

Michael's last week at school was a curiously unreal experience. As fast as he marshalled the correct sentiments with which to approach the last hours of a routine that had continued for ten years, so fast did they break up in futile disorder. He had really passed beyond the domain of school some time ago when he was always with Lily. It was impossible after that gradual secession, all the more final because it had been so gradual, to gather together now a crowd of associations for the sole purpose of effecting a violent and summary wrench. Indeed, the one action that gave him the expected pang of sentiment was when he went to surrender across the counter of the book-room the key of his locker. The number was seventy-five. In very early days Michael had been proud of possessing, through a happy accident, a locker on the ground-floor very close to the entrance-hall. His junior contemporaries were usually banished to remote corridors in the six-hundreds, waiting eagerly to inherit from departed seniors the more convenient lockers downstairs. But Michael from the day he first heard by the cast of the Laocoön the shuffle of quick feet along the corridor had owned the most convenient locker in all the school. At the last moment Michael thought he would forfeit the half-crown long ago deposited and keep the key, but in the end he, with the rest of his departing contemporaries, callously accepted the more useful half-crown.

School broke up in a sudden heartless confusion, and Michael for the last time stood gossiping outside the school-doors at five o'clock. For a minute he felt an absurd desire to pick up a stone and fling it through the window of the nearest class-room, not from any spirit of indignation, but merely to assure himself of a physical freedom that he had not yet realized.

"Where are you going for the holidays, Bangs?" someone asked.

"Switzerland."

"Hope you'll have a good time. See you next—oh, by Jove, I shan't though. Good-bye, hope you'll have good luck."

"Thanks," said Michael, and he had a fleeting view of himself relegated to the past, one of that scattered host—

Thick as autumnal leaves that strew
the brooks
In Vallombrosa—

Old Jacobeans, ghostly, innumerable, whose desks like tombstones would bear for a little while the perishable ink of their own idle epitaphs.

Lucerne was airless; the avenue of pollarded limes sheltered a depressed bulk of dusty tourists; the atmosphere was impregnated with bourgeois exclamations; the very surface of the lake was swarming with humanity, noisy with the click of rowlocks, and with the gutturals that seemed to praise fitly such a theatrical setting.

Mrs. Fane wondered why they had come to Switzerland, but still she asked Michael and Stella whether they would like to venture higher. Michael, perceiving the hordes of Teutonic nomads who were sweeping up into the heart of the mountains, thought that Switzerland in August would be impossible whatever lonely height they gained. They moved to Geneva, whose silverpointed beauty for a while deceived them, but soon both he and Stella became restless and irritable.

"Switzerland is like sitting in a train and travelling through glorious country," said Michael. "It's all right for a journey, but it becomes frightfully tiring. And, mother, I do hate the sensation that all these people round are feeling compelled to enjoy themselves. It's like a hearty choral service."

"It's like an oratorio," said Stella. "I can't play a note here. The very existence of these mobs is deafening."

"Well, I don't mind where we go," said Mrs. Fane. "I'm not enjoying these peculiar tourists myself. Shall we go to the Italian lakes? I used to like them very much. I've spent many happy days there."

"I'd rather go to France," said Michael. "Only don't let's go far. Let's go to Lyons and find out some small place in the country. I was talking to a decent chap—not a tourist—who said there were delightful little red-roofed towns in the Lyonnais."

So they left Switzerland and went to Lyons where, sitting under the shade of trees by the tumbling blue Rhône, they settled with a polite agent to take a small house near Châtillon.

Hither a piano followed them, and here for seven weeks they lived, each one lost in sun-dyed dreams.

"I knew we should like this," Michael said to Stella, as they leaned against tubs of rosy oleanders on a lizard-streaked wall, and watched some great white oxen go smoothly by. "I like this heart of France better than Brittany or Normandy. But I hope mother won't be bored here."

"There are plenty of books," said Stella. "And anyway she wants to lie back and think, and it's impossible to think except in the sun."

The oxen were still in sight along the road that wound upwards to where Châtillon clustered red upon its rounded hill.

"It doesn't look like a real town," said Michael. "It's really not different from the red sunbaked earth all about here. I feel it would be almost a pity ever to walk up that road and find it is a town. I vote we never go quite close, but just sit here and watch it changing colour all through the day. I never want to move out of this garden."

"I can't walk about much," said Stella. "Because I simply must practise and practise and practise and practise."

They always woke up early in the morning, and Michael used to watch Châtillon purple-bloomed with the shadow of the fled night, then hazy crimson for a few minutes until the sun came high enough to give it back the rich burnt reds of the day. All through the morning Michael used to sit among the peach trees of the garden, while Stella played. All through the morning he used to read novel after novel of ephemeral fame that here on the undisturbed shelves had acquired a certain permanence. In the afternoon Stella and he used to wander through the vineyards down to a shallow brown stream bordered by poplars and acacias, or in sun-steeped oak woods idly chase the long lizards splendid with their black and yellow lozenges and shimmering green mail.

Once in a village at harvest-time, when the market-place was a fathom deep in golden corn, they helped in the threshing, and once when the grain had been stored, they danced here with joyful country-folk under the moon.

During tea-time they would sit with their mother beneath an almond tree, while beyond in sunlit air vibrant with the glad cicadas butterflies wantoned with the oleanders, or upon the wall preened their slow fans. Later, they would pace a walk bordered by tawny tea-roses, and out of the globed melons they would scent the garnered warmth of the day floating forth to mingle with the sweet breath of eve. Now was the hour to climb the small hill behind the peach trees. Here across the mighty valley of the Saône they could see a hundred miles away the Alps riding across the horizon, light as clouds. And on the other side over their own little house lay Châtillon cherry-bright in the sunset, then damson-dark for a while, until it turned to a velvet gloom pricked with points of gold and slashed with orange stains.

Michael and Stella always went to bed when the landscape had faded out. But often Michael would sit for a long time and pore upon the rustling, the dark, the moth-haunted night; or if the moon were up he would in fancies swim out upon her buoyant watery sheen.

Sometimes, as he sat among the peach trees, a thought of Lily would come to him; and he would imagine her form swinging round the corner. The leaves and sunlight, while he dreamed of her, dappled the unread pages of his book. He would picture himself with Lily on these sunny uplands of the Lyonnais, and gradually she lost her urban actuality; gradually the disillusionment of her behaviour was forgotten. With the obliteration of Lily's failure the anguish for her bodily form faded out, and Michael began to mould her to an incorporeal idea of first love. In this clear air she stood before him recreated, as if the purifying sun, which was burning him to the likeness of the earth around, had been able at the same time to burn that idea of young love to a slim Etruscan shape which could thrill him for ever with its beauty, but nevermore fret him with the urgency of desire. He was glad he had not spoken to her again after that garden interlude; and though his heart would have leapt to see her motionable and swaying to his glances as she came delicately towards him through the peach trees, Michael felt that somehow he would not kiss her, but that he would rather lead her gravely to the hill-top and set her near him to stay for ever still, for ever young, for ever fair.

So all through that summer the sun burned Michael, while day by day the white unhurried oxen moved, slow as clouds, up the hill towards the town. But Michael never followed their shambling steps, and therefore he never destroyed his dream of Châtillon.

As the time drew nearer and nearer for Stella's concert, she practised more incessantly. Nor would she walk now with Michael through the vineyards down to the shallow poplar-shadowed stream. Michael was seized with a reverence for her tireless concentration, and he never tried to make her break this rule of work, but would always wander away by himself.

One day, when he was lying on a parched upland ridge, Michael had a vision of Alan in green England. Suddenly he realized that in a few weeks they would be setting out together for Oxford. The dazzling azure sky of France lightened to the blown softness of an English April. Cloistral he saw Oxford, and by the base of St. Mary's Tower the people, small as emmets, hurrying. The roofs and spires were wet with rain, and bells were ringing. He saw the faces of all those who from various schools would encounter with him the greyness and the grace of Oxford, and among them was Alan.

How familiar Oxford seemed after all!

The principal fact that struck Michael about Stella in these days of practising for her concert was her capacity for renouncing all extravagance of speech and her steady withdrawal from everything that did not bear directly on her work. She no longer talked of her brilliance; she no longer tried to astonish Michael with predications of genius; she became curiously and impressively diligent, and, without conveying an idea of easy self-confidence, she managed to make Michael feel perfectly sure of her success.

During the latter half of September Michael went to stay with Alan at Richmond, partly because with the nearness of Stella's appearance he began to feel nervous, and partly because he found speculation about Oxford in Alan's company a very diverting pursuit. From Richmond he went up at the end of the month in order to pass Responsions without difficulty. On the sixth of October was the concert at King's Hall.

Michael had spent a good deal of time in sending letters to all the friends he could think of, inviting their attendance on this occasion of importance. He even wrote to Wilmot and many of the people he had met at Edwardes Square. Everyone must help in Stella's triumph.

At the beginning of October Mrs. Ross arrived at the Merivales' house, and for the first time since their conversation in the orchard she and Michael met. He was shy at first, but Mrs. Ross was so plainly anxious to show that she regarded him as affectionately as ever that Michael found himself able to resume his intimacy at once. However, since Stella was always uppermost in his thoughts, he did not test Mrs. Ross with any more surprising admissions.

On the night before the concert Mr. and Mrs. Merivale, Mrs. Ross, Alan and Michael sat in the drawing-room, talking over the concert from every point of view.

"Of course she'll be a success," said Mr. Merivale, and managed to implicate himself as usual in a network of bad puns that demanded the heartiest reprobation from his listeners.

"Dear little girl," said Mrs. Merivale placidly. "How nice it is to see children doing things."

"Of course she'll be a success," Alan vowed. "You've only got to look at her to see that. By gad, what an off-drive she would have had, if she'd only been a boy."

Michael looked at Alan quickly. This was the first time he had ever heard him praise a girl of his own accord. He made up his mind to ask Stella when her concert was over how Alan had impressed her.

"Dear Michael," said Mrs. Ross earnestly, "you must not worry about Stella. Don't you remember how years ago I said she would be a great pianist? And you were so amusing about it, because you would insist that you didn't like her playing."

"Nor I did," said Michael in laughing defence of himself at eight years old. "I used to think it was the most melancholy noise on earth. Sometimes I think so now, when Stella wraps herself up in endless scales. By Jove," he suddenly exclaimed, "what's the time?"

"Half-past eight nearly. Why?" Alan asked.

"I forgot to write and tell Viner to come. It's not very late. I think I'll go over to Notting Hill now, and ask him. I haven't been to see him much lately, and he was always awfully decent to me."

Mr. Viner was reading in his smoke-hung room.

"Hullo," he said. "You've not been near me for almost a year."

"I know," said Michael apologetically. "I feel rather a brute. Some time I'll tell you why."

Then suddenly Michael wondered if the priest knew about Lord Saxby, and he felt shy of him. He felt that he could not talk intimately to him until he had told him about the circumstances of his birth.

"Is that what's been keeping you away?" asked the priest. "Because, let me tell you, I've known all about you for some years. And look here, Michael, don't get into your head that you've got to make this sort of announcement every time you form a new friendship."

"Oh, that wasn't the reason I kept away," said Michael. "But I don't want to talk about myself. I want to talk about my sister. She's going to play at the King's Hall concert to-morrow night. You will come, won't you?"

"Of course I will," said the priest.

"Thanks, and—er—if you could think about her when you're saying Mass to-morrow morning, why, I'd rather like to serve you, if I may. I must tear back now," Michael added. "Good night."

"Good night," said the priest, and as Michael turned in the doorway his smile was like a benediction.

Very early on the next morning through the curdled October mists Michael went over to Notting Hill again. The Mission Church stood obscurely amid a press of mean houses, and as Michael hurried along the fetid narrow thoroughfare, the bell for Mass was clanging among the fog and smoke. Here and there women were belabouring their doorsteps with mangy mats or leaning with grimed elbows on their sills in depressed anticipation of a day's drudgery. From bed-ridden rooms came the sound of children wailing and fighting over breakfast. Lean cats nosed in the garbage strewn along the gutters.

The Mission Church smelt strongly of soap and stale incense, and in the frore atmosphere the coloured pictures on the walls looked more than usually crude and violent. It was the Octave of St. Michael and All Angels, and the white chrysanthemums on the altar were beginning to turn brown. There was not a large congregation—two sisters of mercy, three or four pious and dowdy maiden ladies, and the sacristan. It was more than two years since Michael had served at Mass, and he was glad and grateful to find that every small ceremony still seemed sincere and fit and inevitable. There was an exquisite morning stillness in this small tawdry church, and Michael thought how strange it was that in this festering corner of the city it was possible to create so profound a sense of mystery. Whatever emotion he gained of peace and reconciliation and brooding holiness he vowed to Stella and to her fame and to her joy.

After Mass Michael went back to breakfast with Mr. Viner, and as they sat talking about Oxford, Michael thought how various Oxford was compared with school, how many different kinds of people would be appropriate to their surroundings, and he began with some of the ardour that he had given hitherto to envy of life to covet all varieties of intellectual experience. What a wonderfully suggestive word was University, and how exciting it was to see Viner tabulating introductions for his benefit.

Michael sat by himself at the concert. During the afternoon he had talked to Stella for a few minutes, but she had seemed more than ever immeasurably remote from conversation, and Michael had contented himself with offering stock phrases of encouragement and exhortation. He went early to King's Hall and sat high up in the topmost corner looking down on the orchestra. Gradually through the bluish mist the indefinite audience thickened, and their accumulated voices echoed less and less. The members of the orchestra had not yet entered, but their music-stands stood about with a ridiculous likeness to human beings. In the middle was Stella's piano black and lifeless, a little ominous in its naked and insistent and faintly shining ebon solemnity. One of the orchestra threaded his way through the chairs to where the drums stood in a bizarre group. From time to time this lonely human figure struck his instruments to test their pitch, and the low boom sounded hollowly above the murmurous audience.

A general accession of light took place, and now suddenly the empty platform was filled with nonchalant men who gossiped while they made discordant sounds upon their instruments. The conductor came in and bowed. The audience clapped. There was a momentary hush, followed by a sharp rat-tat of the baton, and the Third Leonora Overture began.

To Michael the music was a blur. It was soundless beside his own beating heart, his heart that thudded on and on, on and on, while the faces of the audience receded farther and farther through the increasing haze. The Overture was finished. From the hall that every moment seemed to grow darker came a sound of ghostly applause. Michael looked at his programme in a fever. What was this unpronounceable German composition, this Tonic Poem that must be played before Stella's turn would arrive? It seemed to go on for ever in a most barbaric and amorphous din; with corybantic crashings, with brazen fanfares and stinging cymbals it flung itself against the audience, while the woodwind howled and the violins were harsh as cats. Michael brooded unreceptive; he had a sense of monstrous loneliness; he could think of nothing. The noise overpowered his beating heart, and he began to count absurdly, while he bit his nails or shivered in alternations of fire and snow. Then his programme fluttered down on to the head of a bald violoncellist, and the ensuing shock of self-consciousness, that was mingled with a violent desire to laugh very loudly, restored him to his normal calm. The Tonic Poem shrieked and tore itself to death. The world became very quiet.

There was a gradual flap of rising applause, and it was Stella who, tall and white, was being handed across the platform. It was Stella who was sitting white and rigid at the black piano that suddenly seemed to have shrunk into a puny insignificance. It was Stella whose fingers were causing those rills of melody to flow. She paused, while the orchestra took up their part, and then again the rills began to flow, gently, fiercely, madly, sadly, wildly. Now she seemed to contend against the mighty odds of innumerable rival instruments; now her own frail instrument seemed to flag; now she was gaining strength; her cool clear harmonies were subduing this welter of violins, this tempest of horns and clarionets, this menace of bass-viols and drums. The audience was extinguished like a candle. The orchestra seemed inspired by the angry forces of Nature herself. The bows of the violins whitened and flickered like willows in a storm, and yet amid this almost intolerable movement Stella sat still as a figure of eternal stone. A faint smile curved more sharply her lips; the black bows in her hair trembled against her white dress; her wonderful hands went galloping away to right and left of her straight back. Plangent as music itself, serene as sculpture, with smiling lips magically crimson, adorably human, she finished her first concerto. And while she bowed to the audience and to the orchestra and the great shaggy conductor, Michael saw ridiculous teardrops bedewing his sleeve, not because he had been moved by the music, but because he was unable to shake by the hand every single person in King's Hall who was now applauding his sister.

It was not until Beethoven's somber knock at the opening of the Fifth Symphony that Michael began to dream upon the deeps of great music, that his thoughts liberated from anxiety went straying into time. Stella, when for a little while he had reveled in her success, was forgotten, and the people in this hall, listening, listening, began to move him with their unimaginable variety. Near him were lovers who in this symphony were fast imparadised; their hands were interlaced; visibly they swayed nearer to each other on the waves of melody. Old men were near him, solitary old men listening, listening ... old men who at the summons of these ringing notes were traversing their past that otherwise might have stayed forever unvoyageable.

Michael sometimes craved for Lily's company, wished that he could clasp her to him and swoon away upon these blinding chords. But she was banished from this world of music, she who had betrayed the beauty of love. There was something more noble in this music than the memory of a slim and lovely girl and of her flower-soft kisses. The world itself surely seemed to travel the faster for this urgent symphony. Michael was spinning face to face with the spinning stars.

And then some thread of simple melody would bring him back to the green world and the little memories of his boyhood. Now more than ever did it seem worth while to live on earth. He recognized, as if suddenly he had come down from incredible heights, familiar faces in the audience. He saw his mother with Mrs. Ross beside her, two figures that amid all this intoxication of speeding life must forever mourn. Now while the flood of music was sounding in his ears, he wished that he could fly down through this dim hall, and tell them, as they sat there in black with memories beside them, how well he loved them, how much he honoured them, how eagerly he demanded from them pride in himself.

After the first emotions of the mighty music had worn themselves out, Michael's imagination began to wander rapidly. At one point the bassoons became very active, and he was somehow reminded of Mr. Neech. He was puzzled for awhile to account for this association of an old form-master with the noise of bassoons. '*For he heard the loud bassoon.*' Out of the past came the vision of old Neech wagging the tail of his gown as he strode backward and forwards over the floor of the Shell class-room. '*The Wedding-Guest here beat his breast, For he heard the loud bassoon.*' Out of the past came the shrill sound of boys ruining The Ancient Mariner, and Michael heard again the outraged apostrophes of Mr. Neech. He began to create from his fancy of Mr. Neech a grotesque symbol of public-school education. Certainly he was the only master who had taught him anything. Yet he had probably tried less earnestly to teach than any other masters. Why did this image of Mr. Neech materialize whenever his thoughts went back to school? Years had passed since he had enjoyed the Shell. He had never talked intimately to Neech; indeed, he had scarcely held any communication with him since he left his form. The influence of Neech must have depended on a personality that demanded from his pupils a stoic bearing, a sense of humour, a capacity for inquisitiveness, an idea of continuity. He could not remember that any of these qualities had been appreciated by himself until he had entered the Shell. Michael regretted very deeply that on the day before he left school he had not thanked Neech for his existence. How nebulous already most of his other masters seemed. Only Neech stood out clear-cut as the intagliation of a sardonyx.

Meditation upon Neech took Michael off to Thackeray. He had been reading Pendennis lately, and the book had given him much the same sensation of finality as his old form-master, and as Michael thought of Thackeray, he began to speculate upon the difference between Michael Fane and the fourteenth Earl of Saxby. Yet he was rather glad that after all he was not the fourteenth Earl of Saxby. It would be interesting to see how his theories of good-breeding were carried out by himself as a nobody with old blood in his veins. He would like to test the common talk that rank was an accident, that old families, old faiths, old education, old customs, old manners, old thoughts, old books were all so much moonshine. Michael wondered whether it were so; whether indeed all men if born with equal chances would not display equal qualities. He did not believe it: he hated the doctrine. Yet people in all their variety called to him still, and as he surveyed the audience he was aware from time to time of a great longing to involve himself in the web of humanity. He was glad that he had not removed himself from the world like Chator. Chator! He must go down to Clere and see how Chator was getting on as a monk. He had not even thought of Chator for a year. But after all Oxford had a monastic intention, and Michael believed that from Oxford he would gain as much austerity of attitude as Chator would acquire from the rule of St. Benedict. And when he left Oxford, he would explore humanity. He would travel through the world and through the underworld and apply always his standard of ... of what? What was his standard? A classic permanence, a classic simplicity and inevitableness?

The symphony stopped. He must hurry out and congratulate Stella. What a possession she was; what an excitement her career would be. How he would love to control her extravagance, and even as he controlled it, how he would admire it. And his mother had talked of taking a house in Chelsea. What various interests were springing into existence. He must not forget to ask Alan what train he was going by to Oxford. They must arrive together. He had not yet bought his china. His china! His pictures! His books! His rooms in college! Life was really astonishing.

The concert was over, and as Michael came swirling down the stairs on the flood of people going home, he had a strange sensation of life beginning all over again.

THE END OF THE
FIRST VOLUME

NOTE
The second and final volume of SINISTER STREET, *containing Book III: Dreaming Spires and Book IV: Romantic Education, will be published early next year.*

Printed in Great Britain
by Amazon